INTERIM SITE

3 1192 00471 7714

x398.20975 Jagen.M
Jagendorf, M. A.
Folk stories of the South

D1801086

Other Books by M. A. Jagendorf

The Ghost of Peg-Leg Peter and Other Stories of Old New York
Noodlehead Stories from Around the World
The Priceless Cats and Other Italian Folk Stories
Sand in the Bag and Other Stories of Ohio, Indiana, and Illinois
The Merry Men of Gotham
Upstate, Downstate: Folk Stories of the Middle Atlantic States
The Marvelous Adventures of Johnny Darling
New England Bean Pot: American Folk Stories To Read and To Tell
Tyll Ulenspiegel's Merry Pranks

By M. A. Jagendorf and R. S. Boggs:

King of the Mountains: A Treasury of Latin-American Folk Stories

By M. A. Jagendorf and C. H. Tillhagen:

The Gypsies' Fiddle and Other Gypsy Tales

FOLK STORIES OF THE SOUTH

FOLK STORIES

Illustrated by Michael Parks

The Vanguard Press, Inc., New York

M. A. JAGENDORF

OF THE SOUTH

Copyright, © 1972, by M. A. Jagendorf

Published simultaneously in Canada by
the Copp Clark Publishing Company, Ltd., Toronto

All rights reserved. No part of this publication may be
reproduced or transmitted in any form or by any means,
electronic or mechanical, including photocopy, recording,
or any information storage or retrieval system, or otherwise,
without the written permission of the publisher, except by
a reviewer, who may wish to quote brief passages in
connection with a review for a newspaper, magazine, radio,
or television.

Manufactured in the United States of America
Library of Congress Catalogue Card Number: 70-134672
SBN 8149-0716-4

Designer: Ernst Reichl

This book is dedicated
to the people of the South,
whom, in the ten years I have
spent collecting these tales,
I have come to love, respect,
and admire.

CONTENTS

List of Illustrations — xiii

Foreword — xv
   by Professor George F. Reinecke,
   EDITOR, *Louisiana Folklore Miscellany*

Preface — xix

Alabama

   The First Tale of Alabama — 3
   Fearless Emma — 4
   Don't Drop Into My Soup — 10
   Railroad Bill — 13
   The Face in the Courthouse Window — 16
   How Far Is It to Jacob Cooper's? — 17
   The Battle of Bay Minette — 19
   The Smartest One in the Woods — 22
   False Alarm — 24

Arkansas

   The Arkansas Traveler — 29
   How Red Strawberries Brought Peace in the Woods — 33
   The Proud Tale of David Dodd — 35
   The Bull Didn't Have a Chance — 42

CONTENTS

The Sad-Lovely End of Wilhelmina Inn	44
The Judge and the Baseball-Pitching Indian Chief	47
Sam Hudson the Great	49
In Arkansas Stick to Bears; Don't Mess with Swampland Skeeters	51
The Daring of Yellow Doc	54
A Tale of Steep-Stair Town	57
The Colonel Teaches the Judge a Lesson in Good Manners	59
The Lost Treasure	62

Florida

The Great Conjure-Alligator-Man of Florida	67
Nobody Sees a Mockingbird on Friday	69
The Tale of Lura Lou	71
Dixie, the Knight of the Silver Spurs	77
Way Deep Down in the Okefenokee Swamps	79
The Bridal Chamber of Silver Springs	82
Daddy Mention and Sourdough Gus	87

Georgia

The Song of the Cherokee Rose	93
Dan McGirth and His Gray Goose Mare	95
The Tale of the Daughters of the Sun	97
Georgy Piney-Woods Peddler	99
The Curse of Lorenzo Dow	105
Hoozah for Fearless Ladies and Fearless Deeds	108
Fearless Nancy Hart	118

Louisiana

The Silver Snake of Louisiana	123
Fairy Web for Mr. Durand's Daughters	125
The Life of Annie Christmas	128
Gray Moss on Green Trees	133
The Bridal Ghost Dinner	135
One Pair of Blue Satin Slippers and Four Clever Maids	138

The Silver Bell of Chênière Caminada	140
Three Great Men at Peace	143

Mississippi

The Song in the Sea	149
The Living Colors of the Twenty-first	151
The Ghost Wedding in Everhope	153
The Ring Around the Tree	155
Tar-Wolf Tale	157
Mike Hooter and the Smart Bears in Mississippi	162
The Sad Tale of the Half-Shaven Head	164
Guess Who!	168

North Carolina

The Savage Birds of Bald Mountain	175
The White Doe	178
The Tale of the Hairy Toe	180
The Revolution of the Ladies of Edenton	182
Nollichucky Jack	184
Pirate Blackbeard's Deep-Sea End	187
The Ways of the Lord	190
The Man, the White Steed, and the Wondrous Wood	193
The Mystery of Theodosia Burr	199

South Carolina

Shake Hands With a Yankee	205
The Tragic Tale of Fenwick Hall	207
Emily's Famous Meal	210
Chickens Come Home to Roost	213
Ah-Dunno Ben	216
The Tale of Rebecca Motte	219
The Perpetual Motion in the Sea	224
Young Sherman and the Girl from Charleston	226

Tennessee

Kate, the Bell Witch	231
The Best Laugh Is the Last Laugh	234

Fiddler's Rock	236
Trust Not a New Friend	239
Come and Laugh with Bobby Gum	242
The Ghost Who Wasn't a Ghost	244
Big Sixteen	247
The Ghost the Whole Town Knew	250
The Power of Woman and the Strength of Man	254
The Gladiator, the Belle, and the Good Snowstorm	257
Beale Street Folks	260

Texas

The Karankawa from the Great Gleaming Oyster Shells	269
How Joe Became Snaky Joe	271
The White Buffalo	275
The Ghosts of Stampede Mesa	277
Only in Texas	281
Texas Centipede Coffee	284
Of Sam Bass	287
Horse Trading in Wichita Falls	290
Lafitte's Great Treasure	292

Virginia

Hercules of Virginia	297
All on a Summer's Day	302
The Merry Tale of Belle Boyd	304
Two Foxes	306
The Black Ghost Dog	308
Grace Sherwood, the Woman None Could Scare	312
. . . Thanks to Patrick Henry	314

Notes	319

ILLUSTRATIONS

So they stopped and called the place by the Indian word "Alibamu," which means "here we rest."	5
"Who are you? Where are you going?"	39
There was a fierce battle between the hurricane and the "Lura Lou" . . . and the hurricane won.	75
Holding the rim with one hand, she walked slowly out, as she had done many times before.	113
When the sons went off, the barge began to move—no man knows how.	131
"Let go my foot and hands," Br'er Rabbit hollered.	159
When the horse saw its master, it reared up wildly.	195
"We'll fire them from rifles, General Lee. Let us do it at once," said Rebecca.	221
He brought back a catfish big as a boat.	261
"Yippee-eye-ay! Go it, Joe! Y'll git that rattler yit!"	273
Peter raised the frightened animal with one mighty effort and flung it clear across the fence after its master.	299

FOREWORD

BY GEORGE F. REINECKE

Editor, *Louisiana Folklore Miscellany*

A few years ago there was a professor of medieval studies at one of our great universities who was fond of rural solitude, but felt he had grown too old for roughing it alone. He therefore compromised by hiring one of his graduate students to accompany him on a spring camping trip to the shores of a nearby lake. This lake was much frequented in the summer months by vacationing families but deserted when the two campers pitched their tent. As the first day progressed, the student grew more and more puzzled by his elder's activities. The professor would poke about the rubbish heaps left behind by the previous summer's vacationers, and from them remove old tennis shoes, which he stacked carefully in little piles.

Placing a generous interpretation upon the terms of his employment, the graduate student decided to join in the old man's game, whatever its purpose. He walked off in a wide circle, glancing right and left, and at length collected a dozen old sneakers from the underbrush. Returning to the camp, he dropped these on the nearest of the professor's piles. But instead of the anticipated thanks, he received an impatient growl. The old man stooped down, tossed the offending dozen as far away as his old age permitted, and muttered only half apologetically, "*Your* damn things don't fit my categories."

Let me now hasten to declare that though my anecdote is as true as any folktale, its hero was certainly not a professional folklorist. But he could have been. This founder of "sneakerology" had more points in common with some of our academic folklorists than we care to admit. These nearly spoil the folklore game by excessive attention to nomenclature and methodology—and folklore, for me at least, is a much better game than tennis shoes. They are a little like Keats's Appolonius, the philosopher at whose profound glance the palace of imagination disappeared and the wedding feast vanished.

In studied contrast, Moritz Jagendorf, an advocate of the folktale as an art, has in his most recent collection avoided almost all structure and codification in this monumental collection of Southern stories. True, they do break down alphabetically by states, but otherwise there is no geographical scheme, time scheme, or any other scheme that my own medievalist mind, with its crypto-sneakerological slant, can detect. Genres, too, are not broken down. Anecdotes stand elbow to elbow with Indian myths, noodle-tales, ghost stories, tales of magic, border episodes, strong-man tales, and the adventurers of local war heroines—all in a rich and overwhelming stream.

Dr. Jagendorf is one who rejoices in oral tradition and the folk mind, and his desire is to join and perpetuate any tradition he encounters. This state of mind, reflected in the author's book, sets him at some distance from the indexers of motifs. He has given us the Southern tale as it crosses and penetrates his own consciousness. The result is "God's plenty," though invested with a very personal touch.

Since I myself do professionally much the same sort of thing the indexers do, though in the field of written literature, I can appreciate and often utilize their able work. Still, I am sufficiently an amateur, and indeed a parochial amateur, in folklore to sympathize with and endorse Dr. Jagendorf's more organic relation to his materials. If the academic folklorists approach the folktale like collectors for a great museum, Dr. Jagendorf treats it as might the keeper of a national park, anxious for the propagation of the creatures in his charge, living in their midst and to a degree sharing their experiences.

As the editor of a Southern folklore publication, I often hear from contributors the theme of the gradual demise of folklore. This note of discouragement is rife among those with one foot in the folk-world and the other in the university, even here in the South. To such persons, this book should give heart. In past years the South has had a better base for the preservation of tradition in its social and economic structure than had the rest of the nation. Here is evidence that changes toward urbanization and long-needed social reform have not destroyed the tradition. For these stories were orally collected. If one compares the contents with those of other well-known collections of Southern material, it becomes clear that here are not merely the recurrent characters and themes, but also a body of little-known stories, and old ones told in a different way, as well as some doubtless new to the printed page.

Those who know Moritz Jagendorf, personally or through his other books, will find his inimitable personality carrying over into the narrative enthusiasm of this latest work. Since he has incorporated himself into our traditions, making himself a member—you can't have that sort of thing conferred—it is only proper that he should leave a personal mark on these tales, as did the long line of conteurs from whom he received them. This is a welcome, a copious, an entertaining book.

G. R.

New Orleans

PREFACE

For nearly fifty years I have gone up and down the United States seeking folk tales. I began in 1922, when I heard the first earthy American tall tale from a native up in Vermont. The story was a revelation and opened for me a folk-literature as big as the world.

I began exploring the states for more tales. I heard those remembered by word of mouth. I read them in old diaries, county histories, and old newspapers. And so I came to the southern states—eleven of them from which I gathered the folk tales found in this book.

As usual, in addition to the pleasure of the actual collecting of the stories, there was also the pleasure of gaining knowledge from them. For example, I learned that there was a marked difference in the stories in the South from those I heard in the North. The southern folk tales have a closer and more personal meaning than those in the northern states. Also, down South I found a large number of what I would call "historical-folk tales." By this I mean tales based on historical incidents, which, by constant repetition by word of mouth and the written word, have become folk tales in the accepted definition.

Folk tales in the South are treated differently from those in the North. They are more common, more frequently told, and they are taken as part of daily *present* life. There is a personal intimacy between the teller, the tale, and the characters in the tale. It is not just a story—but almost a personal experience or participation on the part of the teller.

I have often heard the statement that the battles with the North are still being fought down South. Quite true. That is the southern way of life—to consider time—years—as unimportant (which they are) as compared to feelings and emotions. In the great realm of folk tales, Southerners, high and low, lettered and unlettered, tell them with sincerity, reality, belief, and conviction.

For me, this approach made these tales more exciting and more real; they were as good as fresh corn from the cob.

As usual, the stories of the South go through the same categories as the stories of the North. Some are purely American; some show European influences; and some are European tales transformed and amalgamated to fit the American scene. And, of course, I must add that there are also pure southern tales.

I owe thanks to each and every person in the South, man and woman, to whom I spoke and to whom I wrote asking for stories and help in my work. There was always a warm friendship and co-operation that made my task a delight and a happy adventure.

I cannot and should not single out any individuals, for all deserve the same gratitude. Individual ladies and gentlemen, historical societies, officials, newspapermen and -women, all helped.

In the notes at the end of this book I have thanked those who went far out of their way to aid me.

My only regret is that I cannot include all the stories I collected, for they run into the hundreds.

It was truly a great, exciting pleasure to "live" through the incidents of these tales, and I hope readers will share my pleasure.

MORITZ JAGENDORF

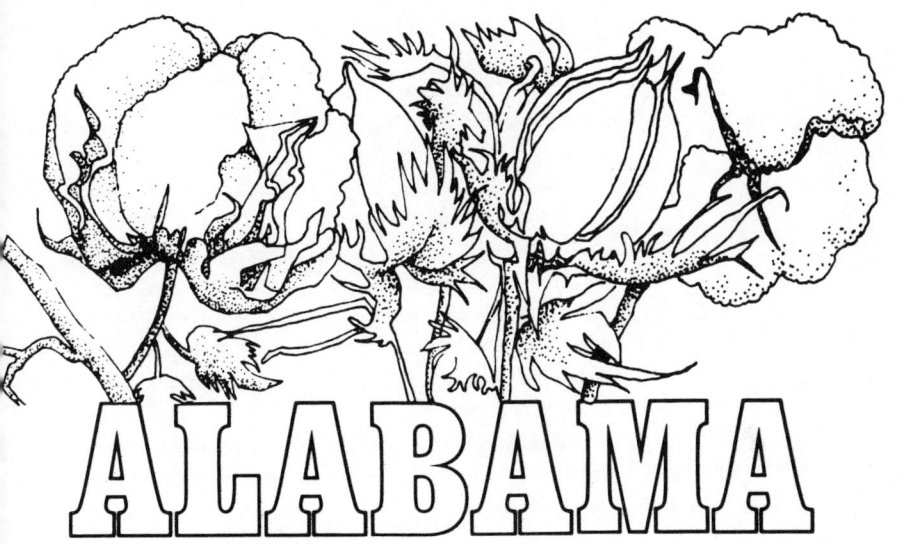

The First Tale of Alabama

I'll begin my tales of Alabama by telling you how Alabama got its name.

There's many a story of how that lovely name came to be, but I'll tell you the one I like best.

A great tribe of Indians, men, women, and children, were slowly on the march from far-down Mexico. They passed moon after moon in weary wandering, hunted by men, driven from place to place through forests and streams and desert plains.

They moved slowly, for they were weak from hunger and sad with worry. Finally they came to a land of fresh green and good water, the land that is now Alabama.

It had taken a long time traveling up from Mexico, battling with men and hunger. The place they saw was richer than any they had seen, rich with grass and flowers, trees full of fruits, rivers full of fish, and woods full of game. They sat down to rest.

The prophet of the tribe spoke: "Maybe this is the land for us. I shall ask the Great Spirit to tell me."

He took a long wooden pole and tied to its end a white leather medicine pouch. Then he put the pole straight into the ground, straight as the falling stars over Alabama. The pole was seen all over, the medicine pouch white against the sky.

"Let the pole stay here overnight and let my medicine pouch speak to the Great Spirit in the sky. Maybe He will speak to us. If He wants us to stay here, the pole with the medicine pouch will stand straight and unbending. If the pole bends to the east, then the Great Spirit wants us to go to the east. If it bends to the north or west, then we must go in that direction."

They went to sleep, and when the sun rose over the trees and water and the birds began to sing, they got up to learn where the Great Spirit wanted them to go. There the pole stood, straight as an arrow on a bow.

"*Alibamu*," the Prophet cried, "*Alibamu*"—which means "here we rest." All the tribe cried: "*Alibamu*."

So they stayed and called the place by the Indian word for "here we rest." And so it has been called ever since, with only a slight change in spelling.

Fearless Emma

This is a tale folks like to tell down in Alabama, for it is about a brave girl who did a brave deed, and Alabama is proud of her.

Americans from the North were battling Americans from the South, and each side believed in the truth of its claims. The fighting was hard and folks at home on both sides were full of worry and fear for those in the battlefields.

It all happened on a hot day when Emma Sansom was coming home from Gadsden. Her home was just two miles west of it, not far from Black Creek. She was lovely to look at on her horse, riding high, with flashing eyes and fearless face. At their cabin, her mother was waiting anxiously.

"Emma, did you get news in Gadsden?"

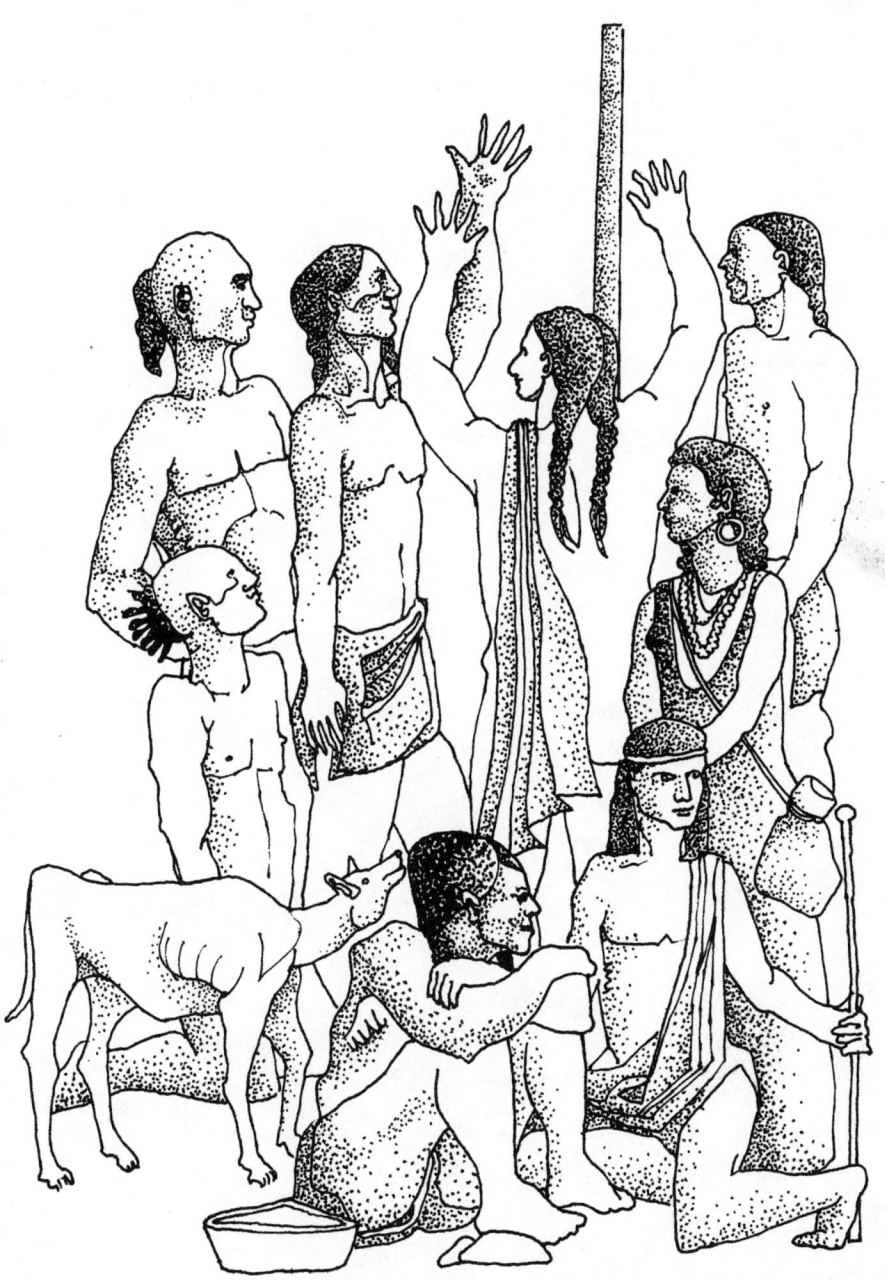

So they stopped and called the place by the Indian word "Alibamu," which means "here we rest."

"I did, Mother. Yankee General Streight is around here and General Forrest is after 'm. They said—"

She didn't finish, for there was firing, and down the road came galloping a troop of Northern soldiers, shooting their muskets in the air. They came racing up to the cabin where Emma and her mother were standing. Two men jumped down and shouted:

"Hey, you women, we're gonna take that horse of yours. Come, hand it over."

Instead of handing the horse over as the soldiers had expected, Emma got hold of the horse's reins on one side, and Mrs. Sansom, her mother, took tight hold of the other side.

"You're not going to take my horse," Emma shouted. Her eyes shot fire and her face was bright red.

"Keep your hands off our horse, Yankee," screamed Mrs. Sansom. "We need it more 'n you do."

The two men tugged at the horse, while the other soldiers watched, laughing.

"Go it, Jerry," one of the men shouted. "Two women agin two men. Let's see who'll win."

"Tom, don't look at the pretty girl; we need a good strong horse," another cried.

The tugging and the banter went on. But daughter and mother were furious, and anger gives strength. They held on fiercely and the soldiers could not get the horse from them. The men were losing their tempers.

Just then a keen-faced man, followed by some soldiers, all on horseback, dashed up. When the men around Emma and her mother saw them, they made way for the newcomers respectfully.

"What's going on here?" the one in front said.

"We need horses, General, and here's a fine beast. We've been trying to take it without hurting the women," said Tom, who was tugging at the horse.

"We need that horse more than anyone," Emma said defiantly. "It's all we've got to work our land. We're two women here, all alone."

"Have you no brothers or father?" the General asked.

"Yes, I have a father and brothers, and they are fighting you Yankees."

The General smiled. "If they are as fearless as you, young lady, they must be good fighters." Then, turning to the men, he added, "Let the women have their horse. Come, we have more important work on hand."

He rode off, the men following. More Northern soldiers came up, and they all dashed over the bridge that ran over Black Creek.

Some women and old men had come up to the Sansoms. Said Mrs. Sansom: "That's the way to treat 'em. If you don't show the white feather, you kin beat 'em."

"Mother, I brought some bacon. Let's put the horse in the barn and let's thank God."

Emma was leading the horse to the barn in back of the house. She had just gotten inside when she heard her mother screaming:

"Lord, they are burning the bridge and the timber on it!"

Emma rushed out. True, the bridge was on fire! The flames blazed high in the air, for the wood was bone-dry. Both the women and the neighbors looked on it unhappily, when suddenly there was great shouting.

A cavalcade of Confederate soldiers came dashing up, and the one who rode at their head was begrimed and covered with dust.

"Ladies," he said, coming up to the crowd, "I'm General Forrest. I'm after General Straight and his men. They're across the creek, but the bridge is burning. If any of you knows a place where we can get across, I'll be obliged if you'll show me the way."

"Yes, General," Emma said quickly, "there is an old fording place not far from here. I know where it is, and I can lead you to it."

"Come, a horse for this brave girl," the General said.

"No need to take a horse from one of your men, General. I can ride behind you."

"Emma!" came the mother's reproving voice. "It's riding with a stranger."

"I'll trust myself to a Confederate soldier," and she jumped up on the horse behind the General.

The Confederates were off, going toward the creek. Bullets greeted them from the other side of the river, where the Blues were all safely hidden on the hill.

General Forrest stopped, ordering his men to halt.

"No good, no use losing lives. Let's dismount. I must find the ford on foot."

"I'll lead you to it, General. I've been there many times. Let me walk in front. I know the way better, and even Yankees won't shoot at a woman."

"Young lady," General Forrest said with a smile, "I'll accept a woman as a guide, but not as a shield. You stay behind. I'll reconnoiter."

Bullets continued to come their way from the hill that rose on the other side of the creek.

The General dropped on his knees and began crawling along the bank, looking for the place to cross.

Suddenly he heard Emma's voice behind him.

"There it is. I know it. Our cows have crossed there often."

The General turned his head. "You here, child! I told you to stay behind."

"I wanted to be near you, General, in case you were hurt. Now we can go back and get the men. They can cross here easily. I knew we'd find it."

She was so pleased and excited, she leaped high in the air, waving her straw bonnet at the soldiers firing on the other side of the water. For a time, the bullets kept coming.

"Ho, there, Yankees," she screamed. "You're wounding my dress!"

The Yankee soldiers cheered and stopped the firing, and this gave General Forrest a chance to get back. Emma ran behind him.

General Forrest and his men crossed Black Creek hot after General Streight and his men. In the end, the Confederates cornered him, as you can read in history books. But Emma is the heroine in story books, and there isn't anyone in Alabama who doesn't know the tale of fearless Emma and doesn't like to tell the story of her great courage, as I have told it to you.

Don't Drop Into My Soup

Once there was was a family who lived in a big house. They were very rich, but they lived just the same as other folks. They died, one after another, until there wasn't a one left of that immediate family. That's the way things always happen.

The house was empty, with no one living in it. But there were all kinds of noises heard in the night, and all kinds of things happening there. Nobody wanted to live in it.

So the distant relatives, to whom it belonged, nailed boards on the windows and doors and stuck up a sign outside that said:

"Anybody who'll stay in this here house three nights kin have it an' all that's in it."

But nobody came to try. This went on for a long time.

One day, a poor boy who lived nearby in the village passed the house and saw the sign.

"I'll sleep in this here house three nights, hants or no hants; then it'll be mine and I'll be a rich man."

That boy was sharp as a briar and wasn't scared of playin' with wildcats.

He went into the house to stay there, not for three nights, but for good.

The first night he made a fire in the chimney and was cooking his supper. There were no lights except the light from his fire. When the soup was done, he put it into a plate and sat down to eat.

Just when he raised the first spoonful to his mouth, there was an awful racket in the chimney and someone was shoutin' to beat Jerusalem. The boy looked up the chimney and there were two legs hanging down. The someone was screaming, "I'm gonna drop down! I'm gonna drop down."

"That don't matter," the boy said. "Drop down, but have a care not to drop into my soup."

The legs dropped plumb down and lay quietly on the wooden floor, and the boy began eating his soup and bread.

Pretty soon there was a ruckus again up that chimney and big hollering! The boy looked up, and there were two arms, each separate from the other, screaming, "I'm gonna drop! I'm gonna drop!"

"That don't matter," the boy said. "Drop, but have a care not to drop into my soup."

The arms dropped plumb down, not far from the legs, and lay quietly. The boy took a few more spoonsful, but soon there was a worse bellowing than ever from that chimney. He looked up and saw the hulk of a body wedged in tight and heard a voice howling, "I'm gonna drop! I'm gonna drop!"

"Don't care if you do, just so you don't drop into my soup."

That big body came down with a big bang, right between the arms and legs, and they came up to it quick, fitting just right.

"Only the head's missin' t' make a man," the boy grumbled.

When the last word was out of his mouth, there was the wildest screaming yet.

"I'm gonna drop! I'm gonna drop! I'm gonna drop!" it went on without end.

"Drop, and stop the hollerin', only don't drop into my soup," the boy said.

The head came down with a crash, right over the body lying on the wooden floor, and fit on like a pea in a pod. The man—for a man it was—sat up and looked at the boy.

The boy put spoon after spoon of soup to his mouth; then he said to the man, "Do you want some o' my soup? It's good soup."

No answer.

"You ain't got much manners, Mister," said the boy, and ate his soup to the end.

The boy made himself a good bed of blankets and, just as he was lying down, he turned to the silent fellow, who looked like the Devil come from fire, and said:

"If ye want, I'll make room in the bed for you."

No word.

"You sure ain't got no manners, Mister, though I was civil. Stay on the hard floor; I'll sleep in my warm bed."

Just as he lay down, ready to cover up, the ghost—for a ghost it was—got up.

"Boy," he said with a voice like thunder in a holler, "boy, since ye ain't scared o' me, I'm gonna reward ye for it. Folks call me a hant and say I'm awful. Well, I ain't. I just cain't rest. You was polite and asked me to share your soup and bed; that shows ye got a good heart. For all that, I'll give ye the treasure that's in this house. Ye kin have it and then I don't have t' watch it no more and kin rest in peace. Come."

The boy went with the ghost, who led him down the cellar and gave him a shovel.

"Dig here," he said, showing him the spot.

The boy dug in that place, and pretty soon he hit an iron chest, and when he opened it, it was full of gold.

"It's yours, boy," the hant said. "Take it. Now I kin rest in my grave and don't have to watch that treasure no more." Then he floated away.

The boy went back to sleep, figuring the gold wouldn't run away. There were no more noises, and he slept all the night. He slept there two more nights.

He got that house and he got that gold and he got to be a rich man. Then he married a nice Alabama girl, and they had many children and a fine life. That's the end of my story.

Railroad Bill

In the olden days there was many an outlaw in Alabama unafeared of the law, of man, or the word of the Lord, and there is no end of tales folks tell about them.

There was Steve Renfro, the outlaw sheriff, who came a-riding into Livingston on a snow-white horse. He had long hair and silver spurs on his boots. Bolts and locks melted before him like butter in the sun.

There was Rube Burrow, the "lone wolf," without fear in any part of him, ever helping the poor.

There was John Murrell, who was a preacher of the gospel. He was always traveling with a pretty girl, singing songs sweet as a nightingale.

And there was Railroad Bill!

Bill was black as ebony and strong as Samson of the Bible. One day he got in a blazing argument with the law and had to flee for his life. From then on, railroad freight cars were his hunting ground and shacks in the dark woods were his home. In the dark woods he learned hoodoo and magic. Then no sheriff, no posse, no "man," could catch Railroad Bill. Every sheriff swore he'd get him, but their words were like water in the Alabama River.

Ed McMillan became the guardian of the law and he, too, vowed he'd get that outlaw man.

"Bill worked for me in my turpentine still; I know his ways and and I'll bring him to the law," said Ed to his brothers.

"Have a care, Ed. Bill is the worst bad man Alabama ever had; have a care, Ed," his brothers warned him. But you couldn't stop

Ed from what he had a mind to do. He had the courage of an army, and fear hid far down deep when Ed was around.

Railroad Bill, sitting in a tumbledown shack with some friends, was told what Ed had said:

"Ed McMillan is after you. He's got a sure hand an' a sharp eye an' he is big and tough. Best hide away for a time or go to Floridy."

"Ed McMillan can't get me, just as no man kin get me. All I needs is change myself to a sheep or dog, then nobody kin git me. But I likes Ed McMillan. I worked in his turpentine still and he's a fine man. He mustn't come after me, or I'll have to use my gun. I'm gonna write him a letter."

He got an old piece of paper and the stub of a pencil and wrote in big letters:

"Don't come, Mr. Ed. I love you."

"You git that paper to 'm," Bill said to his friends, "before he sets out lookin' for me."

One day, Sheriff McMillan found the paper and told his brothers about it. They listened with silent faces.

"Ed, don't you think it'd be better if you let Railroad be?"

"I'm sheriff here, and I got to uphold the law. I'm gonna get Outlaw Bill as I said I would. Escambia County 's suffered long enough."

One day the sheriff learned Railroad Bill 'd been seen around Bluff Spring.

"Now's the time," said Ed, and he and two men set out to hunt the outlaw, Railroad Bill.

They set out walking with care, guns in hand, eyes and ears wide open.

A black man was walking through the woods and Sheriff Ed stopped him.

"Black man," said he, "where's Railroad Bill? You tell me quick or to jail you go."

The black man was silent a long time, white men talking all the time. Then they raised their guns and the black man stuttered with fright:

"He's outside Bluff Spring, in a shack not far from the fork of the road."

The sheriff and the two men took up the trail, silent, with guns held tight. They saw the shack through the trees, and each came from a different side, hiding behind the thick trunks.

Suddenlike, there was a thick voice crying, "Who's there?"

Before there was an answer there was a shot, but no one was hurt. Sheriff Ed stepped from behind the sheltering tree, gun high in hand. There was a second shot and the sheriff fell on the leaves. The two men fired into the cabin, but it did no good. No one was in the cabin now; only a little red fox with a thick bushy tail ran out. The two men were too busy with the dying sheriff to even see the little fox. Let me tell you, that little fox was Railroad Bill. He had worked his hoodoo to change himself to an animal to keep off the manhunters.

There was a great funeral in Escambia County for Sheriff Ed McMillan, for everybody liked him, and white men swore they'd get that outlaw come hell or high water. The whole county was now after that conjuring outlaw man.

One day, a spell after Sheriff Ed's funeral, Railroad Bill came to Tidmore's store not far from Atmore town, to get some vittles.

White men followed him behind the trees like ghosts. A white man sat in the store, a rifle by his side. When the big black outlaw was looking the other way, there was a shot! And then another! And then another! . . . Railroad Bill was on the floor, breathing his last breath. And this time he didn't have time and strength to work his hoodoo and change himself into an animal.

That's what white folks said, but black folks in Alabama, they just laugh and tell another tale. They say Railroad Bill is still roaming around Bay Minette, Flomaton, and Bluff Spring, only now sometimes he's a sheep, sometimes he's a dog, sometimes he's a hog or a rabbit, laughing at white folks' talk.

The Face in the Courthouse Window

The Yankees were on the march in the South, fighting all and anything that came their way. Nothing was safe—not even houses. So they got to Pickens County in Alabama, a county of green pastures, rich rivers, and rolling valleys, where folks worked good and lived happy. But war is black as the devil's kittle. Raiding parties swarmed all over, bursting in like bulls into a flower garden, ruining everything, taking food and cattle and burning buildings. War's worse than the devil in the belfry.

The Blues came to Carrollton, too, the white-honey town near Tuscaloosa, and fought and then burned down the fine old courthouse.

Folks said two black men, Henry and Bill, helped in the burning and the looting. That stayed in the memory of Carrollton folk.

Right after the war, the citizens of the town began rebuilding the courthouse. When it was up a good bit, one day the sheriff found Bill and Henry and put them in jail. Bill was sent off to the penitentiary; Henry got away, but not for long. He was caught and brought back to the Carrollton jail.

Men in blind anger heard of this and gathered round the jail to get the prisoner. But the law was there to protect as well as to punish. To make sure Henry would be safe from the angry crowd, the sheriff took him to the new, near-finished brick courthouse and put him in the small room high up in the attic. There he'd be safe from the mob in the street.

The crowd soon learned of this and began milling around the courthouse, shouting and yelling for Henry. But high up above them another judgment was decreed!

A roaring storm came up with a tearing wind and thunder and lightning and rain by the bucket. Henry stood at the window watching the mob below and the storm above with white fear in his heart. There was no mercy in either the storm or the people.

The storm kept on raging and the crowd below kept on yelling. Suddenly there was a clap of thunder to wake all the dead and a long zigzaggin' streak of lightning to light up all the world.

Henry's face was right close to the window, his nose touching the glass. There was a terrible fear in his face at this wild howling all around. The great streak of lightning shot through the sky into the window, and he fell plumb to the wooden floor!

The rain kept on pouring in great swashes and swishes and the crowd around the courthouse got tired of waiting and shouting, so in the end they went home.

When the sheriff came up to fetch Henry, he was stretched on the ground—still! The lightning from on high had struck him and saved him from the mob and the law. Nobody could do any harm to Henry now. He had gone to a better world.

But not all of him. There on the window of that far-up attic was a picture of Henry's face in terror of man and God. People looking up from below could see it clear, and there it's been ever since.

Folks say they can see it even today. The man who told me the tale said he'd seen it. And if you go to Carrollton in Alabama, maybe you, too, will see that face in the window of the courthouse.

How Far Is It to Jacob Cooper's?

One time there was a judge, Robert Dougherty by name, who lived in Macon County in Alabama. Judge Dougherty was a fine big man with a big booming voice. There were two things he liked all the years of his life: taking long walks in the woods and playing good jokes on his friends.

One spring, he was in need of a milch cow. His old one had gone dry and there was little milk in his home. One day the judge was standing in the street talking to an old friend, Sampson Lanier, telling him he was looking for a good cow.

Said Lanier: "Jacob Cooper, 'bout three miles down on Fort Decatur Road, has a fine two-year-old cow for sale. Think you kin get it cheap."

"If it's only three miles off, I don't mind walking there, but cain't do it now. I'll walk there tomorrow."

Then they spoke of this and that and each went his way.

Now, this Sampson Lanier also liked to have a little fun with his friends, specially with the judge, who had played many a trick on him. Lanier knew Jacob Cooper had a cow that wasn't worth peahulls and that he lived plenty more than three miles away. But the judge did not know this.

Next morning the judge was up before cock's crow and started off without breakfast, figuring the walk before the heat of the day would give him a good appetite and he'd have his coffee at Cooper's house.

He walked full three miles on that road, and when he asked for Jacob Cooper's farm he was told he had to walk a good ways yet, at least four miles more.

He was tired and hot and madder 'n a wet hen when he got there, and he was even madder when he saw the sort of cow Cooper had for sale. She was all skin and bones that wouldn't give as much milk as an old goat. He walked back, sore as a dog covered with ticks, knowing full well Sampson had been out just to flamdoodle him. He swore he'd get even for it, if it took him a month of Sundays to do it. But to Sampson he just said the cow wasn't the kind he wanted. He was biding his time, figuring if any man waits long enough he is sure to get the long end of the stick.

Sometime later the two men met on the road out from Montgomery.

"On the way, Judge?" asked Lanier.

"That I am, going as far as Tuskegee."

"Why don't you come in my carriage? I'm going that way. It's a good five miles and the day's hot. I'm waiting here for my man with the carriage."

The judge quickly agreed. They stood there talking for some time. Then the judge said:

"Tell you what, that fellow's taking his time. I'll go fetch him, I don't mind walking. Sit down in the woods yonder off the road and rest till I bring the carriage. I'll remember the place; I've been there before."

Lanier agreed, for the day was a scorcher. The judge went back and Lanier went into the woods, which were a little way off, lay down in the shade, and soon drowsed off.

Pretty soon the judge met the driver with the horse and wagon.

"Fellow," the judge said, "your master's gone off to a friend. You can drive me to Tuskegee; he'll meet us there."

The driver knew the judge well, so he didn't say anything.

The judge got into the carriage and told the driver to go "easy like" when they passed the place where Lanier had gone into the woods. There was no sign of him, and the judge smiled pleasantly. Thus they came to Tuskegee, and he sat down on the hotel porch waiting for Lanier.

Two hours later Sampson Lanier came up to the hotel on a freight wagon, sitting astride on a sack full of salt, holding over his head a blackjack bush for an umbrella. He came down and looked at the judge with blazing fire in his eyes. The judge looked at him and smiled friendly-like.

"Sampson," he said, "just how far d' you think it is to Jacob Cooper's, eh?" And he laughed, and so did Sampson Lanier, for he knew it was coming to him.

The Battle of Bay Minette

I told you the tale of battling Railroad Bill the Outlaw, who lived around Bay Minette in Baldwin County, and it was a tale stronger 'n bullhides. Now I'll tell you another tale of battling at Bay Minette, but this time it'll give you a good laugh instead o' cold shivers.

It's all about the county seat.

Daphne, a softlike name, on the shores of Mobile Bay, was the first seat of the county, but the business folks, lawyers, and judges from all over didn't favor it. It was too far away for traveling.

"Why not have the county seat more up north that's easier to reach?"

Folks at Bay Minette thought their town, up in the northern part of Alabama, was just the right place for the honor. It had been growing so fast they lost count how many were there. Besides, they had a few strong friends in the legislature, and pretty soon it was decided to move the county seat up to the northern town. Businessmen, lawyers, teachers, judges, all were in favor of it.

But the folks of Daphne didn't see it that way at all and swore they wouldn't let the county seat be moved.

Then the folks of Bay Minette went to court about it. The Minettans had friends in the court rooting for them, so they won. But do you think that bothered the people of Daphne?

"We'll never give 'em the court records and we're not gonna let 'em take a prisoner from the jail. The county seat 'll stay right here," they said.

Minette folks took the fight to a higher court and won the right again to move the county seat to their town.

But the folks of Daphne were stubborner than a mule stuck in the mud. They said that folks in Bay Minette were cutting big hogs with penny knives.

"We ain't givin' up no records and the jail stays right here. Let 'em take this for gospel."

Folks in Bay Minette were getting mad as rabbits running in a briar patch.

"We got to do something. The law's on our side, but we must help the law. We'll get the records and the prisoners if we have to go through roarin' fires and ragin' water."

There was one smart man there named David Quick.

"We don't need to murder cats t' git skins. I've been studying this thorny argument, and there's a simple way to put an end to it. Here's what I got in mind; it's simpler 'n Simple Simon."

Then he told them just what was in his mind, and everyone agreed it was a fine scheme.

They'd pretend they had a prisoner to go to jail, and the sheriff of Minette Bay and four other big, strong men would bring him to the Daphne prison in a buggy. A piece behind them would follow a dozen or two other men on horse or in wagons. Those with the "prisoner" would go to the Daphne jail and ask the sheriff to take him in. When the sheriff opened the jail door, they'd go in and lock the sheriff inside. By that time all the other Minette men would be there to help. They'd take the prisoners and records and maybe even the judge and bring them all to Bay Minette. After that, there'd be no arguments. It was a fine idea.

Next day, early, before cock's crow, men were up in Bay Minette, milling around. Horses were hitched to wagons. Saddles were fastened and talk was high.

"We'll git 'em this time," was the word all around.

The sheriff with four big fellows, one a Negro, who knew what was up, went in the first buggy and rode off. Soon after came a troop of Minette citizens a-horse. Everybody was feeling wild and windy.

Soon they got to the Daphne courthouse and jail. The sheriff sat at the door.

"We got a prisoner here for stealing. We want him put in jail," said the Bay Minette sheriff.

The Daphne sheriff opened the door, and the four Minette men got hold of him and held him fast. They took his keys and locked him in prison and went into the courthouse.

"We'll soon let you out, Sheriff," they said.

The other men of the Bay town had now come up. Quicker 'n greased lightning, they got the records and then they went into the prison, set the sheriff free, took the four prisoners there, and dashed wildly back to Bay Minette. By then, the men of Daphne were up and around and mad enough to eat toads. But they saw there was no use fighting the men of Bay Minette. They had the law on their side and prisoners and records were gone. Right then, the judge came along.

"Might as well go with us," shouted the Minette men. "We got the records and prisoners and the law's on our side. From now on, Bay Minette is the county seat." The judge agreed with them.

So off they all went to Bay Minette, rejoicing like King Solomon in the Bible.

Ever since then, Bay Minette has been the county seat of Baldwin County—and a good county seat it is.

The Smartest One in the Woods

One day, long ago in Alabama, when the leaves shone green and the streams glistened in the sun, Deer was walking slowly, nibbling young leaves.

Through the shadows of the trees came Sun's young daughter, beautiful as a rainbow. Deer looked at her, and she looked at Deer.

"I love Sun's daughter," Deer said very softly. "I want to marry her."

But Deer was timid and would not ask Sun's daughter, the shining girl, to be his wife. He just walked in the woods all day, slowly, head down, nibbling young leaves. Br'er Rabbit came lopping along.

"Br'er Deer, why do you look so sad?" asked Br'er Rabbit.

"I am sad because I want to marry Sun's daughter and I'm afraid to tell her."

"Why don't you write her a letter? I'll take it to her."

"Thanks, Br'er Rabbit; you are a good friend."

Br'er Deer wrote a letter and gave it to Br'er Rabbit.

Br'er Rabbit lopped away. It was a hot day.

"The road to Sun's house is long and it's hot. I'll ask Br'er Frog to take it to that girl. He's wet an' cool and don't mind the heat nohow."

So Br'er Rabbit went to the spring where Br'er Bullfrog lived.

Said Br'er Rabbit: "Br'er Bullfrog, I done you many favors and I want you to do one for me."

The Smartest One in the Woods 23

"That I sure will," bellowed Bullfrog. "What is it?"

"Br'er Deer, he's in love with Sun's young daughter but he's scared to tell 'er. So he wrote her a letter an' he asked me to take it to her. It's too hot for me to go to Sun's house. But you're cool and wet and don't mind the heat. Will you carry this here letter to that pretty girl?"

"I'll do this for you, Br'er Rabbit."

"Watch out you don't get it wet."

"I'll watch," said Br'er Bullfrog.

Sun's daughter came to the spring to get water. Bullfrog saw her, put the letter in his mouth, and sat watching.

The pretty young girl, Sun's daughter, filled her pail with water. When she turned the other way, Bullfrog, holding the letter high in his mouth, jumped into the pail of water. Sun's daughter did not see him. She took the pail and walked home, thinking of Deer all the time.

She came into the house and put the bucket on the ground and Bullfrog jumped out and put the letter on the table.

The girl saw it and read it quickly.

Her father was coming from the sky into the house for the night.

"Here's a letter Br'er Deer sent me."

Sun read it slowly, then he said, "Br'er Deer is a fine young man and you couldn't marry a better."

"Do you give your consent?"

"That I do."

"I'll write him a letter and tell him the news. It'll reach him same as his letter reached me."

She wrote a letter and put it on the table. Bullfrog, sitting in a corner, took it in his mouth and went back to his corner. He wasn't going to walk all the long way to the spring.

"Soon that girl 'll need water an' I'll let her carry me just as she brought me."

He waited, and sure enough, the pail was soon empty. Br'er Bullfrog jumped in and the girl took the pail to go to the spring for water. When she got there, Br'er Bullfrog jumped out and the girl filled the pail and went home. Bullfrog waited with the letter in his mouth. Soon Br'er Rabbit came lopping along.

"Did you give the letter to the pretty girl?" Br'er Rabbit asked.

"She got that letter all right," Br'er Bullfrog boomed.
"What did she say?"
"She answered that letter; here it is."

He gave Sun's daughter's letter to Br'er Rabbit.

Br'er Rabbit said thank ye and ran off in the woods, shouting for Br'er Deer. Br'er Deer heard him and came racing along, and Br'er Rabbit gave him the letter. Deer jumped six feet in the air.

"She'll marry me!" he shouted. "An' it's thanks to you, Br'er Rabbit. You are the smartest one in the woods. Thanks for helping me. I'll do the same for you."

Br'er Rabbit licked his whiskers and laughed low.

Br'er Deer went to Sun, and the day for the wedding was set. It was a grand wedding, and all the animals were there, eating cake and dancing all night. Everybody was happy. Br'er Deer told all how he got his bride, thanks to the smartness of Br'er Rabbit, and everybody said Br'er Rabbit was the smartest one in the woods. And that he sure was.

False Alarm

The day was sunny and warm around Locust Branch in Cherokee County in Alabama. The air was thick with perfume from the flowers, and the birds were singing to beat the band. Everything and everybody were just fine. Menfolk were working in the fields and womenfolk were working in the cabins. High up, the winds were sleeping lazy-like in the clouds. That's the kind of day it was around Locust Branch in Cherokee County in Alabama.

Out of the clear sky, bang! there came a shouting into that fine day. A man came along on horseback, tearing through the fields and roads. His face was covered with grime and dirt, and his horse was wet and foaming. The man waved his hand high in the air, shouting scary words at the top of his voice. He'd been going that way all morning through the settlements of Cherokee County.

"The Indians are on the warpath! They butchered Cozard and his family and set his house on fire. To arms! To arms!"

Then he raced through the fields and streams to warn other settlers.

Men ran home as fast as they could, fear and worry on their faces. The women stopped their housework and children ran home frightened. Everybody began working faster than hounds after 'coons. Guns were examined, bullets were poured fast, knives were tested. As soon as a man felt ready to go, he told his wife how to barricade the cabin and how to fight for children, home, and possessions in case the Indians attacked.

But there was one woman in Locust Branch who wasn't a fighting woman and didn't hold for fighting. She was Mrs. Holmes, the good wife of the minister. Instead of barricading her cabin and getting ready knives and boiling water, she took her large family of children and led them into the cornfield not far from her home. The corn was green and strong and high, near eight feet tall. (That's the kind of corn that grew in Cherokee County in Alabama.) Mrs. Holmes took her brood of children and went deep into the cornfield where neither man nor beast could see her. She gathered her children around her and counted them twice to make sure no child had remained behind. When she got to her son Warren, she let out a long gasp!

"Land sakes, Warren!" she shouted, "you forgot your coat in the cabin. There you are in the clean white shirt I washed yesterday, and the Indians 'll see you first a mile off. You'll make a fine target to aim at. May the Lord save us!"

"Do you want me to go home for the jacket?"

"Heaven preserve us! You'd be without your scalp quicker 'n a passing swallow. You're staying right here with me. I've an idea to fix it so no Indian 'll see you miles off. I just hate to dirty that good clean shirt o' yours I washed only yesterday, but it must be done to save your life from these savages who want to murder us. I'll paint that shirt so's they'll never see it or you."

It had been raining for a long spell, and the ground was soft and oozy. She took the black mud and smeared it all over the white shirt until it looked as black as the earth in which the rich corn was growing.

Then they all sat down deep in the lovely green waving leaves and stalks, frightened and shivering and waiting to hear the war yells of the Indians. But the broad corn leaves rustled softly as if saying to one another, "Folks are mighty foolish sometimes."

So Mrs. Holmes and her children waited and waited and waited, but all they heard was birds singing and insects zumming. Just the same, everyone listened sharply and with fear in his heart. They were listening for a long time when at last they heard cries of men. But there were no Indian yells or shots of guns, only men's voices shouting:

"Open your doors! Come out from hiding! 'Twas only a false alarm! The Cozards are all in good health. We found 'em working in the fields."

Doors were opened, women and children appeared everywhere, and Mrs. Holmes came out of the corn. All were happy except . . . Mrs. Holmes, the wife of the Reverend Mr. Holmes. For she had covered her son Warren's shirt with black mud to no purpose at all, just for a false alarm!

The Arkansas Traveler*

There is an Arkansas tale that's been told the length and breadth of the great land of North America, and now I will tell it to you. It is the tale of the Arkansas traveler.

One time there was a rich planter in Arkansas in Chicot County and his name was Colonel Faulkner. One day he had to go somewhere, so he got on a fine white horse, put his good gun across his saddle, and set out early in the morning.

He was riding, riding all the day, and when he came to the hills of the Bayou Mason country, which was pretty late in the afternoon, he lost his way. He rode all around but couldn't find a road in sight anywhere. He was tuckered out and hungry and he was looking for a place where he could stay for the night.

Pretty soon he thought he heard fiddling, and he followed the welcome sound until he came to a small clearing where there was a squatter's log cabin.

It was a true Arkansas log cabin, with wide chinks welcoming sun and wind, and with plenty of leaks on the roof for friendly calls of rain and snow. In front of the cabin sat the squatter on an empty

---

* Most of the language, punctuation, and spelling follows the first published script of this famous dialogue-story.

barrel, fiddle in the bend of his elbow, fiddling the beginning of an old jig over and over again. In the open door stood his wife, and behind her was the eldest daughter combing her hair with a wooden comb. Around were the other children listening to their father fiddling the beginning of that tune over and over again.

Master Faulkner rode up to the cabin and stopped before the fiddling squatter.

"Hello, stranger," said he. Children and all just stared at him.

"Hello, yourself," said the squatter, who kept fiddling all the time. And he kept on fiddling the self-same tune over and over again through all the talking.

Traveler: "Can I stay all night with you?"

Squatter: "No, sir, you can git to."

Traveler: "Have you any spirits here?"

Squatter: "Lots uv 'em. Sal seen one last night by that thar hollar gum, and it nearly skeered her to death."

Traveler: "That's not what I mean. I'm weary and cold and a good drink would set me right."

Squatter: "Had some, but I finished the last this morning."

Traveler: "I'm hungry, hadn't a thing since morning; can't you give me something to eat?"

Squatter: "Hain't a durned thing in the house. Not a mouthful uv meat, nor a dust uv meal here."

Traveler: "Well, can't you give my horse something?"

Squatter (*fiddling all the time*): "Got nothing to feed him on."

Traveler: "How far is it to the next house?"

Squatter: "Stranger! I don't know. I've never been there."

Colonel Faulkner was getting cross at that unreasonable man and the never-ending scraping of the fiddle. Said he in an angry tone: "Well, do you know who lives there?"

Squatter: "I don't know, I've never been thar."

Traveler: "As I'm so bold then, what might your name be?"

Squatter: "It might be Dick and it might be Tom; but it lacks right smart uv it," and he kept on fiddling.

It was getting more than the colonel could take, so he said: "Sir! will you tell me where this road goes to?"

Squatter: "It's never gone anywhar since I've lived here; it's always thar when I git up in the mornin'."

Traveler: "Well, how far is it to where it forks?"
Squatter: "It don't fork at all, but it splits up like the devil."
Traveler: "As I'm not likely to get to any other house tonight, can't you let me sleep in yours, and I'll tie my horse to a tree and do without anything to eat or drink."
Squatter: "My house leaks. Thar's only one dry spot in it, and me and Sal sleep on it. And that thar tree is the ole woman's persimmon; you can't tie to it, 'caze she don't want 'em shuk off. She 'lows to make beer out'n 'um."
Traveler: "Why don't you finish your house and stop the leaks?"
Squatter: "It's been rainin' all day."
He never stopped fiddling that tune one minute.
Traveler: "Well, why don't you do it in dry weather?"
Squatter: "It don't leak then."
Traveler: "As there seems to be nothing alive about your place but children, how do you do here anyhow?"
Squatter: "Putty well, I thank you. How do you do yourself?"
Traveler: "I mean, what do you do for a living here?"
Squatter: "Keep a tavern."
Traveler: "Well, I told you I wanted a drink."
Squatter: "Stranger, I bought a bar'l 'n more 'n a week ago, but we folks are pretty thirsty and now it's all gone."
Traveler: "I'm sorry it's all gone, but, my friend, why don't you play the balance of that tune?"
Squatter: "It's got no balance to it."
Traveler: "I mean, you don't play the end of it."
Squatter: "Stranger, can you play the fiddle?"
Traveler: "Yes, a little, sometimes."
Squatter: "You don't look like a fiddlur, but if you think you can play any more onto that thar tune, you kin just try it."
Colonel Faulkner got down from his horse, smiling a little, took the fiddle from the squatter, and, knowing the tune well, began playing it. He was a pretty good fiddler and played the tune clear and lively to the end.
Well, you should have seen the faces of these Arkansas folks. It was a caution. Eyes and ears were owl-open and feet were tapping lively, dancing in time to the music. For these Arkansas folks loved music as a cat loves cream. They'd rather hear a lively tune than a

long "politics" speech, and the quickest path to their hearts was with a happy song.

When Colonel Faulkner was done, the squatter cried:

"Stranger, take half a dozen cheers and sot down. Sal, stir yourself round like a six-horse team in a mudhole. Go round in the hollar whar I killed that buck this mornin', cut off some of the best pieces, and fotch it and cook it for me and this gentleman d'rectly. Raise up the board under the head of the bed and git the jug I hid from Dick and give us some cheer. Till, climb up the loft and git the rag that's got the sugar tied in it. Dick, carry the gentleman's hoss round under the shed, give him some fodder and corn; much as he kin eat."

"Dad," spoke daughter Till, "they ain't knives enuf for to sot the table."

Squatter: "Whar's big butch, little butch, ole case, cob-handle, granny's knife, and the one I handled yesterday. That's enuf to sot any gentleman's table. Durn me, stranger, if you can't stay as long as you please, and I'll give you plenty to eat and to drink. Just you plays us good tunes now and then. Will you have coffee for supper?"

Traveler: "Yes, sir."

Squatter: "We'll give you mighty good sweetnin'. And while the women folks bestir themselves, play away, stranger; you kin sleep on the dry spot tonight."

While the women hustled about, the colonel kept on fiddling the tune over and over and many more besides, to the joy of the squatter and all his family. By jiminie criminie! feet moved faster, eyes looked brighter, and faces had a Sunday shine.

He played while the roasting venison smelled sweeter than flowers.

They all sat around a log for a table and had their fill. The colonel sat back well satisfied.

"My friend," said he, "can't you tell me about the road I'm to travel tomorrow?"

Squatter: "Tomorrow! Stranger, you won't get out of these diggin's for six weeks. But when it gits so you kin start, you see that big sloo over thar, well, you have to git crost that, then you take the road up to the bank, and in about a mile you come to a two-acre-and-a-half corn patch. About two miles from thar, you'll come to the damndest swamp you ever struck in all your travels. It's boggy enough to move a saddle blanket. Thar's a first-rate road about six feet under thar."

Traveler: "How am I to get at it?"

Squatter: "You can't get at it nary time till the weather stiffens down some. Well, about a mile beyont, you come to a place where thar's no road. You kin take the right-hand or you kin try the left, but you'll always find the road'll be runnin' out. You're mighty lucky ef you kin find the way back to my house whar you kin come and play on that tune as long as you please."

So the colonel stayed as long as he could with that music-loving family in Arkansas. But in the end he had to leave and, with good wishes and thanks, go to the place he had set out for. And that's the famous tale of the Arkansas traveler.

How Red Strawberries Brought Peace in the Woods

There is a river in Arkansas called Strawberry River because its bank is full of wild strawberries. It is a strange stream because near its mouth it flows forward and backward, which no other river in Arkansas does. The Cherokee Indians who used to hunt around the Strawberry River tell a good story of how the strawberries came to the land.

The Great Spirit looked around and saw the endless sky and the green land, and he said man and woman were needed on that land. So he created a warrior and gave him a squaw for a wife.

The two lived together in peace for a long time. He hunted and fished and the woman planted and reaped and cooked food.

Then one day they had a quarrel about a little thing, and so the trouble began. Every day they quarreled a little more. Soon they quarreled about everything.

This kept on for a long time until one day the woman was so angry, she left the man when he was out hunting. She set out for the Sun land that was far off in the east.

When the man came home, he did not find his wife in the wigwam. He looked all around; she was not there. Only her footsteps showed where she had gone. He followed them, but even though he ran fast he could not reach her, she was so far ahead.

She was far, far ahead, running all the time, not looking back.

The man ran all the time too. He ran so fast, he became tired and hungry. The Great Spirit saw him and was sorry for him.

"Why do you run like that?" he asked the man.

"I am running to catch up to my wife who ran away from our wigwam."

"Why did she run away?"

The man was silent.

Then the Great Spirit said, "She ran away because you two quarreled all the time."

"That is true," the man said. "I will not quarrel again. I am not angry any more."

"If you will not quarrel and not be angry, I will bring her back to you."

The Great Spirit ran in front of the woman and put before her a fine patch of elderberries blooming blue and ripe. She looked at them and kept on running.

Again the Great Spirit ran before her and set in her path some bushes full of blackberries.

The woman came to them, looked at them, and ran on.

The Great Spirit raced ahead of her, all the time putting in her way bushes of all kinds of berries, but she just looked at them and kept on running very fast.

Then the Great Spirit put before her, low on the ground, a bed of beautiful red strawberries. She had never seen the glossy red fruit and had never smelled the strawberry perfume. She bent down to pick some and put them in her mouth. They tasted sweet and good, and she kept on bending down to pick them and eat them. This gave the man a chance to come nearer. One time, as she bent down, she looked backward and saw him running to her.

Then the years they had lived together without quarreling came back to her. She saw the many days they had lived in peace. She forgot all about the quarrels and wanted to go back to him. She sat down near a river where the water flowed forward and backward and waited. He came nearer all the time and she wanted more and more to go home with him. She picked up many strawberries and held them in her hands, waiting for him. He came up and she held the red berries up to him. He took them and ate them. They were sweet and smelled nice. He thanked her.

"These berries are very good and I am glad that you gave them to me. I will not quarrel again with you," he said.

"No, we must not quarrel again and be angry," the woman said.

They ate more strawberries together and then they went home.

The strawberries spread all over, and Indians and white folks have been eating them ever since. That is why near the river in Arkansas where the water flows forward and backward so many wild glossy-red strawberries grow and people call it the Strawberry River.

The Proud Tale of David Dodd

There's a tale of a young boy's courage during the War Between the States known in every Southern state, and particularly in Arkansas. For it happened there, right in the state's own capital, in Little Rock. It is a tale that has been told for so many years, in so many places, and so often that it has become a folktale.

There lived in those sad and scorching days in Little Rock a family by the name of Dodd. They were well known and respected by all. David Dodd, one of the sons in that family, had not joined the Southern army because he was too young. He left St. John's College when the war broke out to work in a telegraph office where there was need of help.

The Northerners came marching down and the Confederate Army had to retreat farther south. Many families in Little Rock followed the Southern army, the Dodds among them.

When they were about sixty miles from Little Rock, David's father said:

"David, I've forgotten some papers in the drawers of my desk. I need them now. Go back to the city and to our house and get them and bring them to me."

David was under age and, according to the military custom of those days, all he needed was a pass from the Confederate commander stating his age. With that he could pass through the lines.

"Now, David, you go to see General Fagan, who's my friend, and he'll give you the proper pass so you can get through to Little Rock."

David, who was bright as a drop of water in the sunshine, didn't let grass grow under his feet. Soon he stood before the general and told him what he had come for.

The soldier listened and then, after a little silence, he said, looking straight at him:

"Davy, you're bright, smart, and I can trust you, I reckon."

"That you can indeed, sir. I wish I were in uniform. The only reason I'm not, is I'm under age, sir."

"I know that, boy. But you can do as fine service for your country out of uniform as on the fighting line."

"I'm working in the telegraph office, sir."

"I know, but now you are going on an errand and you can be of service there too."

"How, sir?"

"By keeping your eyes and ears wide open."

"That I'll do gladly."

"And what you see and hear, you just dig deep in your memory."

"I sure will, sir."

"If ever there is anything you see and hear you think is important, you might put it down in the telegraph code, which you know."

"I sure will."

"And here is something even more important, Davy. There's a man in the enemy camp there who is on our side. He's spying for us. He'll get word that you're coming and he'll give you a report for which I'm waiting."

"I'll gladly take it and bring it safely back."

"I know you will, Davy. Remember: eyes and ears wide open and lips tight closed, except with such you know you can trust."

"Trust me, sir," David said. "I have many friends in Little Rock —one in particular," and he blushed. "I'll bring you back all the information I can get. I hope it'll be what you want."

David left. With his pass he got through the picket lines and into the city. The first thing he did was to go to see his sweetheart, a girl a little younger than he was. He told her proudly what the general had asked him to do.

"I can help you, David," she said eagerly. "All I have to do is keep my eyes and ears wide open and I am working hard for our cause. I know the soldier who is helping us; he's an officer, and I'll get the report for you. You go home and get the papers for your father and I'll go on my errand. Then you come back here."

The girl was off and David went his way. He walked slowly through the streets, noting all he saw. Now and then he stopped, talking to some of those who had stayed behind.

In his home he found some soldiers, and when he told them what he was there for, they let him go to his father's room. Alone, he quickly set down in telegraph code what he thought important in the city. Then, taking out his father's papers, he mixed his notes with them and left. In a short time he was back in the girl's home. She was there waiting for him.

"David," she said, "I have the paper for you. I know what's in it. It has a report of the whole Northern army that's in the city and the plans of what they're going to do. Hide it well."

David took the papers and carefully put them together with his own into a cloth bag and hid it under his shirt. Then, greatly pleased, the two bade each other goodbye, and he started back.

When he reached the city limits, the guards stopped him and he gave them the pass that allowed him to go through.

He was trudging along the road happy in his success when suddenly the sky blackened and one of those wild winter storms came up. Day turned to night; a cold, wild, whipping rain came down, hiding roads and paths. David did not know where he was going. He wandered back and forth through woods and fields and suddenly he found himself at the picket line again. He had gone backward instead of forward!

Two sentries stopped him.

"Who are you? Where are you going?"

David told the truth, that he had come with a pass and had given it up to go back and was now lost in the storm.

"I don't trust you Rebs. You better come with me and tell yer cock-an'-bull story to an officer."

There was no escape, so David had to go along.

He knew well that if the papers were found on him, it meant death. One soldier was in front of him, the other at his back. He watched closely and when he thought the man behind him was not watching, he tried to take out the papers to destroy them. But the man in the rear saw this and before David could do anything, the soldier got hold of the papers.

"So, little fellow, you thought you could fool us. Bet you are a spy. You come right to prison." David was taken to prison and the papers found on him were quickly read. They told everything about the Federal army there: strength, position, plans. Only a high officer could have given that information. Nothing could have been more accusing than such papers.

Trials of such deeds moved swiftly. David was taken before a court and condemned to be hanged—unless he would tell who had given him the paper.

David refused to tell and so he was ordered to be hanged the next day.

The news of David's trial and sentence spread like wildfire through the city. The Dodd family was well known and David was much liked. A committee of citizens went to General Steele, who was the commander in charge, to ask for clemency.

General Steele listened carefully to the speaker and then said:

"Who are you? Where are you going?"

"Gentlemen, I'll pardon the boy and let him go free, but he must tell who gave him the papers with our plans. I'll order him to be brought here and give him another chance. To know who gave that secret information is more important than the life of that young boy." Then he ordered the sentry to bring David before him.

"David," said the general, "your friends came and begged me to pardon you. I'm willing to do so, and I will let you go free, back to your parents, but only if you tell me who gave you that report."

David looked fearlessly at the general.

"Sir, I will not betray my friends and those who are helping our Southern cause."

"David, you are young and I do not like to see you hanged. If you will give me the name of the traitor in my ranks, you will be free to return to your father and mother and friends."

"Sir, I said I cannot and will not betray our friends. The papers were given to me in full confidence and I will not betray that confidence."

"You know you will die for this, boy."

"I know it, sir."

David was taken back to prison and the Little Rock citizens left in sorrow.

The next morning—it was a cold morning in January—David Dodd was taken from prison and died right in front of St. John's College where he had been a student. To him death was better than betraying friends who helped the cause in which he believed.

Whenever tales of bravery are told in Arkansas, and all over the South, you are sure to hear the tale of David Dodd.

The Bull Didn't Have a Chance

One time, way back, there was a man who lived in the Boston Mountains in Arkansas. That man had a fine, strong bull and he opined it was the finest bull in all the state. Maybe that was true or maybe it was not, but, good or bad, that animal had one bad fault. He was a very independent bull and did just as he pleased whether folks liked it or not. Well, you know independence and doing as you please are the great "ornaments" of our land, but they aren't much good if they step on your toes. Then there's trouble. And there was trouble. That bull was starting trouble all around. No garden or field was safe. The critter would just go in and eat up anything he liked. Fences didn't matter. He could knock down a fine rail fence as easy as a morning cobweb.

Near neighbors and friends of that man with the bull were ready to forgive and forget, figuring that, after all, you can't teach a dumb animal human behavior. But there was one neighbor who thought differently. The bull got into his corn patch, on which he had sweated many a long day, and ate his corn, stems and all. He needed that corn bad and his dander was up to treetops.

He went to the man who owned the bull and said, "Your fine bull et up all my corn that I worked a long time on. I need that corn and I ain't got it. Now, pay me for that corn so's I kin go out and buy some."

The man said he wasn't going to pay for what a dumb beast ate up. Dumb beasts didn't know what they were doing anyway.

This made the man who lost his corn even more angry, and he went straight to the judge and swore out a warrant for the bull, trespasser and robber. The sheriff came and dragged the bull to the prison yard. Court was then in session and so the case against the bull was up for trial the next day.

Everybody had heard about the coming trial against the bull and the green where court was held was thick with folks from as far as fifty miles to see and hear that queer case.

A jury was picked and the lawyers for each side rolled up their sleeves and opened their vest buttons and got to work.

It was a hot day and the clacking of those lawyers filled the air with "hot coals." All the time the bull was bellowing in the prison yard, but no one paid any heed to him. Folks never thought that maybe *he* wanted to be heard in the business that concerned him.

There was no end to the talk, and sweat was running down those lawyers' faces like water from a crick. When the sun was low they were hoarse from bawling and you couldn't tell their talk from the bellowing bull, so the judge thought it was time to give the case to the jury. They went in a huddle and soon came back with a verdict of guilty. The judge said the man who owned the bull had to pay the man for the corn and a fine to the court for letting such a wild beast run loose.

Well, that man just saw red powder and razor knives! He hollered he wasn't "gonna pay no fine for no corn to nobody"; besides, he had no money anyway.

The judge scratched his head and then he decided the best thing would be to butcher the bull, since it sure was a menace to the community and the meat would pay for the fine and the corn. Besides, they might even roast a piece and have a friendship feast.

And that's exactly what they did.

Only there was one man didn't agree. He was a good American and didn't think it was a fair trial because the judge and the jury hadn't listened to what the bull had to say even though he was bellowing all the time. But folks don't worry about fair trials so long as the end is to the liking of the majority.

The Sad-Lovely End of Wilhelmina Inn

One time there was a fine hotel on top of a high mountain, not far from where the city of Mena, in Arkansas, thrives.

That hotel was built by immigrants who had come to this land of North America from far Holland. They called it the Wilhelmina Inn, to honor their Queen, whose name was Wilhelmina. It was a great building with many big rooms and broad stairways. On one floor some rooms had been set aside for the Dutch Queen when she would come to visit Arkansas.

To that inn came rich folks like bees to a hive, even though it was not so easy to get there. First you had to go by train to the foot of the mountain, then you had to get on top of a donkey to take you up to the top of the mountain to the inn. But they came there just the same, spending all the hours of the day in fun and frolic.

One time there came to that Wilhelmina Inn the wife of a rich man who owned a couple of railroads. She dressed like a rich woman and she spoke like a rich woman, telling everybody how much money her husband had. With her she had brought a maid to help her dress, as if folks couldn't dress themselves, and also her little dog. It was a very small dog that didn't look like any dog in Arkansas, and that rich woman said she had gotten it in Europe. That little dog was always in her lap and never went hunting, or watching, or anything like all good dogs in Arkansas did.

The first night that woman came in for dinner in the big dining room hung with glass chandeliers and full of people, she held that little dog in her arms. She was nearly covered with diamonds and pearls, around her neck and on her fingers, and her little dog in her

The Sad-Lovely End of Wilhelmina Inn 45

arms had a collar with diamonds and pearls. When she came in, everybody stopped eating. She was used to people looking at her, so she just went to her table, nose high in the air and her little dog in her arms. She didn't know the real reason folks were looking at her. They were used to seeing diamonds and pearls; fact is, they all had some anyhow, but they were not used to seeing a dog brought into the dining room. There was a sign on the wall that said no dog was permitted in that room. And when she sat down and let the little dog lick some cream out of her *own plate,* you could have heard an elderblossom dropping on the grass. Every crystal from the hanging chandeliers was looking down on the rich woman; all the people all around were just staring like owls with candles in their eyes. The woman with the little dog didn't know what it was all about, and she didn't care anyway.

The Wilhelmina Inn had the most polite gentleman hotel manager in all the land. Through the dining room, which was now silent as a grave, came this most polite hotel manager. In his black frock coat and white tie he walked to the table where the lady sat with her dog at the table. He bowed low and said:

"Sorry, Mrs. Pepper, to disturb you, but the rules of this here establishment are not to bring dogs into the dining room and *not* to let them eat from the plates used by the guests."

"Well, I never . . . This is my dog, Mister Manager, and I am paying good money. It's my darlin' and he goes where I go and eats from the plates I use. And he's goin' to eat with me right here whether you like it or not."

The manager bowed politely and said, "Sorry, Ma'am, but the rules of this establishment have to be followed and nobody can bring a dog into the dining room. I must be polite to *all* my guests. We can feed your dog for you with anything you want and in special china dishes, if you'll pay for 'em, but it's got to be outside of the dining room. Many guests in the Wilhelmina Inn don't like to see a dog in the dining room."

"Mister, they're going to like it this time. I'm paying good money for board and keep and, if you want, I'll pay extra for my darlin', but she and I ain't gonna be parted for a thousand inns, and we're staying right here."

With that she gave that man a look that would sour milk fresh from the cows.

The manager did not know what to do. He couldn't put that big, fat woman out, because her husband was a very rich railroad magnate—and, besides, the manager was a gentleman. So he held his temper tight, as a gentleman should, and said:

"Madam, you have to take that dog out of our dining room, I tell you. I must follow my orders."

"This time, Mister, you'll follow *my* orders, I'm telling you."

The manager in his black frock coat walked politely away but mad enough to bite snakes' heads. First he sent a telegram to the railroad man who was the husband of the woman with a thorn in her head. He told him she was behaving contrary to the regulations of the inn and asked him what he was to do about it.

The answer came back in no time. "You better do just what my wife wants."

But the railroad millionaire didn't know the kind of man the manager was. His dander ran high. He would teach that unmannerly woman and that hen-pecked husband a little politeness.

First he called the chef and the housekeeper to his office and talked over the whole business with them. Then he called in all the men and women working in the place and gave them a long talk about politeness and consideration for other folks. The result was that if that woman wouldn't get the misbegotten dog out of the dining room, he and the chef and the butlers and the head housekeeper would leave the place. Then that rich woman could do things herself, as she did before her husband made his money. Another place had asked him to work there and he'd take all the help with him.

Everyone agreed with him because they said they "liked to serve ladies and gentlemen who know how to act like ladies and gentlemen."

That evening no wood was put on the fire and no water in the pitchers. The next morning the manager got on a donkey and so did all the help. They all went to the railroad station and took the next train out and the stubborn woman and the rest of the guests were left to take care of themselves.

Well, the guests, seeing how things turned out, figured they had come to rest and not to work, so they packed their things and got on the donkeys to take them to the train. And the woman with the dog had to do the same, swearing she would get even with the manager.

The beautiful Wilhelmina Inn never got over that. From that time on no guest came there, only the winds and the sun and the rain and animals from the woods. Folks didn't come again, and the wind and the wood creatures broke it up; only some of the strong walls were left. So the place was made into a beautiful park where people come to rest and to have nice picnics. And the park is called Wilhelmina Park.

The Judge and the Baseball-Pitching Indian Chief

Judge Isaac C. Parker of Arkansas was a famous judge, one of the most famous in the land. He held his court in Fort Smith in that state, and he became so well known for getting rid of desperate men with guns and masks * who plagued honest men that he was called the Hanging Judge.

In those years, that territory had many horse thieves, cattle thieves, bank robbers, killers—it was like a snakehole full of varmints, and Judge Parker got it all cleaned up like a fresh-mown field. He tried twenty-eight thousand criminals and suspects and was fair to all of them.

But Judge Parker liked many other things outside of law and judging. Most of all he liked a baseball game. And among the many, many tales told of the Judge, one about a baseball game is the best known.

He was often ready to cry quits at a most important trial to see

---

* Many bandits wore masks on their faces when they held up banks and travelers.

a good game that was played anywhere nearby. For in those days, like today, each settlement had its own team and there were always great rivalry to see which was the best.

One time there was a great game between the team of Fort Smith and the team of Van Buren, a place nearby. These two were the best during the whole summer and now they were fighting to see which was the better of the two.

Judge Parker was sitting with friends talking politics when three young fellows came up to him. They were from the Fort Smith team.

"Judge," one of them said, "we're gonna play the Van Burens for the championship, but our best pitcher, the Indian, Flatfoot, is in jail for violatin' the law. If he don't pitch, we lose. If he pitches, we're sure to win."

Judge Parker sat there just looking at the young fellows.

"Judge, couldn't you let 'm out just for practicin' an' pitchin'?" another of the three said.

Judge Parker didn't say anything. He wasn't one for talking till he had something to say. After a time, he answered.

"I'll see about it. One of you fellows go and get a ball an' glove an' bat. Bring it in the jail yard. We'll be there waiting for you."

The men with the Judge went to the prison where there was housed a collection of bobtail and ragtail that beat Babel. They stayed in the courtyard. The Judge called one of the guards and asked him to bring the Indian out. The three fellows with ball, glove, and bat had come back. The Indian was brought out.

"Now you pitch a few balls," the Judge said to him. "I've seen you play in games and you played good, but I want to make sure."

The Indian pitched a few balls to the man with the glove and the second man swung the bat, hitting the air mighty hard.

"That's good," said the Judge. "Now, listen, Flatfoot. You kin play, but I'll be there mighty close watching you with a forty-fiver on my hip. If you try to escape, you won't run far, and if you don't pitch the best game of your life and win that game, you'll stay in jail for a mighty long time. Just think of that all the time. If you win . . . well, let's talk about it when we get to it."

The Indian listened and did not say anything. He went out with the other fellows to practice, but a guard followed him.

The next day, the day of the game, Flatfoot was out on the diamond with the team. There was a big crowd, the Judge sitting in front.

It was a great game, I can tell you, and those watching made more noise than Indians at a war dance.

Flatfoot pitched as he had never pitched in his life. Not a Van Buren man got a run and the Fort Smith team won the championship because nobody could beat them with that Indian pitching. They yelled and cheered him so you could hear it in the next state, which is Oklahoma.

The next morning Judge Parker was in court and the Indian stood before him. The case against Flatfoot was sure as a rooster's crow. He'd been selling what the law forbade to sell. The Judge listened. That morning he was filled with the forgiveness of the Lord and the justice of the law.

He gave Flatfoot a long talk, telling him that cats always look big till dogs come barking, and the law is a big, big dog and no man doing wrong can escape for long. If he'd travel the path where honest men go, he'd never get into trouble. In the end he told him he'd let him go this time to do more such fine pitching and less prowling in the devil's hunting fields.

Sam Hudson the Great

I'll tell you a story about Sam Hudson, the Davy Crockett man of Arkansas who never knew the word fear from the day he was born. That was in the days when men, women, or young ones couldn't afford to be scared. They had to have courage or lose home or head.

Sam Hudson went further than anyone in Arkansas in not being scared.

That man had three different trades. He was a millwright, a bear hunter, and a gunsmith. He hunted down more bear than any man in the state. He cut down as much wood as Paul Bunyan did and maybe there wasn't a log cabin in Arkansas didn't have lumber that came from Sam Hudson.

In gunsmithing there was no better workman in the land. Folks came from far and near to have their shooting pieces fixed, and he made 'em all as good as new. He worked so hard, he wore out three sets of gunsmithing tools.

When he wanted to rest, he just roamed up and down the land, gun in hand. So he found the Diamond Cave of Arkansas that's famous not only through the state but through all the land.

When he worked, he worked like an army. He cleaned up three farms so there wasn't a bit of scrub brush or tree on 'em: all fine grazing land.

He had to do that, for he married three wives and he had forty children.

And when he went hunting, he hunted like an army. He rode down nine packs of hunting dogs, killed over a hundred bears and so many buffaloes you couldn't count 'em. Folks said he had something more than hair on his head. Nothing ever stopped that man. And just to show you that I speak gospel I'll tell you how he got a panther one day . . . without a bullet shot. It's a tale that's been around the Ozarks for many years, and man, woman, and young ones like to tell it.

One time Sam Hudson was busy in the woods chopping down a bee tree that was chock-full of honey. 'Twasn't easy work and the sweat was running down his face and neck.

After a spell he thought to set down for a rest. No sooner was he resting, the ax by his side, than—dancing mill wheels! he saw sitting before him a snarling panther, lips rising and falling, showing his white teeth, while his white claws were going in and out of his furry paws. The big wildcat was just looking him over, swishing its tail, sort of getting ready, but making no move.

Sam eyed that panther and that panther eyed Sam. Then Sam picked up a big chunk of wood he'd chopped off the bee tree and threw it at the wildcat, thinking he might scare him off. But instead, the cat suddenly got ready to leap at him.

Quickly, Sam raised the ax he'd been using and let it fly. But he swung it so hard the handle flew out of his hands.

That made the varmint mad, and with a scream that shook the trees, he made for Sam.

Sam had no shooting piece and there was the beast, with mouth wide open, eyes blazing fire, fangs shiny, coming at him.

As the critter hit him, Sam rammed his fist and arm up to the elbow down its throat! The critter began choking and shortbreathing. Then slowly it let up and began hanging limp-like. Now Sam got to pounding its side with his other fist hard as he could. He kept on hitting harder and harder all the time and soon the beast hung loose without breathing.

Sam got his hand out bleeding and torn. He carried the wounds of that strange battle on his right arm for the rest of his life. But do you think that stopped him from doing mighty deeds? Not Sam Hudson of Newton in the Ozarks. He never stopped till he went to where other kinds of deeds are done and men rest from hard labor.

In Arkansas Stick to Bears;
Don't Mess with Swampland Skeeters

Back in the old days there lived a squatter in the Delta region not far from what is now the city of Helena. That squatter called himself Major Jones and he said he was slicker than a weasel, but his neighbors said he was a living bobcat that's dragged its tail through a briar patch. He wasn't a neighborly neighbor. He was forever complaining, but his biggest complaint was against Delta mosquitoes that were making life hard for man and beast.

They were as plentiful as ants at a picnic and big as wild turkeys. Some of them were nearly as big as deers in the woods.

One hot night the squatter set out to hunt bear. He was always bragging about his shooting strength. Truth to tell, he was lazy as pond water, so, instead of using his shooting piece on critters, he set bear traps deep in the swamps where he was sure bear were plentiful. After setting the contraptions he returned home. It was then nearly late candle-time, and it was mighty warm. Best time for mosquito-hunting. They were out thick as barn hay. They were zooming louder than frogs croaking. The squatter was hopping faster than a fox with a bumblebee in his tail, to steer clear of 'em. But those varmint mosquitoes smelled blood and they were hot after it. And I tell you when skeeters are on your trail, it's worse than snakes.

The man had come to his canoe, jumped in, and set down to paddle. But the crick skeeters were after him like a mighty army with banners, as it says in the Holy Book. Their zooming seemed like thunder in the springtime. The squatter fought them with paddle and gun to keep them off, but they were coming at him like a herd of buffalo. Major Jones was getting madder by the minute; he thought it was time to use powder and lead. He raised his hunting piece and began to fire. He brought down one or two of the zoomers and scared the rest, but only for a short time. Pretty soon they were at him again. By now he had come to where his cabin was. He leaped out of the canoe, ran to the door quicker than a jack rabbit, and put on the latch behind him, thanking the Lord for his safe escape.

The next morning early he went to the trap to see if it had caught a fat brown bear, for he was in need of meat and oil.

When he got there and saw what he saw, his face looked like soot on a stick.

That bear trap had caught . . . a skeeter the size of a young heifer.

Major Jones's face was fit to scare black cats at night. He held his teeth tight, threw a rope round the neck of the skeeter, tied a log to its borer, and hobbled its hind legs good. Then he got the varmint out of the trap and dragged it home slow-like. It wasn't easy, for that skeeter was bucking and rearing to beat running fire.

"Jest you keep on rearin' and buckin'! I'm gonna train you to be gentle as a lamb and I'm gonna train you to drill holes with that borer of yourn. Maybe I'll find oil."

In the end he got the varmint in the barn, but he put the boot on the wrong leg.

That critter began tearing and ripping around the barn like a bull with hornets all over. It was making such a racket with zooming, nobody could sleep. The third night the squatter couldn't stand it any longer.

"I'll teach that toad blister somethin'," he said to his wife. He took an old mule harness that was lying in the lot back of the cabin and went cautiously into the barn. With dodging and cross-running he got it on the skeeter, tied the skeeter to a post, and went to his cabin.

The mosquito didn't like the queer contraption one bit. So he began smashing it right and left and made enough noise to wake the dead. In the end Major Jones went to the door of the barn. Inside, the skeeter was banging and hitting away. Before Jones's hand touched the wooden latch, the door came down with a bang. The critter had broken the door and had got the harness off its neck.

Major Jones's eyes popped open big as goose eggs, for the next thing that happened no man in Arkansas had ever seen.

Before you could say Jehoshaphat that skeeter was up in the air flying in the moonlight. It was aiming straight for the pasture where the squatter's cow was mooing for the calf. Down went that critter in the pasture and, come gunpowder!, if it didn't get hold of that cow with its hind legs and begin lifting it off the grass.

Now, it is common knowledge in Arkansas that it needs two Bear State mosquitoes to carry off a fair-sized cow, and here just one skeeter was doing it! Major Jones was so flabbergasted that he didn't even run for his shooting piece. It wouldn't have done him any good anyway.

That skeeter with the cow in its hind legs was so high up by then, no lead could catch it.

"Wal!" Major Jones growled like a bobcat with a thorn in its leg, "wal, that'll teach me to stick to bears and not mess 'round skeeters in Arkansas swamplands."

The Daring of Yellow Doc

This is a tale good to tell, good for a good laugh and good for worship of a fearless hero. It's a tale of Doc Rayburn, born in Texas and famous in Arkansas for his daring, his recklessness, and his bravery.

He was a little fellow, weighing just about a hundred pounds. His yellow hair hung long and loose around his shoulders, as men wore it in those olden days. On his head he wore a giant sombrero with little bells, and around the brim were scales of Texas rattlers he had killed.

He had a passion for giant-size horses and they were the only kind he would ride. To see him come along on one of those big horses made you think of a little boat rolling along in a great water. But you know looks are deceiving.

When the War Between the States broke out, he was made lieutenant in Parson's Cavalry Brigade in his own state. He rode a giant chestnut horse, called Limber Jim, in a giant saddle on which he looked lost. On his boots were two huge spurs; at his side hung a big long saber, and two great Colt revolvers stuck out of his belt. But, funny as he looked, not a one laughed when they saw him. He was famous as a tough *hombre* and there was a steel look in his blue eyes that said a bookful.

He and his troop were ordered to Des Arc on the beautiful White River in Arkansas, and when they got there they were welcomed and feasted as all the Confederate troops were wherever they came to a Southern place from hamlet to city.

Yellow Doc—that was his nickname—was a favorite with all and particularly with the ladies. He danced too much every night and ate and drank too much every day and in the end he took sick with a bad fever. When his company left for the field of battle he had to stay behind in the town with one of the families. He was miserable to be left behind, but the people with whom he lived treated him as if he were their son, and under their kind care he soon got well. But he couldn't go back to his troop, for the Northerners had taken the state.

Yellow Doc wasn't the kind to stay still when patriotic work was on hand. In no time he organized a small band of Southerners who weren't scared of panthers, men, or snakes. They began a guerrilla warfare that was a sharp thorn in the side of the Northerners. Day and night they attacked the enemy when and where they least expected it and zoomed off like mosquitoes before the Federals knew it.

The war dragged on. One December day, Yellow Doc and his band were camped along a small stream not far from Des Arc. The sun shone clear and cold and bright, but the hearts of the men were damp and dull. There were thoughts of Christmas and home and loved ones. Nobody said much—they were just lolling around with a bitter word now and then of what Santa Claus would bring them for Christmas and what they would give to dear ones.

Doc Rayburn had a keen mind even as he had a fearless disposition.

"Reckon I got to be Santa Claus if White-Beard forgot us," he was thinking. Then suddenly he said, "I've got an idea, men! How would every one of you fellows like a fine fresh horse for a Christmas present?"

Some laughed, some were silent, some said, "Not by a year's growth. How you gonna do that?"

"Easy as ketch a willipus-wallipus. Tomorrow Yanks are gonna have a dance with a Yankee fiddler. I'm goin' to that dance an' I'm gonna dance to Yankee tunes till mah boot soles 're worn out. An' then I'm gonna bring you back fine Yankee horses as a Christmas present."

"How you gonna do it?" It came from all sides.

"Tell you when it's all over. Now, just keep your lips tight buttoned."

Rayburn set to work next day toward evening. First thing, he went to the house of a friend he could trust and asked for the loan of his youngest daughter's best party dress and shoes and bonnet. He put them on, combed and braided his long, yellow hair, and put it around his head.

"Why, Lieutenant, you look pretty as any girl hereabouts on White River," said his admiring friends.

"Suits my purpose fine," he answered, thanked them, and was off to Des Arc.

There he went to the commander and asked for a pass to go through the lines. He-she said she was a farmer's daughter and wanted to go to the dance she'd heard so much about. Everybody was talking about it. The pass was written out. Night had come and Emma-Lou—that's the name Doc Rayburn had taken—was allowed through the sentries. Fact is, when the two sentries heard she was going to the dance both said they were sorry they couldn't go with her-him.

Rayburn went slowly to the building from which he heard music coming. There was a girlish skip in his walk, but even without it no one would have guessed that Emma-Lou was dreaded Yellow Doc. That skipping walk was really due to the two .45 Colt revolvers tied to his legs just below the knees.

The soldiers at the door let him pass and he came into a room that was all lit with candles. Everything had a gay Christmas feeling. All were merry, and it took no time before he was asked to dance. He looked very much like a pretty young girl. Emma-Lou said she was a farmer's daughter, she had heard about the dance, and thought she might come and have a little fun like the others.

Many danced with "her," and many asked if they couldn't see her again. She promised they'd see her soon and mighty often. The officers and the pretty farmer's daughter were having a mighty fine time.

It was getting late and she said she had to go home or her father and mother 'd be scolding her. And maybe she couldn't come again. She left quickly when no one was noticing her.

Out in the fresh air it was quiet, and Rayburn found his way quickly to the horses. He untied the animals and picked out the one he thought the biggest and the best and mounted it. Then he swiftly stamped the other horses, driving them off before the guards knew what was happening. Shots were fired after him, but it was a dark night and soon rider and horses were completely lost to sight in the woods.

You can figure just what happened when he brought the fine beasts to his patriotic companions. Now there was Christmas cheer among them. Christmas cheer and love and admiration for their leader. They believed no man in the North or South equaled their fearless, smart leader. And maybe they were right.

There are many more tales about Yellow Doc, but we'll leave those for some other time.

A Tale of Steep-Stair Town

In Arkansas there is a town that has the most famous windy-curly streets in all America—maybe in all the world. It is a climbing, curling town up along a steep mountain, turning and twisting over three hundred streets and not one meeting another. The name of that town is Eureka.

Folks coming there need a lot of time to find where they are going to, or from where they are coming. Just the same they come by the thousands and thousands all the time from all over the country. They come to Eureka because it has no end of crystal-clear springs that bring health to sick people. There are sixty-three of those singing springs chock-full of healthy water that will cure almost any sickness.

There are many hotels built along that mountainside that are different from any hotel anywhere else. They are different because every floor, no matter how many floors high, leads you right into a street. You can go into some of those hotels even from the chimney.

And when you look up the chimney of some of those hotels or homes you can see the cows coming home from pasture.

That town built along the mountain is so strange that you can walk from the garden of a house onto the roof of the next, and the young ones can let themselves from the chimney into the living parlor. You can even go in that town to church through . . . the steeple. That town has been called the Steep-Stair Town.

Well, one time there lived in that stair-full town a cantankerous woman who was always at odds with all her neighbors and relatives. She was giving lots of trouble to folks living around her, and they kept out of her way. It was no use crossing her; she wouldn't change anyway. She was always throwing dirt where it shouldn't be. You'd think she came from the middle pit of a mire.

When someone spoke to her about it, she said the Lord made dirt and folks had no right to go against the ways of the Lord. As for her husband, he didn't say much in the house.

One time she had cooked greens and pork for supper. When they were through eating, she put cold spring water in the pot in which she'd been cooking. Then she took that pot full of slop, leftovers, and bones and went to the door and threw it outside, never looking where it fell.

Now, I told you the streets were mighty queer in Eureka, and in many places, if you stood in front of your house, you could look down the chimney of your neighbor. That cantankerous woman had thrown the slop down a neighbor's chimney!

It so happened that the stove in that house had been taken away to be fixed and so the slop went over a nice clean floor and over good furniture. This made the folks in that house mighty mad. They hollered at the slop woman and told her she'd have to come down and clean the place and give them new material for the parlor chair, because the grease would never come out of it.

Neighbors, friends, strangers, and visitors there for their health had come out at the ruckus, and when they heard what happened, they were all on the side of the woman in whose house the slop had been thrown. But the woman who had done it only sassed back and said she wasn't going to pay anything, and the best thing was not to put the chimney at her front door.

"Then I'll have the law on you," screamed the woman through whose chimney the slop had come.

And that's exactly what she did. The next morning she went to a lawyer, and when the next court session was held, the case came before the judge. Every neighbor was there with the woman whose house had been dirtied and the judge got an earful about the slop that was thrown down the chimney.

The slop woman screamed that the chimney was right before her door and if folks didn't like slop water down their chimneys they could move their chimneys away.

But the judge didn't think so at all. He said neighborly folks should be careful of other folks' property. She'd have to pay to fix the chair and if she didn't act decently from now on she better move to the woods with trees and animals that didn't care what was thrown around.

The husband of that woman had to pay good, and from that time on the slop woman didn't throw things around any more. The husband learned it was cheaper to watch his wife than to pay money for her cantankerousness.

Folks in Eureka liked this story so much, they've been telling it ever since.

The Colonel Teaches the Judge a Lesson in Good Manners

This happened in the early days in a town called The Post in Arkansas, and folks still tell the tale to this day.

There lived in those days, at that place in Arkansas, a fine man folks called Colonel Walker. He was a little man with big ideas of honor and of how folks should behave. But many of his neighbors did not agree, so they said he was queer. That's what folks always call you when you don't agree with them. He said he loved every living thing in life and called them all beautiful except whistling women, crowing hens, fire dogs, popcorn, and scratching fiddlers. That was too much even for the Lord on high, so Colonel Walker was punished for it. His own pretty daughter Jane ran away and married a scratching fiddler.

Just the same, everybody liked little Colonel Walker for his good heart that saw beauty in everything around him.

When the Arkansas seat of government moved to Little Rock, Colonel Walker bought a farm there to live on.

Not many folks lived in that section in the old days, and the Colonel's nearest neighbor, about two miles away, was a man called Judge Rover.

One day Judge Rover came to Colonel Walker.

"Colonel," he said, "I'm in need of a yoke for to hitch my oxen to do the plowing. Mine just broke in two. Wonder if you'd lend me yours for a spell."

"Ye can have it, Judge, and use it all you want."

Rover took the yoke, used it for quite some time, and then "forgot" to return it.

The Colonel waited and waited. When he was in need of it, he sent word for Rover to return it. Rover was feeling mighty mean that day, so he growled, "If he wants it so quick, let 'm come and git it or send for it."

When little Colonel Walker heard this, he was ready to burst through a five-foot wire fence. He took his well-oiled shotgun and walked the two miles to Judge Rover's home. It was a broiling hot day, but he didn't think of the sun.

When he got there, Judge Rover was in his backyard looking at a young colt.

"David Rover," said the Colonel, leveling the gun at his head, "pick up that yoke you come to borrow from me and carry it right back to my house or you'll be fit for nourishing the black earth."

Rover looked at the hole in the gun and said: "That's a fine way to visit a neighbor. You'd think I'd robbed an altar in the church. I'll send yer danged yoke back with my man."

"Y' ain't gonna send it back with nobody. Ye got to learn something about neighborliness and manners. Pick up that yoke with yer own hands and carry it to my yard, or . . ."

Rover looked at the Colonel, gun set against his shoulder and his lips tight closed, so he picked up the heavy yoke, set it on his shoulders, and began the two-mile walk in the sizzling sun. The Colonel walked close behind him, the gun at his shoulders.

Rover walked slowly, because that yoke was growing heavier every five steps. Three times he tried to drop it, but every time the Colonel set the barrel of the gun at his neck and said, "Keep movin'."

They had now come to the Colonel's house. At the gate Rover dropped the yoke against the fence.

"Ye didn't get it at the fence," the Colonel said grimly. "Ye got it in the barn. Bring it to where ye got it." He spoke in a way that didn't allow any arguing.

Rover picked it up and carried it to the barn.

When he set the yoke in the proper place, the Colonel dropped his gun and said quiet-like: "Now, Judge Rover, come on the porch where there's plenty of fans on this scorchin' day. I'll tell my wife to fetch cold water from the well and make us a cool drink."

The two sat down, and the Colonel called his wife and she prepared a cool drink for the two.

The Colonel spoke of this and that about the farm and then he said, "Rover, y're always welcome to use my ox yoke, but you got to return it when y've done with it, so's I don't have to ask for it. That's the beautiful neighborly way."

Then the two men parted good friends.

The Lost Treasure

There lived a man in Washington, Arkansas, by the name of James Black. He had mountain sense and he was a fine, upright man. Everyone called him the salt of the earth, and no one in the state of Arkansas could forge a finer knife than James Black could.

Day and night he was forever tinkering with black iron and forging to make the best kind of steel that could be made. Those were the days when men put work before money.

One day there came to his smithy a Mr. Reason Bowie, a fine, decent man.

"Black," he said, "I want you to make for me the finest hunting knife man ever made and I'll pay you a good price for it."

"I kin try, Mr. Bowie," Black said. "You just give me a little time."

James Black wasn't the kind to waste time making kitten britches for tomcats and so he set to work right away. He worked in that forge from dawn to dark mixing metals in white heat, putting in a little of this and a little of that.

After many days of working and mixing, he was satisfied he had made the best knife that ever came from his smithy. It was long, a little curved, sharp, and good for hunting and fighting.

Reason Bowie came to the smithy.

"Mr. Bowie," said Black, "I made for you the best knife I ever made, just as you asked. Here, look at it."

Bowie took the knife and examined it a long time.

"It's a knife 'll stand anything."

The Lost Treasure 63

"It's the first I made like it; guess it's as good a piece of steel as ever was."

Bowie's knife soon became famous for keenness and strength. He was forever boasting about it and showing it to everybody. Soon men came from all over to Mr. Black to have a knife made like "Mr. Bowie's" and after a time they just called it the Bowie knife. Black charged a good price for his work, but folks didn't mind that at all, so long as they got a knife of the same steel and in the same shape.

Other blacksmiths tried to make Bowie knives, but they couldn't. They couldn't make the same kind of steel. Men said Black had discovered the great secret of making Toledo steel such as they made in Spain hundreds of years ago. That steel was famous in the whole world. Black would never tell how he mixed his metal; he wasn't much of a talking man anyway.

So the years went by and Black became an old man and lost his eyesight. He couldn't work any more and couldn't make any more Bowie knives.

But folks wanted those knives. The governor of Arkansas heard about it. Maybe he, too, wanted a Bowie knife. So one day he went to see James Black.

"Mr. Black," he said, "you've made the finest knives ever made in Arkansas, maybe in all the country. Folks call it the 'Arkansas Toothpick.' Now we don't get any of your fine knives any more. Won't you tell me the secret of how you mixed your metals, Mr. Black? It would be a shame if the way these great knives you made would be lost when you go to a better world. The way you mixed your metals is truly a great treasure and should not be lost. Tell me how you mix your metals for this great knife."

"Governor," said James Black, "I'm old and blind and I can't work any more. It's time for me to tell others how to make that blade. Go and get ink and paper and I'll tell you exactly how I fixed things to make those blades. You can put it down in writing."

The governor went out to get paper and ink. Old man Black was sitting, his head low, thinking hard to remember how he mixed his metals. Again and again he shook his head.

The governor came back with paper and ink.

"Here I am, Mr. Black," he said, "now, you tell me and I'll put it down."

Black was silent a long time, then he said slowly:

"Sorry, Governor, I don't recollect any more. My head's gone on me. I just can't remember. There was lots o' things that went in that steel, but I just disremember what it was. Don't remember the parts! I'm sorry, Governor!"

James Black died, and the treasure of the combination of how to make his famous steel of the Bowie knife is lost. All that remains is to tell the tale as I told it to you.

The Great Conjure-Alligator-Man of Florida

Long ago there was a great conjure man in Africa. He was a good conjure man and he also was a good friend to animals, most of all to alligators, and he could change himself into one whenever he wanted to. He said the alligators were his brothers.

One day slave traders caught him like an animal and brought him to our land to be a slave. He was sold to a master in Carolina. But he wasn't the kind to be a slave. Soon he fled to Georgia and then to Florida. There he became a great conjure man, always helping those in need everywhere, and folks called him "Uncle Monday." They called him by that name because they said he was as fresh every day of the week as a man is on Monday after a good Sunday rest.

Those were the days when the Seminole Indians were fighting against being driven from their homeland by the white folk. They said it was their land where they had always lived and where they wanted to live. Uncle Monday had become friendly with the Indians, helping them first with conjuring and then in their just struggle. He became a fearless and wise warrior and aided them in their combats, but the Indians lost battle after battle. The white army had trained men and no end of guns, and the Indians and their black brother had to retreat until they came near Maitland Lake. There they fought and lost again.

Uncle Monday was wise even as he was fearless. Or maybe his conjuring power showed him. He told the Indians there was no use fighting the white man. They couldn't win. But he wasn't going to be a slave to any man in any land. He was off to his friends where no one could harm him and he was going to stay there until there was peace among all folks, black, red, and white. The Indians heard his words and said little. They were bitter against the white people for taking their land from them.

One day Conjure Man said he was leaving, and the Indians made a great feast for him for the last time.

When night came, all the Indians were there beating their drums and chanting Indian songs. And as is the way of Indians, they danced their war dances. But the one who danced most was the black conjure man from Africa. He danced slowly and he danced fast. He leaped high, roaring and shouting words none understood, and he whirled and twisted, around and up and down. You could hear that singing and shouting deep into the lake and far into the woods.

Then the Indians saw a thing by the light of the fire they had never seen! That wild dancing man from Africa began to change. He was turning kind of brown. His face got longer and longer, coming near to a point. The sides of his mouth got kind of thick-lippy, hanging down, and his teeth got long and pointed. His legs and arms got smaller and smaller, and thick, and long claws were coming from them.

He kept on dancing, and his body was growing thick and long, and scales were coming out on the back, and a long tail like an alligator's tail was growing from his back. The conjure man had turned alligator! The biggest alligator that ever was. He was still dancing and leaping and flapping around on his short legs, bellowing like thunder so that trees and leaves shook.

Then the Indians saw another strange sight and they stopped their dancing and shouting. First they heard from the river an answering roar that made the lake's waves rise high as the trees. From the water two long lines of alligators swam out, their mouths wide open, roaring and bellowing. The air and the woods were full of the noises. Then that conjuring man, now an alligator, slid slowly into the water between the two rows of alligators and—all the alligators went under the water. It became still on the water and in the woods. The Indians were still, too. They knew they had lost a good friend and a fearless warrior.

But that man from Africa wasn't lost. He's still in the waters of that lake. Sometimes he changes himself into a man and goes among his folks, conjuring to help them and conjuring to punish those who should be punished.

When he's away from the lake, the alligators bellow louder than they do at other times, and that's their way of telling the biggest alligator of all Florida to come back to them, to come home.

Nobody Sees a Mockingbird on Friday

Folks in Florida say nobody sees a mockingbird on Friday in the woods, and now I'll tell you why. But first I should tell you that the boys and girls of the state of Florida chose the mockingbird as the loveliest bird of the state, and with good reason. It is a very clever bird and can imitate the song of any other bird that sings, and even the whistling of people. One time a man who came from Europe said to folks in Florida that the mockingbird did not sing as beautifully as their nightingale. They made a bet on that. The man from far Europe went back and brought some nightingales to Florida. The birds were let loose in the woods, and what do you think happened! The mockingbird soon imitated the song of the nightingale and sang even more beautifully.

But one day a week the mockingbird does not sing at all, and that day is Friday. Fact is, you don't even see much of that bird on Friday. Why?

Well, it was this way. Once there lived a very bad man deep in the Everglades or maybe it was up north in the Okefenokee. I don't exactly know where, but it doesn't really matter. He had a terrible temper and was at war with man and beast. He'd fight to shoot whatever man or beast came in his way. He was very strong, too, so that everyone was scared of him.

But there was some good in him, too. He loved birds, all birds, but the mockingbird most of all. He said the singing of that bird was much like himself. Sometimes it screamed harsh and croaking and then it sang so sweetly your heart would melt. He liked to sit on bright moonlit nights and watch the pale-gray bird with the long tail and the white patches on his wings singing sweet songs, screaming hoarsely, and imitating other birds. That man with the terrible temper would sit for hours listening. He'd break up stale bread to feed the mockingbirds, and sometimes they'd hop on his outstretched hand for crumbs.

One day that bad man went a little too far with some good folks and they decided the best thing for everybody would be to get him out of the way. And that is what they did.

Everybody was glad when that bad man was gone, everyone except the birds, and most of all the mockingbirds. They were very sad. They flew all over to learn where he was, and in the end they learned he'd gone where it is hotter than any other place in the world. Then they were even sadder.

"We must do something about it," they twittered. "We must get him out of that terribly hot place!"

They went there by the thousands and tried to pull him out. But the fire burned their wings, and the heat and the smoke hurt their eyes, so in the end they had to fly away so as not to be burned altogether.

But the mockingbirds weren't ready to give up.

"We must get our good friend out of there," they twittered all together. So they held a great meeting.

"If we can't get him out of that terrible place, we can put out the fire so he doesn't burn," said the wisest bird. There was much talk and twittering, and in the end they decided the best way to put out the fire was with sand. They would all fly to the shores of Florida and bring the sand from there, to put an end to the fire in that terrible place. That would save their good friend.

They flew to the seashore by the thousands and, bringing grains of sand, dropped them on the fire.

But mockingbirds, like all creatures in the world, must build houses, take care of their children, and do the many other things all of us do. So they had to stop flying to help their friend so as to do the other things that must be done. But still they wanted to help their old friend. Again they had a meeting of all the birds. There was much talk in mockingbird language, and in the end it was decided that the best thing was to take off one day each week and bring the sand to their friend. That day would be Friday. And so it was done and is still done to this day, for that hot place is a very big place.

Six days a week mockingbirds work at what they have to do and sing, but on Friday they fly off to the shores of Florida to get grains of sand to put out the fire in that hot place—to save their friend.

That's why you don't see mockingbirds on Fridays in the woods of Florida.

The Tale of Lura Lou

Listen and you will hear the story that is often told on the southern end of Florida. It's a tale of love and of a phantom ship and a slaver-pirate that's as good as any that was ever told. It happened in the days when slave-bringing to America was still a common thing, though the law had forbidden it. Savage white men without pity in their hearts committed this inhuman crime in hidden ways and places.

Such a man was LeComet. He had a great plantation way down in Florida. His mansion was big and beautiful and there he lived with his only daughter. She had the lovely dove name Lura Lou, and she was very beautiful and very proud, as you would expect the daughter of a rich planter to be. She did not know her father's brutal business.

He got his slaves from "Red Luck," a famous slaver captain and pirate. Folks called him that for the color of his hair and because luck was always on his side. He was a big fellow with flaming red hair and blue eyes, even though his father was a Cuban. He was strong and fearless and without pity in his heart.

Late one night, guided by arranged signals, he brought his schooner full of slaves to the usual landing place near LeComet's mansion. The overseer met him on shore to greet him, but the planter wasn't there.

"He had to go to the city on important business for our trade," the overseer said. "It looks as if someone has been telling the government watchdogs something about our doings. He went to see some friends about it. Come, let's first get the 'goods' in."

The slaves, in chains, heavily guarded, were taken to their quarters.

"You and your men, Red Luck, come in the white servants' dining room. I got a good meal ready for you."

"I don't eat in servants' quarters," Red Luck roared. "I'm going to the big house as I always do."

He was not a man to cross. Without saying another word and to show the overseer how the captain of a ship should be treated, he went up to the big house and began banging on the door.

When a black man opened it, he stormed in. But no sooner did he enter the wide hall than he stopped short. There, at the top of the broad stairway, awakened by the banging on the door, stood a beautiful young girl. She was tall, with thick black hair and eyes deep and dark.

Red Luck stood speechless for a time. Then he said quietly and slowly:

"Who are you?"

"I am Lura Lou, the daughter of Mr. LeComet. Why were you banging on the door in the middle of the night? Who are you?"

The Tale of Lura Lou   73

"I am Red Luck, captain of a schooner. I come from Cuba and I trade with your father." He did not tell her what kind of trade it was. He did not tell her he was a slaver.

She came slowly down the steps and ordered the black man to set the table and bring some food and wine, which she offered to Red Luck. He ate and drank. They spoke for a long time and in the end Red Luck told her fearlessly that he had fallen in love with her and on his next journey to her father's house he would ask him for her hand.

Lura Lou did not say much, but her eyes showed she did not look unkindly on him.

The pirate-slaver left, but it wasn't long before he returned with a fresh cargo. LeComet was at home and Red Luck quickly told him what was in his mind and heart. He wanted Lura Lou as his wife.

The planter flew into a wild fury when he heard this. To give his daughter to a pirate-slaver!

Red Luck listened, and at first he did not say anything. Then he spoke:

"Why don't you ask your daughter? She'll have something to say about this."

LeComet called his daughter, and when Lura Lou said she loved the captain, her father was stunned. For a time he was silent. Then he spoke:

"Red Luck, you can see this is a terrible surprise to me. I need a little time to get used to the idea."

He was trying to gain time. Red Luck agreed and said he'd return in two weeks with his boat, which he had now rechristened the "Lura Lou."

Red Luck left. No sooner was he gone than LeComet got in touch at once with government officials who, he knew, had been trying to capture Red Luck and his boat for a long time.

Quickly two government cruisers were in the waters where Red Luck would come with his ship.

But the planter made one bad blunder. When the government officers were at his mansion for dinner, he told them, before his daughter, what a great prize they would soon gain: the clever slaver-captain and pirate, Red Luck. He was sure his daughter could not warn Red Luck. And there he made his mistake.

No sooner was Lura Lou alone than she rushed to the village where the fishermen lived. They were all Red Luck's friends, many of whom were his countrymen. She came straight to the one who was the headman of the village and told him the danger that threatened his friend and hers.

The headman lost no time. He roused the whole neighborhood and gave orders to the men to get their boats ready.

The fishermen came from far and wide at the call of the headman. They were told the news and were ordered to go out to sea, spread in all directions, and find Red Luck's vessel and warn him before the cruisers would sight him.

The boats started out to sea at once, and Lura Lou, silent and pale, was in the one with the leader. The fishermen fanned out in all directions and it was not long before the "Lura Lou" was sighted. The boats rowed up fast, signaling their friend to warn him.

In a short time Lura Lou and the boatmen were on the schooner. They told Red Luck the danger threatening him. The other fishing boats had also come up, surrounding the schooner. Then Red Luck promised and swore to the men that in return for warning him and saving him and bringing him his love, he would always warn them and save them when they were in danger.

The schooner, now led by the fishing boats, was directed into a cove where neither friend nor enemy could find it.

The government cruisers waited and waited and LeComet stormed like a madman trying to find his daughter. But all his fury and fuming and all the searching did little good. Lura Lou and the boat that bore her name were safely hidden away where none could find them.

In the end the cruisers left. Red Luck was told of it by his fishermen friends and he set out for Cuba. It was in August, the month when the hurricanes begin coming to Florida, and one of them hit the "Lura Lou." For once luck deserted Captain Red Luck.

There was a fierce battle between the hurricane and the "Lura Lou" . . . and the hurricane won. The schooner, Red Luck, and his beautiful bride went down to the bottom of the sea.

*There was a fierce battle between the hurricane and the "Lura Lou"
. . . and the hurricane won.*

The storm passed on, the sun shone warm. Months passed away, years passed away, but the "Lura Lou" did not pass away. The "Lura Lou" with Red Luck and his bride always comes back to the southern waters of Florida to warn the fishermen of coming storms and hurricanes. When a boat is caught in a storm, Red Luck knows how to keep the waters around it calm and save the fishermen in it.

That was Red Luck's promise to them when they warned him of the government cruisers, and he keeps his promise to this day. Any good, old fisherman along the southern coast will tell you this. And these old fishermen know.

Dixie, the Knight of the Silver Spurs

The armies of the North called him "Dixie" and Southerners called him "the Knight of the Silver Spurs," and when folks in Florida want to bring you a pleasant smile, they'll tell you grand tales about him. His real name was Captain John Dickison and, like the knights of olden days, he performed many daring deeds. Folks in Florida said he was better than any knight of any land.

He was captain of a small cavalry troop that brought no end of trouble to the Northern fighting men.

One night the Captain came to a ball given by Federal officers. Before the pleasant evening had passed, he was off with eighteen horses, a dance band, an ambulance, and forty men. Could any knight of old beat that!

But the tale folks of the Golden Sand State like most to tell is how he and his cavalry band captured a ship of the deep blue sea. And this is how he did it.

Day and night he gave no rest to the Northern army that tried to stop supplies coming to the Southern fighting men. He was everywhere along the St. Johns River and its many offshoots of rivers nearby. He gave no rest to the soldiers on the land or on the water.

On a lucky day Dixie and his daredevils captured a Federal post at the mouth of the Oklawaha River, which made the Federals hopping mad. The commanding officer ordered two boats, the "Columbine" and the gunboat "Ottawa," to capture Captain Dickison and his rebel band. The Captain learned of it and, hidden by the thick growth along the river, followed the two boats that were after him. When they reached a narrow part, his men opened fire. The boats answered, but the cavalry was getting the better of the fight.

The two captains of the vessels decided their boats were more important than victory over Dickison, so they separated to lead the fierce Captain off their track.

But you know success sharpens wits. Captain Dickison thought quickly and decided to follow the "Columbine," steaming southward. Hiding in the deep growth along the shore, this was a simple task. When both boat and cavalry reached Horse Landing where the river is very narrow, Dickison and his men opened fire. The boat tried to escape, but hit a sandbar. Dickison and his men kept up the attack fiercely, and soon the "Columbine" had to hoist the white flag of surrender.

Captain Dickison and his triumphant cavalrymen boarded the boat, took away all supplies useful to the Southern cause, removed the wounded prisoners, and burned the boat.

Thus it came to pass that a troop of cavalrymen commanded by a daring soldier conquered a vessel of the sea.

So proud and so grateful were the Southern folk of Florida for this heroic deed that the ladies of Orange Springs took all their silver treasures and heirlooms and melted them down to make a pair of silver spurs for Captain Dickison. And so he was called the Knight of the Silver Spurs.

The Union soldiers called him Dixie because he came upon them from Dixie Land, as the Southern states were sometimes called.

But, by whatever name, his is the fame.

Way Deep Down in the Okefenokee Swamps

There are many, many miles of the Okefenokee swamps in Florida and Georgia, and people tell many, many tales about these places. If you go there and meet the folks and act friendly-like, they'll tell them to you, as they told them to me.

You take a boat to go through the waterways under the hanging green boughs of cypress, pine, and oak, and the guide who is with you, whether a black man or a white man makes no difference, will have a head full of tales ready to spill. Or, if you want, you can hear them in the evening when you sit in the cabin listening to the mighty music of birds and insects and animals.

The stories are like the Okefenokee swamps and trees and animals. They move without end, but it's a kind of lazy moving.

It's a queer, thick, hot laziness. The sun burns lazy, the heavy shadows move lazy, and the stories have a kind of lazy life too. It's a dream life and the storytellers tell their tales in slow, lazy words that's like a drowsy music.

Maybe they'll tell you about Diddy-Wah-Diddy. That's a fine place that's always busy, with a nice busy laziness. . . .

It's a place for boys and girls and grown folks when they stay good all the time. Then the Lord gives them their reward right on this earth—right in Diddy-Wah-Diddy. He doesn't wait until they die and go to heaven.

Nighttime, when the moon shines big, the good Lord leads them to Diddy-Wah-Diddy. It isn't so easy to get there. There's hard traveling through blueberry bushes, cypress, live oak, and gallberry bushes. It's a long way, and they meet wildcat and deer and water moccasins and alligators and many other kinds of water and land creatures. When they get there, sweating and huffing and puffing, there's a fine reward. First thing, there are strong wooden benches and tables, all set with tablecloths and knives and forks. In the middle there are pots of fried chicken, hog jowls, and chitlins. And there are sweet potatoes and pies. And all the time there's a song going on over and over again: "Eat me! eat me! eat me good!" So they eat, and the more they eat, the more chicken and pie comes on that table. When they can't eat any more, they close their eyes and everything goes off that table. Then they take a nice nap and rest their bones in peace. When they wake up, they go back home, to do good and stay good. Those folks are the good folks in the Okefenokee in Florida.

Or that riverboatman will tell about the Okefenokee Heaven full of Florida black folks. In that Heaven there is a great big water with no windings and twistings like the Okefenokee waters. There are no winds there; it's just a big clear sea of glass where the angels have plenty of sporting fun, sliding around when they have no work to do.

There are broad streets of gold that sing hymns and psalms when folks walk on them. Near every step brings a song with it.

And then there's the "other place" too. Way down deep, far away. It's called West Hell. It's the hottest place in all the world. The Okefenokee on the hottest day is mighty cool alongside that deep place.

One time, a long time ago, John, big "John de Conqueror," was walking in the direction of West Hell. He was the biggest black man that ever lived. He was tall as the tallest tree and so black it got dark wherever he went. As he was walking he happened to wander into West Hell. It was mighty hot and he was fanning himself with his big hands. The devil's youngest daughter was taking a walk the same time and came where John was. She was the prettiest black girl you ever laid your eyes on. Big John de Conqueror took just one look at that girl and fell in love with her.

"I'm gonna marry you, pretty girl," John de Conqueror said.

"You can't marry me, big black man," the gal answered, "'cause my pappy wants me to marry a king."

"I'm no king, but I'm John de Conqueror and I'm gonna marry you."

He went to the devil's stable and took out the two finest horses, called Hallowed-Be-Thy-Name and Thy-Kingdom-Come.

"I'll get on the bigger horse and you get on the smaller one and we'll go to my country and we'll be married," John said.

They both got on and went speeding through West Hell. The devil was just coming home from business and saw the horses' tails waving from side to side. He got on his black bull that could run faster than the fastest train and soon that black bull caught up with the two just as they were about to get out of West Hell.

"Big John, you let my daughter go," the devil roared, "and gimme back my horses. An' you, hussy, you come right home."

Big John de Conqueror jumped off his horse and tore off one of the devil's arms and got to beating him with it. He beat him and he beat him until the devil cried for mercy.

"I'll give you mercy," John de Conqueror said, "but I'm gonna keep the horses and I'm gonna keep your pretty daughter, an' you got to turn down them dampers of your hot stoves so 'tain't so hot when I an' your daughter come visitin' here. Right now you hand me some ice water so's I can drink somethin' cool, I'm that hot."

The devil promised everything John asked, and he got the ice water too.

Then John and his bride left that hot place and went on to an island in the Okefenokee where they've been livin' happy ever since.

When John de Conqueror and his bride come visiting West Hell all the dampers are pushed down and it's a mighty pleasant place for resting.

The Bridal Chamber of Silver Springs

Silver Springs, in Florida, has perhaps the clearest water in all the state, if not in all the world, according to folks living around there. You can even count the pebbles at the bottom of the water that keeps bubbling up.

The waters are full of all kinds of gleaming fish and giant brown-backed turtles, swimming and crawling all over. And there are also sweet-smelling flowers and many kinds of colored plants in that water. Folk come from all over to look at those wonderful springs and the colored life in them.

Years ago Captain Harding Douglas, a proud man and a rich one, lived there. He had an only son named Claire, who was good to look at and who was a fine gentleman. His father was proud of him, as he was proud of everything that belonged to him.

Not far from their mansion lived a beautiful girl named Bernice Mayo. When Claire saw her, it was love at first sight, for she was very beautiful. First they thought of nothing but their love. But when folks saw them together and gossip began to spread, Claire knew he would have the devil's own time with his father when he told him that he wanted to marry Bernice Mayo, for she came from poor folk.

The two saw each other near Aunt Silla's little cottage that stood right off crystal Silver Springs Lake. One sunny day they sat at the water's edge watching the floating flowers and the colored fishes darting around like lightning. They were speaking of the gossip that was going the rounds.

"I'll speak to my father before the talk comes to his ears. I'll tell him I love you and will marry you."

Bernice was not much of a talker, but she said enough with her eyes. She looked long at Claire, smiled sweetly, and then looked at the magic springs, bubbling without end from the deep cleft in the bottom of the lake.

"You do what you think is best, Claire, and I hope God will help us."

Claire spoke to his father and there were angry words between them. The Captain had different plans for his son. He did not want him to marry a poor girl.

Captain Douglas argued with Claire for days, but the son would not give in to his father's wishes. In the end the Captain remembered that there were many ways to catch flies, and one of them was with honey. Said he:

"Son, I see you love the girl deeply and so I'll not stand in your way. But before the wedding, you must go to Europe for me on important business only you can attend to. When you return, Bernice and you can get married."

Claire told this to the girl. She had her misgivings, but she did not speak of them.

The day for saying goodbye came and they were walking in the woods.

"Come, Bernice," Claire said, "let us take a boat and go out on the water."

Soon they were in the center of the lake where the water was dancing upward from deep below, like jewels and pearls.

Neither said much; it was hard to speak at the parting time. There were tears in Bernice's eyes. She had a feeling that they were parting forever on this earth. They just looked at the silvery, bubbling water and at the ever-moving life of fish and flowers in it. Then Claire took a little golden chain from his pocket.

"Here, Bernice, this is a little present for you. Wear it on your wrist until I come back to you. I'll return quickly. I'll write to you often."

He rowed back and they bade each other goodbye with heavy hearts. . . .

Paris and London are gay cities and Claire found pleasure in the excitement of the new sights. He wrote to Bernice, but his father saw to it that the letters did not reach her. Besides, Captain Douglas arranged that Claire had to be away a good long time. Days, weeks, months went rolling on and Claire was enjoying himself as he never had before. He didn't give too much thought to Bernice Mayo. But not so with her.

Every morning she waited hopefully for a letter, and in the evening, when none had come, she thought, "Perhaps tomorrow!" She ate little, spoke little, and slowly pined away.

Often she rowed out to the center of the Silver Springs, sitting there for hours, watching the life of the water and the fish and the plants and flowers . . . dreaming. But there was no joy in it.

Sometimes when Aunt Silla passed Bernice's cottage, she would try to comfort her.

"Honey child, stop your worrying, young Claire's true to you and he'll write to you."

"I haven't had a word from him since he's gone."

"You look bad; you mustn't worry."

But the advice did little good. Bernice was hurt and unhappy and became ill from worry. Her cheeks lost their color and her eyes their brightness and soon she was so ill she could not do her daily work. She was becoming weaker all the time. She felt her end was near.

"I want to die at the Silver Springs where we sat together so many times and where Claire last promised me that he would soon return."

She went down to the springs where they usually were together, and sat down. She was too weak to row out.

Aunt Silla was out fishing and saw Bernice. She went to her quickly and her old eyes were wet with tears when she saw her.

"You're eating your heart out too much, Bernice, honey child. No use pining away for what you can't have."

"He promised he'd come back soon; he never writes to me."

"There's plenty others 'd be glad to have you."

"There is no other for me. I want to die."

"You are too young to die. Leave that to old folks like me."

"I don't want to live. I know I'll die soon. There's something I want you to promise me, Aunt Silla. When I'm dead, you take me out in your boat right to the middle of the lake where the springs come up. It was there Claire said goodbye to me and gave me the golden wrist chain." She began to cry.

"Stop the silly talk, Bernice honey. You ain't gonna die. You mustn't say such words."

Aunt Silla argued till her throat was dry, but it did little good. All she got from Bernice was:

"I'm dying for sure and it won't take long. I prayed to the Lord and He spoke to me and told me I'd die soon. He said Captain Douglas could keep me from Claire on this earth, but he could not keep us apart in heaven. Now, you promise me you'll let me go into the lake. After I die Claire will come to me there and we will be together forever. Promise me you'll drop my body in the bubbling water. He'll come to me there. Promise me! If you don't, I'll haunt you for the rest of your life."

Aunt Silla thought it best to humor Bernice, so she promised.

A few days later Bernice went into the woods, lay down on the soft grass, closed her eyes, and breathed slowly. Soon she did not breathe any more. So Aunt Silla found her and covered her. Then she came back at night when the moon was full in the sky, put the body in her boat, and rowed it to where the water came bubbling and whirling from the deep cleft in the bottom. There she dropped the dead girl. No sooner did the body reach the bottom than the cleft closed. The old woman went home crying, praying to the Lord.

Claire came back. In the excitement of his homecoming, he didn't think of Bernice at first. Besides, his father saw to it that there was a pretty girl in the house, a distant cousin, whom he thought Claire would find pleasing. She was pretty enough to be liked by any young man, and Claire found her gay company. The next morning, at breakfast, Captain Douglas said:

"Son, I have a brand-new skiff, pretty as a daisy. Let me take you two young folks out for a ride in the springs."

The girl quickly said yes, but Claire suddenly became silent. Now he thought of Bernice and the hours they had spent on the water together and where he had seen her last.

"Yes, Father, let us go," he said quietly.

It was a beautiful sunny morning and the water of the springs was clear as crystal. The fish darted around and the flowers and the colored plants shone brighter than ever.

They rowed around slowly and Captain Douglas and the girl did all the talking. Claire sat silent. Suddenly the girl cried out, white with terror.

"Look! there is an arm in the water! There is a gold chain on the wrist!" All looked down in horror.

They saw a thin, white hand waving in the water, and on its wrist was a golden chain—the chain Claire had given to Bernice the day they parted. Claire looked at it in frozen horror.

"That is the chain I gave Bernice when I said goodbye to her," he whispered.

He couldn't take his eyes off the bubbling water with the waving arm. Then . . . a big rock in the bottom parted and the three, speechless with fear, saw the swaying body of a girl.

"Bernice!" Claire cried, and before his father could stop him he dived in the water to his love. When he reached her, he took her in his arms and Captain Douglas and the girl saw Bernice's arms twining around Claire. Then the walls of the cleft closed. The water, boiling and bubbling, shut off the sight of the bottom. . . .

That spot is called the Bridal Chamber, ever bubbling, ever murmuring the tale of these two lovers. Tiny shells come up like Bernice's tears, and on the rocks grow little white flowers with leaves like lilies. Folks call them Bernice's bridal wreath. Any girl who gets these flowers as a gift knows she'll be a happy bride in a year.

Daddy Mention and Sourdough Gus

Down in Florida, nearly every swamp man, pinewoods man, or fisherman can tell you about Daddy Mention if you can just get them into friendly talk. And the telling will always come with a good bellyful of laughter, for Daddy Mention was just such a kind of man.

He was a "natchral man" as the saying goes. He was every bit as strong as John Henry. He could drive a ten-pound hammer better than a machine. And he was wiser by three thousand miles. That's what folks in Florida, in Polk County, say, and when I heard the tales they tell about him, I agreed. Those tales would fill a fat book, and I'm going to tell you just one of them to give you an idea of the kind of meat they're made of.

Like many a time before, Daddy Mention was in deep trouble with the sheriffs of Florida. This time it was something about catching baby alligators and selling their meat for beef or maybe cutting trees folks weren't allowed to cut, or something. The sheriffs were looking for Daddy Mention for a long time until one day three of them caught up with him.

The name of one of those sheriffs was Moonlight Cooligan, the second was Alligatorface McNutt, and the third was just called Sourdough Gus. That last one had the sourest, longest face in all Florida and even that didn't describe the sour, mean disposition of the fellow. He had never laughed from the day of his birth and he dreamed every night of dark, dank dungeons. The other two sheriffs were just common folk who took their job as a patriotic duty and as a handle for a living.

Sourdough had it in for Daddy Mention and had sworn if he ever got him behind bars he'd keep him there till doomsday. When the three caught the luckless man, Sourdough told it to him in such a way that it left no doubt.

Daddy Mention walked along the road with the three sheriffs, thinking deeply, for he knew he sure was in trouble. He scratched his head until it near bled from thinking. Then he spoke to the sour-faced fellow:

"Brother Officer Sourdough Gus," he said, "I don't know just why you're lookin' so mad at me an', to tell you the truth, I don't mind if you take me to jail and keep me there till judgment come. I don't mind it one bit. You just go ahead an' do it. But I'll tell you somethin'. You must be a sad man, for you got the saddest face I ever did see. The kind o' face that says, 'I ain't had a happy minute for many years, not for a long time . . . long as Methuselah.' That ain't good for your disposition, Sheriff. Now, if you had just one good laugh, all the sadness would fly away from you and never come back no more, sure as gourds is gourds. I know that.

"Tell you something, if I make you laugh and bring a little sunshine on your face, you let me go free this time and I promise I'll never do no wrong in this world again. If I don't, you kin keep me under lock and key for the rest of my natchral life. I'm willin' to stake all my life in a dark dungeon for givin' you just one good laugh."

Well, Officers Moonlight Cooligan and Alligatorface McNutt were all for it, but it took a long time to make Sourdough Gus see it. Laughing was as far from him as chicken from fox, with a dog in between. But it takes lots to discourage a man from Florida, and the two sheriffs hammered away at Gus, telling him that a good laugh was even better than Florida sunshine, and in the end he said he'd agree to the bargain.

Daddy Mention felt better, but as often happens he couldn't think of anything funny at the moment. So he started scratching his head all over again, only in a different place. In the end he said:

"I just cain't think of something real funny right now and what I'm going to tell you holds no salt, but it's try or bust.

"Now, you know when the Lord got to makin' folks, He thought it would be easiest to make 'em o' dough. Just like the kind that's used for making bread.

"First He made lots o' dough, for He was goin' to make many folks, like the sands o' the sea. He made a lot o' shapes, but, when He came to putting 'em in the oven, the oven was too small, so He thought He'd bake 'em in batches.

"He put the first batch in and after a time He took 'em out. But you know what happens the first time you try somethin'? They came out half baked, kind o' yellowish. So He said, 'You be the yellow folks, like the Chinese.'

"Then He took the second batch and put 'em in and He thought He'd now wait a good long time. When He took 'em out there was a fine batch of dark, crusty, baked folks. And the Lord said, 'You be the African black folks.' And the good Lord He was mighty pleased with that batch and He said, 'Yum, yum, yum, yum, yum, yum. . . .'

Daddy Mention kept on saying yum, yum until all the three sheriffs got tired of listening. So Alligatorface McNutt cried out:

"For Pete's sake stop yer yummin' and get to the next batch. What happened to them?"

"Well," said Daddy Mention kind o' slowly, "That batch had gotten all sour waiting so long and He left it sour and unbaked and made out of it all the sheriffs that's got sour faces."

You should've heard Moonlight Cooligan and Alligatorface McNutt roar with laughter when they heard this, and in the end Sourdough Gus, he began haw-hawing.

Of course they had to let Daddy Mention go free, and there wasn't a sheriff in all Florida could lay hands on him ever since that time.

The Song of the Cherokee Rose

There are tales and tales of the Cherokee rose, each as lovely as the little, white, sweet-smelling flower. Three states claim it as their own and one, Georgia, has made it the state flower. For that reason I will now tell you the tale of the Cherokee rose as folks tell it in that state. It is a tale the Indians told long before the white man came.

The Indians of the swamps were on the warpath with bows and arrows, and many a life was lost. One Seminole brave was captured by the Cherokees. He was tall and strong, with black hair and black eyes. As was the custom, he was condemned to be burned. But the condemned man became sick, too sick to stand on his feet. The Cherokees wanted to see an enemy "warrior" die, not a sick man weak as a woman.

"Let him be fed until he is strong again and then we will punish him," the chief said.

So it was decided. The young Seminole warrior was brought to the home of a Cherokee to be nursed back to health. In that Indian home lived a warrior and his wife and daughter. The daughter saw the young captive and felt sorry for him. Then sorrow turned to love—for both.

"You must not die," she said to him. And he did not want to die; he wanted to live with his love.

"I am getting well," he said. "But I know the dry wood is ready to send me to the Happy Hunting Grounds."

"We must run away together," the Indian girl said. "When night comes, we must go, or it will be too late."

When night came and the bellowing of the bull alligators was heard from the distance, and the never-ending song of the frogs came through the dark air, the girl crept to where the young warrior was lying, eyes wide open.

"We must fly now while the noises are loud," she whispered. "We will not be heard now. Everybody is sleeping."

The two crept out slowly and, once out, they began running swiftly through the paths in the swamp. The girl was in the lead, for she had known these paths since early childhood.

There were as many noises in that swamp as there were stars in the sky. The night wood was thick with sounds. The two had gone a way, she in front, he following, when suddenly she stopped.

"Why do you stand still?" the young warrior asked.

"I feel sad to leave my tribe and my father and mother."

"Do you want to go back?"

"No, I will go with you, but I want to take something from my home so that I remember it and them."

"Go," he said, "I will wait here. You must take care."

She went swiftly and he waited in the dark. After a time she returned with something in her hand.

"What did you bring?"

"I took a vine with the roots that grew on my father's home. It has a small white flower with a little yellow sun in the middle that smells sweetly. By the flower and the sweet smell I will remember my home and my father and mother."

When the two came to the warrior's home in the Seminole tribe, she planted the vine, the little white flower, near her own hut where it grew and flourished and spread all over the land of Georgia like a lovely white song.

White folks called it the Cherokee rose for the Indian bride who planted it.

Dan McGirth and His Gray Goose Mare

In the early days, a fine woodsman came from North Carolina to settle in the wilds of Georgia, and his name was Dan McGirth. He was tall and straight as a sapling, fleet as a deer, and strong as a panther. No man was a better shot or knew the woods and the swamps better than he. He was one of the finest scouts in the state.

When the Revolutionary War broke out, he was on the side of the American patriots and gave no end of help to the Colonial troops fighting and scouting.

Dan had a horse he called Gray Goose. She was a beautiful glossy mare, strong and fleet as an arrow. She could almost understand when her master spoke, and she seemed able to think. Dan loved that horse like a child and the two were always together in peace and in war.

One day Dan and his Gray Goose came to a fort on the St. Illa (it is now called Satilla). There were many of the Liberty Boys there, ready to battle the English. As usual, Dan's horse was admired by everyone, among them a Colonial officer, a mean and ugly fellow with the temper of a wolf at the end of a long winter. He looked at the horse like a fox at a hen.

"What'll ye take for the horse?" he growled.

"This horse ain't for sale. I love that mare as a father loves a child. Fathers don't sell their children."

The officer had as much understanding of such feelings as a scorpion has for its young.

"I want that horse. I'm an officer and ye better sell her to me," he snarled.

"I'm an American and a patriot and I'm 's good as you are. This is my horse and I'm not gonna sell her to you or to anybody else. Besides, I need her for scouting for our cause."

Hard words followed and the officer called Dan ugly names. It made Dan angry and he struck the churl. A fight began and soon the two were on the ground.

Soldiers standing by jumped in and separated them, and since Dan, who was just a scout, had hit an officer, he was put under arrest. A court martial was held and Dan was sentenced to be flogged in public for hitting an officer. He was to be flogged twice, in public.

Many were angered at this, but nothing could be done, and so part of the sentence was carried out. Dan McGirth was flogged before all and then taken back to prison to wait for the second part of the sentence to be carried out. Dan did not speak but there was a black burning fury in his heart. He swore he would be revenged on that officer and on the whole American army.

He was kept in prison for some time. One day he was looking through the bars of his window, his eyes and face full of bitter hatred. Suddenly he saw Gray Goose tied to a tree not far from his prison. Someone had ridden her.

"Maybe that accursed scoundrel," Dan breathed. No one was around and he called his beloved horse softly, as he had done so often. Gray Goose knew her master's voice and when Dan kept on calling the horse, she tore the rope that held her and ran up to the window.

Seeing the animal he loved within reach and feeling a wild, fierce anger in his heart gave Dan the strength of ten men. Getting hold of the bars at the window with both his hands, he tore them apart and in a moment he was out and on the back of Gray Goose.

"Go, go like the wind," he whispered to the mare, touching her sides with his boots. Gray Goose understood she had to run faster than she ever had and was off like a streak of lightning. Men had come out and Dan McGirth shouted his curses and yelled he'd pay 'em back a hundredfold.

Shots flew after him, but neither horse nor rider was hurt. Soon they were in the woods where none could find them. Dan McGirth went straight to the British camp, to the officer in charge. He stood before him, black anger in his eyes, and spoke:

"I'm Dan McGirth, the scout. I've come to join your side. I know I am a traitor, but I have sworn to be avenged on a Colonial officer for what he did to me."

The British officer knew of Dan McGirth and his ability, and when he heard the whole story, he understood. He was mighty glad to have the famous, fearless scout on his side.

So Dan McGirth joined the British forces against the Colonial army. He found a number of men who felt as he did and formed a company of Rangers who gave no end of trouble to the Americans fighting for freedom.

But, for all that, folks in Georgia and folks in Florida like to tell the tale of fearless Dan McGirth and his Gray Goose mare. They feel that Dan McGirth had a little right on his side.

The Tale of the Daughters of the Sun

A long time ago, some Indian warriors went hunting deer and birds. It was not easy hunting in the Okefenokee waters and swamps, which were always turning and twisting like an angry snake. They went through cypresses and hanging moss and shrubs and flowers. They went over rivers and logs and lakes and moving land, but they couldn't find anything for their bows and arrows. Their village was now far, far away, and they were hungry and tired, so they sat down on logs lying on the ground. One of the warriors raised his head to speak, but his mouth stayed open for a time, then he shouted "Look."

All the others looked up. At a distance there was a large island, all green with trees, and in the center was a big, still lake. It seemed a fine place fit for homes and hunting and fishing.

They all leaped up and began running to the island. But no matter how much they ran, they did not get any nearer to it. It was always the same distance away as when they first saw it.

They walked for a long time toward that island but they did not come to it.

"This may be a bad island full of evil spirits," they said. All were very tired and hungry so they sat down on the leaves. Some closed their eyes. When they opened them, they did not believe what they saw.

Around them stood the most beautiful women they had ever seen, tall and straight, with black hair and black eyes.

"They must be Daughters of the Sun," the warriors said.

"That we are," the women said.

"Come with us," the warriors shouted. "You will be welcome in our tribe."

They got up and went toward them.

"You must not come near us," the women cried.

"Why not?"

"Terrible things will happen to you if you do. Stay where you are."

"We are not afraid," the warriors said.

"Our husbands are fierce men and will kill you. They have done this to other strangers who came to us."

"We are not afraid."

"We can see this. You are fine warriors and we don't like to see you dead. Go from here. Go quickly before our men come. We do not want to see you dead."

No matter what the warriors answered, the beautiful women repeated the same words over and over again. After a time, the Indians said:

"Since you beg so much, we will go now." But in their heads they were saying, "We will come back with others of our tribe and take you with us."

"We will go," the warriors said again, "but we are hungry. We have not eaten all day."

The women went away, but the warriors did not see where; it

seemed they had vanished into the air. Soon they were back with cooked deer meat, cooked corn, and berries. The Indians ate while the women looked on. When the warriors were finished, the women said:

"Now you must go quickly before our men come. They will soon be here and they must not find you. We will show you the path to take."

And the women showed them a path and gave them food to take along, and then ... they weren't there any more!

The warriors followed the path and soon came to their village. They told everybody what had happened and all about the beautiful women.

"Rest a few days," the chief said, "and then we will go to the island and bring them here."

After a few days the chief and the warriors set out to find the island and the Daughters of the Sun.

They walked a long time, guided by the warriors to whom the adventure had happened, looking for the trail to the island. But all the looking did not help. They could not find the island with the Daughters of the Sun. Nobody could find it, and to this day no one ever has.

Georgy Piney-Woods Peddler

Listen:

Way down in Georgia lived Georgy Piney-Woods Peddler. He peddled his wares up and down the roads, up and down rivers, through the swamps and through the woods, always swapping and trading.

There wasn't a thing he wouldn't trade, except one—his darling daughter Annabell. He loved her more than words can tell or pen can write.

One day Annabell said:

"Pappy, get me a big, bright, shiny silver dollar to buy me pretty things for my wedding day."

"A big, bright, shiny dollar I'll get ye and pretty soon to boot," said her pappy.

Off he and his horse went to see what they could do. The pig-frogs were a-grunting and the herons were a-flying while he was a-singing:

> With a wing, wang, waddle
> An' a great big straddle
> An' a Jack-fair-faddle,
> It's a long way from home.

Soon he met a barefoot woman leading a fat, brown cow. Said Georgy Piney-Woods Peddler to the Cow-Woman quick-like:

> Trade ye mah horse,
> Trade ye mah ring.
> Trade ye all an' everything,
> For a shiny silver dollar,
> Mah daughter to bring.

Answered the Cow-Woman: "Got no shiny silver dollar to trade, got nothing at all to trade. But I'll swap you my good fat cow for your strong big horse."

So Georgy Piney-Woods Peddler swapped his horse for the cow and went on.

Cherokee roses smelled sweet, cham-chack woodpeckers pecked, and the Peddler was a-singing,

> With a wing, wang, waddle
> An' a great big straddle
> An' a Jack-fair-faddle,
> It's a long way from home.

Along came a thin man with a beard, leading a glossy black mule.

Said Georgy Piney-Woods Peddler to the Mule-Man quick-like:

> Trade ye mah cow,
> Trade ye mah ring.
> Trade ye all an' everything,
> For a shiny silver dollar,
> Mah daughter to bring.

Answered the Mule-Man: "Got no shiny silver dollar to trade, got nothing at all to trade. But I'll swap you my glossy black mule for your good fat cow."

So Georgy Piney-Woods Peddler swapped his cow for the mule and went on.

Yellow-tailed bees were zumming, and bull 'gators were thundering while he was a-singing:

> With a wing, wang, waddle
> An' a great big straddle
> An' a Jack-fair-faddle,
> It's a long way from home.

Came along a barefoot boy with a fine hunting dog.

Said Georgy Piney-Woods Peddler to the Hunting-Dog-Boy quick-like:

> Trade ye mah mule,
> Trade ye mah ring.
> Trade ye all an' everything,
> For a shiny silver dollar,
> Mah daughter to bring.

Answered the Hunting-Dog-Boy: "Got no shiny silver dollar to trade, got nothing at all to trade. But I'll swap you my good hunting dog for your glossy black mule."

So Georgy Piney-Woods Peddler swapped his mule for the dog and he went on a-singing:

With a wing, wang, waddle
An' a great big straddle
An' a Jack-fair-faddle,
It's a long way from home.

Along came a red-haired man carrying a fine cypress-wood stick.

Said Georgy Piney-Woods Peddler to the Cypress-Wood-Stick-Man quick like:

Trade ye mah dog,
Trade ye mah ring.
Trade ye all an' everything,
For a shiny silver dollar,
Mah daughter to bring.

Answered the Cypress-Wood-Stick-Man: "Got no shiny silver dollar to trade, got nothing to trade at all. But I'll swap you my fine cypress stick for your good hunting dog."

So Georgy Piney-Woods Peddler swapped his hunting dog for the cypress-wood stick and went on and on, a-singing merrily:

With a wing, wang, waddle
An' a great big straddle
An' a Jack-fair-faddle,
It's a long way from home.

Along came a big Seminole rattlesnake, rattling his rattlers, a-calling his diamond-back snake wife.

Said Georgy Piney-Woods Peddler to the big Seminole rattlesnake:

Trade ye mah stick,
Trade ye mah ring.
Trade ye all an' everything,
For a shiny silver dollar,
Mah daughter to bring.

But the Seminole rattler rattled angrily, "Got no silver dollar, got nothing at all to trade, but I got my sharp teeth full of strong poison. I'll take your cypress stick and never pay you anything."

With that he darted at the stick and sank his fangs filled with poison deep, deep, into it.

He sank his teeth in so deep he couldn't get 'em out. So Georgy Piney-Woods Peddler lifted the stick high up in the air and flung it round and round. Then he flung that Seminole rattler so far away he never was seen in that part of Georgia again. Then he went on and on a-singing merrily:

> With a wing, wang, waddle
> An' a great big straddle,
> An' a Jack-fair-faddle,
> It's a long way from home.

But as he sang, his cypress-wood stick began to swell. The poison of the snake in it was so strong it would even make wood swell.

The poison of the Seminole rattler worked stronger and the stick grew bigger.

Soon it swelled big as a tree.

Soon it swelled big as two trees.

The poison worked harder and the stick swelled big as three trees.

Then it swelled bigger than that.

Came along the Railroad-Ties-Man.

Said Georgy Piney-Woods to the Railroad-Ties-Man:

> Trade ye mah stick,
> Trade ye mah ring.
> Trade ye all an' everything,
> For a shiny silver dollar,
> Mah daughter to bring.

Answered the Railroad-Ties-Man: "Deed, I got a fine, shiny silver dollar and I'll trade it for your cypress-wood stick, for to make railroad ties from it."

Sang out Georgy Piney-Woods Peddler:

"I knew I'd get that shiny silver dollar for my lovin' daughter Annabell, if I'd trade long enough. Here's my cypress-wood stick. Give me my shiny silver dollar."

"We-uns don't carry shiny silver dollars 'round in the pocket. I'll take your stick and tomorrow I'll bring ye the finest, biggest silver dollar ye ever saw in your life."

So Georgy Piney-Woods Peddler went home a-singing on top of his voice, he was that happy.

> With a wing, wang, waddle
> An' a great big straddle,
> An' a Jack-fair-faddle,
> It's a long way from home.

The Railroad-Ties-Man cut the great big cypress-wood stick into three hundred and three good railroad ties and laid them along the railroad bed near the Suwannee River.

When he was done, the rain began to fall. It rained hard, like it rained in the days of Noah's Ark, and it all came down on the railroad ties along the Suwanee River.

It rained so hard it washed the poison of the Seminole rattler out of them railroad ties. And as the poison washed from the ties, they began to shrink.

They became smaller.

The rain fell harder and they became smaller.

The rain poured on and they became smaller and smaller.

The rain poured harder and they became smaller than that, until they were no bigger 'n little toothpicks.

The Railroad-Ties-Man saw the toothpicks and ran to Georgy Piney-Woods Peddler's house and cried:

"The railroad ties cut from your cypress-wood stick shrunk to little toothpicks. They ain't worth a big silver dollar. They're worth no more'n a thin silver dime."

"Let me see that silver dime," cried Annabell of the lovely eyes and lovely hair.

The Railroad-Ties-Man took out a new dime from his pocket and gave it to her.

She held it in the sun and it shone and glittered like the evening star.

"It's beautiful and shiny and silvery and I like it as much as a shiny silver dollar. Maybe better," said Annabell.

"Then keep the dime, my lovin' darlin' daughter," said Georgy Piney-Woods Peddler, "and I'll start in tradin' all over again and get you your shiny silver dollar yet."

So he kissed her goodbye and went off on the roads a-singing.

> With a wing, wang, waddle
> An' a great big straddle,
> An' a Jack-fair-faddle,
> It's a long way from home.

The Curse of Lorenzo Dow

Lorenzo Dow was a little man in size, but he was a great fiery preacher, like a prophet in the Bible. He went up and down the eastern states of our land preaching the word of the Lord and pleading with men to live as the Lord desired them to live. Some loved him and followed him; some hated him and jeered him.

So he came to Jacksonboro, down in Georgia, a thriving, roaring town; a county seat, about halfway between Augusta and Savannah. It was a wild, rough town. There were brawls and battles and broken heads and gouged eyes.

Lorenzo Dow wanted to preach to these rough men and show them the True Light.

There was a Methodist church in the town and it was there he decided to preach to that wild crew. But no sooner did he open his mouth to speak the word of God, to tell them to mend their ways, to repent, and leave the road of brimstone and pitch, than they began hooting and jeering and drowning out his voice. But he kept on pleading with them and they threatened him. It was a rough crowd and it looked bad for Preacher Dow. But the Lord was watching over him. In that crowd there was one man and his sons, Goodall by name. He was a big, strong man and so were his sons, and they were God-fearing men. They got the preacher between them and safely led him to their home to stay overnight.

The next morning Lorenzo Dow tried to preach again, but the mob began howling and screaming and in the end Mrs. Goodall said the wisest thing for Mr. Dow was to leave the town.

With the preacher in their midst, the Goodalls, around him as a bodyguard, led him through the howling mob to the bridge that spanned the little creek at the beginning of the town.

The mob followed behind, hooting and howling and roaring for him never to return, or he'd be tarred and feathered.

Lorenzo Dow went across the bridge filled with righteous anger and indignation against the unkindness and ungodliness of these folks. He stood on the other side of the bridge while the hooting rabble milled across the water, bawling and jeering. The preacher faced them fearlessly. Then he took the shoes off his feet and shook the dust of Jacksonboro from them. He raised his voice, and it sounded like a roaring out of darkness.

"I pray the Lord will deal with you as He did with Sodom and Gomorrah. He will bring darkness unto you and destroy you and lay your homes to waste. He will bring the wrath of fire and wind and water on your heads. You who find pleasure only in drinking and rowdying will dry up like the sea. Your cursing voices will be thorns in your throats and you will be plucked from the earth for your inhospitality. I curse you for shutting your ears to the words of God and reveling in evil doing and corruption. Only one house will remain in this Gehenna; only one family will prosper in this den of iniquity, and that is the Goodalls and their home, for they are full of charity and kindness!"

The crowd continued hooting and mocking and sneered and laughed at his words and his threats.

Lorenzo Dow turned his back on them and went his way.

The Curse of Lorenzo Dow 107

But from then on, strange things began to happen in Jacksonboro. Fires would break out and folks never knew how. House after house was burned down to black ashes. But, strangely enough, no fire ever came to the Goodalls. It seemed as if that house was protected by God.

One day when the sun was shining clear, darkness suddenly spread over Jacksonboro and a wild wind roared out of the heavens. Giant trees with black roots were twisted out of the earth, roofs were torn off houses, and some houses flew through the air like weird birds. There wasn't a house that did not have wounds from that fierce storm—except the house of the Goodalls.

People now became frightened at these fearful happenings. They saw the hand of the Lord in it. They did not speak loud, but they thought deep. They remembered Lorenzo Dow, the preacher, and his words across the bridge!

One afternoon a small rain began to fall. Folks of Jacksonboro went to bed same as usual. But soon they were awakened by a raging storm. The little creek over which the preacher had been driven became a roaring stream rushing wildly through all the town, through the houses and barns. Soon buildings rose from their holdings, lurching in the swirling waters. Cattle were bellowing in terror and horses were screeching, trying to find a safe place. It was like the last Day of Judgment. When quiet set in again, there was not a house that was not damaged—exeept the house of the Goodalls.

People had white fear in their hearts and there was a great exodus. Those who had jeered and scoffed at Lorenzo Dow were going away without saying much. Jacksonboro, which had been the county seat, was becoming desolate. The houses were dead empty and decayed and began falling down. Only one house, a simple, sturdy two-story building, stood unharmed and untouched by wind or weather, the house of the Goodalls who had given a night's friendly lodging to Lorenzo Dow.

The county seat was moved to another town. Jacksonboro slowly decayed, died, and became a ghost town.

During the War Between the States, when General Sherman marched through the South burning and destroying everything in his way, he heard the tale of Jacksonboro and left the Goodall house standing. It was not burned.

Hoozah for Fearless Ladies and Fearless Deeds

There are many tales in history folks don't like to see buried in books, so they keep on telling them from one generation to another. Fathers tell them to sons, and friends tell them to friends. That's the way history tales become folktales. Such is the tale of the two fearless women Mammy Kate and Agnes Hobson and the two fiery steeds Silverheels and Lightfoot, and Captain Heard of Georgia. Now I'll tell you the story which anyone 'll tell you from one end of Georgia to the other.

Silverheels was a beautiful horse, a big gray stallion, strong and glossy. He and another horse named Lightfoot came from General George Washington's own stable. The great General had given them to Captain Heard, who had fought under Washington in many of the early battles. The two animals had Arabian ancestors, and folks say Arabians are the finest horses in the world. They can run fast as the wind and walk silent as cats and understand when spoken to.

Captain Heard treasured these two horses and had them with him when he settled in Georgia. He and Silverheels were inseparable in peace and war. And there was war in those days: the Revolutionary War. The British were all over the thirteen colonies and there was fighting everywhere, most of all down in the South during the final days of the struggle.

Captain Heard was now a general and was in every battle, always riding Silverheels, who saved his life many a time. One day the General was badly wounded and captured by the British. He was taken to Fort Cornwallis in Augusta and put in prison. The fort was commanded by General Brown, a hard and ruthless man.

Hoozah for Fearless Ladies and Fearless Deeds 109

Those were black days for the Americans. Tories, British soldiers, and their Indian allies were plundering and burning homes and fields. No quarter was shown to the American rebels and General Heard was promptly condemned to death.

The terrible news quickly reached Fort Heard and the Heard plantation which was nearby. There was sadness and sorrow at the plantation. The mistress of the house, relatives, friends, and Negro slaves were unhappy and brokenhearted. General Heard treated his slaves like friends and they all loved him.

Among the slaves there was a woman named Mammy Kate. She was big, strong, and unafraid. Her face was not handsome but she had a ready wit and a quick mind and everyone liked her.

As soon as she heard the misfortune, she went to her mistress.

"I'll get Massa free," she said, "but I'll need Lightfoot to help me. The rest you just leave to me."

"How can you, Kate? How do you know you can?"

"Saw a white horse and made a wish and it got to come true. You just leave the rest to me." Then she told her mistress what she intended to do. Mistress Heard, seeing no other way, agreed.

Mammy Kate mounted Lightfoot, a horse nearly as good as Silverheels, and was off for Augusta, which, about fifty miles from the Heard plantation, was where Fort Cornwallis was.

When she came near the city, she stopped with some friends and left her horse there, telling them to hide it and that she would soon return. Then she got a big, strong clothesbasket, put it on her head, and walked straight to Fort Cornwallis.

Mammy Kate was a smart woman and quick with her tongue. She went to the officer in charge of the fort and said she was looking for washing. She'd be glad to wash the officers' sheets and shirts.

"Can you iron our ruffled shirts well?" the officer asked.

"I'm a big possum and I kin climb a tree good. There is nobody in Georgia can iron ruffles better than I kin. They'll be white as new when I bring 'em back."

The officer liked her open face, her big smile, and her ready wit.

"If you are so good, how is it you must come begging for work?"

"Mighty poor bee that don't make more honey than she needs."

"You said you can iron ruffled shirts well."

"That I can 'deed, but don't like to praise myself. Crows don't sing sweet, but you kin depend on 'em to make noise."

The officer agreed with a smile. It was not easy to find women who could do that work well.

She was given the work and did it well indeed, and from then on she was free to go in and out the fort.

Every day she came with her big washbasket, took away soiled linen and shirts, and every evening she returned them, taking whatever soiled clothes and linens there were.

Everybody liked her, for she was forever laughing and joking. She became friends with every man—even with those who guarded the prison doors. Soon she could go in and out of the prison as she went everywhere else.

General Heard recognized her, but a wise look from Mammy Kate's eyes warned him not to show it.

One day she said jokingly to General Heard in front of the guard, "How'd you like me to wash yo shirts, Massa Heard, while you is in prison?"

"Very much indeed, good woman, and I'll gladly pay you."

"You can't do that," said the guard, "unless you get permission from General Brown."

"I'll get it, sure 's squirrels crack nuts," Kate answered smilingly.

A few days later she brought General Brown's frilled shirts with which she had taken particular care. He seemed quite pleased and complimented her on the excellence of her work.

Mammy Kate's face beamed with pleasure. She thanked him and she added:

"General, that prisoner you got in prison you're gonna hang soon asked me to wash his shirts for him. You'll not mind it. He says he can pay me. I got an itchy palm and enough pennies added make nice guineas."

General Brown laughed and said, "Well, I've got 'm safe enough and he won't wear shirts much longer. You can wash them for 'm if you want to. He might 's well go with a clean shirt for his long journey."

From then on Mammy Kate saw General Heard often, and when they were alone, she outlined to him her scheme. He shook his head and didn't think it possible, but Mammy Kate seemed so confident and since it was the only straw that might save his life, he agreed.

It wasn't long after when the plotting woman heard that the General would be shot in a few days.

Mammy Kate came quickly into the prison.

"Did you hear the ringing, General? There's a church 'round." Then she whispered, "Tomorrow when I bring your shirts, you be ready."

The next day Mammy Kate came late in the afternoon to deliver her wash. When she had given it to the British officers and taken up the things to be washed, she came into the prison to give General Heard his belongings.

It was pretty dark and the two were alone. Kate emptied the soiled wash on the floor and set the basket on the ground.

"Quick, Massa, you curl up like a puppy in here. Git in that basket quick."

"Are you sure you can carry it? I'll be heavy."

"You is a little man with a smart head and I's a big woman with a strong head. You just get in quick." This was true.

General Heard got into the clothesbasket quickly and curled up. Mammy Kate threw the dirty wash carelessly over him. Then she raised the basket with both her hands and put it on her head. Holding the rim with one hand she walked slowly out as she had done many times before.

The guard stood at the door.

"I got a heavy load, young fellow," she said.

"Since you come, these officers wash their shirts more than they did before," the soldier said.

"Let 'em give me the wash, so long as they pay good for it. Guess I'll raise my price for my work."

"Don't raise the price for us soldiers."

"No, I'll take my gravy from them with the gold braids and you just give me a little grease."

The soldier was pleased at what she said and she went out, through the courtyard, through the gate as she did every day.

For a while she walked slowly, but when she was where the fort was hidden behind the trees and she knew she was safe from guards, she set the basket on the ground. General Heard jumped out. It was pretty dark by then.

"You wait here behind the trees, Massa. I got 'em to send up Silverheels from yo stable an' I came here on Lightfoot. We got two horses nobody kin beat. Ah'll fetch the horses."

She ran off, and in the shake of a lamb's tail she was back with the two fine steeds. The General leaped on Silverheels and Mammy Kate mounted Lightfoot. The two horses understood the importance of the moment. They went off like lightning and in due time they arrived at the plantation.

The joy for the escape was unbounded and the praise and thanks to Mammy Kate the same. There was a great feast for the General and Mammy Kate and—Silverheels and Lightfoot.

But the war was still going on. General Heard was back in the midst of it. Brave and fearless he led his men. But bullets know no pity and he was wounded twice in action, the second time in the leg.

Things did not look too good for the Americans. General Greene was now in North Carolina directing the American soldiers. General Heard was doubly unhappy, for he had to stay home, inactive because of his wound.

One day a soldier came to the Heard plantation with dispatches from General Elijah Clark of Georgia, to be forwarded to General Greene. Every man on the Heard plantation was away. General Heard could not move. He was desperate. No man was in the neighborhood.

Not far from the Heard plantation was the Hobson plantation. There Mrs. Agnes Hobson was working as all the women of the South were working. Agnes Hobson was a fine lady, an expert horsewoman, and she loved all animals. She was strong and fearless and a good patriot.

When she heard of General Heard's dilemma, she came to him at once and offered to carry the dispatches—if he would let her use Silverheels.

"Only that horse can do it," she said.

"Mistress Hobson, it's a very long ride and a very dangerous one. Even a man's strength might not hold out."

"I am not afraid and I can live for days on a horse. I know I can

Holding the rim with one hand, she walked slowly out, as she had done many times before.

trust myself to Silverheels. She is the finest mare in all of Georgia."

"You are a lady."

"A Southern lady, and so much the better, and—safer. As a woman I'll be permitted to go where a man wouldn't be allowed to go. I'll say I'm on my way to Carolina to visit relatives...."

"But..."

"It'll be easy for me to hide the dispatches in my hair where no one 'll ever look for 'em. Just you let me take Silverheels. We two can do it."

There was no one else to send, so General Heard gave her the dispatches and with a heavy heart he bade her and his fine horse goodbye.

It was a long journey for a woman. All day in the saddle with enemies all around. She rode the day long and put up for the night with friend or foe. No one would deny a lady a night's lodging.

The third night came and she had to stop at a strange house. The barking of a dog brought a man to the door and she asked for a night's lodging.

Yes, there was a room with a clean bed in a shed that led off the main living room. She accepted this gladly, for she was tired. The man invited her into the living room where there were some other men who had come a-horse. She ate a little and then begged to be excused, for she was very tired and wanted to go to bed. The host pointed to a door off the main room, lighted a lantern, and told her she would find a clean bed there. She thanked him and, taking the lantern, first went out again "to look after my horse." Soon she returned, carrying her saddle.

"I always sleep with the saddle near me for convenience," she said quietly. Then she bade all good night and went into the room where she was to sleep. She closed the door first and then, by the light of the lantern, she looked around. Besides the door to the living room there was only one window with a shutter over it. A narrow bed stood in the corner. She blew out the light and without taking off her clothes, she lay down on the bed. The saddle she put next to the bed on the ground. She felt nervous and could not tell why. From the living room came low voices and she listened to them.

Soon she heard some more men coming in. Suddenly she was wide awake. One of the voices was saying:

"I know that horse in the stable. It belongs to the worst rebel in the country. It's the fastest horse in the state. Bet you the rider is carrying military dispatches somewhere."

"It's a woman," someone said. "She says she's goin' to Carolina to visit friends."

"I know everybody living hereabouts. Just let me have a peep at her and I'll tell you quick if she is for the king or the rebels."

"Guess you are right. She must be traveling for the rebels sure as roosters crow."

"Come, let's see." Then there was silence.

Mistress Hobson closed her eyes quickly and began to breathe deep and regular.

She heard shuffling about and tiptoeing towards her door. Then for a time there was silence. They were listening. Then the door was opened very slowly. She lay still. The door opened and three men came in slowly, the first carrying a lantern, which he was shielding with the palm of his hand. He tiptoed to the bed, raised the lantern, and looked at Mistress Hobson for a few moments, then he turned around and walked out, the others following him. They closed the door softly. Agnes Hobson was at the door at once listening at the keyhole.

"I know her," the man with the lantern said. "She's Agnes Hobson and a rebel if ever there was one. She must be carrying something to the enemy. She's got to be searched."

"Let's take her to the camp," said another. There was a British camp nearby.

"It's late o' night and I kin keep her here safe till the morning," said the owner of the place. "I'll lock the door and I'll put my dog before the window; anyone kin pass that beast 's got to be smaller than an ant."

The others seemed to agree, for the next thing she heard was the key turning in the door. Soon after she heard a growling at the window and the tying of a dog.

Mistress Hobson was thinking fast. She could not break the door. The only way out was through the window. The dog! She loved animals. All animals understand and are good to those who love them, she thought.

She waited a long time until all was still and everyone was in bed. When all was silent, she crept to the window and opened the shutters. There was a growling and she saw a big black dog. She began calling softly to him and talking. The growling kept on and so did her soft, gentle speaking. The dog came slowly to the window. She had it wide open and put her hand out. The dog came up and she stroked his head, and kept on talking gently. The dog began wagging his tail. She kept on stroking his head for some time. Then she slowly began to climb out of the window, dragging the saddle with her—and talking to the dog, scratching his head, and stroking him.

She was out! and she untied the dog. Then she walked slowly to the stable, the dog following. She opened the stable door and a low whistle brought Silverheels out. Slowly she put on the saddle and mounted the horse and walked him slowly, the dog following quietly.

When Mistress Hobson felt she was at a safe distance, she just touched the horse's flanks with her heels and off he was like a shot! The dog remained behind.

Mistress Hobson reached General Greene safely with the dispatches, thanks to Silverheels and her courage.

Since then the tale of Silverheels and the courage of two women, one black and one white, has been told over and over again in Georgia and all the South.

Fearless Nancy Hart

Down in Georgia and in most other Southern states they tell tales of Nancy Hart, of her great courage and fearless acts. She lived in Elber County and she was red-haired, six feet tall, and no man her size could beat her in strength. Each of her eyes looked in a different direction, but no man could sight a gun better than she. Folks everywhere liked her, for she had a heart of gold, ready to do good all the time, and she was a staunch patriot.

There are many tales of adventure and courage about Nancy, and now I'll tell you the one folks tell more than any other.

The Harts lived not far from Augusta, in that lovely, golden state, which the British had overrun. That was during the Revolutionary War. One day six British soldiers, straying from the main body of the army that was on the march, came upon the cabin of Nancy Hart. The menfolk were away in the fields and she was there with her children. The Redcoats came on her unawares, else she would have fought them off. But six guns and bayonets pointed at her.

"So you are Nancy Hart," the leader of the men said. "Well, we're here to see you don't help any rebels to escape as you've done before. And you can't escape either. We're hungry. Give us food. Good Mistress Hart, cook something for us, we've plenty of time," and they laughed at her.

"I never feed the King's men," she said fearlessly. "Ye've stolen all we have. There's only an old gobbler left."

"Well then, you cook the old gobbler. I'm sure you'll make it soft and succulent. I'll get the old bird."

The man went out, while the others stacked their guns carefully against the logs of the wall of the room.

Nancy stood quietly looking at them. She was thinking fast. The man came in with the dead fowl. Suddenly she had a plan.

"Aye," she spoke, "I'll cook the fowl for ye."

"Fine," said the fellow, handing her the fowl. "Let's see, Mistress, if you can cook as well as you kin fight," he added laughingly.

Nancy Hart busied herself with the fowl, while her older daughter Sukey stood near her.

The soldiers sat down to wait for the meal. They passed their flasks around, laughing and jesting. Nancy Hart watched the men from the corner of her eye—and the guns stacked against the log wall. She walked back and forth near those guns getting things needed for her cooking and making a great deal of clatter with her pots and pans. Altogether there was a great deal of noise in the room.

"Sukey," she spoke low to her daughter, "I'm gonna send you out for water. The conch shell to call your father from the fields is at the spring. You know the call. When I send you to the well, you take that conch shell, go a ways off from the house, and blow it for your father. He'll understand." Sukey was smart and just nodded her head.

Nancy kept on working with the food and walking all the time back and forth between the soldiers and the guns. Near where they were stacked there was a wide crack between the logs. When she was sure no one was looking, she quickly slipped one of the guns through the opening of the logs. Then she went on with her work, talking and jesting with the soldiers. They were drinking and making themselves comfortable.

Soon Nancy saw another chance and she slipped another gun through the wall. Only four guns were left. The soldiers were deep in their cups.

"Now, Sukey girl," she said, "I need water. Go bring it." Sukey understood. Nancy was standing with the guns behind her; the soldiers were busy talking. She picked up another gun to slip it through the opening and one of the soldiers saw her. He leaped up yelling:

"She's taking our guns!"

Quick as a flash the gun was at her shoulder.

"Any Redcoat that moves is a dead man," she cried.

The other soldiers were up. The one who saw Nancy first made a run for her. There was a flash and a shot and the soldier fell to the ground. Nancy dropped the gun, picked up another and it was at her shoulder. Another soldier moved toward her. Another flash and the second man fell. "I told ye not to move," Nancy said coolly. "Sit down quick. All of ye are prisoners." The four soldiers sat down.

"Father and the men are coming," Sukey screamed, rushing in.

The four men tried to make a leap toward the door, and Nancy fired again. There was shouting outside and Nancy's husband and some other men came in. In no time the Redcoats were tied, and Nancy was hailed as a heroine.

This was only one of Nancy Hart's heroic deeds; she was just as brave at other times. No wonder Georgia folks tell stories about her to this very day.

The Silver Snake of Louisiana

Here's the first tale I heard in Louisiana, the tale of the Bayou Teche. The Indians tell this story of those Indians who lived in Louisiana long, long before the white man came.

It was many years ago—no one can remember how many, maybe it was in the beginning—there lived a giant silver snake in that land. The snake was so big that when you stood looking at the tail, you could not see the head; and when that snake opened its mouth, it could swallow three deer at once.

When it writhed through the woods and water, it shone like the full white moon—and animals ran from it in fear. And so the Indians had no game to hunt and were hungry.

The Indians were afraid of that snake. They feared it more than the dark-winged creatures who flew wildly over the dark water. It was not good to live with such fears.

The medicine men beat the drums day and night and all the Indians came to hold a war council. Many spoke and everyone agreed the snake must be destroyed.

Warriors came by the hundreds, armed with bows and arrows.

From afar, through the green grass and the green wood, came a great white light.

"It's the silver snake!" the Indians shouted. "It's the silver snake!"

The chief rushed up a hill, and all the warriors followed. The Chief put an arrow in his bow and raised it level with his face. All the hundreds of warriors did the same. The Chief stood still and waited, and so did all the others. The silver snake, shiny white, writhed through the green growth. Soon it was in full sight of the warriors. All eyes were on the snake, every bow ready.

The Chief gave the signal and an army of arrows was let loose. There were so many they were thick as a cloud. The aim was sure, the arrows were sharp, and they all pierced the silver skin of the great snake. The snake began writhing fiercely, lashing its body deep into the earth.

A new volley of arrows was shot. Still the snake kept on writhing wildly, deep in the green grass, in the brush and woods, in the black earth, in every direction, forward, backward, round about, and downward, cutting gulleys and gulches everywhere. A third volley of arrows came, and little by little the great writhing became slower . . . then it stopped!

The Indians rushed out with their clubs and put an end to the monster.

The twisting and the turning, the writhing and the lurching of the silver snake had made gulches and chasms and ravines in the plains and in the woods. Soon these were filled with running water. When the rains came down, the waters grew higher, and after a time there was a giant stream rambling and twisting and turning— just as the silver snake had done. The Indians called that stream "Tenche," which means snake, and then when the French came, they called it "Tesh" or "Teche." We call it "Bayou Teche," the beautiful winding stream with giant live oaks, cypresses, palmettoes, and canes spreading along its banks. On it there are fields of purple water hyacinths and blue and copper-colored irises, looking up at the blue sky and down into the dark-green and dark-brown water. Folks in Louisiana say it is beautiful water, and I say so too.

Fairy Web for Mr. Durand's Daughters

In the young days of the country, our land seemed bigger than it does today because there were so few people in it. And everybody felt a great urge for doing marvelous deeds, like Mr. Durand, who lived on the Bayou Teche.

Mr. Durand came from France to America, and when he arrived, every inch of his short body became truly American. He could do more boasting than any man along the water; he could do bigger things than any man; and he could shout more (in a high, squeaky voice) than anyone along the Teche in Louisiana. He married two times and had twenty-four children, and all of them obeyed him and loved him, as did all his slaves. Everybody thought Mr. Durand was the greatest man in Louisiana.

Sometimes Mr. Durand got lost in the many names of his children, except when it came to an important event. Then he not only remembered their names, but he also remembered to do something good for them. And when two of his daughters were to marry two fine gentlemen on the same day, Mr. Durand came forth in all his glory.

But first I must tell you that a wedding in Louisiana was the most important time in folks' lives. Every father and mother tried to have a bigger, better, and more exciting wedding than had ever taken place before.

"We'll have a wedding the like of which was never seen in all Louisiana or even in France," shouted little Mr. Durand, thumping his chest. "Two daughters married at the same time! *Hein!* This is something that does not come to a father every day. It'll be double big and double marvelous. These two pretty girls and all my family are the *crème de la crème* of Louisiana, and I must make a wedding that fits my position. I must think about this."

He went to his room, sat down in a soft chair and began sipping a fine brandy brought from France, and thought and thought and thought. And when Mr. Durand thought so long, a great idea was sure to be born.

"Ah! It must be a great secret," he said softly to himself. Then he called in some of his slaves and explained something to them very carefully, and swore them to secrecy. They went off on good strong mules.

"Where did you send them, and to get what?" asked his wife, daughters, old aunts, and cousins.

"I sent them to Cathay to fetch some riches that will be the greatest surprise in your life. This will be a wedding the like of which the Teche has never seen, and the like of which the whole world has never seen. And don't ask me to tell you about that surprise. Just wait!"

When a French father gave an order to his family, no one ever disobeyed.

Now began wedding preparations that could only be seen in Louisiana. Dressmakers and hairdressers came from New Orleans; fancy cakes and nougats were ordered. At the plantation of the Durands, aunts and cousins, relatives, friends, and slaves—everyone worked day and night with baking, broiling, cooking, and cleaning.

Three days after Mr. Durand had sent the men away, they came back with big paper boxes, well covered, so no one could see what was in them. Toward the evening, when family and slaves were in their rooms, Mr. Durand and the four black men came out with the boxes, unseen by anyone.

They walked along the avenue of giant shade trees nearly three miles long which led to the great house. As they came near each tree, the men would climb up with one of the boxes and let out some dark insects that were in them. This was done on each and every tree; then they all went back into the house.

As the days went on, and everybody was busy with the preparations, there began to spread a beautiful silver woven lace between the branches of the trees, and from one tree to the other, even across

Fairy Web for Mr. Durand's Daughters

the avenue. Big spiders were weaving! It was the spiders for which Mr. Durand had sent the slaves.

White folks, black folks, old and young, everyone looked in open-eyed wonder at the silver-laced canopy growing over the trees and in the branches of the long avenue. When the sun or the moon shone on it, it was as if fairyland had come to the Teche. Nothing like it had ever been seen before.

It was still five days to the wedding and the big mansion was like a giant ant heap full of excitement. But no matter how busy, everyone was always looking at the sky. For the great question was: Will it rain, or will it not rain; will a wild, strong wind come up, or will no strong, wild wind come? If either happened, the marvelous lace canopy, swinging and swaying and gleaming like jewels, would be destroyed.

Mr. Durand looked at the sky, hands in the pockets of his lavender pantaloons.

"It will not rain until after the wedding, and there will be no strong winds until after my daughters' wedding day."

When Mr. Durand spoke in those sharp tones on his plantation, it was law.

And it did not rain! And there was no wind! Day after day, it was clear and calm.

Early in the morning of the wedding day, Mr. Durand came out with some of his slaves, each carrying bellows filled with—silver and gold dust. And gently, gently, they began spraying the silver-gray lace, spreading nearly three miles over the avenue. No one in all Louisiana, perhaps even in all the world, had ever seen anything like this. Then a carpet was laid along the long road under the silver and gold canopy, up to the very altar, which was near the house. Mr. Durand truly had done something no one had ever done before!

Giant tables were set between the trees, laden with every kind of food, fruit, wine, and cake. It was truly a kingly setting! Everybody, far and near, was invited, and everybody came. They came by boat and they came by horse, they came in carriages and on mules. There were nearly five hundred at that wedding. And no one could find words for the wonder of that beautiful gold-and-silver canopy woven over the trees by the spiders.

"Only Mr. Durand could have thought of this and done it," everyone said, and praised him to the skies.

"I brought these spiders from Cathay," Mr. Durand said proudly. But some said they came from the forests in nearby Cataboula. Wherever they came from, they had obeyed Mr. Durand's orders, as everybody did.

The couples were wedded and blessed, and folks ate and sang and danced and drank.

Then a white, gleaming boat came along the Teche and took the newly married couples on their honeymoon trip. But the guests stayed and made merry for many a day, eating, drinking, and dancing. Everybody was happy, even the spiders in the trees that had made for Mr. Durand the greatest wonder on the Teche.

The Life of Annie Christmas

One time there lived in Louisiana a woman they called Annie Christmas. She was the strongest woman in that state.

Have you ever heard any tales about her? If you haven't, you'll hear them now, just as folks have been hearing them for years and years. Every kind of tale, by every kind of folk. White folks say she was a white woman, and black folks say she was black as shining coal. Both say she was nearly seven feet tall and weighed over two hundred and fifty pounds. She had a mustache like a man, and sometimes she put on man's clothing. Then she'd fight with the keelboatmen, a dozen at a time, and lick 'em so hard they looked as if they had had an argument with screaming wildcats. Mike Fink, the greatest of all keelboatmen, never came down Louisiana way because Annie said if he ever showed himself around the New Orleans

The Life of Annie Christmas

levee, he'd go back looking as if he'd gone through a five-rail fence.

Now I'm going to tell you how she beat someone of whom all were scared!

One time Annie Christmas dressed up fancy. She shaved her mustache, put on a red satin dress, and stuck purple plumes in her black hair. She took half a dozen of her best lady friends, got on a keelboat, and went pleasure-riding up the Mississippi. At each landing they rested, and one or another of the ladies found a man to suit her taste and bade goodbye to the rest.

When they came to Red River landing, Annie Christmas was alone and felt lonesome-like. There was an old paddle wheeler boat waiting to go off, heading for New Orleans, and she took passage on it, tying her keelboat to the stern of the paddle wheeler.

It was grand, riding like a lady as the boat went, the water chugging and blogging, and Annie Christmas had a bully time.

The captain-pilot of the boat was a mean man—meaner than a bear clawed in a trap. But he kept out of Annie Christmas's way. She was known the length and width of the Mississippi and he knew what was good for him. The weather, though, was as mean as the captain-pilot. They had come to a new cutoff (that is, a place where the land was cut through for the Mississippi to flow and so save time going around big bends of land), and the old paddle wheeler was the first boat to try to go through it. Night came on and the sky was full of clouds, like torn blankets flying all over. The yellow river was tearing around like a wild witch, making deep holes, welling and gurgling. Some folks say the Devil and the Mississippi are first cousins.

The captain-pilot was working hard, trying to run that boat through the newly-made cutoff. There were snags and sandbars, and floating, knobby dead stumps, and it was hard going. The captain-pilot was getting madder and hotter by the minute.

Annie Christmas was standing near him, never saying a word.

Then the boat hit a bar. The captain-pilot roared hard words and swung the boat back, crunching and groaning. It hit a new bar. Sweat poured down the captain-pilot's neck and he bellowed words to burn air and hens' feathers. These words were meaner than poison snakes and they made Annie Christmas mad.

"You hold your tongue," she screamed. "Stop calling the Devil from hell, or he'll come to fetch you."

"Don't care if the Devil takes me, takes the boat, takes the crew, and all on it. Wish the Devil would take the Mississippi and pour it in a sand hole a thousand feet deep."

"Look out, man, your wish 'll come quick."

"Let 'm come and take us all. Don't care if he brings hailing brimstone with 'm and pours it all over."

"Did you hear that, Devil? What this blaspheming man said," Annie Christmas screamed. "Old Nick 'll get you, but I'm a God-fearin' woman, and I'm not goin' with you."

She leaped off the side-wheeler into her keelboat, and poled it away quicker than a bullet leaps from a trigger.

"Captain-pilot, you'll get your wish. Captain-pilot, your wish'll come sure as snakes crawl. There's three black crows flyin' overhead and that's black luck for you. There's hant in that screamin' wind. There's your man, hant! The captain-pilot's waitin'."

She was now out from the cutoff, as easy as if led by the best pilot in the land, and she kept on going. But her boat was going slow. So you know what Annie Christmas did? She tied the rope round her boat, jumped on shore, and tied the other end around her waist. Then she began towing that keelboat, running in long steady strides. The boat flew over the water like a swallow flies, till it and Annie came to New Orleans, where all were ready for that black woman heroine. Folks still tell about this great boat-pulling. And they still tell about the captain-pilot and his side-wheeler, who have never been seen since except on dark and foggy nights when you can hear that side-wheeler clanging and chugging hoarsely, and the godless captain-pilot blaspheming and bellowing.

Annie Christmas lived a lusty life until the day she died. Some folks say it was of love, some give other reasons. When she felt the end coming close, she called her twelve sons to her bedside. There they stood, all seven feet tall, six on each side. She told 'em how she wanted to be buried and they promised to obey.

Came the day. All the folks of New Orleans and every boatman from the levee were there. They stayed around the door of Annie Christmas's house till the sun had sunk down deep.

Then from the house came the twelve sons, dressed in black,

When the sons went off, the barge began to move—no man knows how.

carrying their mother in a black coffin in which she lay clad in a black satin dress. They put the coffin in a coal-black hearse, drawn slowly by twelve black horses. Six sons walked on each side. So they came to the levee, the great crowd following. A coal-black barge was waiting on the dark water. The black coffin was put on that barge by her sons, and they came back to land. No man nor beast was on that barge.

When the sons went off, the barge began to move—no man knows how. It floated out into the sea, until it couldn't be seen any more. . . .

Black folks say Annie Christmas is still sailing around the levees of New Orleans, and that the black barge can be seen on moonless nights, just the same as the side-wheeler can be seen on foggy nights in the cutoff on the Mississippi.

Gray Moss on Green Trees

The Indians tell a tale down in Louisiana. Maybe it's the Choctaw Indians, maybe it's the Chitimacha Indians, who battled with the French for many years when they were not busy making fine baskets and bright copper things. It might even be another tribe that tells this tale, or it may be all the tribes.

There was an Indian mother working in the field along the river. Near her, her two children played with bows and arrows, and with blue and purple flowers.

Suddenly, cold Wind came racing in the air through the trees. Then Rain came on, sharp rain, running in all directions. Water in the river rose, high and cold.

The mother took the children by the hand and ran toward her

hut of palmetto leaves. But she could not run as fast as the flying Wind, or as fast as the racing Water. Water was all around her, coming higher and higher, and held her feet down.

The mother climbed up a thick oak tree, holding the younger child in her arms. The older one followed her slowly. Soon they were high up, where Water could not reach them.

Wind kept on howling and Water kept on rising. Then Rain stopped, but cold Wind still ran wildly in the trees and around the three high up in the branches. The mother and the children were very cold and the children began to cry.

"Mother, I am cold, my feet are cold."

"Mother, my hands are cold and I can't hold on to the branches."

Moon came out over the black, flying clouds. Its white light was sharp and bright.

"Mother, I am cold," both the children cried.

The mother, too, was very cold.

"Man in the Sky," the mother prayed, "my children are very cold and will die. I am very cold and I can't keep them warm. I don't want my children to die from the cold. Take pity on them, they are very young. Take pity on me, so I can be with them. Be kind to us and don't let us die."

So the Indian mother prayed to Moon, while black and gray clouds flew all around the sky.

Moon spoke to Clouds, and to Wind. They listened. Moon shone strong on the mother and the children, and they fell asleep. Then Moon wove and wove and wove. . . .

Morning came. The sky was clear and warm. The Indian mother and her children awoke and were warm. They looked on the branches and saw what they had never seen before. All over the trees, in the branches and around them, was a thick green-gray blanket that had covered them. It was not made of cloth, but of grass, and Moon had woven it. The Indian mother looked and looked, and so did the children.

"Mother," cried the older boy, "it's a blanket all around us. It kept us warm all night. Moon heard you pray and tore up the clouds to make a blanket for us. Moon hung it on the tree to keep us warm."

"Yes, son, that's what Moon did for us. The sky is clear and the clouds are now on the tree."

They came down and went home.

The "Cloud-Cloth," folks call Spanish moss. It has been on the trees in Louisiana ever since and has spread to trees in other states.

The Bridal Ghost Dinner

I went to New Orleans and there a lawyer friend told me the ghost tale of the Mardi Gras dinner that has been told for many years.

New Orleans is the gayest city in Louisiana, and it is famous for its ghosts, its conjuring, and its Mardi Gras (which is Shrove Tuesday). People come to the Mardi Gras from every part of the country, and there is always a great ball at the French Opera House. On the stage, actors show beautiful living scenes of history and Greek tales, and the great crowd, dressed in silks and satins, watch and talk and make merry.

Many years ago, there sat in that gay Mardi Gras crowd at the Opera House a young gentleman who had come from up East. He didn't know anyone, so he sat alone and just looked at the gay goings on. Accidentally, his eyes wandered up to the boxes of the theater, and he saw in one of them the most beautiful girl he had ever seen in his life. She was a Creole, with eyes like black stars. He could not take his gaze off her. Soon she looked at him, and the moment their eyes met they fell in love with each other.

He left his seat and went into the lobby where the chandeliers sparkled and gleamed. Soon the girl entered, blushing like a rose in in the morning.

136 LOUISIANA

"I should not have come," she whispered. "I left my parents and a young gentleman who was with us. He is courting me."

"I love you," he said, "and that excuses everything."

"My parents will be angry and worried."

"I will marry you, and I know they will forgive you." He took her arm. "Come, let us go, I am hungry," he said. "We will eat and then we will go to the church and be married."

She went with him without saying a word. They walked from the Opera House to Royal Street and went into a brilliantly lit restaurant and sat down at a table.

"Waiter," the young man said, "this is our bridal dinner. Put flowers on the table and bring us the finest meal you have."

The flowers were set on the table, and the waiter brought food fit for such a celebration.

They ate and they drank and talked of how much they loved each other. The hours passed quickly as they sat happily at that dinner and, before they realized it, there was a rosy dawn in the sky; it was Ash Wednesday.

The two went to the beautiful St. Louis Cathedral for early Mass, and then they went to the priest and were married.

Hand in hand, both came back to the girl's parents and they were forgiven.

Soon after, the newlyweds said goodbye to all and went up North where the groom had his home.

It was cold up in the North and the lovely Creole bride began ailing. Before long, the girl wilted away like a delicate flower taken from its warmth and sunshine. She died and the young husband's heart was broken. Nothing could console him.

Shrove Tuesday, the day when he had first set eyes on his beautiful bride who was no more and the time of the Mardi Gras in New Orleans, was nearing.

"I will have dinner with her at my side, like the first night I met her . . . in my imagination . . . in my memory," he said to himself.

He wrote a letter to the restaurant man on Royal Street and sent him the exact amount of money the dinner had cost that night. In the letter, he said:

"Set the table for the same dinner I had with my bride at your restaurant last Mardi Gras. Set it with flowers and the same food we ate that night. The finest food you have. My bride and I will be there, though you won't see us. Whatever is left, give to a young couple who have no money for a dinner that night."

The restaurant man did as he was told. He set flowers on the table and the finest food in the house. The waiter stood behind the chairs with a napkin on his arm. He stood there a long time, as had been ordered, but no one came. He felt cold and eerie standing there, with no one in the seats. It seemed like a death-dinner.

The restaurant man found a poor young couple and gave them the food that had not been touched by human hands.

The next year, the restaurant man again received a letter and money ordering him to serve the meal, just as he had done the year before. There were to be flowers on the table and fine food and wine and a waiter in attendance. Then the food was to be given to a poor couple.

The restaurant man did as he was ordered, but this time the waiter thought there were two ghosts sitting at that table. He felt the air moving over the food and all around him. . . .

Every year thereafter a letter came to that restaurant with money for the same order, and the table was set accordingly. Folks in all New Orleans knew of that ghostly dinner for the beautiful dead Creole girl and her lover. And everyone believed her ghost and her husband's ghost came to that dinner.

One Mardi Gras the restaurant man received a letter from a lawyer up North telling him the man had died and had left an order, and money, for the dinners to be continued every Mardi Gras, just the same.

And so it was done for many, many years. Folks spoke about this strange bridal ghost dinner and came to see it set with the waiter standing behind the empty chairs. Many said they saw the flitting ghosts of the lovely Creole and the handsome young man at that table. Whether they saw the ghosts or not, the dinner was served on Mardi Gras night and people still tell of it in New Orleans.

One Pair of Blue Satin Slippers and Four Clever Maids

In the early, early days, there lived on the turning, twisting Teche every kind of Louisiana folk. There were strong, rough-handed Acadian farmers, sturdy enterprising Americans, and noble Frenchmen and Spaniards. The country was beautiful and rich, even as it is today. Folks worked hard and brought great riches to America.

There lived in those days on that twisting river a family by the name of Conrad. They had no riches, but they had an honest name and were known as fine folk everywhere.

Around their house was all the beauty of Louisiana's bayous. There were great, colored flowers, and willows with lacy strands of thin leaves; there were tall, dark cypresses and oaks. And there were the four Conrad daughters, dainty and pretty as anything on the bayou. Their cheeks were rosy as fresh roses, and their laughter rang all the day through the plantation.

One evening when the moon was big, four bright young men came courting the four Conrad girls.

Now, courting in Louisiana was a little different from courting up North. Here, down South, when a favored young man came to see his favorite girl, she would dress as if for a ball. Out came her prettiest dress and her best lace shawl; her feet were shod in the finest, pointed satin slippers, perhaps sent from France.

The four Conrad sisters dressed that night the proper way, but, alas! only one of them had shining blue slippers fit for a courting evening. But these Conrad girls had minds bright as their eyes. Before the gentlemen visitors came, they and their favorite maid had many secret talks, giggled with laughter, blushed from excitement.

One Pair of Blue Satin Slippers and Four Clever Maids 139

The four young men came dressed in their finest tight trousers and coats and sat down on covered chairs, waiting for their chosen ones to enter.

Soon the first pretty miss, small Mary Clara, came tripping down the stairs in shining blue satin slippers, her face radiant as the North Star.

The four young men rose from their seats and the tallest of them all, David Weeks, turned red with joy. They bowed low and the girl greeted them with a winning smile. She smiled most at young Weeks, and then led him off to a seat near one of the large windows where they seated themselves behind the curtain. She began talking merrily and the young man said little. While she chatted about this and that and everything, she slipped off the satin slippers and slid them out of the window.

The maid, who knew the scheme, stood under the window and caught the little slippers and ran quickly back around the house, up the back stairs, and soon . . . there came down the broad stairway pretty Conrad girl number two, her feet shod in gleaming blue satin slippers.

The three young gentlemen rose courteously and bowed deep and then one of them, who got the nicest smile, followed the lovely girl to another large window where the two sat down, forgetting everyone but themselves. And while the girl chatted brightly and the young man looked at her with wide-open eyes, she deftly slipped the satin slippers off and, bending out of the window under a pretty pretence, dropped them to the maid waiting underneath.

Swiftly the maid ran around the house, through the back door, up the back stairs. A few moments later, down from the wide, lighted stairway came pretty Conrad maiden number three, her lovely feet in blue satin slippers.

The two young men rose, bowed low, and when they looked up, one of them got a sweet inviting smile and followed right to a window that looked out on the dark green grass. The pretty Conrad maiden number three chirped gayly, like a bird, and the young man's eyes never left her pretty face. Off came the satin slippers and they were slipped through the open window and soon . . .

Down the stairs came pretty Miss Conrad number four in blue

satin slippers. Up rose the young gentleman, bowed low, and the two sat down together in a love seat in the center parlor.

The four couples had a gay and happy evening. Cake and drinks were served—by Conrad Maiden number four in blue satin slippers, while the others sat near the windows in merry-hearted conversation, in their stocking feet. But that did not prevent the four young gentlemen from telling of their love and proposing. And it did not prevent the young ladies from accepting.

In later years the four Conrad sisters told of the single pair of courting slippers and the gentlemen laughed and thought their wives were as clever as they were pretty.

The Silver Bell of Chênière Caminada

Grand Isle is one of the Louisiana Islands along the Gulf of Mexico. Chênière (the oaks) Caminada (the name of a merchant) was a little town across from Grand Isle. Many folks lived in each place, working in the sunshine and fishing in the dancing water for redfish, sea trout, pompano, and other kinds of fish. The people were all happy and contented. And who wouldn't be, living in that Louisiana paradise, full of richness, wonder, and beauty? There were vast stretches of oaks twisted into shapes of dancing witches and wondrous beasts; palms, strong and tall; and endless other green life. There were so many pelicans you could not count them, and pale pink herons, and flocks of other birds that came to the Island for food and drink and chattering.

In Chênière Caminada there was the clearest silvery-sounding church bell of all Louisiana. It weighed seven hundred pounds and was made of silver given by kind people and a generous priest.

The Silver Bell of Chênière Caminada   141

Every Sunday young Father Grimeaux preached in the church where the bell hung. Folks even came from Grand Isle to listen to his good words.

So everyone lived without care and with many pleasures—until the day of the terrible storm. That was in 1893.

The winds raged and roared, the water rose high and tore everything in its path. The folks of Chênière Caminada fled to Grand Isle, where there was greater safety.

When the storm died down, they went back to their homes. But while they were dancing to celebrate their safety, the storm returned a thousand times more fiercely than before. The winds howled wildly and the waves rose mountain high. The silver bell tolled on and on and on, to warn folks, and young Father Grimeaux was everywhere, praying, consoling, pleading with men and women to be courageous and have faith in the Lord. Houses were ripped out of the ground and swirled wildly away. People fought the rising waves and were pulled down to the depths. But the silver bell tolled on and on and on. Suddenly the silver tone in the screeching wind stopped! The wild water had torn down the church, and the bell lay silent on its side, waters surging wildly over it.

When the storm was still and the sky was blue, there was desolation all around. Torn houses and weeping folks were everywhere. Many left Chênière Caminada to go to towns where storms would not tear life into shreds. Many went to Westwego, not too far away, and they took their silver bell with them, hiding it to keep it until they could build a new church.

One day, an order came from the bishop for the folk of Chênière Caminada, now living in Westwego, to give their beloved bell to another town. They were sad and angered, but they had to obey the orders. So the bell was put on an oxcart and the drivers set out on their slow, sad journey.

But there were some from Chênière Caminada who were rebels and would not see their bell taken away. These men followed the cart unseen, at a distance.

The cart, with its treasure, moved along the dusty roads at a slow pace until it was dark. Suddenly strange noises were heard in the woods and there were queer calls of birds. A man came up to the cart and spoke to the drivers; then they all went off to see what had caused the weird sounds. They searched here and there, and when they came back—the bell was gone! The drivers did not say a word, they just returned to town. Even there, they did not talk of what had happened. People were silent and shook their heads when the word "bell" was mentioned. Even the sheriff made no search for it.

So the years went by, and the bell of Chênière Caminada was nearly forgotten by outside folks, but not by those who had come from Chênière Caminada and now lived in Westwego. Then one day word came that a new church in Grand Isle needed a bell. That would be the right and proper place for the old silver bell, near where it had first hung, calling people to God's service.

In Grand Isle they thought so, and went to Westwego to talk it over with the old folks who had come from Chênière Caminada. Quickly they all came to an understanding. It would be much nicer to have the beautiful old silver bell hanging in a church looking at the little lost town than buried in the deep dark earth. But first the bell that had disappeared on that dark night would have to be found. So they went out with spades and shovels, and many black townsfolk were with them.

They went to the Westwego cemetery and began digging deep here and there. Soon they hit something hard! They worked more carefully, and lo! there was the bell in the dark earth, no worse for wear after hiding for many years. There was great rejoicing everywhere when the silver bell was seen gleaming in the sunlight. It was placed on a cart, decked with flowers, and taken to Grand Isle, where it was hung in the new church. Everyone rejoiced, and so did the silver bell when it looked once again on old Chênière Caminada with its twisted oaks and giant palms waving high.

The good people of Grand Isle decided to ask Father Grimeaux to come and bless the new church with its wonderful silver bell, but they did not tell him where the bell came from. That was to be a surprise.

Father Grimeaux came in a boat, for he had a new parish now. With him were many other church dignitaries, all in gleaming vestments. When they got near Grand Isle, the silver bell began to toll. Father Grimeaux became alert at its first ring. Wasn't this the same tolling he heard the night of the terrible storm? He had never forgotten the sound of that bell. Now he heard it on an occasion of joy, not tragedy and sorrow! Tears came to his eyes—tears of gratitude—that he could hear the silver bell of Chênière Caminada on such a joyful occasion. He fell on his knees and prayed for those for whom the bell had tolled at that tragic time, and that it might never happen again.

The silver bell of Chênière Caminada is still at the church of Grand Isle, in Louisiana, and you can hear its sweet ringing if you go there now.

Three Great Men at Peace

This is a tale of three great men in the world who did deeds few men ever have done, and in the end, they came to rest together in a little cemetery in the town of Lafitte, Louisiana. The cemetery is still there under the large, thick live oaks, right at the foot of the bridge that crosses the Bayou des Oies (which, in French, means the Bayou of the Geese, because thousands of geese came there in their wandering flights).

In that small plot of ground rests, first, Jean Lafitte, a great hero of Louisiana (though some call him a pirate), for, except for him, General Andrew Jackson would surely not have beaten the English; not far from him there lies buried John Paul Jones, the American hero of the sea; and finally, there also is buried the Emperor Napoleon, who, so the folktale tells, nearly conquered the world.

The French say the great Emperor's body is in France, but folks in Louisiana say he is buried in the Lafitte cemetery, and who are you or I to argue that which folks have told for many, many years?

In the olden days, Jean Lafitte was fighting in the waters around

Louisiana and other states. Then, too, John Paul Jones was winning battles in many waters and many lands. Often these two great seamen performed great deeds together, so folks say in Louisiana.

John Paul Jones was honored by many countries, from the United States to Russia. He fought many battles and won all of them. Then he died and folks around Barataria say it was Lafitte who had Jones's body brought there and buried in the little cemetery so that he could be with his friend whenever he pleased.

There were great wars in Europe in those days, and Napoleon won more and more lands for the French people. Lafitte, like most people then, loved Napoleon for his fearlessness and his wisdom. Then luck turned against the Emperor and he was captured and sent to St. Helena as a prisoner.

"He must be freed," Lafitte said a thousand times over, and his lieutenants and crew said the same.

Lafitte sent a sloop and a trusty crew to St. Helena to rescue the great Napoleon. On board was a patriotic Frenchman, who looked like the Emperor and was ready to lay down his life for him, as so many Frenchmen were. The sloop came to the island in the dark of night and the Emperor was smuggled on board and his double was left behind in prison.

But luck was against the great warrior and he died on the way. When the sloop came to Barataria and Lafitte heard the news, he arranged a great funeral to which every man of his crew came.

"Bury him close to the grave of John Paul Jones," said Dominique You, Lafitte's fearless lieutenant, "and leave room for a grave in between. We all must die in the end."

And so it was done. Now there was a little cemetery under the waving live oaks. The dark cypresses rose over the graves of two great heroes of the world.

The years went on, and Jean Lafitte performed many more memorable and daring deeds for himself and his country; he fought battles and became more rich and powerful all the time. It seemed he could conquer anything. But one day something came along he could not conquer: the call from the other world! He died, and the men who had followed him through every field of life knew a great man had passed away and therefore must be buried with great men. To them there was but one such place in Louisiana: the little cemetery in Lafitte, between the other two great warriors: John Paul Jones, who conquered all on sea; and Napoleon the Great, who conquered all on land.

There Lafitte was buried and there he rests. When you come to Bayou des Oies, the grave will be shown to you. If you come on All Souls' Day, you will find candles burning on these graves, set there by some pious woman who remembers.

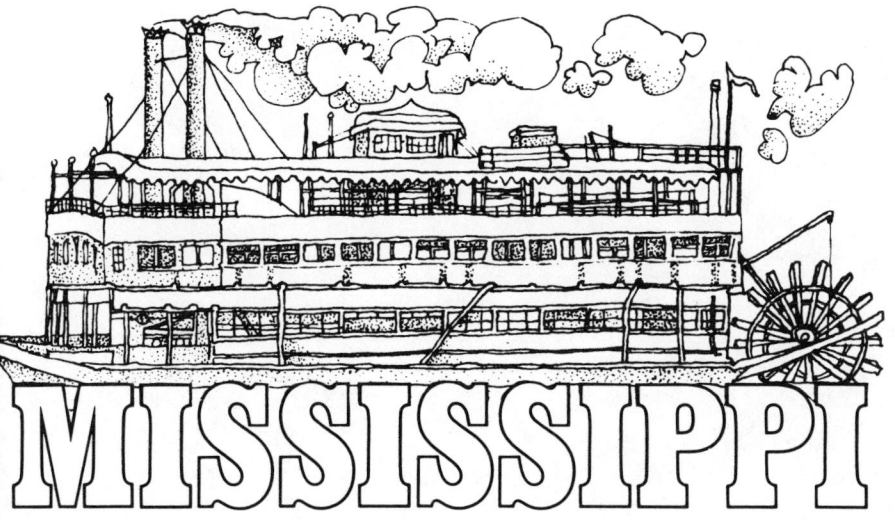

The Song in the Sea

Long before the Spaniards came, the Pascagoula Indians lived in the land white folks now call Mississippi and Alabama. They were strong, they were handsome, and their life was good.

One day, Olustee the strong, son of the chief of the Pascagoula tribe, went into the green woods to hunt.

He walked lightly on the leaves, ears and eyes wide open, listening to the never-ending talk in the woods and looking at the birds in the branches and the flowers on the earth. It didn't take long until he had a fine deer on his shoulders and turned homeward.

As he walked along the water, Miona, daughter of the chief of the neighboring Natchez tribe, came walking the opposite way. They looked at each other and they knew they were made for each other. But neither spoke.

Miona had been promised by her father to Otanga, chief of the Biloxis, a tribe of great warriors who were always on the warpath, and Olustee had heard of this. But love knows no fear. They looked at each other and loved each other.

Again and again Olustee went hunting where he had seen Miona and she came often to the water.

"Come to my people, Miona," Olustee said at last. "We will marry. My people will love you as I love you."

Miona listened and went to the Pascagoula tribe. When the chief and the warriors saw her, they greeted her with gladness. Everyone thought she was a fit wife for their future chief.

Otanga, the Biloxi, heard of this, and he went to Miona's father.

"Your daughter, whom you promised me for wife, has run to a Pascagoula dog, the son of their chief. Let us attack them and take their land."

So they attacked the Pascagoulas. The tribe fought hard, but since the enemy warriors were much larger in number and were fierce men, the Pascagoulas were losing ground. Olustee saw this with bitter sorrow, and he knew they would all perish.

Said Olustee to his father: "Father, it is better to live in the deep water than to be killed or made slaves by the Biloxis."

"That is true, my son." Then he cried aloud, "Pascagoula men and women and children, let us walk into the water where the Biloxis can't attack us."

They began singing and chanting . . . the song of death! The waves rose and fell gently, joining the song of the tribe. And if you listened closely you could hear a song coming from the deep sea; it, too, joined the song of the Pascagoulas. But it was not a song of death, it was a song of life, of another land where there was no war and hatred. The winds, coming from high far-off lands, also joined in that loud song, and so did the darting, quivering hot rays from the big golden sun.

The women, Miona, and the children, singing, went into the green water first. The warriors came next, singing, and at the end followed Olustee and his father, chanting the death song loud and strong. They all sang together with the sea and the wind, the waves and the sunrays, as they went deeper and deeper into the blue-green water. . . . Then the water closed over them with gentle waves.

The Biloxis could not hurt them now.

Other Pascagoulas have lived near these blue-green waters since that time, and when the sun is blue and the stars fall, you can hear singing coming from the sea, the death song of the Pascagoulas down in that deep water.

The Living Colors of the Twenty-first

Sometimes a ray of sunshine broke into the dark days of the great struggle between the North and South of our land. Here is one of those golden rays clear as a church bell ringing on a spring morning.

Soldiers' regiments are named by numbers, and there was a Twenty-first Regiment in Mississippi. It was a member of Lane Brandon's Company.

In that regiment there was a colored sergeant called Big Buck. He was a large lumbering man who was renowned as a bear hunter. And he was famous in other ways, too—for his kindliness, his readiness to help anyone in need, and for his generosity and honesty. He believed the Southern cause was a just cause, so he had volunteered to fight for it.

Big Buck was always in the thick of battle, and there was plenty of battling. But the Northern army was forging ahead and the Southerners had to retire. They fought every inch of the way to hold up the marching enemy and allow the Southerners to retire safely. The Twenty-first of Mississippi was the very last regiment fighting off the victors.

Big Buck was standing behind a frame house firing at the Northerners. Suddenly, when he was reloading, he saw a sight that wiped war and battles from his mind and eyes. There, from an alley, came toddling toward him a little girl no more than three years old, followed by a big Newfoundland dog trying to catch a rolling cannonball.

Big Buck forgot cannons, forgot everything, even the advancing foe. He saw only the little girl, the shaggy dog, and the murderous cannonball. And through his head kept running:

"She's 'bout the same age as my little girl I left home, God bless her soul! There's innocence for you. No hate! No shootin'."

The Northerners were getting nearer, shooting death all around, but Buck didn't give it a thought. He rushed out from behind his shelter, never noticing bullets, picked up the child to get her out of danger, then dodged behind the house, joining his Southern comrades. The dog followed him, barking.

From that day on, though bullets hailed down and though Northerners besieged them, pouring shell and hell into them, that little girl was taken care of as if she were in the hands of angels, not in the hands of rough-handed and rough-faced men. She was the mascot of the Twenty-first Regiment. She slept soft and warm when men lay on the hard ground; she ate well and plenty when the men went without food. That whole regiment was father and mother to the little girl; her own parents could not have done as well by her.

Came the day when the Yankees gave up trying to drive the Confederates from their position and withdrew, leaving the field and town to the Southerners. The honor of leading the men back into the city was given to the Twenty-first of the Magnolia State for its great bravery.

The sun was shining in the blue sky, band music was playing in the wind, and all the soldiers stood ready. But the officer did not give the order to march. Men were wondering what was wrong. Then the word spread: The colors of the Twenty-first Regiment could not be found. The men stood and waited, Big Buck among them, the little girl on his arm, the big dog beside them wagging his tail. The big soldier, child, and dog were always together.

Men were searching all over for the flag. Some had become impatient at the delay. Suddenly Big Buck had an inspiration. A thought had gone through his mind like a bullet—an American Mississippi thought. He ran to the front, holding the child with flying golden hair and fluttering dress like a banner over his head:

"Forward, Twenty-first," he roared, "here are our colors!" and he waved the laughing child high above his head.

The men fell in and marched behind them, hurrahing and shouting the good rebel yells of the South.

So they came into the city, Buck leading with the little laughing girl high in the air, gay as any banner that ever waved before a marching regiment. A crowd of people smiled and cried and cheered the soldiers.

Suddenly there was a wild scream in the crowd; a woman broke through, rushed up to Big Buck, threw her arms around him and the child. There was a small happy cry of "Mommy," and the woman fainted. It was too much for the mother, who had thought her child dead—and now saw her alive and happy!

The mother soon was well again, and Buck gave her the little girl, the standard of the Twenty-first Mississippi Regiment.

The men of the Twenty-first of Mississippi have never forgotten the lovely child who was their banner and brightened a few days of the horrible war when they were fighting for what they felt was a just cause. The members of the regiment, their friends and relatives and endless others tell the tale, and here it is for you.

The Ghost Wedding in Everhope

Folks down in Mississippi who live near Lake Washington in the Delta country say it's the most beautiful lake in the world. That's what Junius Ward, who came there first to hunt poodle-doos—a kind of duck—and mallard ducks, and water turkeys, said, and he settled there. Soon many other families came down that way and, seeing how beautiful the water and the fields were, settled there too—among them Andrew Knox. He came with his family, chose his land, and began building a fine red-brick house.

Knox had a young son whom he loved; the boy was the apple of his eye.

He said to his son:

"Someday these lands and this fine red-brick house being built will be yours. But first we'll all have many happy days here."

Then, young, and full of eager excitement, he instructed the men working on the house to leave spaces in the brick walls.

"I'll put bottles of wine in these holes, and they'll be opened at my son's wedding," he said, laughing. "It'll be a mighty rich wine by then and worthy of a great celebration for a son of mine."

Mr. Knox was a jolly and happy man and kind to all, black and white.

It was done as he ordered, and many a bottle of good wine was put in between the cool bricks for aging and strength.

The boy grew up in Everhope, as the house was called, and everyone loved him, just as they did his father.

Then one black day young Master Knox took ill. All kinds of doctors were called, but none could help him. No one could save him, and he died. It broke his father's heart, and he sold the plantation and the house, and soon he followed his son.

But Everhope, the red-brick house with the bottles of wine set in the walls for Master Knox's wedding day, remained strong and untouched by weal or woe, though it was closed up.

Then, on Christmas day, a strange and weird life came into the empty house. A ghost life! A great celebration, as Andrew Knox had planned for his son's wedding day.

Suddenly the whole house was alight with candles! Mostly the great parlor. Lit up as if for a Christmas ghost wedding—a wedding for young Knox, as his father had planned. Servants dressed in their best moved around dusting and polishing furniture clean and bright. There was hustle and bustle. Then they began setting the great table with gleaming glasses, china, and silver. Soon Andrew Knox and his wife and guests surrounded young Knox leading a lovely bride on his arm as he came in. Friends and relatives, all gone, filled the big room. All were dressed in their finest. Everyone was gay, jesting and laughing and talking.

Then Mr. Andrew Knox and his wife sat down, and with them young Knox and his radiant bride. Friends and relatives also sat down. You would never think these folks were specter-ghosts from a world we know only in our dreams.

Then there was another wondrous change in this phantom

world. The brick walls where the bottles had been placed for the wedding opened up, and the bottles set away by Mr. Knox for his son's wedding came floating through the air and placed themselves on the table in silver holders in their proper places. The corks came out and the servants poured the wine into the shining glasses. Food was served, there were toasts, and the wine was drunk.

So the evening went on gaily, in celebration, eating, drinking, and cheerful conversation. In the end, bride and groom left, and so did the guests, one after another. Plates were removed, the corks went back into the bottles, and the bottles rose in the air and floated back into their places in the red-brick walls where they had been put years before by Andrew Knox for his son's wedding day. The walls closed up . . . until the next Christmas day.

Every Christmas the same Christmas ghost-wedding dinner takes place all over again. And each Christmastime, the bottles come floating out of their brick hiding places to fill the glasses for the wedding feast of young Knox in Everhope.

The Ring Around the Tree

There is a lovely tale about the Indians told down in Biloxi on the Gulf of Mexico, which shows that Indians are no different from white folks or any other folks except for the color of their skins. They think the same way and do the same things as we do. They are always warring, the same as we, and loving, too, even when they are at war.

The Indians living in the Bixoli region were always battling the other tribes around them. One day the son of an Indian chief who had battled against the Biloxis was hunting in the woods. In a clearing near a spring was the daughter of the Biloxi chief. And, as so often happens, they fell in love with each other. Love cares little about war.

These two met often in the woods where they thought no one saw them. But one day a Biloxi hunter did see them and told the chief.

The chief told his daughter she could not see the son of his enemy again. The girl was very unhappy, but love does not worry about difficulties, and one day the young brave dared come to the Biloxi chief to tell him of his love.

The chief was standing in a grove of oak trees, the young Indian before him.

"I love your daughter and I want to marry her."

"You are my enemy and you cannot marry my daughter. I forbid her to see you."

The young brave pleaded again, saying they were not enemies if they loved each other.

The chief was silent, looking at one of the oak trees. Then he said:

"You will marry my daughter only when a ring grows around this tree," and he pointed to a thick oak and walked away.

The young Indian left in anger.

That night a great storm came by, twisting trees and branches in fantastic ways. Some strong branches were twirled around the oak tree to which the chief had pointed and had formed a circle around it.

In the morning the daughter of the chief saw the ring around the tree and showed it to her father.

The chief looked and was silent. Nor did he say anything when the maiden went off with her young warrior.

That ring stayed around the oak tree for years and years. No storm could tear it off.

With the years it became tighter and tighter, until it became a solid ring. Just as the chief had required.

The tree is still there. It is on the lawn of the historic Episcopal Church of the Redeemer, and everyone who visits Biloxi goes to see it, even as I did.

Tar-Wolf Tale

One summer, way back, there was a hot shining sun all the time. It just didn't stop shining; you'd think that sun was getting big wages for shining all the time. So every bit of water dried up. The river dried up, the springs dried up, and the swamps dried up. Everything was dry as bone. All the animals suffered because they were thirsty. They were getting thinner all the time.

But there was one animal that didn't look bad a bit, and that was old Br'er Rabbit. He was sleek and shiny like a snake come out of the water and was always lippidy-lopping along, singing a little song to himself.

"How come?" all the animals asked. "You look fine and fat and slick. Where do you get your water?"

"I drink dew on the grass that comes from heaven, that's what keeps me so fine."

"Don't believe it," the animals said. "We lick the dew every morning and none of us looks like you."

Br'er Rabbit, he just twitched his ears and lippidy-lopped off.

"That rabbit isn't telling the truth," the animals said. "We must watch him. He's getting water someplace. We'll watch him all night to see."

They went near Br'er Rabbit's house and sat around watching.

When the sun was sliding behind the trees, the animals saw Br'er Rabbit coming out of his cabin holding a big jug and looking all around him. He started walking and walking, the animals following, following all the time.

Pretty soon they saw him going into a patch of blackberry

bushes, and after a little time he came out with the jug full of fine water.

The animals let him go home first, then they all ran scram-bang into the blackberry bushes. And what do you think! There under the blackberry bushes was tucked away a spring chock-full of bubbling, good water.

All the animals drank and drank and drank the good water. My, it tasted fine! Then they said:

"Rabbit's mean and we got to teach 'm a lesson."

"That we must," all said. "How?"

They thought a long time, then they all agreed the best thing would be with a Tar Wolf.

"What's a Tar Wolf?" a young animal asked.

"Well, a Tar Wolf is a wolf made o' tar. That's all."

They made a Tar Wolf that looked like a real wolf and put him in the bushes right alongside that spring with the cool sweet water. Then they went home to sleep.

Next morning when Sun was up, Br'er Rabbit went to the spring for his morning drink.

First thing he saw was that Tar Wolf looking black and bad.

"You go from here, Mister Black Wolf," Br'er Rabbit said.

Black Tar Wolf just said nothing.

"You go from here, Black Wolf, or I'm gonna slap you. I ain't scared o' you."

Black Tar Wolf didn't open his mouth.

"Ain't gonna answer won't help you; you go just the same," Br'er Rabbit said. "Or..."

No noise at all. Then Br'er Rabbit slapped Black Tar Wolf a hard slap. He wanted to take his paw back, to slap him a second time, but couldn't, for his paw was stuck deep in the tar.

"Let go my paw, Black Wolf, or I'm gonna hit you with my other paw! That's stronger and hits harder."

Black Tar Wolf didn't say anything. That made Rabbit good and mad.

He swung back with his left paw and struck Black Tar Wolf with all his might. His paw went deep into the tar and he couldn't get it out.

"Let go my foot and hands," Br'er Rabbit hollered.

"Let go my paws," Br'er Rabbit screamed, "or I'm gonna kick you hard."

Not a mumbling word, so he raised his left foot and kicked Black Tar Wolf with all his might. Then he couldn't get his foot out.

"Let go my foot and hands," Br'er Rabbit hollered, "or I'll kick you with my right foot, and anyone I kick with my right foot's sure to die."

But Black Tar Wolf didn't answer just the same, and you know why. So Br'er Rabbit gave him the hardest kick he could with his right foot!—and there he was, feet and hands deep in the black tar, dangling like a big catfish on a hook. Then there was laughing all round him, for all the animals had come early to see what would happen.

"Now we got you, Br'er Rabbit. Next time you'll tell us when you got a spring full o' fine water and we are dying for a drink! But there isn't gonna be no next time. We're gonna finish you right now, break your neck so you don't do no harm to nobody again. We're gonna finish you for good."

Br'er Rabbit was thinking hard and sweating all over.

"I know I done wrong, and you got the right of the Lord to punish me. But breaking my neck'll not do it. I can grow another new neck quicker 'n you can say Jehoshaphat."

"Then we're gonna cut off your ears."

"That's fine. Cut 'em off. I got new ones all ready and they are longer 'n better than the old ones."

"If you can grow back things, then we'll do something to you that'll hurt you good and strong. We'll throw you in a briar bush full of the longest stickers. When they stick you long and deep, it'll hurt till you scream."

"Oh please! don't do that. I don't want to be hurt. I hate briars stuck in me. Don't throw me in the briar bushes! Please!"

"Ha! that's just what we're gonna do," the animals cried.

They threw him and the Tar Wolf into the briar bushes. The stickers stuck deep into Tar Wolf, who couldn't move and stayed stuck. And that let Br'er Rabbit tear himself away from Tar Wolf. He leaped out, shouting and laughing, even though the briars had stuck him pretty bad.

He ran off crying, "Thank you all for helping me get away from that bad Black Tar Wolf. I couldn't 've done it without you. Next time, try something better."

Mike Hooter and the Smart Bears in Mississippi

There are bears and bears—smart bears and foolish bears. Folks in Mississippi used to say Mississippi bears are the smartest bears in all these United States.

That's what Mike Hooter, the great Bear-Hunter Preacher of the Magnolia State, used to say when he was alive, and he sure knew all anybody ever knew about bears. Fact is, he was the greatest bear hunter ever was in Mississippi. Ask any man in the state and he'll agree mighty quick.

Some folks called him Mike Shouter, for he was forever roaring louder than ten waterfalls when he got to preaching sermons or when he was arguing about the smartness of the Mississippi bears. If you tried to argue the point about bears, he'd come 'round quick with the tale of Ike Hamberlin and his funny bear hunt in the cane. It's a good tale worth telling.

One time Mike Hooter and Ike Hamberlin got to talking about bear hunting and they planned to go out together one day after the big game. But Ike was monstrous jealous of Mike, so he thought he'd steal a march on his friend and go out alone before him. He set out early in the morning, he and his dogs, without Mike.

But Mike had got wind of this, so he got up crack early himself that morning, took his two-shooter, and went off looking for Ike. But he didn't take his dogs along.

After a time he sighted Ike and just followed him right along a ways off.

Ike had gone pretty deep in the canes when his dogs started growling and barking. Their hairs began standing straight on their backs like tomcats in a fight. And there was another kind o' deep noise too, something a-tween a grunt and growl.

"Run, git 'm," Ike shouted to the dogs. But the dogs wouldn't. They just ran around Ike yapping and crying, as if they were scared to death, tails stuck a-tween the hind legs.

"Sic 'em! Sic 'em!" Ike kept on hollering to the dogs, but they minded him like birds in flight.

Mike was watching all the time, wondering what was coming next.

Ike was mad as a hornet, but he kept his temper, coaxing and coaxing the dogs to stir up the bear that was somewhere. Those dogs wasn't acting natural. Mike, watching, felt kind of sorry for Ike.

There was the man out hunting for bear! There was a bear for sure somewhere 'round the canebrake! There were bear-hunting dogs to stir the bear! And instead of doing their duty as good hunting dogs should, they just kept on whining, tail a-tween the legs. It sure was not right. You'd think a hant was on 'em.

Ike was mad fit to kill.

"I'll make you good-for-nothin' critters tend t' your business as you oughta," he shouted. Then he took his flintlock, leaned it against a tree, and ran to the creek and began picking up stones and throwing 'em at the dogs.

Well, when Ike Hamberlin got busy picking up stones and throwing them at the dogs that were howling t' heaven, there was suddenly heard an awful noise in the cane. A crackling and breaking and crashing like a hurricane, and out came the biggest and most powerful bear ever seen by Ike or Mike. He was a great giant standing on his hind legs. And what do you think that critter did! He just walked up to the tree where the gun was standing, picked it up with his front paws and looked at it, and then blowed into it with powerful breaths—blowing all the powder out!

Right then, Ike Hamberlin, his back to the bear, thought he'd thrown enough rocks at his cowardly or bewitched dogs and started out for his gun. When he turned around and saw the bear with it, he stood stock still. His hair stood up on his head, his mouth was wide open, and his eyes were ready to jump out of his head. And Mike, watching, was just as numb.

The bear looked at Ike with a bear grin, kind of plumb unconcerned, then he put the rifle back against the tree, turned around, and began easy loping off.

Ike rushed up to the gun, grabbed it, aimed straight at the bear, and snapped the lock! . . . Not a sound from the trusty old piece! But there was a sound of laughing afar off. Mike had seen what the bear had done and was laughing fit t' kill. The bear turned around and looked at the aiming Ike. His jaws opened wide in a bear laugh, one of his front paws went to his nose and—he thumbed his nose at good Ike, who was snapping and snapping. Then Ike turned the gun 'round and saw the powder was gone! His face looked like it'd been soaking in vinegar for six months. He shook his fist at the bear, shouted a few strong words, and turned 'round to go home. He'd had enough bear hunting for the day.

Mike turned home too, laughing till the tears ran out of his eyes.

He told the story for the rest of his life, just as I'm telling it to you. And it always brought a good laugh.

Now, wouldn't you say that Mississippi bears are mighty smart bears?

The Sad Tale of the Half-Shaven Head

This happened years ago down in Mississippi, in the days of the carpetbaggers, and folks still love to tell about it. If you don't know what a carpetbagger was, I'll tell you. They were fellows coming from the North after the Civil War, with baggage light as a bird's wing in wide bags made of carpet. They mixed in affairs they had no

The Sad Tale of the Half-Shaven Head 165

right to mix in. They drove tough bargains, often cheating folks. Worst of all, they tried to tell people how to live and what to do. They sure made life miserable for Southerners. Southern folks didn't like these fellows, and you can't blame them.

Well, one of those carpetbaggers, named Woodmansee, had come to Aberdeen in Monroe County, Mississippi. He'd become chancery clerk and was making himself about as friendly and popular as a mule in a beehive. He was a funny-looking fellow, with long hair down to his shoulders, as was the custom in those days, and he was very proud of those locks. He was forever mixing into other folks' business, sticking his nose where he shouldn't have. There wasn't a soul in the whole county had a good word for him, leastways the lawyers.

One day after sunset he went to the office of two lawyers, Mr. Beckett and Mr. Barry, to have a piece of business settled. They had their office over a store, up one flight of stairs.

Woodmansee had been drinking more than was good for him and he was going along like a rowboat on billowing water. He worked hard to get upstairs, and when he arrived and came into the room not a soul was there. They'd gone home for the day. He snooped around a bit, looking at things he had no right to look at, and then he began to walk down. I told you that carpetbagger wasn't too steady on his feet and he slipped on one of the steps and rolled all the way down, cutting the side of his head. It was a pretty big cut, and it started to bleed. He lay there. Right then there came by Mr. John McCluskey, another lawyer of the county, and saw the fallen man. He at once got some black folks standing around to help him pick up Woodmansee and take him back to the lawyers' offices, where there was a couch. They laid him on it. He was moaning and groaning and mumbling he was sure going to die.

"You ain't gonna die," John McCluskey said, "but that bleeding's got to be stopped." He was examining Woodmansee's head and saw that the cut was not really deep and wouldn't do any real harm.

McCluskey had a quick mind and was the kind of fellow who liked a good joke. He saw a chance to play it on the man who was making his and other folks' lives miserable.

"I've got to stop the bleeding, Woodmansee, or you might bleed to death. To do it right, I'll have to shave the hair around it."

"Do anything, but stop the bleeding quick!" Woodmansee groaned.

McClusky went to the little cupboard on the wall where he found court plaster and razor and soap.

Woodmansee lay face down, eyes shut, and didn't see what was going on.

McCluskey first took court plaster and put it over the cut to stop the bleeding. Then he soaped the fellow's head and began shaving his hair off . . . on the opposite side. Soon he had one side of Woodmansee's head shaven off clean and shining like a peeled onion. Then he bandaged the side with the cut and, with the help of the two men who had brought Woodmansee up, took the carpetbagger to his own room and put him to bed. There he fell asleep quickly.

The next morning, when Woodmansee saw himself in the looking glass, he roared like a gored bull. The long hair on one side of his head was gone and his half-bald head glistened like a yellow apple. The other side was bandaged. He looked worse than a clown in the circus.

"That McCluskey. . . . I'll put enough bullets in 'm to turn 'm into a sieve," he roared. "I'll have his head for committing a crime." Then he grabbed his gun and ran to find John McCluskey.

The news of the trick John had played on the carpetbagger had spread as fast as August goldenrod.

The lawyers, as well as townfolks, were on the lookout for the Yankee, and they saw him running along, roaring-red, looking for John McCluskey.

The two lawyers Woodmansee had gone to see stopped him as if by accident.

"Lord above," cried Mr. Barry, one of the lawyers, innocent-like, "what happened to you, man! Who cut half your fine long hair offa your head?"

"That so-and-so and so-and-so scalawag McCluskey! Where is he? I'll blow his head off when I catch 'm. Have you seen 'm? I'll put a dozen bullets through his vile carcass."

"Well," said Barry slowly, "maybe it'll give you mighty fine satisfaction to blow his brains out, but then he'll be dead. I kin tell you a better way to get even with him that'll torture him good for a long time to come."

Woodmansee stood silent, glaring at the two men.

"There's a better way to hit John . . . in his pocket. He loves money more 'n his life. Sue 'm, sue 'm for lots of money! You're sure to win in court. And when he has to shell out money, it'll hurt 'm for the rest of his life."

The two kept at Woodmansee until they made him believe that suing would hurt McCluskey more than shooting.

Angry as he was, he agreed and told the two lawyers to bring suit against John, which they did.

Now, you know how court cases go. They don't go; they crawl along slower than snails. Week followed week while Woodmansee was walking around, his whole head in a white bandage to hide the one shaven side that made him look like a freak at a fair. Folks stopped him as if they didn't know what had happened and asked him in what battle he had fought.

All the time McCluskey was telling black and white that he couldn't be blamed for Woodmansee's "accident." It was dark when it happened and he was so excited when he saw the poor bleeding man that he didn't know what he was doing. He was truly sorry for having made the mistake of cutting the Northern gentleman's hair on one side—and the wrong side at that!

But the whole county and many outside the county knew what had really happened.

The weeks dragged along and Woodmansee began to feel that everyone was just making sport of him. He fretted and he fumed, but it did him little good. Life had become for him dark as the hour before dawn, the darkest hour of the night. Wherever he went he saw only smiling faces!

One day he just faded out of Monroe County—out of Mississippi—like a bad hant. He left the Magnolia State. But the tale didn't leave. It's still there and told to this day and always brings a good laugh.

Guess Who!

Once there was a very nice young black girl, and she was a mighty pretty girl, with laughing eyes and dancing feet. All the fellows were crazy about her and they let her know it. There were always a few hanging around wherever she went. They'd much quicker look at that girl than work. But she couldn't make up her mind which one to marry. She was kind of uppity. She just kept looking and judging 'em all. You can't blame her; there were so many, it was hard to choose.

But there were four suitors courting her she favored more 'n any of the others, only she couldn't make up her mind which one she'd marry.

"Well, maybe I'll marry the one who can do things the quickest," she said to herself and her friends.

All four were big and strong and not afraid of anything. And all had plenty o' honey words for that pretty black girl.

One morning she was walking to a spring for water, a wooden bucket in her hand.

Along came one of the young suitors she favored. He was the oldest of the four and he was a carpenter.

He knew all about that pretty girl and what was in her mind, so he sang out just for fun, "I'm a mechanic without a trade, an' now you just tell me where you is goin', honey."

"I'm going to get water."

"I'll go with you. Gimme, I'll carry the bucket for you."

He took the bucket and they went to the spring and he filled it full o' fresh water. Then they walked home, and I can tell you that young fellow's mouth wasn't clamped. He was telling her all kinds o' nice things and asking her to marry him.

While he was deep in love-talk, kerplunk! the bottom of that wooden bucket full o' water began falling out.

What do you think that young smart carpenter fellow did? Quicker 'n you can wink an eye he found a plank. Quicker 'n you can open your mouth he cut it to fit the bottom o' that bucket. And quicker 'n your breath 'd come out o' your mouth he put that bottom back in the bucket, tight as bark on a tree.

He did it all so fast, not a drop o' water fell out.

"I may be a mechanic without a trade, but that's the kind of carpenter I am, honey. Now will you marry me?"

"You're the finest carpenter in the state, but I got to think more 'bout it. Just wait a little longer and I'll tell you for sure."

Time went on and so did the pretty girl. Winter came and it was mighty cold. One day that pretty girl was sitting in the house with the second young fellow she favored. He was a woodcutter.

He knew all about the pretty girl and what was in her mind, so he sang out just for fun: "I'm cuttin' wood without a trade." Then he talked warm words, but they weren't warm enough to make that room warm.

"Think you might get some wood for the fire; there isn't a stick in the house."

"I sure can; I'll make you nice and warm, sugar plum," he chirped lovingly.

He took his ax and went out. There was an old tree standing near the house. It was near ten foot thick. He tried his ax for sharpness, and right then there began one of those queer winter storms with thunder and lightning and no rain.

Just as he raised his ax a streak o' lightning showed high up in the sky coming down toward that tree.

Up went the ax, down came that ax. Up and down a thousand times, quicker 'n the lightning.

Bang! Bang! Crack! Crack! The tree was down.

Cut! Cut! Cut! Splitting right and left.

And what do you think! Before that bolt of lightning got near that tree that young woodcutter had a good cord o' wood all cut, running with it into the house.

"There, sugar plum, 's enough wood to keep us warm so I can tell you how much I'm longin' for you to marry me. Maybe I'm cutting wood without a trade, but you can see I'm the finest woodcutter in all Mississip."

"You're a mighty fine woodcutter for sure, but I got to think 'bout that marryin' business. Just wait a little longer and I'll tell you for sure."

But time doesn't wait for anyone, not even for pretty girls. Spring came to Mississippi and everything was green and fresh. One morning that pretty girl and the third of her favorite suitors were walking in the woods. He was a blacksmith by trade.

The sun was shining and the birds were singing and it was a good day. A fine day to ask a girl to marry. That's what the young blacksmith was doing, asking the pretty girl same as all the others had. That girl was the most marrying-asked girl in the state of Mississippi.

He knew all about that pretty girl and what was in her mind, so he just for hi-de-do cried: "I'm shoein' without a trade; but just you marry me an' I'll show you what I can do." Catfish an' crabs! He was always carrying hammer, nails, and iron hoof-shoes with 'm. While they were talking, there leaped a deer afore their eyes.

"Honey, I'll show you what shoein' a fine blacksmith without a trade kin do."

He ran after the deer, took out hammer, nails, and iron hoof-shoes and shod that deer . . . while it was running mighty fast!

When he was done, he cried: "See, hon, the kind of workman I am. Will you marry me fast as I can shoe a deer?"

"You're a fine blacksmith and there is none better. But when it comes to marryin', I got to think 'bout it. It's different from a-nailin' hoofs on a mule or a deer. Just wait a little longer and I'll tell you for sure."

So time went along and fall came in. One day the fourth young fellow who was a-courtin' her came her way. This one was a barber.

"Angel face, I'm shavin' without a trade," he shouted. "I sure love you and 'll keep you in clover." And he kept on talking about what young folks talk about: love.

Sudden-like there leaped out of the bushes a plump rabbit with long ears.

"Angel lamb, I'm gonna show what I kin do at shavin' without a trade!"

Out came the razor, soap, and water he always carried with him.

Before that rabbit could run across the green patch, his face was clean shaven, and even behind the ears.

"See what I can do! Now will you marry me?"

"You're the best shavin' man that ever was, but marryin' ain't the same 's shavin'. I got to have a little time to think about this. Just you wait a little and I'll give an answer for sure."

So that pretty girl was thinking and thinking and thinking a long, long time. She was thinking so long, I couldn't wait to find out which one she married in the end. The best I can do is guess, and so can you. And when you tell me, I'll tell you.

NORTH CAROLINA

The Savage Birds of Bald Mountain

This is an old-time story. It happened long ago when Bald Mountain in the Blue Ridge of North Carolina was covered with green-leaved trees and low shrubs full of berries. Then it wasn't bald as it is today.

At the base of the mountain lived the Indians, hunting and planting. They had plenty of everything and no hostile tribes tried to take away their hunting grounds.

One day the women were in a field hoeing and planting, the children were playing, and the warriors were busy with bows and arrows, getting ready to hunt. There was good peace all over.

Suddenly a wild, high screaming came from the sky and it became dark. The mountain and the valley were in deep shadow.

They looked for the sun and saw a giant bird flying to the mountain and their homes. The bird was so big it hid the sun. It was screaming fiercely, full of evil. At the mountain it flew down amid the trees.

The sun shone again. The evil bird was quiet and there was peace.

Day after day there was quiet, but in the heart of all the Indians living around that mountain there was fear.

"No good will come of this."

"Days of trouble are ahead of us," all said.

But life around the mountain was peaceful. The squaws worked in the gardens, the children played in the woods, and the warriors were busy hunting, bringing meat to eat. But never did one go up the mountain where that giant bird was living.

One night when the yellow moon wandered in the sky between the stars, the sleeping tribe was awakened by wild screeching and the earth shaking. All rushed out in white terror! There was the giant bird, screaming so loud and flapping his wings so powerfully that the earth shook. Leaves flew all over and trees leaped out of the earth—with roots like long hair.

The lashing bird was screeching loud as thunder. It swooped down into the valley over the huts of the Indians who had fled in fear. It flew around and around, roaring and flapping, diving and soaring, then . . . it flew high up, back to the top of the mountain, and again there was silence.

Warriors, women, young men, and girls slowly came back to their homes and then saw that one of the children was missing.

The wild, roaring bird that brought the thunder had carried it off to the mountain!

There was terror in the hearts of all and they were afraid to attack the giant thunderbird. The moons passed on and there was silence in the mountain and peace in the valley—for one year.

Then, one night, they all were awakened again by the wild screeching and the thundering noise. When they rushed out, there was the giant bird roaring and thundering and flying around and around. It came lower and lower into the valley and when it flew off again, another child was missing. And so it happened every year. But the Indians were afraid to battle the monster. Day and night they were in terror.

They prayed to the Great Spirit to help them, but the Great Spirit did not listen to them.

Then one day a new chief was the head of the tribe and he was not afraid.

"We have suffered too long from this fierce bird. If the Great Spirit won't listen to us and help us, we must help ourselves. The time is near when the bird of screeching and thunder comes to rob us of our children. We must battle the beast, and destroy it."

The warriors took heart and armed themselves with their strongest weapons.

"We will battle that evil bird and win," the chief said. "Let all the women and children go deep into the woods and wait until we come for them. If we don't win, we will die like warriors."

The braves spread around the mountain and began climbing up. Slowly they went up higher and higher through brush and trees.

They were near the top when they suddenly stopped and stood still like the trees in the earth. Before them was a sight to put fear into the heart of the most fearless. Instead of one fierce bird with flaming eyes there was a whole tribe of them standing close together, beaks bent forward, eyes boring, ready to attack.

The warriors stood frozen with fear! The weapons dropped from their hands—all except the chief's.

"Great Spirit," he shouted, "you won't let our whole tribe who worship you be destroyed by these evil birds. You must come to help us or we will be lost!"

The Great Spirit heard the prayer of the chief. Suddenly fires flashed from all over the sky. They flashed down on the birds and they all burned to the ground. Then the fire spread through the green trees of the mountain and through the shrubs. The flames reached to the sky and when they died down there was not a tree left on the mountain, even as there were no birds left.

The Indians sang songs, and danced dances of thanks and praise to the Great Spirit. They could now live in peace, and they did.

But when spring came, everything was green except the mountain. There was not a leaf on the trees or a blade of grass on the earth, and the shrubs were shriveled and black. All was bare and bald. The fire of the Great Spirit had burned deep.

There have been no trees on that mountain since and so it is called the Bald Mountain.

The White Doe

Along the yellow-gray sand hills and dunes of Nags Head and Kitty Hawk, and all along the thin island shores of North Carolina, and in the swamps of the Islands there is a tale of a wonder-white doe. Folks who live in the cranberry bogs and who have magic sight can see at midnight that pure-white doe, standing still as a statue and looking out into the far, far ocean. She stands all alone, her moist, wistful eyes gazing longingly far away, where the Old Country is.

There is no end of tales running in those yellow sands of the North Carolina coast and other places about the White Doe. One story, sad and lovely, about Virginia Dare, the White Doe, has been told for more than three hundred years and is still told today. For it is a living tale that stands out like a white church spire in thick gray clouds.

Perhaps the most famous early settlement in the southern part of our land is the lost colony of Roanoke. There are many mysterious tales about this lost community and the first child born in it: Virginia Dare, the White Doe. Let me tell you the one I like best.

Soon after the settlers founded Roanoke, they were greatly in need of food and supplies, and when none came from England, Governor White went to get them. It took a long time and when he returned . . . three years later . . . there was no sign of the men, women, and children he had left behind. They had gone to the Indians and could not be found. The baby, Virginia Dare, was among the Indians and they called her the White Fawn, even as her mother was called the White Doe.

The White Fawn grew up lovely to see and soon she became known as the White Doe.

Two Indian braves courted the young White Doe—Okisco, a fearless young chief and a fine warrior, and Chico, who was the medicine man, the magician in the tribe. The young White Doe favored young Okisco.

There was hard feeling between the two rivals and anger flew like cold, fall winds between them.

When Chico, the priest-magician of the tribe, saw that Virginia, the White Doe, would not have him, his anger was like a wild storm on the water. He spoke words of black magic and young Virginia turned into what the Indians called her. She really became a pure-white doe, beautiful to see and fleet as the wind.

With magic feet she roamed through the green woods like a great gleaming white jewel. Lone hunters and whole tribes saw that wonderful white creature and tried to hunt it down, but no one ever succeeded.

Okisco was in wild sorrow and anger when he saw his love was gone. But no brave could battle the medicine magic man of the tribe. Chico had great secret power; only the medicine magic man of another tribe could challenge him. So Okisco went to see Wenando, also a great medicine-magician of a neighboring tribe, and told him his tale. Wenando listened and then he said:

"I will give you an arrow made of silver that has magic powers. Watch for the White Doe and when you see her, shoot her with your silver arrow into the heart. She will then become the girl that she was and you can marry her."

Okisco watched and waited. He followed the White Doe day and night until one day came his chance in a bright clearing in the green woods. He aimed steady and straight, and there was no wind. Swift and straight the silver arrow went, hitting true. The White Doe fell down, Okisco ran up and . . . instead of the White Doe, a young white woman lay dead on the ground and . . . a White Doe was galloping with great leaps swiftly into the woods. . . .

Since then, those who have magic sight have seen, at midnight, the White Doe fleeting among the sand hills and the dunes. Sometimes she is seen in the valley where the city of Raleigh now stands, sometimes in the swamps of the islands, sometimes in the cranberry bogs. She is seen everywhere, leaping, running, or standing still, and looking sadly and wistfully out on the ocean in the direction of the land from which her parents had come.

And even to this day, folks along those narrow islands of North Carolina say that those who have magic sight can see, at midnight, the White Doe, the ghost of Virginia Dare.

The Tale of the Hairy Toe

There was a young woman in North Carolina whose hair hung straggly around her face. Or maybe it was an old, old man who always hobbled around with an ash-tree stick in his gnarled hand, who went to the field to get potatoes, or maybe it was chick peas. And while grubbing around for food to live, that person saw a HAIRY TOE lying in the muddy black field. It was a long, hairy, scary toe with long, sharp, crummy claws! The hair was black and brown, and hung all around in sticky, clammy tangles.

But just the same that person picked up that dank, black, hairy, scary TOE and took it with the eats and began going home.

The road was dark and dank and windy, and the trees and even the mountains were bending and creaking and crowing and shrieking in the wild wind. Black birds flew in the air so fast you couldn't tell what they were and little animals scuttled all over, and ran all around, and away from that person with the HAIRY SCARY TOE.

Then from far, far away came the words "Who's got my HAI-AI-AI-R-Y T-O-E? Who's got my HAI-AI-AI-R-Y T-O-E?"

The words came in the whizzing wind from far, far away.

The person ran and ran and the voice followed and followed. So the person came to the dark-brown wooden cabin, rushed in, and

The Tale of the Hairy Toe

slammed the door behind him with a bang. The door was locked and the windows were tight, but through the chinks of the boards came the cold, hard wind with the words "Who's got my HAI-AI-AI-R-Y T-O-E!"

The person made the fire quick and, shivery, cooked his eats with the wind coming sharper and the words coming nearer—nearer—

The person ate quick and, shivery, swallowed the eats, half choking from the hurry because the windy words were coming nearer, nearer! "Who's got my HAI-AI-AI-R-Y T-O-E! Who's got my HA-AI-AI-R-Y T-O-E!"

The person jumped into the bed, clothes and toe, without bothering about pots and fire, and pulled the quilt over his ears, scared, so as not to hear. But just the same, that screaming wind with the screeching voice, coming from the black clouds and the creaking woods, was howling all the time. "Who's got my HAI-AI-AI-R-Y T-O-E!"

The person shivered and shaked and quivered and quaked and his teeth rattled against each other like witches against cauldrons.

Now that roaring voice was very near—right at the cabin door!

Then, suddenly the door opened with a crash; the wind from the woods and the mountains came in with a rush and a roar and with it . . . the strangest creature ever come to North Carolina.

The person was so scared no sound could pass his lips. Eyes just stared out of the quilt and looked, and saw . . .

A big, strange beast, long and fat and bent down like an orang-utang, limping and looking all over; slowly looking and limping . . . as if one toe on his hairy leg was missing.

But even more terrible was his face. Two fiery red eyes flashed out of his tangled, knotty hair.

"You sure got fiery eyes," the person said with teeth chattering like pots and pans.

"So I can look through you. Shoot fire into you. Who's got my HAI-AI-AI-R-Y T-O-E!"

"Why 've you got such long fat arms with such thick strong muscles!"

"So's I kin put 'm around you an' squeeze an' squeeze till there's no breath in ye! Who's got my HAI-AI-AI-R-Y T-O-E!"

"Why 've you got such long hairy claws with sharp sticky nails!"

"So I kin scratch ye all over, an' scratch your grave open! Who's got my HAI-AI-AI-R-Y T-O-E!"

"Why've you got such long fangs hanging out o' your mouth!"

"So's I kin chew your bones!"

He was crawling nearer and nearer to the bed and the quilt where the person was lying, teeth banging against each other.

The strange creature came nearer and nearer. Now his long hairy arms were on the quilt and . . . he tore it off! and there was . . . the HAI-AI-AI-R-Y T-O-E!

"You've got my HAI-AI-AI-R-Y T-O-E!" and he grabbed the person with the HAI-AI-AI-R-Y T-O-E under his arm! . . . and raced with the screaming wind into the woods and was never seen any more. . . .

The Revolution of the Ladies of Edenton

This is a velvety tale that actually happened down South in North Carolina. Folks there and folks in every other Southern state love to tell it, for it is a happening of which every man, woman, and child in North Carolina, as well as every other state, is proud. To this day, wherever the story is told, it brings a warm and grand smile to the face and to the heart: the Edenton Tea Party, the first famous revolution by women in our land.

Surely you have heard of the Boston Tea Party, where merchantmen and citizens decided to throw the English tea into the bay rather than buy it and pay the tax. The same was done by the Edenton ladies—just as patriotic and just as determined to forego tea drinking until the unjust taxes by the English were lifted.

There were Penelope Barker and Elizabeth King, there were

The Revolution of the Ladies of Edenton

Sarah Valentine, Miss Johnston, and a host of others with equally rounded names who cried that America must be free of British tyranny.

The whole town of Edenton in North Carolina was boiling with political fervor and fury. Old and young were set to free themselves and run their own government. And when the women were not asked to the political meetings that were going on, they decided to have their own political meetings. So they met in their homes when they came together to knit and embroider, to talk, and to drink tea.

At all these get-togethers there was tea—English tea! No social visit or friendly gathering was ever complete without tea. Now, with talk of British tyranny, talk of throwing off the British yoke—what of British tea?

One day, in that eventful year of 1774, Mistress Penelope Barker and Mistress King and a few other fine ladies were sitting over sweet cakes and cups of tea. They talked, not of laces and recipes and fashion, but of British tyranny and American determination to be freed from it.

"We too must join our men fighting for freedom," spoke Mistress Barker. She was fearless and free in her talk.

"That we certainly must. I don't know just what we can do, but there must be some work for us women," said Mistress King.

Such was the talk throughout Edenton. The seed was planted deep, and soon the fruits began to grow.

The next afternoon when the ladies were together, they decided to form a militant patriotic organization to help the men ready to fight at the battlefront. Thus began the famous feminine revolution of the ladies of Edenton against "British Tea."

The women were gathered at the home of Mistress Elizabeth King. There was a large number of them, over fifty. Talk was loud and strong. Eyes shone and faces flushed. Mistress Penelope Barker was elected president.

The talk was different from the talk men had at their patriotic meetings and soon they formed their own plan of battle against the British.

"The Ladies of Edenton," for reasons of patriotism and the desire to help the fight of the thirteen colonies in their battle for independence, decided unanimously they would not conform to the pernicious custom of drinking the tea come from England. And the aforesaid "Ladies of Edenton" would not promote or encourage "ye wear of any manufacture from England until such time that all acts which tend to enslave this, our native country, shall be repealed."

These were the very words the ladies of Edenton used on October 25, 1774, and all the women of the town, high and low, lived up to the resolution fully.

Instead of tea they now brewed dried leaves of raspberry vines and to them this tasted sweeter than the tea from England, for it was sweetened and flavored with patriotism and love of country.

The fervor of action burned high after this patriotic deed. When the ladies declared their tea-independence of England, the men of Edenton dispatched to beleaguered Boston a shipload of corn, flour, and pork. One of Edenton's merchant princes gave one of his ships for George Washington to use, and Dr. Williamson, at his own cost, bought cargoes of medical and other supplies for the Revolutionary army. Many others followed suit.

Such were the results of the revolution of the Edenton ladies. Do you wonder that the story is in the land of folktales where such stories are told over and over again!

Nollichucky Jack

This happened in North Carolina when the state was much bigger than it is today, for then a big piece of Tennessee was part of it.

In those days, there lived a man who was famous in all the state and loved by all the folks of the state. His name was John Servier. John was renowned for his looks and his strength. Most of all he was famous for his smart head and fearless deeds. No man fought harder than he at the Kings Mountain battle when the good mountain men were fighting the British under Ferguson. Everybody knew him, loved him, and called him jokingly Nollichucky Jack.

Now, folks in the Blue Ridge Mountains, and all around, were too far removed from the government either to receive orders or to make complaints. The law was far away and of little use to them. This raised the dander of the folks along the Holston and they felt they had to do something about it.

"The law down in Raleigh ain't gonna bother us no more. We're gonna make our own law."

Nollichucky Jack and all his good mountainfolk neighbors got a-going on the idea and it wasn't long afore they set up a state of their own and a government of their own. They called their new state "Franklin" in honor of Ben Franklin, who was the smartest man in our land in those early days, and Nollichucky Jack was made governor.

News moved slowly in those days, but pretty soon it leaked out about that a brand-new state was stuck in the Blue Ridge Mountains of North Carolina. Some folks thought it was a right smart thing, some laughed, and some got doggone mad—particularly the lawmakers in the capital. They said those dilly-headed mountainfolk 'd have to stop that monkeyin' with law and order or that passel of fools up there 'd all be clapped in the jug.

Now, if they had known anything about North Carolina mountainfolk, they'd have known it's easier to go to Heaven than lay the law down to one of them mountaineers.

The law fought 'em and they fought back, because they were used to battling. One time there was a real pitched battle between the law of the United States and the law of Franklin. Four long years there were strife and combat between these two forces until the lawmakers in Raleigh got blazing mad. They sent soldiers to the Blue Ridge Mountains, and Nollichucky Jack was arrested for high treason against the state of North Carolina. He was taken to Morgantown for trial before the court.

The news of the coming trial spread quicker than the devil could scorch a feather. Folks from far and near came on horse, on foot, and in wagonloads. Neighbors, friends, strangers all were there to see and hear. But there wasn't much talk. Those mountaineers didn't like a man they loved and respected in the claws of the law.

But the closest friends—the bodyguard of the "governor," they called themselves—were nowhere in sight. They were in the woods, guns oiled and loaded to rescue their leader. They weren't gonna let their "governor" be manhandled by the law!

They had two plans. First they'd try to rescue him from the courthouse. If that didn't work, they'd fire the town and in the excitement they were sure they'd get Nollichucky Jack where none 'd harm him.

When the crowd on horseback came near Morgantown, they stopped and two men leading the "governor's" fine racing mare got ready.

"Heard a cricket in my cabin last night," said the one leading the mare; "that's a sign o' good luck."

"Hope they break a mirror in the courthouse," one of the men said grimly.

"Ye just git ahead. Found an old penny this morning and you know that's always a sign o' good luck! Jack'll be free before the sun'll be over the middle, I know that for sure."

The two men with the three horses, their arms hidden under their shirts, set off and were soon in Morgantown. The town was full of folks milling around the courthouse as if it was Fair Day.

The two "Franks" (that's what they called the folks who lived in the new state of Franklin) came up to the courthouse. The rider in front got down and handed the reins of his horse to the other man, who was leading the riderless horse. Then he walked through the wide-open door into the courtroom where the trial was moving along like babies jumping from tree stumps. There was much noise and much smoke.

The Frank moved close to where the prisoner could see him and pretty soon caught his eye. With a turn of his head toward the door he showed the "governor" that his own mare was right outside held by a Frank, waiting for him.

I told you Nollichucky Jack was smart as a whip and he quick understood what was afoot. The Frank waited a little time listening to questions and answers and when there was a minute's pause and the lawyers were putting their heads together, he walked right up to the wooden railing behind the prisoner, where he could see the judge better; then, raising his voice so all could hear him, he spoke to the judge:

"Are you done with that there man?"

For a minute it was quiet as a dark cave. Folks kind o' looked straight ahead. Nobody seemed to know just what to do.

Right then Nollichucky Jack leaped over the rail, lit out through the door, the Frank behind him, and before you could wink an eye he was on the mare racing away to beat the wind across the mountains.

Not a man in Morgantown raised his foot or his voice or his shooting piece. All were only too glad to see Nollichucky Jack get away. Well, maybe even the judge was glad too.

No one ever bothered the "governor" again. Fact is, when the new state of Tennessee was formed, John Servier, Nollichucky Jack, was made the first governor of the state.

As for the state of Franklin, that just kind of died out in the face of the bigger state of North Carolina.

Those were the kinds of things that happened in olden days when each man fought for what he thought was right.

Pirate Blackbeard's Deep-Sea End

When men come down to the sea, where it edges the sand, to fish, tales of piracy and the deep ocean are sure to rise up like leaping porpoises. Particularly after a good meal—well washed down—there comes the drawing of the long wind-whistling: tall tales, taller than the tallest masts! That's what these men like to hear and tell, and one evening I led the way. So come along—this one is a gem of the deep blue ocean.

There are ninety-nine tales, more or less, of how Blackbeard, (Edward Teach was his born name), the fierce pirate, met his death. I'll tell you the one I like best because it is a screamer, as tall tales ever are, even as it is savage.

Merchantmen, captains, and governments were after that pirate who was robbing and murdering on the big billowing seas. But that human sea-shark—whose black beard began under his eyes, running down to his chest, braided into pigtail braids and curled around his ears—was afraid of neither man nor devil. Prizes and purses were set on him, brought in dead or alive. But that scourge of the sea, running around North Carolina and all the Atlantic seaboard, slithered through inlets and coves, through harbors and high seas, untouched and unhindered. Fearlessness and connivance with those who worked for the British Crown always helped him to escape—until one day. . . .

A wild wind flew around the sea, bringing high white waves with whitecaps, and the sun shone bright and sharp as a saber. Captain Blackbeard with his hard black eyes was on the lookout for his next victim, a fine India merchantman filled with silks and gold, that he knew was coming along the sea. He didn't know this was an unlucky day for a man who married thirteen wives, as he had. He didn't know this was the day when the Devil lay in wait for pirates of the sea, ready to swallow pirate ships and pirate crews! No, he didn't know that. He and his crew were too busy scanning the horizon for the victim vessel to be captured. So they didn't see a fine ship lying hidden in an inlet of the North Carolina shore watching its chance to put an end to Blackbeard and his crew.

Blackbeard and his men did not see the fearless master of the boat and the chosen crew of men, armed to the teeth, lowering a yawl and rowing quickly toward them. In between deep green vales of frothing billows, they were coming to the pirate boat.

Thus there are three vessels in this tale a-sailing the high seas, with sea gulls screaming in the sky: the rich India merchantman under full sail; the pirate Blackbeard in his craft to rob silks and spices to sell and bribe, and gold and silver to hoard; and the yawl coming up to end that pirate on his unlucky day.

Quickly the yawl came nearer while the pirates' eyes were glued on a distant sail that they took to be the ship laden with riches.

The yawl careened and rose and rolled around in the whooping billows, getting closer and closer to the pirate ship. Then . . . sharp iron hooks were hurled and the master of the yawl and his men raced fearlessly on deck with pistols and cutlasses all ready.

"Villain, fight like a man for your life!" shouted the master.

Blackbeard and his men turned and saw flashing blades and cocked pistols. The enemy on their deck!

"Avast you and all o' you! No quarter! Send them down to feed the sharks! Cut 'em to pieces," roared Blackbeard, angry as a bull. His tricorn hat flew off, his head bent forward. Cutlasses and dirks flashed and pistol shots rang out. Close, fierce fighting began.

Pirates and attackers stood their ground, neither giving nor asking for quarter. The deck was covered red and strewn with cut-down men. Then came the great sight: Pirate Blackbeard and the young ship's master, Lieutenant Maynard, facing each other; the pirate's mouth and eyes shooting poisonous fire and the young seaman, open-faced, laughing at his fury. The good sun in the sky watched the two and soon it was shining cruelly in the pirate's eyes while the young man saw clear and sharp in front. Then—of a sudden—he had an opening! His saber flashed like lightning and off flew the pirate's head, pigtail braids, fiery eyes, and all. It rolled along the bloody deck to the shouting triumph of the young master of the yawl.

Then up leaped Blackbeard, without his head and braided beard, and dived into the foaming green-blue water. The head lay on the deck, black eyes watching all those around and its body in the water. And you know a body without a head is as poor as a minnow in the sea.

Then was seen the strangest thing ever in the waters around Ocracoke Inlet. The headless body in the water began swimming with strong strokes around the ship; the head on the deck began roaring words that can't be writ with ink: cursing, screaming, threatening all of North Carolina and all the world. Three times the pirate's body swam around with strong big strokes, while the head on the deck roared scorching curses on all and every one. Then the Pirate Blackbeard's body went down in the dark blue sea, as a bloody pirate should, never to be seen again. But the doughty young master of the ship put up the head with the pigtail braids for all to see and for a warning to all.

Some folks say Lieutenant Maynard of Virginia killed Blackbeard, but I'll let you decide who is right—the teller of the tale or history.

The Ways of the Lord

I'm telling a tale that truly happened.

There was high talk and good talk in and around Swanquarter and Swanquarter Bay and Swanquarter Island in North Carolina. Folks were trying to decide where to build the new Methodist house of worship.

All of them had spots they thought best, so in the end they agreed to appoint a committee to choose the place. The word was said and the deed was done.

After a little time the committee came back and said that Sam Sadler's empty lot, high on a hill and in the center of the town, was the best place. Folks could come there easy from the islands, from the lakes, and from the swamps.

But Sam Sadler thought the idea was worth as much as two whoops in the lower land. He wanted that piece for himself and he needed it for his own use.

"There's a hundred other places to build a church and I won't have it on my land."

Friends and neighbors were surprised and said Sam Sadler had gone cross-eyed in his head. The minister spoke to him, but Sam avowed he'd spoken the last word and didn't want to be bothered by prickly-pear words.

"Ye'd better look in some other place."

Nobody in town could understand such job turkey talk. The minister wasn't feeling too chipper about it.

"Can't understand why a rich man like Sam Sadler won't give a piece of land to Him who is the giver of all. I'll pray to the Lord to soften that stone heart of his, for it is a golden crown to have the house of the Almighty on your land. I'll pray to the Almighty to make him see his error."

The minister prayed, but Sam Sadler's heart remained stony.

Folks began looking for another place for their house of worship. In the end, a high-minded merchant offered a good piece of his land for the church and it was taken with good will.

Men, carpenters, all kinds of workers put their heads down and hands to work and soon there was a goodly wooden house for Sunday prayer. Folks came from all around for the first worship in the new home of God.

Now, you know Swanquarter is right on the bay of the same name, and there are other bays, Juniper Bay, Rose Bay, and the great Pamlico Sound with a long string of islands. It is a great water country and the living water is part of the life of the land all over. The voice of the water, the never-ending moving of the water, the ever-rolling soundings are part of the day and the night life and in it are the screaming and crying of feathered creatures coming from Mattamuskeet Lake. Folks, birds, water, winds, sun are like a great family all living together.

Maybe it was the birds in the heaven who told the waters of Sam Sadler's hardheartedness. Maybe it was the winds running high over the trees, earth, and sea who spoke out. Or maybe it was the One even higher up in the heaven who whispered the tale to the rising and falling waters. They all sure knew about the goings on in the Swanquarter church-building argument.

The waters heard and talked their own talk. They saw in the hearts of the townsfolk and the minister that the church was not in the right part of the town. . . .

The first worship was done and folks all went to their homes while winds and waters were still talking about the goings on.

Then . . . the winds began loud talk. They blew up hard, and swift rain began falling; and the swells from the waters were rising and roaring. The winds roared back in their own language.

Folks didn't understand the words, but they did understand the wild galing. So did the many creatures: the swans, the herons, the loons, the gulls, and the sandpipers. All the waterfowl understood the voices and words of water and wind.

The waters of the sound and the bay were churning and rolling and twisting in great, great swells. Then the thick, moiling, rolling swell rose and rolled towards Swanquarter! Every drop of water in that giant mass knew its place and knew exactly what to do.

It rolled and swelled and thundered, coming closer and closer, and then . . . into the town.

Folks cried: "A tidal wave!"

That tidal wave came into the town, rolled through the houses, not harming anything. Then it rampaged up to the new church. Folks stood at windows, fearful, watching. The roaring wind and the wild clouds in the sky watched, too. The swell raised the new church high up, then turned it this way and that way, elbowing that wooden building through the streets straight to that welcome spot where folks wanted that church to be: right on Sam Sadler's piece of land! Right on the piece he wouldn't give to build the church!

Then the waters rushed gurgling, satisfied, out of the town back to the bay. The winds too ran out into the world of the sea and the sun came out shining, mighty pleased at the sight. So were the good folks of Swanquarter mighty pleased and so was the minister. All came out and stood around the sight of the miracle. The hand of the Lord had set His home where the good people wanted it.

Sam Sadler came too. First he spoke to the minister, telling him the Lord had shown him He wanted His house to be on his, Sam Sadler's land. Then he went to the deed office and told the man to deed the piece of land to the church and the Lord. And so it was done.

To this day you can still see the old wooden church on Sam Sadler's land, which he deeded to the Lord. Now it is a part of a brick church that was built later.

The Man, the White Steed, and the Wondrous Wood

Years ago there lived in North Carolina a man who had two great loves in his life: trees and a white horse.

He had been a very poor boy, but he worked hard and became rich, and with his money he bought land—much land covered with giant oaks, and silver birches and pines, and many other trees. Trees that had lived with the wind and the sun, with the rain and the Indians for endless years.

In the midst of those trees he built a rich house and a fine stable. For the stable he bought many horses because he loved horses. He was always buying horses as he was always buying more woods.

One day he found and bought a royal horse, a pure-white mare with its head held high in the air as if it were the ruler of all around. He loved that horse and the trees in his woods as a man loves his wife and children. They were his children and his wife. Though he wooed a lovely lady, he never married her.

Day in, day out, he sat on his white horse riding through his beloved woods. Slowly, swiftly, in sunlight and moonlight and gray light, in fair weather and stormy weather, he was always talking with his horse and his trees. The leaves spoke to him with ten thousand lips and caressed his face as he moved among them; the creature under him whinnied and nuzzled him. Everything in the woods had a meaning for him; the mist, rising all around him with a sweet green smell of leaves, and the moss spoke to him in soft words. The dew and the raindrops hanging all around were lovely to him as pearls in the ocean.

He had a terror of the ax and saw and would not let anyone cut down any of his tree-friends.

When people laughed at him because he told them that the tree-folks were more loving and kind than humans, he'd smile and say: "That's because you aren't as smart as my horse and I. We hear the talk of the trees and see how they live every day just the same as you and I."

Folks in Raleigh thought William Pool was a queer man.

But that "queer" big man was a very happy man with his beautiful white horse and the big silent trees and all the creatures who lived in the woods. They would have lived happily together all their lives if man had not come in to destroy their paradise.

There came a horrible and tragic war, which makes brutes of men and breeds destruction and tragedy. Brother battled against brother. Houses and lands were destroyed. Human beings did not count.

William Pool thought long and carefully. He was a rich man.

"If the Yankees come they'll take everything away on which they can lay their hands. First I will give money for the cause in which I believe, the rest I'll hide where none can find it."

When he heard the enemy was approaching, he hid his silver and the money he had left deep in the woods. Then he went in deeper and deeper among his trees till he found a fine open space hidden between oaks and birches.

"Here you will stay and no enemy will find you," he said to his beloved horse.

He brought water and hay to the place, enough to last a few days. Then he tied the horse carefully, giving plenty of space to graze, eat, and drink. He petted the glossy skin with loving hands, and spoke to it softly.

"You'll stay here and soon I'll return and you and I will again be together. You'll be safe here. No Yankee 'll find you. They'll be gone soon. Just have a little patience."

The horse looked at him with its large soft eyes and whinnied and nuzzled his hand, as if it understood every word he said.

Then William Pool returned to his home and sat down grimly on his porch awaiting the enemy he was sure would come.

And come they did, for William Pool was known far and wide

When the horse saw its master, it reared up wildly.

The Man, the White Steed, and the Wondrous Wood 197

in all Wake and Johnson counties as a rich man. A band of marauding soldiers, having heard of his riches, had quietly left their camp to get them. They came in their blue uniforms and with brutal words demanded that he show where his gold and silver was hidden. They had searched the house and had found nothing.

"I haven't hidden any gold, I gave it away to help the just cause." William Pool was not scared.

"You got plenty. Where did you hide it?"

"You better talk or... we'll make you talk," said another.

"We know how to make fellows like you talk!"

But threats and snarling and cursing did not change Pool's words.

"We know you buried your gold. Where is the place?" The leader of the band spoke slowly now.

"I have no gold, I gave it away."

"We got to be a little tough to make that fellow talk," the leader said.

He took a wooden pole from the fence, and the soldier pinned William Pool down (he was a big man). Then they straddled him on it and rode him down a way, all the time asking where the money was hidden. So they came to Pool's mill.

"Either you tell where you hid yer gold or that mill 'll make a good fire."

"I told you I have no gold."

Quickly the building was aflame, burning in the hot sunshine. William Pool looked on with a set face.

"We'll not get anything out of this damned reb. Come, let's look for it ourselves. It's got to be somewheres in the woods."

Off they went into the woods. Pool stood at the burning building, then he went slowly to his house. It was not easy walking.

The Yankees rode through brush deep among the silent trees. Birds were singing and the top leaves were whispering in the wind, but the soldiers did not hear or see. They were blinded by greed.

Suddenly the leader, who rode first, stopped, bent his head forward, and listened. The others had stopped too.

From afar, through the hazy-green air of the leaves and the dark trunks was heard a soft friendly whinnying. A friendly horse was greeting the horses of the soldiers.

Slowly the men rode towards the mellow sound until they came to the clearing! They stopped in surprise at the sight of the magnificent creature!

"Wal, that horse's as good as gold," said the leader. "I'm gonna try it. We kin get a good bit for it."

He changed saddles from his own horse to the white one and got on it, leading his own along.

"C'm on, let's get back to that lying reb and show him what we found."

So they came to William Pool sitting on his porch, eyes straight ahead.

When the horse saw its master, it reared up wildly, letting out sounds of recognition. Pool had turned white as chalk. But what could he do against eight armed men!

"Thanks for the fine mount, Mister Reb," the soldier sneered.

"My horse 'll come back," Pool said hoarsely. "It will be mine when I'm alive and when I'm dead. It's my horse."

The soldier dug his boots into the horse and it raced off wildly.

"It will be forever with me," Pool kept on saying. "It will return."

And return it did.

William Pool left this world for the world where there are no wars. The white steed came to the same world. When the two saw each other there was a greeting as can only be between friends who love each other. Pool mounted his white steed and where do you think they went riding? Right into the woods they both loved so much.

Folks said they saw a ghostly white horse and ghostly rider in the woods at night. They were right and they were wrong, for these two were not just a ghost rider and ghost horse but two friends together again with their friends the trees. And these three, William Pool, his glorious white steed, and the fine old trees, were always together until—again—hard man stepped in and destroyed the trees and shrubs and grass. And so there were no tree-filled lands for the ghost of William Pool and his white steed to ride. They were never seen again. Folks in Raleigh said the ghosts were gone for good. And that was truly a pity.

The Mystery of Theodosia Burr

It was December 31, 1812; the sky was dark gray, wild dog-winds were chasing black ragged clouds all over the sea and heaven. The ocean roared crazy laughter at little men and their boats trying to beat the elements. Just the same, that very wintry day a little pilot boat, the "Patriot," in the harbor of Charlestown, in South Carolina, dancing up and down and lurching back and forth like a pea in boiling water, was getting ready to leave. The captain didn't seem to be worried about the weather. He was watching his men loading bales of tobacco. The most valuable part of the cargo was a beautiful lady, who was already there. She was sitting in the cabin at the table while one of the men was hanging a painted portrait of her on the wall. It was not easy work with the boat swaying and turning wildly.

"Takin' this to your father?"

"Yes, I am taking it to my father in New York City."

"It's a mighty fine picture."

The lady did not answer and soon the picture was hung and the man left.

The woman sat still, moving only when the boat moved.

She was a famous lady of high degree, Theodosia Burr Alston; famous for her wit and beauty, and her marriage to Governor Alston of South Carolina, and famous for her infamous father, Aaron Burr, who was tried as a traitor. Even though he was acquitted and had, after going abroad, returned to the United States, the black soot of turncoat still besmirched him and those nearest to him. But to Theodosia he was her father and now she was going on the little boat to visit him in New York City.

She sat silent and sad, with eyes that told of a thousand sorrows.

The Captain came in, letting in a blast of frosty air:

"Hope you're comfortable, Mistress Alston."

"I thank you, good Captain. I am."

When she said no more, the Captain left for the deck. And, as usual, there was talk among the men of Aaron Burr and his beautiful daughter who was loyal to him, no matter what. But the blowing wind and the rearing waves and the racing clouds cared little about the woes and worries of men and women and kept on going their own wild way.

In a little time it calmed down and at moments a steel-yellow sun gleamed through the black clouds. The Captain ordered the boat to get underway. Carried by a strong wind, it went along.

Most of the time Theodosia sat in her cabin at the little table on which stood soft wax flowers of strange, glossy colors, covered with a glass. She looked at the silent flowers and she looked at a beautifully carved Nautilus shell, and sometimes she looked at her own portrait on the wall, which she was bringing to her father. She rarely spoke to anyone, for her heart was too full of the tragic fate of her father, whom she loved dearly.

The weather had cleared a little and the "Patriot" plowed through the gray-green waters and the dancing whitecaps.

It was the noon hour of the second day and the boat was plunging and plowing, but moving steadily up the coastline of North Carolina. The Captain was on the bridge, standing next to the helmsman, when suddenly he narrowed his eyes and looked sharply on the horizon. Then he took his glass and looked long and keen. The coast all along was infested with pirates and buccaneers who spared neither men nor boats. There was a white speck, a sail on the horizon of the ocean. It looked like a bark moving swiftly in their direction. Any strange vessel was suspicious.

"I fear it's a pirate," he said low, his cold breath coming out like smoke from his bearded mouth. The sea-robbers lay ever in wait for sailing ships.

Soon his fears were fully confirmed. Swiftly before the wind, the boat came bearing down on them. It flew no flag, but they could now see the men on deck and the gleaming of weapons.

Two boats were lowered with fully armed men making toward them.

Mistress Theodosia Burr Alston had come up and stood near the Captain.

A roaring voice came from the bark.

"Surrender or we'll blow you down to the bottom for the sharks."

What could the Captain of the "Patriot" do. The pirate vessel was ten sizes above his own, he was outnumbered ten to one in men and arms, and the pirates were armed to the teeth.

In no time the tough-looking crew of the two boats were on the deck with shrill yells and whoops, cutlasses and pistols in hand. The pirate bark had come up to the "Patriot" and threw grappling irons onto the little boat.

"Out with what you have in the holds," the Captain of the pirate ship shouted.

The Captain of the "Patriot" said grimly: "Get the bales."

As the bales came up they were tossed on the pirate bark.

"Now out with the gold."

"We have no gold," the Captain spoke dully, "we have none."

The pirate didn't believe it.

"Where there is such a fine high-toned lady there must be jewels. Hand 'em out or you'll walk the plank."

"I have no jewels," cried Theodosia. "I am on my way to visit my father in New York. Let us go and I'll see you will be well rewarded."

"You mean we'll be hanged, fine lady."

There was a shout from the lookout sailor of the pirate boat:

"There's a sloop-of-war coming this way."

"We must get rid of 'em quick; dead men don't talk," the pirate Captain ordered.

Again Theodosia offered the pirates rich rewards and freedom if they would let them go free. "My husband is Governor Alston. He will pay you well."

But it was of little use. Either from fear or hardness of heart, the pirates were determined to carry out their cruel threat.

The pirates hustled them on with pistols and cutlasses in hand

and bravely the Captain, Theodosia, and the crew "walked the plank."

"Let's burn her," one of the pirates said.

"No, no burning; it might bring the government boat. Slash the rudder."

The rudder was slashed and the pirates sailed off swiftly.

The dastardly deed was done and the pirate vessel was disappearing. The sloop-of-war, far off, did not come near them. . . .

The lone pilot boat drifted along the rocking waves and so came in to the shores near Kitty Hawk, a few miles below Nags Head in North Carolina.

There the "bankers" * got on it and divided everything that could be moved among themselves as they did with every wrecked vessel. The portrait of Theodosia went to one of the "bankers," John Tillet by name. . . .

That is one of the legends of the mysterious disappearance of Theodosia Burr. There are others.

Maybe the boat was lured to destruction by land pirates.†

Folks who believe that ghosts float around in the world say Theodosia's ghost wanders around the sand dunes of Kitty Hawk and Nags Head.

Only the winds of the North Carolina coast and the moon in the heaven can solve the mystery of how Theodosia Burr Alston met her end.

* People living on the banks were called "bankers."
† At the dangerous points on the coast, evil human beings would flash lanterns on stormy nights, making sailing vessels think they were pilot lights leading to safe harbors. When the vessels were wrecked against the rocks, wreckers would gather the spoils.

SOUTH CAROLINA

Shake Hands with a Yankee

When folks down South sit around their beautiful marbled mantelpieces and richly papered rooms, or when they sit in wondrous flowering gardens under rich magnolia trees, they like to tell tales of bygone days. Many tales tell how the homes they lost in the tragic War Between the States came back to them. None is more heart-warming than the story of how the Paul Hamilton House in Beaufort came back to that family. That Sea Island dwelling is about seventy miles from Charleston.

The cruel war was over, but the Northern conquerors were often hard on the rebels. The government had taken the Hamilton House to use as a hospital. But not for overlong, for soon after, the hostilities were over. The owners could not rent their own property from the government. Such was the hard law, and therefore Mr. Hamilton begged an uncle to rent it for them. He did, and all the family moved back. But it didn't take long before they learned that the house was to be auctioned off, as were many houses. The Hamilton family sat in the large room in sadness and sorrow.

"We must not lose our home," Mistress Hamilton said. "We grew up here, and the house is part of our life, part of us."

"We won't lose it," said Mr. Hamilton. "I'll bid up to a million dollars against any man who wants our home."

"Where would you get the money?"

"I'll find it."

The terrible day came. Mr. Hamilton was there. So were friends, neighbors, strangers—those trying to buy things at little cost. The auctioneer began the sale in his singsong fashion. Many bids were offered for the house, for it was a fine building filled with costly furniture.

The bidding went higher and higher, but no matter how much anyone offered, Mr. Hamilton bid more. Finally he got the house at a much larger sum than he could afford. He went up to the auctioneer.

"Sir," he said, "I have not all the money to pay, but if you will give me a few days, I'll go to Charleston where I have some lots that I can sell at a good price and that will cover the cost of my home."

"How long will it take you, Mr. Hamilton? You know the government can't wait."

"I must have a few days. It takes at least three days traveling back and forth."

"The best I can allow you is three days, sir, and I'm not so sure I can do that. You had better hurry."

Mr. Hamilton left at once, but when the next day came the auctioneer announced that he could not wait. The house would be put up for auction if the money was not paid in a few hours.

Mrs. Hamilton and the whole neighborhood heard the news with deep anger. Mrs. Hamilton pleaded with the mayor to hold off the sale till her husband's return, but the mayor said he could not do anything to interfere with the power of the auctioneer.

When the hour of the sale came, all the town was there, buyers and onlookers. Among them were most of the town merchants, some of whom were from the North and on the Northern side during the war. Most folks sympathized with the Hamiltons. Mrs. Hamilton did not come. She was too unhappy.

"'We can't see those folks lose their home. It would break their hearts," said Reuben Holmes, a Northern Yankee merchant who lived there.

War and anger were forgotten. Everyone thought only of the Hamilton family and their home.

"I agree with you," said another Northern merchant, Simpson by name. Many standing there said the same.

"I'll tell you what," said Mr. Holmes, "let's raise the money right here and pay for it. I am sure Mr. Hamilton will return it to us when he comes back from Charleston."

The feeling of good will, friendship, and kindness spread swiftly among the crowd, and in no time Mr. Holmes and all the neighbors had raised the money. The auctioneer had to take it, and the Hamiltons had their home.

The story of the generous deed came swiftly to Mrs. Hamilton's ears, and she wept for joy and gratitude. She rushed to Mr. Holmes's store.

"Mr. Holmes," said she, and there were tears in her voice as there were tears in her eyes, "Mr. Holmes, I don't know how to thank you for your kindness. I have no words. And I also want to apologize to you. I had unwisely sworn never to shake hands with a Yankee. I was wrong. All people can be kind and generous in any place. Here is my hand, with a gratitude that comes from a loving heart. I will never forget your generosity and kindness."

Mr. Hamilton returned and repaid the money, and in his heart, too, there was a feeling of gratitude that bore the fruit of life: friendship and understanding.

The Tragic Tale of Fenwick Hall

This is a dark tale of the sunny South. It happened in the heart of South Carolina. Some tell it one way, some another; but all folks tell it, and so it is a folktale. Here is the way I heard it told.

There was Lord Fenwick—some called him Lord Rippon—and

he lived in Fenwick Castle, built high on a red brick foundation for protection against water and men. There was a captain's walk high up on the castle to watch for the enemy, and a passage deep under the ground for secret escape in case of great danger.

Lord Fenwick loved hunting and horses, and his stable was full of the finest of the land. But no matter how many splendid steeds he had, he was always looking for others.

One day, he heard of some fine horses in far England. Straightway he purchased them and ordered that they be sent to Fenwick Hall with a proper groom. Groom and horses came in good time, and both were a pleasure to see. Slender of leg, sleek of body were the two horses; and the English groom was tall, blue-eyed, blondhaired.

The handsome young man was treated courteously by everyone in the plantation. He had the freedom of the house and the table. He was almost like one of the family. So he met Lord Fenwick's daughter many a time and oft. They met in the dining hall, and they met in the garden. They were often close to each other when they went riding on those splendid horses, through the green woods and along talking streams. It wasn't long, and it wasn't short, before these two handsome young people fell deeply in love with each other. Their hands touched, and their lips touched, and they promised each other eternal troth.

One day the young Englishman, honorable and fearless, came to Lord Fenwick.

"Lord Fenwick," he spoke open and straight, "I love your daughter, and your daughter loves me. I am not rich, but I can work and I am not afraid of work. I know I can provide for her."

Lord Fenwick went into a wild fury, and he told the young man he had other plans for his daughter. The young man was only a stable groom, and if he wouldn't remember his station, he'd be sent to where he came from.

The daughter came to plead with her father.

"I love him," she said. "We want to be married. Only he can make me happy."

"It's a silly infatuation, just puppy love. You'll get over this as soon as he's gone. I'll send him packing back."

"Wherever he goes, I'll go with him, Father."

"That will be at your own peril," Lord Fenwick spoke darkly.

One night, when the moon was hiding behind wildly running clouds, a savage wind was screaming through the trees. The moss on the live oaks was tossing fiercely against the hard trunks.

Two fleet horses were racing through the woods, racing against man and wind and weather to reach a haven of safety. It was the young groom and Lord Fenwick's daughter, fleeing to be wed.

"We must reach the city of Charleston before my father discovers our flight," the girl said again and again.

"We will reach it," the young man said. "I have friends, and there a ship 'll take us to England, where none can do us harm."

The horses raced on and so did the wind and the dark clouds in the sky, but soon their hopes turned ashes-black!

There was a beat of pursuing horses!

"Faster! Faster!" the girl said. "It's my father, I know. He must not overtake us. He is a hard man."

Both bent low over the racing steeds, urging them on and on. The splendid animals knew what their riders wanted of them and strained every muscle to go faster. Their hoofs hardly touched the leaves and the green.

On and on the two flew, and so did the cavalcade of six behind them. They could see one another now. Then . . . the pursuers caught up with the fugitives and surrounded them!

Lord Fenwick never said a single word. His lips were tight shut, his eyes narrowed down. The five men with him, black and sinister, were silent too. Only the horses neighed and breathed hard and loud and swished their tails. Then Lord Fenwick commanded sharply:

"Tie 'm! Rope 'm."

One of the black men came up to the pale groom, tied his hands with a rope, and put a noose with a long rope around his neck. The girl sat frozen with icy fear. She could not speak. She moved her lips, but no sound came forth.

"To the tree!" said Lord Fenwick hoarsely.

One of the black men led the roped man's horse to an old live oak and flung the end of the rope over a thick limb and tied it down.

Then Lord Fenwick led his daughter, frigid-fixed on her horse, to where her lover's horse was and put a riding whip in her icy hands.

"Lash the horse!" he said—it sounded like croaking in her ears. But her hand did not move. He raised it for her and lashed the horse on which the young man sat.

The horse reared high, the horse cried out, and then ... dashed away! The body of the lover floated heavy in the wild wind.

Lord Fenwick led his cavalcade and his young daughter back to Fenwick Hall.

She sat high on her horse and stared in the black air. Her face was ashen-white. She was stone-silent. And stone-silent she sat for the years of her life.

Folks, black and white, called that tree where the young man paid for loving one high above his station the John Tree, after Lord Fenwick, whose first name was John. Folks went in wide circles to pass it by. There were eerie sounds of moaning, and there were heavy sounds of swinging in the wind on that John Tree.

Emily's Famous Meal

The tale of Emily Geiger! It is a story that happened long ago, and it has been told a thousand times over by many folks. If there is a better tale of courage and daring, I haven't heard it.

Emily lived with her father, John, not far from Columbia, the capital of South Carolina.

When the Revolutionary War against England broke out, the Geigers were on the patriots' side, but alas! John Geiger was an invalid and could not join the American forces. But Emily, his daughter, eighteen, fine to look at, and healthy and strong, was eager to do something for the American cause. Soon her opportunity came.

She heard that the great General Greene, whose headquarters were not far away from her home, had to send an important message to General Sumter, who was in the Wateree Swamp. The distance was honeycombed with Tory soldiers and sympathizers, and no patriot could get through safely. When Emily learned this, she went to her father.

"Father," she said, "General Greene needs someone to send a message to General Sumter. No man can go, but a girl could get through without suspicion. I will volunteer."

"Go with my blessings, daughter, and may the Lord guard you. If I cannot do anything for my country, at least you, my daughter, can."

Emily went at once to General Greene.

"I have come here to offer my services, sir, to carry any message you wish," she said. "I heard you need a messenger to reach General Sumter. I know the road well."

"It is very dangerous work," General Greene said.

"Not as dangerous as what you and your men are doing, sir. I'm not afraid and I know I'll succeed."

General Greene had confidence in her open and fearless talk.

"Very well, Emily," he said. "I'll give you a dispatch to take to General Sumter, which you must deliver to him personally. To be on the safe side, in case you lose the paper, memorize it so you can tell it to him."

"That I can do easily," she said.

The dispatch was written, and then Emily repeated it until she knew it word for word.

She went home, got on the fastest horse in their stable, and set off on her trip of danger and adventure. From the very first, she ran into trouble.

Not far from the Geigers lived a Tory spy, who had his informers in General Greene's camp. He learned that Emily had been sent with a written message and set out after her. But she had a good start and a swift horse to boot. He rode as fast as he could but did not catch up to her.

Evening came, and his horse was tired. He rode to a house

where another Tory lived, also a spy. He told him to take up the chase.

It was deep in the night when Emily stopped at a house where she was known. She told the people she was on her way to friends, who lived a few miles away.

These folks were Tories, but they knew the Geigers and they liked Emily, so they told her to stay until morning. Emily was given a little room off the kitchen, and she lay down to sleep without taking off her clothes.

She hadn't slept long when she was awakened by a horse's hoofbeats and a knocking on the door. She heard but a few words and knew at once an enemy was after her.

Quickly and silently she slipped on her shoes. There was a window on one side. She opened it, slid out, and went into the stable. It was at the back of the house. She led her horse out silently, leaped on, and was away like the wind. It was dark, and no one had seen or heard her. She was off to her patriot friends.

No one pursued her. The Tory looking for her could see no trail in the dark.

She reached her friends at dawn, got a fresh horse, and without any rest started out to the swamps.

But again she came upon trouble. She was on the road only for a short time when suddenly three British soldiers surrounded her. There was no turning back or fleeing. She was covered on all sides.

"Where to, girl?" the one who seemed the leader said.

She was caught unawares and stammered a poor reply.

"Bet she is one of the female spies for those rebels," said the man.

"Aye, that she must be. Let's take her to Lord Rawdon. He knows how to deal with that kind."

She was led between the soldiers to the British camp, before Lord Rawdon. He questioned her closely, and though she gave satisfactory answers—she said she was on the way to visit some friends—he did not trust her. He knew the Whigs were always employing women to carry messages, and that they were very clever. He decided to send for a woman, to have Emily searched. She was locked in a room to wait until the woman came.

Emily was now alone and thinking hard. The message must not

be found! But how to get rid of it? She could not tear it up, for then the pieces would be found! Suddenly her face lit up with a wry smile. She quickly tore the letter into fine pieces, and then, taking small amounts at a time, began chewing them and swallowing them. The dry paper with the ink was not very tasty, but it had to be done! Mouthful by mouthful, she swallowed it all!

The woman came soon after and went carefully through her clothes, and of course found nothing. Lord Rawdon was a gentleman; he apologized and sent an escort with Emily to help her get to her friends.

There she got a fresh horse, and finally reached General Sumter and delivered the message that she had memorized.

To this day, folks tell the tale of the heroic, fearless girl, and the unpleasant meal she ate for the sake of her country and the American army.

Chickens Come Home to Roost

A long time ago there was a smart trader in Ireland named Joseph McCullough. He came to South Carolina and got a good house on the main road leading from Greenville down into Georgia.

The house was an inn and a trading place at one and the same time. Many a traveler rested there and many a barter and bargain was fought out in that inn.

Joseph McCullough was a sharp haggler and could beat any man in buying and selling. He'd trade in any- and everything, and his house was well known by travelers going up and down the main highway.

All kinds of folk, on horse or by wagon, would come to feed

their animals and also to find a night's lodging. Joseph McCullough did a thriving business, but the more money he made, the more he wanted. There was no way of holding him, nohow.

He bought from peddlers and planters everything from pins to barrels. He'd also buy bales of cotton from nearby colonists and then send 'em to Atlanta to be sold at a price. But he always thought the price wasn't high enough. He wanted more.

John had his cousin Read for a partner. One day he said to him:

"Cousin Read, we got to get more for our cotton. We're paying high for sugar in Atlanta and so we got to get more for the cotton."

"They won't pay no more," said Cousin Read.

"Yes, they will. We'll see about it. Just you remember, if you want money strong enough, it'll come your way."

"How you gonna do it?"

"There's many ways to catch flies. I'll show you."

John opened one of the bales of cotton and took out full half of it. Then he said to Read:

"Come with me."

"Where you going?"

"You'll see."

John walked in back of the house to where an old grindstone was lying.

"You help me carry that stone."

"Where?"

"To the cotton bale."

Read and John picked up the stone and brought it to the open bale.

"Now, help me put it in."

The two men put the stone in, and John covered it with cotton and sewed it together.

"They'll never guess that stone's there between the other bales, and it'll weigh pretty heavy," John said.

The bales and other merchandise were loaded and the driver went off to Atlanta with orders to bring back barrels of sugar for the cotton.

Men and wagons rolled along the road where there were many other men and wagons, and in good time they came to the proper merchant in Atlanta. The driver said Mr. McCullough wanted barrels of sugar in exchange. The merchant said that was all right with him.

Then he examined each bale of cotton closer, better than McCullough thought he would, and came to the one loaded with the stone. The weight seemed suspicious. He decided to open the bale, did, and . . . found the stone!

"Ah, good friend Mac," he said, "so that's your little game. I see you can cheat as good as a cat can lick a dish, but I ain't as green as I look to you. You got to catch the bear before you sell the skin."

After unloading the bales of cotton, he began filling barrels with sugar. Into one of them he put one third sugar, then the grindstone, and then filled the top with a thin layer of sugar. Then the barrels were loaded onto the wagon and went off to Mr. McCullough.

Traveling on the highway was slow, but in the end the sugar came to the merchant's inn. Mr. McCullough, who was suspicious of everyone but himself, checked all the barrels. When he came to the one with the stone in it, it didn't seem right. It was heavier than the others. He opened it and there was his own grindstone back again. John McCullough was a sharp trader, but he also loved a good laugh.

"Cousin Read! Cousin Read," he shouted, "come here and see the rooster that's come home to roost."

Read came up, looked, and saw the stone in the barrel. A big grin on his weather-beaten face, he turned to John and said:

"That grindstone looks mighty familiar, John, don't it? Aye, the rooster did come home to roost."

"And we'll let 'm roost here for good," John added.

Guess they didn't load stones for merchandise again after that.

Ah-Dunno Ben

This is a star-shining tale of the dark days of the American Revolution.

The British were driving the Americans from valleys and dales and cities. Charleston had fallen, and the conquering Redcoats did what conquering armies have always done. They went from city to city, from farm to farm, taking whatever they could lay their hands on: goods, cattle, and food. The patriots tried every means to save what belonged to them.

Around Charleston, the fallen city, the soldiery raided many plantations and homes. Folks sought every refuge in woods and swamps, carrying animals and possessions with them.

Now, there was a large plantation not far from the seaport, that was owned by Major Harleston and his family. It was a rich holding that would be a prize for the British. But the Harleston household had fled with all it could carry—to hide in the dark, distant woods and in the deep, murky swamps.

Old Cy and a few stableboys under him were in charge of the fine horses of the plantation. The horses were led into the swamps, and Ben, one of the young boys, was given the work of wiping out the hoof tracks so that the British wouldn't find them.

Ben loved horses, loved his master, and loved his work, and he was determined to do his job so well that no British soldier could find those tracks. Bent down, and face to the earth, he slowly and carefully smoothed out earth tracks and brushed away telltale leaves and twigs. The work took time, and soon the men with the animals were far ahead of him. He was so much interested in his work that he never saw a troop of British soldiers coming his way. He was quickly surrounded and dragged by one of the soldiers before an officer on a horse. The troop of men were on the hunt for horses, which they needed badly.

"I think this black fellow is a stableboy and knows where horses are hid," said the soldier, who was leading Ben.

"Where are the horses and the men from the plantation? Where are they hidden?"

"Ah dunno, sah!"

"C'm on, you must know, young fellow. You know where the horses are hid and maybe cows and chickens, too. Talk up; you'll be well rewarded for your pains. Where are they?"

Ben wasn't going to tell. "Ah dunno, sah!"

The sergeant behind the officer had been watching Ben closely. Getting off his horse, he winked to the officer and began to examine his horse's hind hoof. After a few minutes he dropped the hoof, turned to Ben, and said: "You hold the hoof, it'll be easier for me to examine it."

Ben picked up the hoof and held it like a trained stableman. The sergeant turned to him and said firmly and with an oath: "You are a stableboy, and you know where the horses are hidden. Sir," he turned to his officer, "from the way he picked up that hoof and held it, he's been doing it for a long time. Make him come out with it, or string 'm up."

"Boy, you tell where the horses are, or in a minute you'll be dangling from one of these trees."

"Ah dunno, sah." Ben's face was set.

"Yes, you do," the officer cried angrily.

"Hang him," the sergeant cried.

"Go ahead," the officer said.

A noose was put around Ben's neck, and the rope was thrown over a heavy limb of a tree. The sergeant held the end.

"For the last time, will you tell where the horses are?" the officer asked.

"Ah dunno, sah," Ben said without flinching an eye.

"Pull 'm up!"

The sergeant pulled the rope and Ben was dangling in the air.

"Let 'm down," the officer said.

The sergeant obeyed and Ben's feet touched the ground again.
"Now, will you tell?" the officer said fiercely.
"Ah dunno, sah!"
"Pull 'm up."
Up went the rope again. The officer now waited a little longer.
"Let 'm down," the officer said again.
Ben's feet touched the ground once more.
"Now, will you tell where those horses are?"
"Ah dunno, sah," Ben spluttered.
"Pull 'm up and keep 'm there." Again Ben was swinging in the air. He was there for some time.
"I'll try just once more," the officer said between his teeth. "For the last time, will you tell where those horses are?"
"Ah'm not gonna tell!" Ben said fearlessly.
"Up, and let 'm hang," the officer said harshly.
Up went the rope and, when Ben was in the air, they tied it to a limb and galloped off.
"That'll be a warning to those accursed rebels."
They didn't know that a few patriots and folks from the Harleston household had been watching all the time. The instant the soldiers were out of sight, they rushed up and cut the rope and Ben came down choking and heaving.
It didn't take long before Ben was breathing easily, and he sat up and looked around.
"Those fellows gone?" he asked the friendly folks.
"Dey gone."
"Den ah goes. Got to help Uncle Cy. He wants me t' look after them horses. Yuh clean up them tracks."
Off he ran, as if he had done some common daily chore instead of a heroic, noble deed.

The Tale of Rebecca Motte

The courage and sacrifice of Southern women during the Revolution as well as during the Civil War were fully equal to that of the men fighting on the battlefield. Here is one tale of a woman of South Carolina, told all over the South, the tale of Rebecca Motte.

There was, and still is, a grand plantation on the Congaree River, about fifty miles from Columbia, owned by the Motte family. When the Revolutionary War began, Mr. Motte and all his family were on the side of the Americans. Mr. Motte was out fighting on the battlefield, and Mrs. Motte was in charge at home, on the lookout for whatever she could do to help.

The Americans were on the defensive. Colonel Tarleton had captured the Motte House, and a party of officers was stationed there. Since it was a strong building, the British turned it into a fort. Reinforcements were set up all around, and it was called Fort Motte.

General Francis Marion, who led an army of ragged American patriots and was a deep thorn in the side of the British, decided to drive the Tories from the Motte home. He attacked it without letup and finally captured one of the outposts. Mrs. Motte, who had been living in the main house, was then ordered to leave. The British were afraid to have the wife of an enemy in the fort. When she was told she had to go, she moved to one of the small houses that was not far from the main building. She threw together a few necessities, and among them, accidently, was a quiver with three arrows that came from East India, which a friend had given her. They were poisoned arrows used in war among the natives, and they also had some substance on them which would ignite upon striking dried wood.

She stayed in the small cottage while General Light-Horse Harry Lee and Marion, the "Swamp Fox" as he was often called, kept up their attack on the main house.

The siege had gone on for some time—far too long for the restless Swamp Fox and the equally restless Light-Horse General. They decided to finish it quickly.

The two leaders were sitting together in council, discussing the siege. General Marion, small, dark-faced, but fearless as a lion, was speaking:

"There is one way of ending this long siege, Lee."

General Light-Horse Lee, handsome and eager, questioned:

"And what is this one way, General Marion?"

"Very simple. Burn 'em out. Set the house on fire. Then the enemy will have to run."

"Aye, a good idea, General. But it is our friends' house and Mrs. Motte has been gracious and helpful to us. It would be a rude act of discourtesy to set her house on fire."

"Aye, that's true; but this is war, and it is the only way to end this siege quickly. If the British get reinforcements, it will be an end to our siege. The house 'll then be lost as well."

"Yes, it'll be lost to Mrs. Motte either way, General Marion."

"It's got to be done, Lee, I tell you. And I think we can get Mrs. Motte's consent. I don't believe she'll object. Why don't you ask her, General Lee? You have a way with ladies."

"It won't be easy, but I'll try."

He went at once to Mrs. Motte.

"Madam," he said, "we have come to a decision that I am afraid will be hard for you to accept. General Marion and I feel that the British must be driven out of your fine home before they get reinforcements."

"I can understand that," said Mrs. Motte. "How will you do it?"

"There is only one quick way, Mistress Motte, and that is to destroy your home by fire. It took General Marion a long time to come to this decision, but we know reinforcements are coming, and then your house will be lost anyway. I assure you, I tell you this with great reluctance, but we know of no other plan."

"We'll fire them from rifles, General Lee. Let us do it at once," said Rebecca.

The Tale of Rebecca Motte

For a time Mrs. Motte was silent, then the General got the surprise of his life.

"Sir," Mrs. Motte said, "I heartily agree with your decision and General Marion's. My home is of little importance compared to the freedom of our country. Don't hesitate for a moment in your decision. What is more, I will help you."

"You will help us!"

"Indeed I will. I have something that will facilitate your task."

"That is most generous and self-sacrificing, Mrs. Motte, and does great honor to you. You are a true patriot."

"It is no more than any true American patriotic woman would do. And now I will tell you how I can help.

"Some time ago, a friend who had been in the Far East brought me some arrows as a gift. I still have three of them. They are poisoned and are used in warfare. But they also have another quality. When you shoot them against dry wood, they will ignite it and set it on fire. I happened to take them along when I left my home—I don't know why. Perhaps Providence prompted me. I will give them to you to set my house on fire."

Without another word, the courageous woman left and returned in a short time with the quiver and the three arrows.

General Marion had come in too, and the two men examined the arrows.

"You must be careful, gentlemen," Mrs. Motte said, "the ends are poisoned."

"We have no bows to shoot them with," said General Lee.

"We'll fire them from rifles, General Lee. Let us do it at once."

The first arrow was loaded into a rifle and shot towards the roof of the main house. All three watched breathlessly. The arrow flew through the air and fell on the roof and . . . nothing happened. There was deep disappointment on all the faces.

"Try another," said Mrs. Motte.

The second was fired and . . . the same result.

Said Mrs. Motte: "Gentlemen, perhaps the wood is still wet, it is early morning. Let us wait until after the sun has dried the shingles. I am sure we'll then have better luck."

They waited, and soon after the noon hour, the third arrow was shot.

No sooner did it hit the roof than a little smoke began to curl upward. It didn't take long before the flames were all over the top. The fire spread quickly and the British saw they would be burned out of the building.

The white flag was hoisted and then—war and hatred were forgotten. The Americans who had rushed to the house, and the British who were there, worked with such good will that the fire did not spread. Only the roof was burned. The courageous and generous patriot, Mrs. Motte, had her house back again, undamaged but for the roof.

The Perpetual Motion in the Sea

Many kinds of tales run around Beaufort. Some set folk laughing with salty tears, others set them crying with salty tears.

Many say those tales are wind-lies; others call them gospel truth; but wise men say, when you hear a tale folks tell over and over, shut your eyes and open your ears and just have a good time listening. Here is one of those tales, and you can take it any way you like, but if you are wise you'll follow the path of the wise men.

There once lived a man by the name of Jones, down in that town of Beaufort, where the Islands run in and out and the water runs all around. He was a good planter, but he was forever puttering around with bolts and screws and carts and wheels. When folks asked him the reason, he'd say:

"I want to discover the secret of perpetual motion, where a thing keeps on going forever without machinery of any kind. That perpetual motion trick's more important than making gold through alchemy, for when you get perpetual motion, you won't need no machinery any more. Machines 'll be running on their own power. Look at the money we will save."

Some folks laughed at him; some said: "Maybe John's got something."

Most of 'em would stand around watching his tinkering, as folks like to do.

One fine spring morning, planter Jones went out in his skiff, to fish on the waters around the Island. When he was a way out, he dropped his oars and sat with his harpoon ready in hand, watching the rolling swells of water. He was after a good-sized devilfish. In those days, there were many in the waters and rivers and in the sound around those parts.

It was nice and lulling to sit in the warm sun with the soothing rocking of the skiff on the rolling water. Soon he did not think of the cruel sport of wanting to kill a fish, playing there in the water innocently, but turned his mind inside, to swift wheels whirring around without end. He forgot everything else and so he never noted that his oars were floating away in the gray-blue water. But suddenly he awoke from his daydreaming. He saw the wide, thick wings of a great, giant devilfish. His harpoon flew out and hit deep.

The fish, wild with pain and fury, lashed out right and left. The pain would not go. It only hurt more. He raced down in the water in fierce fury, trying to get rid of the piercing ache. The point would not pull out, so he began speeding like a demon, up and down, and all around the water, dragging Jones and the skiff with him.

Folks on the shore and in fishing boats, saw the skiff without oars flying up and down and around. They recognized Jones and heard him shouting as though he had at last found his secret of perpetual motion. For how else could a boat race around at such fierce speed without oars or sail?

But Jones, in the skiff, was not thinking of perpetual motion. He was frightened white. All he wanted was to stop the wild racing through the water and get rid of the fish that was tugging him.

Now the fish was pulling him out to the wide sea. Jones was terrified. But folks on the shore and in the boats were cheering lustily and hurrahing.

The sea, before the eyes of the frightened planter, looked like an endless grave. He was racing right into it. Suddenly he remembered! He had a knife in his pocket! He pulled it out and worked desperately to cut the line of the harpoon that was tied to the boat. It wasn't easy with the boat tearing at breakneck speed. In the end, he succeeded. The line that held the giant fish was cut . . . the "perpetual motion" slowly stopped. He was dizzy.

Folks came out and brought in the exhausted fisherman, and then they learned the cause of the perpetual motion that had caused the skiff to race wildly on the water.

But that didn't stop Jones from tinkering with bolts and screws in the hope of making a machine that would go forever. People quickly forget.

Young Sherman and the Girl from Charleston

Many are the tales that are written and told about the Oakland mansion, in Charleston County, on Georgetown Road. It has a "ghost room" where a gentle ghost glides in like a little white cloud and prays at the bedside of the one sleeping there. Then there is the tale of the British soldier, who, during the Revolutionary War, rode into the dining room on horseback, drew his sword, and, with the point, picked up a roasted fowl from the platter on the table and rode out laughing at the angry family sitting there.

But the prime tale told of Oakland House is one that perhaps had a bearing on all the South during its tragic War Between the States.

Long before those suffering days, there was stationed at Fort Sumter, which was not far from the Oakland plantation, a young Northern officer named William Tecumseh Sherman.

Young Sherman, fresh and debonair and pleasing, was wel-

Young Sherman and the Girl from Charleston

comed in all the Southern homes around the fort and, of course, in the Oakland House as well. He came often to these homes for their gracious hospitality, and . . . to meet the pretty, young Southern girls.

William liked Southern girls. When he was still at West Point, he was a great admirer of a young Southern belle, who visited there quite often.

To Oakland House there came a young Charleston girl who was noted for her rare beauty, and, even more, for being a merciless coquette. She and the other girls came often to that home, and there they danced and dined with the young officers of the fort and the young neighboring planters.

It was a tale of love at first sight with young Sherman when he saw this lovely creature with glowing face and flashing eyes. She turned his head completely. And she—she loved flirting and teasing and playing with all young men, whether they came from the North or the South. Sherman was fair game.

But he took the affair very seriously, and love is blind and causes blindness. He never saw, or understood, that she was just coquetting with him. She liked the young Northern officer's attention and encouraged him just enough to keep him guessing and worrying. Again and again he spoke seriously to her.

"Will you marry me? Will you marry me?" It was always on his lips.

"What is the rush? There is plenty of time. I am so very young."

Thus saying neither yes nor no, she kept him hoping and waiting.

This went on for a long time, and it had its effect on young Sherman. One day he was sitting with some young fellow officers, glum and silent. Then one of them blurted out:

"William, stop your silly worrying about that girl. Don't you see she is just flirting with you and leading you along, as she does many others? Don't take her so seriously."

"How do you know?"

"She has been boasting to the girls of her conquest and that she is leading you a merry dance at her own pleasure."

Young Sherman was deeply hurt and shocked and humiliated. He didn't speak much to anyone about it, but deep within he brooded over what he called the deception of a girl. But she made little of it. She had too many other admirers.

And so the tale goes that young Sherman never forgot the hurt the lovely young girl caused him. It is said and it is told that he never forgave the humiliation. Some say that the horrid wrecking of the South by his military vengeance was due, to an extent, to the hurt he received from the Southern belle in his youthful days.

Kate, the Bell Witch

Reckon the most famous witch in the state of Tennessee, and maybe the most famous witch in all the land, is Kate, the "Bell witch."

Her real name was Kate Batts, a right proper name for a woman who was forever complaining, forever gossiping, and forever making trouble. There wasn't a neighbor 'd say a good word about her. Bell was the name of the family she was torturing all their lives.

John Bell had come from North Carolina to settle in Tennessee. He came with his big family and his slaves and bought a big farm near Adams. Then he bought a small piece of land that belonged to Kate Batts to round out his holdings.

True or untrue, pretty soon this woman began spreading the news that John Bell had cheated her. No one believed a word she said, because John was an upright and God-fearing man. Just the same, Kate kept up the cantankerous cackling till folks' heads rubbed sore.

When she was on her deathbed, she said she'd come back and hant John Bell and his kith and kin to the grave. And she was as good as her word.

No sooner was she dead and cooled six feet under the ground than John Bell and his daughter Betsy knew about it. They never had any peace from then on. Kate 'd throw the pots and the furniture at 'em. She'd yell and scream at 'em and call 'em names till they got so edgety they couldn't sleep or rest.

Sometimes she'd even take away the food from their mouths and spill their coffee over 'em. That's when she took on as a cat. Sometimes she'd come as a goat with a long scraggly beard and then other times she'd be seen around looking like a dried old hag, which she was. That was when she'd yank their hair or pull their noses or stick needles in their arms. D'you think she stopped with the two Bells? Not she! After a time she began bothering folks all over Robertson County. She'd come to meetings and outholler, outgroan, and outsing any ten sinners in the congregation. Sometimes she'd raid folks' homes of vittles and drink and she let her anger out on John Bell. She was a jumping spider and folks had never known such a contrary witch.

Sometimes out of a blue sky she'd be kind to other kin in the family, often helping 'em when they were in trouble. She had a liking for John Bell's wife; one time when she was sick, Kate fetched her a big basket of fine fruits from the Southlands.

There's no end of tales told about her doings and the one folks tell most often is the one time when she and Old Hickory, General Andrew Jackson, came together head on.

The doings of "Kate-witch" were known from one end of the state to the other and outside o' Tennessee too. Near everybody knew about Kate and so did Andrew Jackson.

One day, out of devilment, he got together a few of his friends and started for Nashville to go to the Bells in Robertson County to meet the famous witch firsthand.

They set out a-horse and a-wagon with tents and plenty of good vittles for the body, bent on a new kind of good laugh. When they crossed the line of the Bells' holdings, the wagon stopped and the wheels wouldn't turn.

It was a straight stretch and the driver whooped and whoa'd and popped the whip. The horses put their heads down, strained their backs, but the wagon wouldn't budge.

All the men examined the harness, took off the wheels, and tested 'em. Nothing wrong; but just the same nothing 'd move that wagon. All put their strength to the back, trying to push and start it rolling. They might as well have tried to push a mountain.

Andrew Jackson was smart 's a catbird after a bug: "Bet it's the doings of Kate the witch," he said.

No sooner were the words out of his mouth than they heard a woman's voice sharp as a hammer on an anvil. "Right, General. Glad ye know me. The wagon 'll be goin' now. See you tonight."

Kate kept her word. The wagon went on, but before telling you what happened that night, I must tell you that the General had brought with him a fellow famous as a "witch-layer," one who could beat witches at their own game and even finish 'em with a silver bullet.

When the famous company got to John Bell's home, they were welcomed with Southern frontier friendliness. Throughout the evening of eating, drinking, merrymaking, and waiting for Kate, the "witch-layer" kept on telling tales of how he had got the best of many a witch. When he was through with all the tales he knew, there was heard, all of a sudden, a screaming razor-like laughter and then . . . furniture began flying around the room, dishes and pots began flying at the men's heads—mostly at the head of the "witch-layer." It was worse than bee hunting in a locust patch.

"Use yer silver bullet," cries came from all around. "It's the witch! Use yer silver bullet!"

The fellow rammed his gun, worked at it, but it wouldn't go off.

There came a screechy female cackle. "Ye did a lot o' word-slingin'; now I'll show ye what I kin do."

Smack! Smack! Bang! Bang! Crash! The witch-layer fell to the ground, then leaped to his feet and began running around. The banging and whacking didn't stop and the cackling laughter kept on, with a blustering chorus of ow's and ouch's from the fellow. In the end, he flew out the door—to the laughter of Kate and the men.

"Enough for the night, General," the sharp thin voice in the air said. "Tomorrow I'll show you a little more."

The men didn't talk much and went to sleep. The next morning the General was for staying longer, but the company said they had

had enough. "Can't afford too big a price for wisdom," one said. And so they went off.

But that was not the end of Kate the witch. She kept making life miserable for John and Betsy Bell till they went to a more peaceful world. Y'd think Kate 'd had enough by then, but not that witch. She's kept on her weird doings down to this very day.

Every now and then folks in Robertson County in Tennessee 'll tell you of some new stunt Kate, the Bell witch, has been up to.

The Best Laugh Is the Last Laugh

Richard Reagan, living near the lakes of Ireland, couldn't be beat in arguing, praying, fighting, or playing a joke that brought a bellyful of laughter. One day he decided Ireland was too narrow for his britches. He gathered kith and caboodle and came to America where, he heard, there was plenty of room for the Irish and the Dutch and every other nationality in creation.

No sooner was he in the great woods with the red Indians and the white settlers than, just as he had done in Ireland, he began working, arguing, praying, and playing jokes that brought good laughter to the hard-working settlers. There wasn't a thing in this great new big land he had chosen to call his own that the man from Ireland missed.

Now, Richard Reagan had three fine sons and one of them was named Timothy. He was the third, and favorite, son of his father, for he was as like his pappy as one pea is like another.

The Best Laugh Is the Last Laugh 235

When Timothy was full grown, he went to Sevierville, in Tennessee, where you can see the Appalachian Mountains standing green and fragrant against the blue sky. He thought it the finest place in all the land for a fighting, arguing, joke-loving American come from green Ireland.

Timothy was a big fellow who loved horses so much he went into the harness-making trade. When harness-making was slow, he cut trees, to make stocks for the law to put sinners in. In those days, fellows sitting in the stocks quickly came to their senses and quit their evil-doing.

In between all his work Timothy found plenty of time for roistering and joke-playing. Sometimes his doings went too far over the fence and there'd be short talk, but the good mountain smells 'd clear the air and folks forgot and forgave. They knew he didn't mean any harm, for Timothy had the kindest heart in the Appalachians and was ready to help when anybody needed it.

One time there was a big trial going on in Gatlinsburg. Folks came from all around, and Timothy Reagan came too. The trial was going strong, and the lawyers and the Judge were sweating, and everybody was listening.

Timothy didn't agree with what one of the lawyers was saying and he said it loud for all to hear.

The Judge didn't like Timothy's remarks and told him to keep his mouth shut. The Judge didn't know there was no shutting up Timothy when he got going.

Every time the Judge or the lawyers said something Timothy didn't like, he'd put in his own Irish bit. This made the Judge madder and madder. In the end, he yelled:

"Timothy Reagan, I sentence you for contempt of court. For the remainder of the trial you will sit in the stocks made by your own hands. That'll teach you to behave proper when court is in session. Sheriff, take him to the stocks."

Timothy came back with some harum-scarum words that couldn't be printed on paper, and went with the sheriff to the stocks on the courthouse green. Folks were curious and followed after them to see what would happen.

Said the sheriff: "Timothy Reagan, git in them stocks as the Judge ordered."

"Guess folks got t' obey a judge of the court," Timothy said meek-like, but there was a sly look dancing in his eyes.

Timothy went to the stocks, sat down on the bench, and put one foot where his wrist should go. Then he put the other foot in the wrong hole and began fumbling around like a newborn calf trying to find its first legs.

"Hurry up," the sheriff said impatiently. "I gotta git back to the courtroom."

But Timothy kept on fumbling and in the end he said, "Sheriff, here's a funny bit. It seems I can't git into me own stocks. The law's the law and I gotta git in 'em. Judge ordered it. Reckon ye'll have to show me the way. C'mon and show me and I'll follow you quick."

The sheriff wanted to get back to the trial, so he pushed Timothy away and sat down on the bench. He stuck his wrists and neck in the right places and before you could say Jehoshaphat, Timothy slammed down the upper halves, snapped the locks, and walked away laughing his head off.

Folks all around howled so hard the Judge came out to see what was going on. When he saw the sheriff in the stocks and Timothy and the crowd laughing, he couldn't help joining in. How can you punish a man who makes you laugh?

So Timothy was once again forgiven—as he had been many times before.

Fiddler's Rock

In Johnson County in East Tennessee there is Stone Mountain, and on that mountain there is a rock sticking six feet high in the air. Folks knew that rock pretty well because it was a place favored by rattlesnakes from all around that came there to let the sun warm their cold blood. The wriggling and the rolling of the glistening varmints in the sunlight was a great sight. After a time, folks called that snake rock Fiddler's Rock because it was the rock where Martin Stone did his last fiddling on a sunny Sunday morning.

Martin peddled glistening wares and pretties womenfolks liked, needed, and bought from him. But that wasn't the only reason why he was dog with the women. Martin fiddled a fiddle better than anyone in East Tennessee. There wasn't a wedding or a play-party or a meeting where he wasn't welcome as rain after a drought. When he began to move that bow, he took folks to lands far over the trees and the mountains. He made 'em feel as if they were in another world. When they heard him, they wanted to cry and sing and whoop it up with jumping feet and shouting sounds.

Now, there was one kind of sport Martin liked better than any other and that was sitting on that sticking-up stone and playing his fiddle. When the rattlesnakes 'd come wriggling and weaving to listen to him, he'd pop them all with his well-oiled Colt. Sometimes he'd just sit and watch the snakes a-writhing and a-glistening.

He was a moody fellow who often didn't know what he wanted or what to do. His mind would wander far away and 'd get kind of jumbled up with the smell of the balsam and the blue of the sky. Maybe he was hearing kind of sleep-music in the smell of the trees and the singing of the birds and in the glistening, wriggling varmints in front of him.

Then maybe he'd turn to fiddling sweetly as if he were at a wedding or a play-party. He'd fiddle tunes to make the feet dance and the heart ache.

I guess those snakes knew the meaning of Martin's fiddling and danced in tune. They'd rise and rear, and wiggle and twist, and crawfish and turn every which way as if celebrating the wedding of a king.

One Sunday Martin wasn't just up to going to church. "I'll pray my own way," he said to himself, and he walked through the sweet smelly woods and brush till he came to the rock that stuck way out. He sat down on the top of it. The sun was shining hot enough to warm the world. Mockingbirds, the singingest birds in the land, were doing their best warbling and cavorting as if trying to tell

Martin something he should know. Towhees and woodpeckers and robins were busy as ants on the run in the balsam and the hemlocks and tulip trees. Martin paid no mind to 'em. He was in one of his faraway feelings. Soon some rattlers came out, rearing their heads and moving their tails. Martin took out his gun, fired a shot, and one rattler did his last wriggling. He fired another shot and missed. His hand dropped down and he looked over the trees.

"No," he mumbled to himself. "That ain't proper work for Sunday mornin'."

For a spell he sat silent, just kind of dreaming, then he took his bow, put his fiddle box on his knees, and began fiddling tunes. More rattlers were coming out from the sides of the rock and he kept on his fiddling. More rattlers! More and more rattlers! A lake of rattlers! Little ones that didn't have their first button, big ones that had enough rattles to put the fear of the Lord in a stronghearted man. But not into Martin's heart. Martin just looked at them and near didn't see them shiny varmints moving like thick candles in a big sunny church. He was playing to beat the singing of angels, for he had a hog-wild feeling in him. He was fiddling to make St. Peter open the gates on high while the rattlesnakes were a-rearing and a-rustling and a-twisting, their slick bellies shining in the yellow sun against the gray rock. Their small heads and little tongues twisted in their own snake speech and their own snake-tongue singing.

A pigeon-crazy feeling was creeping all over Martin and he was getting kind of scrambly-witted. Slowly-like, his fiddle bow dropped from his hands and soon his fiddle box slid along his side. He looked down with big bug-eyes at the wriggling, shiny thick mass o' snakes. He didn't hear the birds a-singing and the wind a-sighing. He didn't see the blue above and he didn't feel the burning sun. He was only seeing the glistening thick candles a-nodding to him with a kind o' calling.

The ledge of the rock was mighty slippery and he began sliding to that slithering messy-looking something. Forgot his gun, forgot his fiddle, forgot himself, forgot everything, just looked at a weaving, dancing lake from which was coming a hissing song. He slid right among them. They wrapped around Martin from one end to the other, popping him all over with their poison fangs like kind o' kisses—for they loved the fiddling and the fiddler.

A few days later, men found Martin, face and head and body lying flat on the ground, dead as Tony, as the saying goes.

But I reckon it takes more than a score of rattlesnakes to shut up a fiddler like Martin in East Tennessee. You'll not hear his shooting, popping rattlesnakes coming out of the sides of the rock, but you can sure hear his fiddling in the light of the full sun or in the shine of the full moon. Folks swear they still hear it today, and I believe 'em.

Trust Not a New Friend

Folks around Nashville, Memphis, and all over Tennessee and other states swear this tale is true and so nobody can say it isn't. What's more, it's a tale that'll bring a good laugh, and such a tale 's got to be true.

It happened when General McCook of the Federal army was in Nashville, where daredevil "Colonel" John Morgan and his raiders gave no peace to the Northerners. You never could tell when that Kentuckian would appear, or in what disguise, to make life lickety-brown-black for the Federals. General McCook tried to keep eyes and ears wide open to capture Morgan and his band, but you might as well have tried to catch lightning gone hog-wild.

Morgan didn't give a thought to watchers and waiters. Fact is,

240   TENNESSEE

it made him more audacious. He was always thinking of some new scheme to harass and beat the Federals.

One time when Morgan and his men were up in Davidson County, in Tennessee, he said, "I'm gonna give you a little present of a hundred and fifty Northerners without firing a shot. Watch me do it."

The next thing they knew, there was John Morgan dressed like a hard-working farmer, sitting on a wagon loaded with sacks of flour.

"What's the game?"

"You'll find out soon!"

The men knew their leader, so not another word was said.

The "farmer" drove his wagon kind of easy into Nashville right up to the St. Cloud Hotel. Outside stood a man he knew could be trusted, so he left the wagon with him and went straight into the dining room. It was the middle of the day and the big tables with chairs around were slowly filling up.

Morgan looked around and, seeing General McCook sitting alone, sat down opposite him.

"General McCook, sir, I reckon," Morgan said, bowing and speaking with the drawl of the farmfolk.

"Right, sir, that's my name."

"Wal, Gineral, if there is none of them rebs * around, I got something to tell ye that's jest fer your ears."

The General looked on both sides. The seats were empty.

"Nobody's near, you can speak freely."

"Wal, sir, my farm is a ways up, close to Burk's Mill that's just full of rebs. They've sworn ye're not gonna get a speck o' meal the size of a pea even if your men starve to death."

General McCook looked at Morgan, all ears.

"That's not my way of thinkin', Gineral. Naturally, I don't speak about it round my way and ye know why. An' t' show ye my heart's in the right place I brought down a wagonload o' flour, the finest y' ever saw and ye can have it for the reg'lar price."

That was "angel's" song to the General's ears. Provisions were low. It was a windfall from heaven.

---

* Southerners were often called "rebels" or "rebs."

Trust Not a New Friend 241

He left the table, ordered the flour to be taken to the commissary, and the good farmer to be paid in hard coin.

Morgan took the money and went away. But in less than half an hour he came back to General McCook's headquarters. He asked to see him quick and was taken in at once.

"Gineral, I got to tell ye something that's jest fer ye and nobody else."

"Come, friend, there's nobody around, you can say anything that's on your mind."

"Wal, Gineral, seein' you've been so kind and paid me good," his voice sank to a whisper, "I kin tell you somethin' worth ten loads o' meal."

"Yes."

"Wal, if ye'll send tomorrow, say a hundred and fifty of your best-picked armed men, to the hill near Burk's Mill, I'll lead 'em to where they kin find a big nest full o' rebs. An' they got lots o' things ye kin use an' need, meal, bullets, powder, ye know...."

The General's eyes lighted up. Here was a collaborator sent from heaven. And right where the need was the greatest.

"The Lord sent you, good friend," he said eagerly. "I want to thank you for your loyalty to the government's cause and I want to thank you personally for what you've done for me. I'll sure have the men there and I know I can trust you to lead 'em to the right place. Come back and you'll be well rewarded for your patriotism." Morgan went off with a pleased smile on his face.

The next morning one hundred and fifty well-armed Federal soldiers led by a young officer were on their way to the mill. As they got near it they were met, not by a farmer, as the General had been told, but by "Colonel" Morgan with a force of men armed to the bootstraps and outnumbering the Federals. The hundred and fifty soldiers were taken without a single shot. They were led to the rear where in time they were exchanged for Confederate men. All except the young officer. Him, Daredevil Morgan released on parole and sent to General McCook with greetings.

"Tell the General it's from his friend, the 'meal-selling farmer' he met in the St. Cloud Hotel dining room, whom he so wisely trusted. And tell him maybe it's not so wise to trust a new friend even if he 'comes from heaven.'"

Come and Laugh with Bobby Gum

When folks down in Memphis want to make friends and kin chuckle, they tell a tale about Bobby Gum. What Bobby Gum'd say or do would make horses and folks haw haw. So I come around to the day that funny fellow hopped in to where Judge Henderson was holding court, shouting, "I'm a horse! I'm a horse! I'm a horse!" Judge Henderson, like all neighbors of Bobby, liked him if he didn't step too heavy on their toes. That day the Judge was trying an important case.

"Quit your horsing, Bobby Gum, we got something to do here," the Judge said.

But Bobby wouldn't quit, he just kept on hopping and shouting, "I'm a horse! I'm a horse!"

"Sheriff," the Judge said, "Mr. Sheriff, seeing that all the livery stables in town are full, I order you to put this here horse in the county jail for ten days." And so it was done.

But that's not the tale I was going to tell you about Bobby. I was just sidetracked by the horse. What I want to tell you is what Bobby did during the great election when Henry Clay and James Polk were battling fire 'n brimstone about who was to be President of the United States. It was a hot fight and folks stuck to sides like bears to bee trees.

Bobby Gum was a strong Clay man and he didn't care if the whole world knew it.

One day, when Judge Henderson, who had given Bobby ten days in jail for horsing around too much, was in court trying a very important case, Bobby was feeling mighty gay, running all over town roaring:

"Hooray! Hooray! Hooray!
"Hooray for Henry Clay!"

He kept on the din, hooraying till he came to the courthouse where the session was going on.

On the steps of the courthouse he roared loud enough to wake the dead:

"Hooray! Hooray! Hooray!
"Hooray for Henry Clay!"

He kept up his bellowing, disturbing the Judge, the lawyers, and everybody else.

"Sheriff, go and tell that numskull to stop the yowling or I'll put him in jail again," said the Judge.

The sheriff went out and told Bobby what the Judge had said. But you couldn't cow Bobby that quick. He kept on yelling and hooraying about Clay so folks couldn't hear a word in the courtroom. It made Judge Henderson mad as a billy goat.

"Sheriff, get that fellow in the courtroom. I'll fix him good."

The sheriff brought Bobby into the courtroom.

"Bobby Gum, quit that cat-on-the-fence yowling so's I can go on with the court or I'll clap you in the caboose for a month."

Bobby looked at the Judge with a twinkle in his eye and a cotton-tail grin on his face.

"Tell you what, Judge," he said with a horse wink, "I'll stop and let you go on with the court if you let me give one more cheer for the man I want to win."

For a minute the Judge was silent, then he answered, "Go on, you crazy fool, you can yell one more cheer for Clay if you also give a cheer for Polk."

For a moment Bobby looked at the Judge, then a sly smile came on his face.

"I'll sure obey your orders, Judge. Come, I'll do it on the court steps."

He went out on the court steps, the Judge and all following to see a Clay man cheering for Polk. When Bobby got to the last step, he filled his lungs with a deep breath and roared at the top of his voice:

"Hooray! Hooray! Hooray!
"Hooray for Henry Clay!"

He roared so loud folks said they heard him two miles away. Then Bobby, looking all around with a foxy grin, took a deep, deep breath again and bellered:

"Hooray! Hooray! Hooray!"

Then, lowering his voice so's you couldn't hear him, he whispered:

"Hooray for James Polk!"

Then he leaped on his horse and rode off laughing with all his might. So did everybody else, even Judge Henderson. You couldn't get mad at a fellow 'd make you laugh. Could you?

The Ghost Who Wasn't a Ghost

In old Gloucester in Tennessee stood an old church called the Ware Church. It was a sad church, for it was forgotten and deserted. The doors were broken and wind and rain came in, wild and roaring, whenever there was a storm. People didn't go there; only sometimes, in bad weather, someone would come in for shelter. Otherwise folks kept away, for they said it was haunted by eerie ghosts.

Now, there lived in that town of Gloucester two young men of fine families and fine reputation, Charles and Avery by name. They were close friends, though they were as different as a cat from a crow.

Avery was the boasting kind, always talking of the great deeds he had done and the great deeds he was going to do, while Charles was quiet and courageous. He didn't talk about his courage. He never boasted.

Often these two had arguments about courage and valor, for you know how, in those early days of the land, courage played a very important part in daily life.

Once both these young gentlemen were invited to parties, each in a different home. It was a night in June and the weather was threatening, but just the same, each went.

While the parties were at their gayest, a storm began raging over the town. The wind blew as hard as a hurricane and the whipping rain tore around trees and houses. But the dancing and the dining went on merrily to the music of the fiddlers and the music of the storm, until the wee hours.

Then the parties began to break up. The one in which Charles was the guest was first. Wrapped in a heavy greatcoat, he set out on his fine white horse in the battling rain and wind. The horse cantered along as best it could.

When he came to the deserted church, which was on his way home, the thunder and lightning and pelting rain were so wild that he decided to look for shelter inside. He rode through the open door and there, among the broken pews, he remained quietly with his horse, waiting for the storm to pass.

Avery had started out a little after Charles, riding head-down through the tearing wind and rain. He also came to the church and decided to go in and stay there till the storm was over.

He led his horse in slowly through an open door. At that moment a great streak of lightning zigzagged through the sky and Avery saw . . . a white horse with a hooded figure!

Fear lay hold on him like an iron-fanged bear trap. For a minute he held his horse with a cold grip. Then, wheeling, he mounted and whipped it into a flying run through rain and wind.

Charles, understanding quickly that he had frightened Avery, shouted, "I am Charles!" But the wind and thunder drowned his voice. Avery thought the ghost of the horse was screaming at him and that devils were after him and he lashed his horse to run faster.

Charles raced after him, shouting all the time, "Stop! Stop! It is Charles!" But Avery heard only screaming in the wind. This frightened him more, and the horse, catching his fear, dashed wildly along until it came to Avery's home and plunged through the gate.

A moment later Charles also reached the gate. He knew Avery had run away in fear and couldn't help shouting through the rain: "Avery! Avery! You silly fool! Don't you see it is me, Charles, your friend?"

Avery was silent. Suddenly he realized the silly part he had played.

"We won't have any more arguments about courage! You surely didn't show any just now! Good night, friend Avery. You needn't be scared. No ghosts are chasing you!" And Charles rode off.

Avery was shocked! He slowly dismounted, led his horse to the stable, and then entered his house and went to bed, spending a restless night.

First thing the next morning he sent a note to Charles, begging him not to breathe a word to anyone of what had happened in the church until he had seen him. Charles sent back a note, promising he would not speak.

Avery had no rest. If the shame of his cowardice became known, it would follow him through all his life. How to hide it? Finally he had an idea.

Two days later he sent a note to Charles, inviting him to a special dinner that evening. Evening came and so did Charles.

Avery had set a magnificent table. Silver candlesticks with lighted candles everywhere, and the finest dishes. They sat down to a rich feast with old wines.

Avery talked of many things—except of what had happened in the Ware Church. So, between wining and dining, the evening passed pleasantly.

The meal was over and they were sitting and enjoying a sweet cordial when Avery sent the servant away. Then he rose from his chair, locked the doors, opened a drawer at a side table, and took out a pistol. He raised it and pointed it directly at Charles.

"Charles," Avery said, "you know I am not a coward, but even a valiant man can sometimes be frightened. I was frightened in the church, but I am not a coward. At this moment I have you at a disadvantage because you are not armed. That is unfortunate for you, but I am desperate and can't stand on politeness. Unless you swear that you will not tell a soul, while I am alive, what happened at the Ware Church, I'll be forced to shoot you."

"My dear friend Avery," said Charles, "what happened at the church is not of such great importance, and I don't think it is worth dying for. I swear and promise you I will never tell anyone what happened at the Ware Church while you are alive."

"I am happy and grateful to you for your decision," said Avery. "You have my permission to tell the story after I have gone to a better world."

They drank a toast, shook hands, and the story was never told while Avery was alive. When he was no more in this world, it came out, and that's how I can tell it to you.

Big Sixteen

"Don't know how old I am, but I am just old enough to know what I seen and heard while I was there in slavery time. We didn't have much dem times. Lived on middlin' and 'lasses. De white folks, they kept the hams for themselves. But we was all fat jest the same.

"De only rest we got was when it rained. Den we was all together. We would sit around and swap tales.

"Heard one about a man. Maybe in Georgia, maybe in Mississippi, maybe in some other place. Dey called him Big Sixteen because he wear dat number shoe. He sure had big feet.

"One day Old Massa say, 'Big Sixteen, I believe I want ye to move dem big sills I had cut down in de swamp. Bring 'em up to the house an' stake 'em proper.'

" 'That's sure what I'm gonna do, Massa,' said Big Sixteen.

"So he went down in de swamp and brought back all dem long big sills. Brought 'em up to the house and staked 'em. Don't know just how many there was of 'em. Maybe a hundred, maybe two hundred, maybe more. Big Sixteen, he was a mighty powerful man.

"So Old Massa said another day, 'Go in the pasture and fetch me the mules. I want to look 'em over.'

"Big Sixteen he went in the pasture, caught them mules by the bridles, but they was balky and wouldn't go nohow. He pulled 'em an' pulled 'em and in the end he tore the bridles to pieces. So he picked up each of them mules, put one under each arm, and brought them to Old Massa.

"Old Massa looked at Big Sixteen an' says: 'Big Sixteen, ef ye kin tote a mule under each o' your arms, we kin do anythin'. Ye kin even tote the debil here. Go catch the debil an' tote 'im here.'

" 'Yes sir, Massa, ah kin bring de debil ef ye git me a nine-pound hammer an' a pick an' shovel.'

"Old Massa give 'im a nine-pound hammer an' a pick an' shovel. Big Sixteen, he went in front of the house an' went to diggin'. He was diggin' nearly a month before he got where he wanted.

"Then he picked up his nine-pound hammer and began knocking on de debil's door.

"De debil answered de door himself. De debil says:

" 'Who dat out dere?'

" 'It's Big Sixteen.'

" 'What yo want?'

" 'Wanta have a word wid y' for a minute,' answered Big Sixteen.

"Soon as de debil poked his head out de door, Big Sixteen hit 'im over the head wid de hammer, picked 'im up, an' carried 'im up to Old Massa.

"Old Massa took one look and his skin got crinklin' all over.

" 'Take dat ugly thing away from here quick. Ah didn't think you'd catch de debil sho enough.'

"So Big Sixteen picked up de debil and throwed 'im back down de hole.

"After a while Big Sixteen died an' walked up to Heben and knocked on de gate.

"Peter, he looked at 'im and told 'im to go on away because he was too strong.

" 'Big Sixteen, ye might git out of order and wouldn't be nobody to handle you.'

" 'Wal, I got to go someplace.'

" 'Try the other place.'

"So Big Sixteen went till he got to the gate of Hell. Behind dem gates the debil's children was playin' hide an' seek.

"Soon as they see Big Sixteen they run to their Mammy an' cry:

" 'Dat big man is dere what near killed Pappy.'

"She called 'em in quick in de house and shut the door tight.

" 'Ye ain't comin' in here,' she cried to Big Sixteen.

" 'Got t' go someplace.'

" 'Wal, seein' it's ye, here's a piece o' red-hot coal, go 'way an' start a hell o' your own.'

"So Big Sixteen went off . . .

"When ye see a jack-o'-lantern in de night, y' know it's Big Sixteen with his piece o' red-hot coal lookin' for a place to go to."

One said, "Give us somethin' to wet our goozles wid so we kin swallow dat lie."

"Yes, everybody believes signs or somepin."

The Ghost the Whole Town Knew

I will tell you the strangest ghost-mystery story I have ever told and I have told no end of ghost stories. What is more, you will agree with me when you are through reading it.

Most ghosts you and I know or have heard about are grown-up or old folks and are found in old deserted houses or churches or in broken-down barns or cemeteries. Not this ghost. This one was a very young girl who came in full daylight to a fine old mansion used as a finishing school for girls of her own age.

This strange tale actually happened in the year 1870 in Memphis, the King Cotton city. The newspapers wrote about it for months, the whole town took part in it, and there are folks today who'll tell you that their grandparents remember the affair as if it happened yesterday.

It begins after the death of little Lizzie Davidson, the daughter of Colonel Davidson, a wealthy planter. She was a lovely child and when she died she was buried in her favorite pink dress.

In the same city and at the same time, blue-eyed, blond-haired Clara Robertson, the daughter of a well-known lawyer, was a student in the most fashionable finishing school in the city. The school was in a fine old Southern mansion with while columns, and was attended by the daughters of the best families.

On the morning of January 1, 1871, Clara was in the music room practicing her piano lesson. Suddenly she heard a slight noise in back of her, turned around—and saw a sight that stopped her heart beating.

There stood a little girl about her own age, but smaller, thin

The Ghost the Whole Town Knew 251

shoulders and shrunken, with dull sunken eyes. She wore a pink dress bespattered all over with greenish, earthy mold. You could not see the flesh on her hands. Her dress smelled of earth and the grave.

Clara was frightened to death. She jumped off her stool and ran to the next room where her teacher was.

"There's a ghost in my room," came from her pale lips.

"There are no ghosts, child," said the teacher, who was busy at the moment. "Don't be afraid, Clara, dear," she added kindly. "You are just a little nervous. Go back to your piano. Don't be afraid. Just go back to your work."

Clara went back slowly; she was a courageous girl. She stopped at the door and peeked into the room. It was empty. There was no ghost!

"Maybe the teacher was right! Maybe I was just seeing things."

She finished her piano practice, a little nervous, then went home and told her parents about the ghost.

Her parents agreed that the teacher was right and tried to make her forget what had happened. Clara, healthy and young, soon forgot the ghost.

A few days later, she was all alone in the schoolyard—and there stood the ghost of the little girl again. Clara turned pale. She was too frightened to run away.

"Don't be scared," the little ghost said in a dull, low voice. "I won't hurt you. I'm Lizzie Davidson. I have come to tell you there is a treasure buried under the big tree in this yard. It's in a big glass jar, the kind drugstores have in their windows. You must dig for it at midnight. Get it and then wait until I come to tell you what to do." Then the little ghost disappeared as if the air had swallowed her.

Clara went home and told her parents what had happened.

Her father listened and then said smilingly, "Well, it can't do any harm digging away. We'll do as your girl friend said."

Mrs. Robertson told the tale to a friend and pretty soon every one in Memphis knew about it.

A few nights later, Mr. Robertson, accompanied by a few friends armed with shovels and lanterns, went out on their strange adventure. Picture their surprise when they came to the school mansion and found nearly the whole town milling all around—white folks, black folks, folks from everywhere who had heard of the ghost and the digging.

Nonetheless, Mr. Robertson and his friends went to work with picks and shovels by the light of the lanterns.

They dug carefully, since the ghost had said the treasure was in a glass jar. Pretty soon one of the men felt something solid and with great care a mud-covered jar was found.

There was dead silence in the crowd when they heard the news. Mr. Robertson put his hand into the jar and brought out a few packages wrapped in brown paper and a big heavy envelope.

"It will be simpler to examine the contents at home by better light," Mr. Robertson said.

They put back the packages and envelope and went home.

Right then the ghost appeared to Clara.

"Clara," she said quietly, "the packages in the jar must not be opened for sixty days. You must obey me, otherwise all will be lost." Then she vanished.

Clara told this to her father.

"Daughter, since what the ghost has said has come true, we might as well obey her and wait." He then announced that the contents of the packages and envelope would not be opened for sixty days.

The whole city of Memphis was now agog. Old and young, rich and poor, white and black spoke of that treasure jar. The officers of the city were so deeply interested that Mr. Robertson decided to engage the Old Greenlaw Opera House on Second Street for the opening of the jar.

Each waiting day brought more nervousness and a weird, eerie fear to the folks of Memphis. The year of 1871 has been remembered ever since.

Folks began to be afraid to go out at night. They were scared to walk in dark alleys. Women were frightened when they heard creaking noises, and children cried when they were left alone. The whole city was under a communal cloud of fear.

In Beale Street folks spoke in low tones. Everyone seemed to have a queer feeling of an unknown dread or disaster. Men in drinking places ordered "ghost drinks."

Day and night folks spoke of the "ghost," and Mr. Robertson became worried. Robberies in Memphis were common in those days. He therefore hid the jar in his garden behind one of the little outhouses.

All the town was waiting for the night it would be opened in the Opera House.

One evening after supper Mr. Robertson thought he heard a noise in his backyard. Worried about the treasure he had hidden, he went out to investigate. . . .

Just what happened he could not explain later. All he knew was that when he walked towards the place where the jar was hidden he was suddenly hit a terrible blow over his head and fell down unconscious. When he regained consciousness, he ran to the hiding place and—the glass jar was gone!

And it was never found. But the ghost was not completely gone!

One day when Clara was walking in the schoolyard with a friend of hers called Lula, there stood the ghost of Lizzie Davidson once again before her.

"Clara," she whispered, "in that jar there was two thousand dollars in gold crowns, a set of jewelry and a diamond necklace, and some very valuable papers."

"Lula! Lula!" cried Clara, "there is that ghost again. Do you see her?"

"No, I don't see her," Lula said.

The ghost vanished and was never seen again, and Memphis slowly returned to its normal life.

The Power of Woman and the Strength of Man

When God made man and woman, he put 'em in a house to live. Woman was just as strong as man and when they got to fighting, they'd always come out even.

One day Man says to himself: "Ah'm gonna see God 'bout this. Ah'm tired fightin' with that woman Ah can't beat." So he went to heaven and came before the Lord.

"Lord," says Man, "nobody can ease man's spirits ceptin' you. With the star shinin' from you, help me. Ah ask you, Lord, t' give me more strength, so's Ah kin beat that woman. You just can't be bothered comin' down on dis here earth all the time to straighten out things between us. Make me stronger so's Ah kin straighten 'em out mahself. Give me just a little more strength."

"All right," says God. "Now you got more strength than Woman."

Man, he run all the way from heaven till he come to his home. Soon 's he got to his house he holler: "Woman, here's yo' boss. God give me more strength and now Ah'm yo' boss."

Woman starts fightin', but he beats her. She tries again, he beats her the second time. Woman starts again, and he beats her the third time.

Man was mighty proud of himself.

"You be good or Ah'll put plenty water in yo' eyes."

Woman was mad. "We see 'bout that," she say.

The next day she goes to the Lord.

"Lord, Ah come before you to give me mah strength Ah used to have."

"You got all the strength you used to have, but your man's got more."

"How come? He can beat me now and he couldn't do that befoh."

"He got more strength because he come and ask for it and Ah gave it to him."

"Please, God, give me the same 's he's got or maybe you take away what you give him."

"What Ah give Ah never take back. You just got to put up with it."

Woman went home mighty mad, and on the way she meets the Devil and tells him the trouble she got.

"Listen to me and you'll make out ahead o' man. Take that frown from yo face, turn around, and go back to God and tell 'im to give you the keys hanging on the nail near the door. Then bring 'em to me and Ah'll tell you what to do with 'em."

Woman, she climbs back to heaven.

"Woman," says the Lord cross-like, "what you want now?"

"Oh God! Master o' the rainbow, you kin put the stars in their place!"

"Woman, Ah ask you what you want."

"Gimme them keys hanging on that nail."

"Well, take 'em and don't be botherin' me no moh."

So Woman take the keys and went clippety clip to the Devil.

"Ah sees you got them three keys," Devil says.

"Ah got 'em all right."

"Them three keys," Devil says, "they got moh power and strength 'n man ever got if you handle 'em right. Now, take them keys and go home. First thing, you lock the door to the kitchen. Man always thinks of his stomach first. Second key is fo' the door of yo' sleeping place. Lock that. Man don't like to be shut off from his sleep. Last key is fo' the room where you rocks yo' cradle with yo' child. Lock that. Man loves his children and want to see his generation."

Then the Devil says: "Now, don't you unlock them doors until Man uses his strength for your benefit and your desires."

Woman run home and did just that. When Man come home, she was setting on the porch, rocking and singing:

> "Peck on the wood
> "An' make the cradle swing."

When Man saw the three doors what used to stand wide open strong locked, he swelled up like pine lumber after rain.

First he tried to break 'em open, for he figured his strength 'd beat 'em.

When he saw he couldn't, he bellered, "Woman, who locked them doors? Where 'd ye get the keys from to lock 'em?"

"God gave 'em to me."

"We see 'bout that!" he cried and rushed to God.

"Woman locked me out from mah vittles an mah generation and mah sleep. She say You give her the keys."

"Deed Ah did. She asked for 'em and Devil showed her how to use 'em."

"God! Give me keys so Ah kin unlock them doors and she don't get no control over me."

"No, Man," said the Lord, "What Ah give, Ah give. Woman got them keys and she kin keep 'em. You go and ask Woman to open the doors fo you."

Man returned, but all his arguments wouldn't make Woman unlock the doors. He kept on asking all the time and when he asked and did what she wanted, she opened the doors.

But Man wasn't satisfied at all. He said to the woman after a little, "Tell you what, Woman. Let's divide up. You give me half yo' keys and Ah'll give you half mah strength."

"Ah wanta think 'bout that."

Woman, she sit and think and Devil pops in at the window and says, "Tell 'm No, Woman. Let 'im keep his strength and you keep yo' keys. Just remember when fly time comes, cow needs a good tail."

So Woman would not trade with Man. Ever since that time Man had to mortgage his strength to live with Woman.

> That's why Man makes
> And Woman takes.

The Gladiator, the Belle, and the Good Snowstorm

This is the tale they tell around Memphis, Tennessee, when it was a small town, free, fancy, and open.

One time the "better folks" of the town decided to have a free and fancy costume ball. There was great excitement among the younger folks, each trying to create a more unusual costume than the others.

Now, among these better folks there was a young gentleman, tall, handsome, and genteel, who was quite proud of his appearance. Whenever he had a chance, he liked to show his muscular body and, therefore, he decided to come dressed as a gladiator to show his fine physique.

He put a crown of leaves around his forehead, arranged a short tunic, white as snow, around his torso, and wore sandals on his feet.

The young "gladiator" naturally invited a Southern belle as his partner for the ball. She had decided on quite a different costume. She was dressed as a Russian maiden. She wore a fine, heavy embroidered blouse, and an embroidered skirt and boots. Over her blouse she had a white sheepskin coat that was also embroidered.

So the two came to the ball as did many other young people of the town, and there was a gay and mirthful evening with flirting, dancing, eating, and drinking. An orchestra of fiddlers, also dressed in costumes, played for the dancers.

It was truly a spirited evening full of Southern glee . . . until there was a cry: "A snowstorm has come up!" So it had, a wild wind and tearing sharp flakes. It soon became a blizzard, a bobcat-wind whipping the snow in all directions. The music stopped and the gaiety changed almost to a panic.

"How to get home!" On every girl's lips and in every male's mind the thought: "How will we get home!"

You must remember that in those days there were no public vehicles to be found in the streets of a small town. Nor were there telephones to ask parents or relatives to come with carriages or horses. So all started out on foot as best they could.

In short time the dance hall was empty except for the gladiator and his Russian belle. The young man naturally was worried about going out into the icy wind and cold snow with near no clothes on. The young lady waited politely, though a little annoyed.

After a time she said: "Charles, I must go home, I can't stay here all night."

"Maybe the blizzard 'll stop!" It came hesitatingly from him.

"It may go on all the night and if you don't want to take me home, I'll just have to go alone."

Of course no gentleman would permit this.

"Very well, let us go," he said.

The two, he with little clothing and barefoot sandals, she in sheepskin coat and good boots, started out bravely in the wildly dancing snow. She held on tight to his arm, for the tearing wind often threw them off their feet. It buffeted them in all directions and nearly tore Charles's tunic off.

Head down, teeth set, and miserably cold, he plodded on, the belle holding on to his arm—until they finally reached her home.

Whether she was angry or displeased with Charles, or disappointed in the evening, or perhaps because she was too cold to think, the pretty belle never asked her escort into the house.

"It's very late, Charles, I just can't wake my pa, my ma, and ask you to come in."

Charles saw quickly there was no use "sowing seeds" in the snow, so he bade her a short good night and began plodding to his own home.

The snow was not falling as thick, but the wind was going like whipped wildcats. His wet, thin tunic was flapping crazy in the wind and his feet in the thin sandals were nearly frozen stiff.

The Gladiator, the Belle, and the Good Snowstorm 259

Struggling, reeling, falling, he made slow progress nearing his home.

In those days, the town had its night constable who walked with his lantern through the streets to see that all was well. Memphis, too, had its constable and his name was Floyd. Right now he too was floundering through the snow in as good a frame of mind as the weather.

When he saw the ghostly half-naked man . . . or woman . . . struggling through the snow, he stopped, mouth and eyes wide open.

"That sure is a ghost with the flopping rags, coming straight from the grave or maybe my eyes have just gone wrong," he mumbled.

He was a brave man, so he stopped grimly and turned his lantern on the spook. Just imagine his shock when he recognized Charles, for he knew him and his family.

"What! . . . Charles, are ye drunk? Have ye gone daffy? Have ye gone crazy? If ye ain't, I'm sure gonna take ye to the caboose and charge ye with parading in the street with indecent clothes."

He ran up to the poor fellow who was standing with teeth chattering like drumsticks and body shaking as if he had St. Vitus dance.

Charles tried to speak, but it was difficult:

"I'm not d-d-d-drunk an' I'm not c-c-c-crazy, I'm freezing! I'm c-c-coming from the b-b-ball."

Floyd looked at him. The poor fellow looked so miserable, he couldn't tell him what a fool he was, so he just took him by the arm to help him battle the wind. Heads down and without talking, they plodded along until they reached Charles's home. . . .

I do not think the young gladiator ever saw the young belle again nor did I hear that he ever went to a ball dressed as a gladiator again.

Beale Street Folks

Ours is a land big as the biggest. Everything is big: we have big rivers and big mountains, big mines and great big woods, and we have big cities and big towns full of big folks. In the cities, in the towns, in the mines, and in the rivers there are big tales about folks and animals and everything.

One of the cities that has no end of tales is the King Cotton city in these United States. One time, long ago, it was called Saktilafa, which means, in Indian language, the banks that have no end of ridges made by the water washing away. But now it is called Memphis.

Every street in Memphis has no end of tales about it, most of all Beale Street. That street is known from one end of the country to the other. It begins right on the Mississippi River and goes down to the muddy bottoms folks call East Street.

In the early days, white folks lived there in great twenty-two-room mansions. But the street was mighty hot. When the sun shone down on it, it was like an iron furnace. So white people moved away and black people moved in, thinking they could cool it off. And they sure did, and brought a different kind of heat, the warmth of great singing and dancing.

There are a thousand stories about that Beale Street, too long for me to tell you all now. So I'll just give you a taste of them, a few little stories about two of the folks who lived there. I'll tell you about Steamboat Bill and Cherry Malone. They still talk about them out there. I heard all about them when I was there.

Now, some called Steamboat Bill by another name; they called

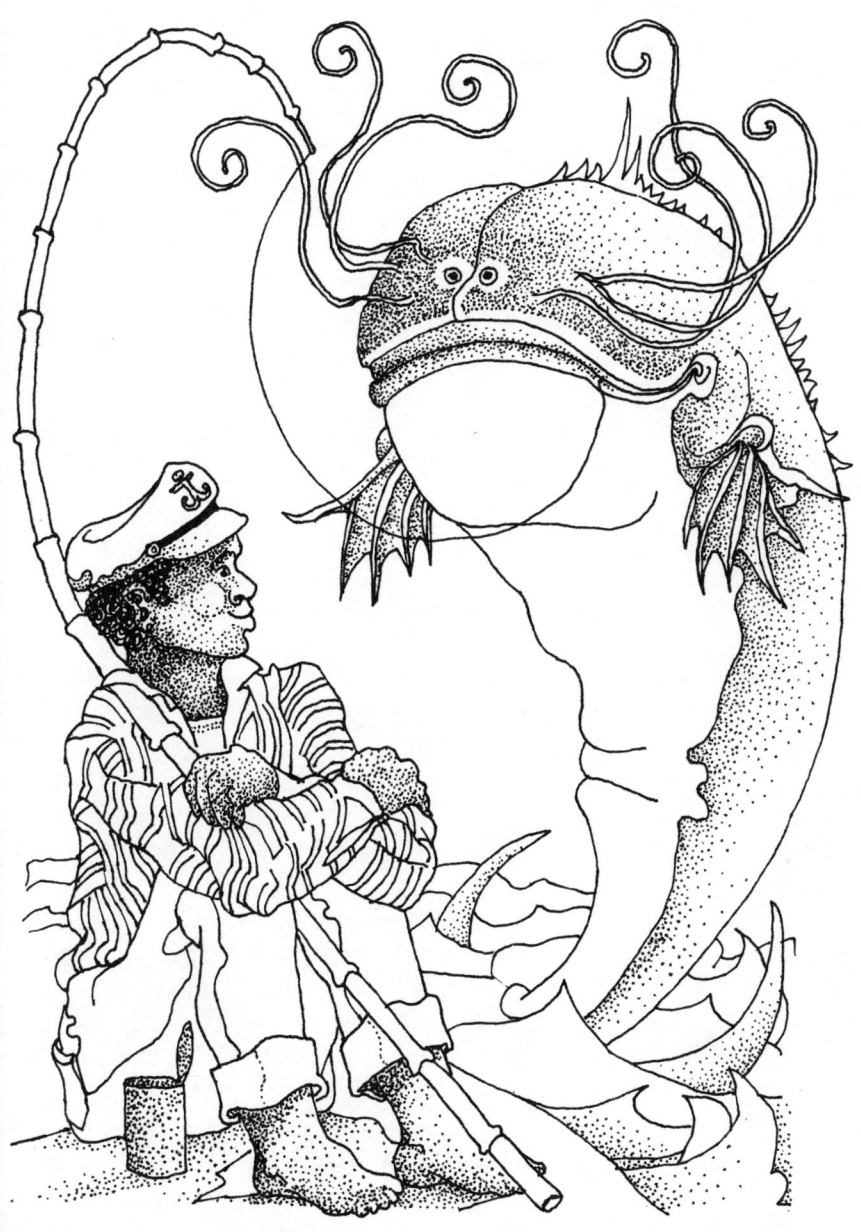

He brought back a catfish big as a boat.

him John Henry. He could outwork, outplay, outfight, outsing all the other rousters on the Mississippi River. They still sing about him, just as they sang in those days:

> Ashes to ashes
> An' dus' to dus'
> If Bill don' get yo
> De river mus'.

And he could eat! Lord, how he could eat! He'd finish more catfish than half the folks on Beale Street. Here's what happened one time.

One day he went fishing and when he came back, he brought a catfish big as a boat.

Folks young and old got around him, looking and shouting:

"Where'd yo git that fish, big as a whale in the ocean? Did you catch 'im with a hook with a rabbit for bait or with an iron cotton hook? Maybe yo finished 'im with a sling and a stone like David did to Goliath."

Steamboat Bill, he just laughed to shake the houses down on Beale Street and said:

"Got a Luck Bag 'round mah neck, big muscles in mah arms, an' eagle eyes in mah head. Ah jest come to that river and throws out mah hook an' looks.

"Pretty soon there come a-swimmin' along that giant catfish and he look at me. Ah look at 'im. Told you ah got eagle eyes. Ah look and says: 'C'm on, you great big catfish! Ah's waitin' foh you!'

"Catfish, he look at me a long time, then he shake his head and says: 'No use battlin' Steamboat Bill. Might as well give in without arguin'.'"

That's how Beale Street had the biggest catfish fry of the year and the best singing and dancing of the year.

I could tell you many more tales about Steamboat Bill, but now I'm going to tell you instead about Cherry Malone.

Cherry Malone was six feet tall and weighed a hundred and seventy-five pounds and no fat on her either. She was a big black woman who could beat every man, woman, or policeman in the King Cotton city. She never needed help of any weapon. She said any rouster who'd fight with a razor, gun, or blackjack was a "low-flung coward" who didn't know the blessing of good strong fists.

The law was her best friend, for she was always helping the police when they had trouble with men working around.

There's still more. She could win more money and quicker than any man in a gambling house. There was no woman like her in all of Tennessee.

One day she learned that a rich lady for whom she had worked had died poor 's a church mouse and was going to be buried in a pauper's grave. There wasn't enough money to bury her decently.

When Cherry heard that, she went straight to the undertaker. Her eyes were blazing and she set her hands on her hips.

"That white woman was to me like a mother. She ain't gonna be buried in no pauper's grave. Don't yo be puttin' mah mistress in a pauper's grave. Yo jest keep her here till Ah come back and it ain't gonna be a long time neither."

She left and went straight to a "fancy" place in the city. Men stood before polished counters with brass rails. Other men with long beards sat before tables playing away their life's work and fortunes. Roustabouts with pants rolled up and cotton hooks * in their belts stood around watching.

Cherry Malone came in, head high, and sat down at one of the tables.

"Ah'm here," she said. "C'm on. Ah'm gonna try mah luck. Got a brand new Luck Bag round mah neck an' got to save mah mistress from a pauper's grave. C'm on, Ah's ready."

She didn't stay long and she didn't work hard, but when she went out, she had five hundred good American dollars. At the door she shouted to the crowd:

"Don't try no 'Gravy Train' † on me! Got to use that money to give mah mistress a decent burial."

She came to the undertaker and put the five hundred dollars on the table.

"Mister, here's mah money to give mah mistress a decent grave," she said.

---

* To pick up bails of cotton.
† When anyone won a good deal of money, his friends would follow wherever he went until he treated the crowd. That was called the Gravy Train.

"Miss Malone, that's too much money for the burial," the undertaker said.

"Put what's left over in flowers foh mah mistress, she sure is worth it."

So Cherry Malone's mistress had the finest burial with the finest flowers ever seen in King Cotton city.

That was the kind of folks who lived on Beale Street in Memphis on the Mississippi, and that's the kind of deeds they did.

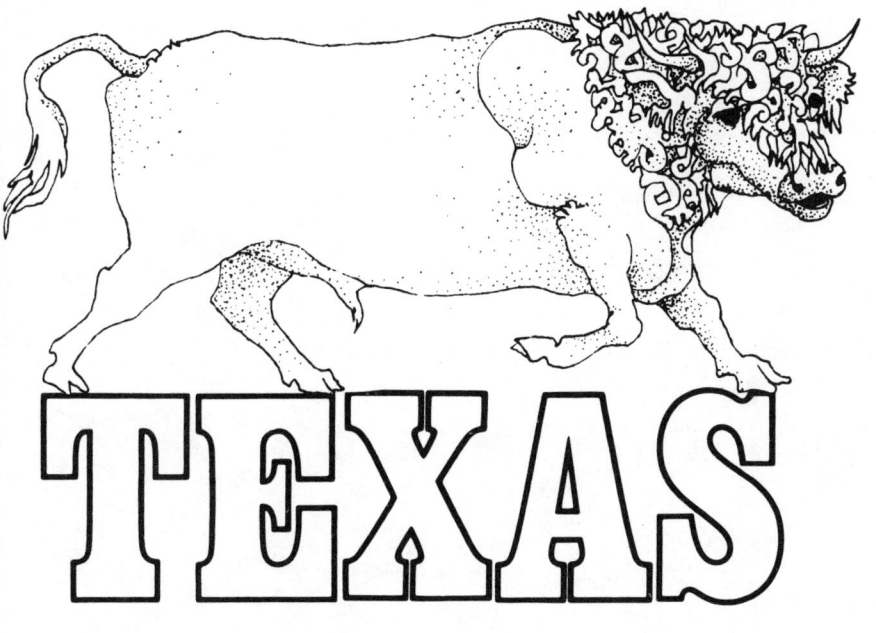

The Karankawa from the Great Gleaming Oyster Shells

Now it is Galveston Island and white folks live there, but in the aforetime years the Karankawa Indians hunted in the cool woods of the long island filled with weaving sunlight. They fished in the ever-moving waters around the rich narrow land. They were happy. How did they come there?

The great golden Sun God and the wondrous silver shiny Moon Goddess, both roaming over land and sea, were husband and wife. Soon they had a son, the first Indian child.

"We must give him a cradle," the Moon mother said. She took two giant oyster shells, pearly gray, shining like her face on summer nights and set them on the white clouds.

"This will be his cradle, and the clouds moving high over the waters will rock him to sleep." So it happened. The white fleecy clouds floated over the glittering gulf and rocked the boy to sleep.

One day the Sun God and the Moon Goddess had a silly, black quarrel. One said one thing; the other, another. And in the green heat of their anger, the gleaming gray oyster cradle was pushed off the white cloud. The oyster shells closed quickly to make sure no harm would come to the cradle and the child when they hit the water.

Down! Down! the cradle dropped until it touched the foam of the Gulf of Mexico. The waves were happy to have the child. They rose and fell softly, just as the clouds had, and the child slept and played to the singing moving of the water.

But in the heaven there was sadness. The Sun God and the Moon Goddess missed their son. The father was brooding in the great silence of the world and the mother was crying streams of tears. The tears fell on the Earth and the Earth drank the good rain that gave life to roots lying deep. (Ever since, there have been rich rains along the lands of the Gulf.)

"Our son is lonely on the great water. He should have a playmate," the mother said. "He is more lonesome than a single bird flying over the world."

"We must send him a companion to play with him," said his father.

So the two, father and mother, sent down a girl, lovely as a seaflower. She came into the Gulf waters in a cradle of glistening pearl-gray oyster shells. The silver-green waves moved the two close together.

They played with the fish from the deep waters and with the gray birds touching the foam that was forever coming and going.

They grew up together, loved each other, and married at the right time. They had many children who lived with them on the long green island in the singing waters of the Gulf of Mexico.

One day the two parents died, and they were buried in the giant gray gleaming oyster shells in which they had come from the clouds.

Their descendants, the Karankawa Indians, who lived many years on the island white men called Galveston, always held the gray gleaming oyster shells in great veneration, for they remembered that their forebears had come in the shells from the white clouds in the Heaven.

How Joe Became Snaky Joe

Up around Big Spring in Howard County, Texas, runs a tale 'd bring a horse laugh to a gang of seven-day-stampeded waddies. It's the tale about Snaky Joe.

Joe was one of the gang in the Road Ranch in the eastern part of the county that was out for a fall roundup and branding. They were sitting around with chow and black coffee. Soon the Bossman sang out:

"There's lots o' calves got to be branded, c'm'on an' get goin'."

The men got up easy-like to get their mounts, most of which were span pintos. There was plenty to do. Many of the hobbles were broken and that meant trouble getting those cayuses.*

Joe, long and lean, with a face that looked like a horse, walked around, lasso in hand, looking for his pony. The ground was pretty broken up, what with the stampeding of the cattle and the digging of prairie dogs. It wasn't easy walking, and pretty soon, plunk! he fell into a gopher hole. There he was, pinned to the ground, never knowing there was a rattler lying in that hole. The varmint got mighty angry for being stepped on, so he dug his fangs into Joe's bony ankle. Joe jumped up mighty scared, seeing what bit him. He yelled once or twice, but every waddy was busy with his own business. There was nothing he could do except pour on the wound all the tobacco juice he could pour out o' him and trust in the good Lord.

He sat there biting his teeth together, but there wasn't any pain

---

* Bronco or Indian ponies. Originally, ponies raised by the Cayuse Indians.

in the ankle, so he figured he was O.K. Up he got and started looking for his pinto again.

He looked and he looked, but that pony of his had gone far away. So he sat down to rest a spell because that ankle was hurting just a little. He was too mad to see where he was sitting and so that fool waddy sat down right on a rattler again. Hard luck was sure following him.

The rattler didn't like Joe on top of him, so he sank his fangs right into the seat of Joe's hard-ridden leather breeches. Those breeches were hard 's an alligator's hide and, once the fangs were in, the critter couldn't get 'em out. When Joe got up, the varmint couldn't get off and hung on like a tick in a fat dog. Joe was so set on finding his pony that he didn't feel the hanging rattler. He had spotted his pony and was hot after it. When he was near enough, he threw his lasso and got that cayuse of his.

Leading the pony, he picked up his saddle and put it on. He tightened the girth and got ready to mount.

The pony smelled the snake hanging on Joe's pants and tried to get away. It pulled hard and ran hither and yon with Joe hanging on.

The rattler, dangling on the pants, didn't like the throwing around right and left and tried to get its fangs loose. But those were tough pants and he was just flinging about. Joe was beginning to feel the weight in the back, so he turned around to see what it was and saw . . . the snake!

He began yelling and jumping up and down to get the snake off while holding the pulling, running, snorting, plunging, rearing pony!

Hearing Joe yell, the other hands rushed up. When the cowpokes saw the queer sight, they began howling and dancing and roaring with laughter. It was a sight to make a solemn preacher hold his sides. They danced around the whirling, yelling Joe trying to pull the snake off his pants and holding the reins of the rearing pinto. They threw their sombreros high in the air, yelling, "Yippee-eye-ay! Go it, Joe! Y'll git that rattler yit!"

Joe was getting out o' breath from running around with that pony and worrying about the rattler in the back. Pretty soon his pinto, near frightened-loco, knocked him down, trampling on him.

"Yippee-eye-ay! Go it, Joe! Y'll git that rattler yit!"

Then some waddies jumped in, got hold of the pony, while others pulled off the dangling snake, making short work of it. . . .

Joe rose after a time and got his quieted pony and pretty soon every waddy, still laughing, was at work lariating and branding.

Come eating time, they sat around, branding irons and ropes on the side, eating "son-of-a-gun" stew and drinking black coffee. The talk was about Joe, now "Snaky Joe," and how he kept going around without a stop. And the story has kept on going around ever since. That's how come you hear it now.

The White Buffalo

White magic has been called good magic, and through the years white animals are said to have had this good white magic. There are endless tales about these animals. There are great stories about white elephants and about white unicorns, those one-horned creatures of medieval days. There is a splendid story of the White Whale; stories about white deer; there is many a tale of white bears; and there is a grand story of the White Buffalo in Texas. It's the kind of tale you would expect in Texas.

It happened many years ago when Texas was still a vast buffalo country, where huge herds moved over the endless plains like giant black clouds in the sky. . . .

Around Wolf Creek, in the most northern part of Texas, Indians, on wild-maned ponies, hunted the buffaloes for food, clothes, and shelter. They followed the tremendous, tramping, roving herds across the green sea of grass.

One day a band of Comanche warriors with bows, arrows, and tomahawks were hunting. Suddenly they halted their wild ponies in wide-eyed surprise! In that black, weltering mass was—a White Buffalo! They never had heard of one, never had seen one. He ran differently from the others. Head high, he seemed to lord them. Now he was stamping wildly on a path made for him by the others. Then he circled around them like a bird floating in the air. A giant white beast-bird!

The Indians regained their courage and charged in the direction of the magnificent creature, but they didn't come any nearer him.

"Maybe it is a buffalo sacred to the Great Spirit."

"No, he just doesn't seem like the others. We will get him."

The ponies dashed and circled with their riders. The Indians shot at the buffalo, threw their tomahawks. Nothing reached him. The giant white animal, head up, came near, then floated away as if playing a game. Darkness came and the men went to their encampment with their booty—but without the White Buffalo.

The next hunt—the same. The great black herd and in its midst the White Buffalo gleaming like a Comanche moon. The Indians hunted wildly, shot arrows, tried to encircle him, dashed at him, but every time they thought they had him, he just floated away. . . .

There was fierce anger in the Indian band, shamed pride. The White Buffalo became a hateful sight. Again and again the men charged, drew their bows with all their might, but the giant beast always floated away.

"He is a ghost!"

So it went on moon after moon. Bands of Comanches came together to hunt the White Buffalo. The chiefs had decided to get him dead or alive. They hunted till their throats were dry and the ponies were stumbling. The White Buffalo never tired; he just stampeded the rest of the herd so they ran wildly in all directions. But he, the great Chief Creature, floated over them all.

Moons and moons and moons went by. The only ones who hunted the great White Buffalo were those who did not know that he was a "ghost buffalo." He was never brought down.

The buffalo herds became smaller and smaller, for now white men were not hunting them, but slaughtering them by the thousands to make big money. But the White Creature was still with his herd, and no man, red or white, could get him.

One day a group of hunters was trying to slaughter a whole herd that had the White Buffalo in it. They felt sure they would get him. Suddenly a wild Norther was seen across the far horizon.

Do you know what a Texas Norther is? The sun is shining hot enough to burn flesh, the sky is clear. Then—black, big, ragged clouds come racing along the blue. It suddenly turns cold enough to freeze boiling water and it begins to blow! Ice-cold wind tearing along madly, breaking, ripping everything in its way! Freezing rain and sleet shoot down from above.

The White Buffalo saw the darkening in the sky. He knew what was coming. In an instant he stampeded the herd! A freezing curtain of cold was coming toward them!

Taking the lead, he rose high in the air! So it seemed! All the other animals raced after him!

Sleet! Rain thick as a blanket poured down! The black water was as thick as black earth. Black rain! Sleet! Fierce wind! Then it cleared. . . .

Indians and white folk say that the furious Norther picked up the ghost White Buffalo and his herd and carried them to happy hunting grounds. There they would be ever at peace from the hated white hunters.

The Ghosts of Stampede Mesa

No cattleman driving a herd will bed them on Stampede Mesa that runs through Dockum Flats down Texas way. It's full of moaning, wild-riding ghosts bringing hard luck to heads and horns.

Cowboys have seen them and heard them. Heard a screaming voice in the black, windy night, calling crazy for cows. Seen a nester * tied to his racing horse, horse and rider blindfolded, and two skeleton riders behind yelling and screaming, driving the horse with lariat and whips. They'd be racing over the mesa till they came to the bluff and there the blinded horse and rider would leap crazy over to be shattered in the wind.

That's the nester's punishment for stampeding fifteen hundred head of cattle in revenge for losing a couple of heifers that had mixed up in the herd, and it's his punishment for bringing death to two good cowboys.

Some folks say it's only tumbleweeds driven by the wind, but others who know tell this tale.

Old man Sawyer, tired and worn, was driving his herd of fifteen hundred cattle to the market. He was frazzled and weary-footed. Not enough hands to help, not enough grass to keep cattle sleek. But that day he felt he had a rabbit's chance. He was coming to a good mesa. A good piece of tableland with a gentle slope off one side, plenty of good grass and water handy. Just the same, he and the men were fouled and frazzled. Cattle were strung out in a long line, trekking slowly. Sometime along the afternoon some cowboys saw five or six cows belonging to a nester straying into the herd. Cowhands didn't like this because it always brought trouble, but they went on just the same.

The cattle were bawling; the men were weary, dusty, and aching for a rest when they saw the mesa in the distance. Just at that time, the nester came racing along. He was screaming like an angry cock:

"Ah want mah cows out o' that mangy herd. An' ah want 'em right now!"

Old man Sawyer was a tough *hombre* and in a mean mood. He'd been looking at his steers that were gaunt and sore-footed.

"Git! Come back when I don't feel like the Devil in the belfrey."

"I'll give you time," said the nester. "If my cattle ain't out o' your

---

* An unwanted farmer in cattle-grazing lands. Cattlemen and nesters were fierce enemies.

The Ghosts of Stampede Mesa

outfit by midnight, I swear by rattlesnakes I'll stampede yer whole blasted herd."

If you don't know what stampeding is, I'll tell you. It's suddenly scaring cattle so they go wild, tearing blindly in any and every way. It often means their death. The smallest disturbance, wild shouting, or a stray shot will start such a stampede. The only way a stampede can be stopped is by "milling" the cattle—making them go round and round in circles. No man in his right senses will ever stampede a herd.

Old man Sawyer looked at the nester, then he said slowly:

"Don't ye be stampedin' my herd. If ye do, it'll be the last stampedin' ye'll do on this earth o' Texas. Git!" His hand was on his six-shooter.

"Ah'm goin', but Ah'll be back midnight fer mah cattle. Ef ah don't git em. . . . Ah told ye." Then he rode off.

The herd struggled up the slope to the mesa. They drank, nibbled a little grass, and nested down for the night.

On the south side of that mesa there was a steep and very dangerous cliff and there Sawyer put two cowboys as guards. He'd have put more, but he was short of men. Besides, he figured the herd was at peace and didn't need much guarding.

The two cowhand guards thought the same and they quickly went to sleep among the cattle.

It was a dark night with no moon and all silent except the breathing of the cattle, lowing now and then.

Midnight came, and there was the nester toting along slowly up the mesa. He rode around, saw the sleeping cowboys, and slowly took out his six-shooter. Then he let out wild screaming yells and began firing!

At the first sound of the shooting, the cattle, wild with fear, began running in all directions away from their bedding, butting one another, tearing into one another and . . . making straight for the steep bluff!

The two guards, Sawyer, and the other cowboys awoke in an instant and tried frantically to mill the herd. But the maddened animals couldn't be stopped! They leaped blindly over the jagged, deep edge of the mesa to their end.

All the shouting and wild riding of Sawyer and his men were of no use. The thunder of the hoofs of the bellowing steers around them was a mad hurricane let loose. In the end, all the cattle were over the cliff!

The two guards were also pulled by the cattle over the precipice!

Sawyer and the men left stood around black and grim, none saying a word. After a time Sawyer said, "Go, git the nester. Bring him alive, on his horse."

The men rode off without saying a word. Sawyer remained on his horse, head down, silent, thinking thoughts blacker 'n thick smoke!

In two hours' time the men came with the nester riding between them. Sawyer was still sitting on his horse as they had left him.

For a time Sawyer looked straight in the nester's face without saying a word. Then he turned to his men and said, "Blindfold the horse and tie the rat to it."

The men did as they were ordered.

"What 're ye gonna do?" the nester cried, turning green as grass.

"I'm gonna send ye to find yer cows and look for the two cowhands ye murdered." Then, to his men:

"Take 'm near the edge and let him see the way."

They took the screaming nester near the jagged edge of the bluff and gave the horse a slight flip that sent it flying over the edge. . . .

In the morning the bodies of the two cowboys were given a decent burial. The nester was left with the dead steers.

Since that time that mesa's been called Stampede Mesa and since then every herd bedded on that mesa has been stampeded before morning.

Cowhands say it's the ghosts of the two cowboys riding after a screaming nester on a blindfolded horse does the stampeding. Others say it's old woman's talk, and that it's the tumbleweeds driven by the wind frightens the herds. Who knows?

Only in Texas

No mess of tales about Texas is full until you have a tale about Roy Bean. Roy Bean, the most famous judge of the biggest state in these United States of North America, until Alaska came limping along and messed it all up.

That man learned to be a lawyer, but he was lots of other things besides. He was a mayor and a teacher and a barber. He was a rustler and a bartender; he was a cook and he was a shoemaker and a preacher. He was almost everything a man could be, jumping from one to the other quicker than a spider on a hot stove. Then he got to be a judge. He was a judge the likes of which the world had never known.

There are a thousand tales of his famous decisions and each one is better than the other. I'm going to tell you about one case, and I know it will teach you all you want to learn about his way of judging. But I've got to tell you first that while he was a judge he also had a famous drinking place called The White Lily. But that wasn't his only business either. He was always ready to turn to any business that came along where he could catch a silver dollar.

One day a man blew into The White Lily who knew Judge Roy Bean pretty well.

"Judge," he said, "I saw a fine piece o' land down the river that 'd be just right for raisin' hogs. Hogs 's bringin' a good price, an' I'd like to go in the hog-raisin' business, but I ain't got the money to buy hogs. You got plenty o' money; lend me the money to buy hogs an' we'll be pardners. I'll do all the work and ye'll get half the profit when we sell 'em."

"Sounds good to me," said the judge, "I'm always ready to go into a business that'll bring shinin' silver dollars."

The man got the money and went out and bought a bunch of fine hogs. Pretty soon that place down the river was just full of fine fat hogs.

Time came to sell, and Judge Bean asked the man how he was doing with the hogs.

"Hogs is sellin' good, Judge, but feed's high as the sky an' our profits go into that feed. But I reckon pretty soon we'll be makin' money. Pretty soon."

"Pretty soon" was crawling like an oxcart. Months passed and then a year went by. More months were marching along and Judge Roy Bean was getting mad. He was thinking hard how to get his money and teach the man a lesson.

First he told the man he wanted to break the pardner business and get his money back.

"An agreement's an agreement, Judge," the man said, "an' no good judge 'd break it. Ye got to wait till times is better."

Judge Bean was thinking hard. Law was law and the judge had to see it through. He couldn't bring the fellow to court because he'd come to trial before himself, since Judge Bean was a partner. It was a hard nut to crack and Roy Bean was doing hot thinking till one day he made up his mind.

"I'm gonna sue that fellow in my own court an' break up that pardner business in the right law way. I'm gonna let Texas show all these United States that justice's got to win in the end. That man's been usin' my money mighty good, but I'm on the short end o' the limb. But I ain't gonna fall. No siree. I'll show 'm."

That's what Judge Bean was saying to his friends in The White Lily, and pretty soon everybody was waiting to see how the hog raising 'd shin up a thorn tree.

Then, one day that hog man got a summons signed by Judge Roy Bean to come to court.

The man was much surprised, but a summons is a summons, so he came to court. The whole town was there wondering what Judge Bean had in his boots.

There he sat before the table with his fat law book before him.

"Court come to order," Judge Bean roared. "Everything's got to be done accordin' to law. First I'm gonna choose a jury o' seven men. Twelve's too many."

He called seven men and they sat down not far from the table.

"Gentlemen of the jury," Judge Bean said, "I want t' bring to your notice a case of dishonesty. This here man"—pointing to the hog raiser—"this here man bought hogs with my good money. We were joined in legal pardnership. I with my money an' he with workin'. Profits from sellin' the hogs to be shared fifty-fifty atween us. This legal pardnership's been going on for near two years and even tho' that man's been sellin' hogs a-plenty, I've never gotten one red copper from him. Therefore, this here man, gentlemen of the jury, 's been guilty of dishonesty, an' I ask you gentlemen of the jury, in the name of justice, to find him guilty for defraudin' me of my share of the profits. What d'ye say, gentlemen of the jury?"

The hog-raiser stood looking from Judge Bean to the jury, not knowing what to say.

"Guilty," roared the seven jurymen.

"That's fine, gentlemen of the jury, and I thank ye for your fine decision.

"An' now," turning to the hog man who was standing open-mouthed, "I'm gonna pass judgment. The decision of this court is that the plaintiff—that is, me—get back from this dishonest man half o' that hog ranch for the money I put in it. Second, since you, my pardner, are guilty of dishonesty in our legal pardnership, I order the constable to sell at public auction your half of the hog ranch. That'll pay for the cost of this here trial and pay damages to me for what I've suffered havin' to go to the trouble of this here trial."

Roy Bean's pardner was still standin' speechless at the strange trial, the like of which had never happened, except in Texas, before Judge Roy Bean.

Texas Centipede Coffee

R. F. Smith, a grand ranger of Amarillo, tells this tale and says it is the kind of story that could happen only in Texas. And to prove it, he tells the exact spot where it took place—right up north, not far from Graham, a little way from Wichita Falls, where the winds are fresh as morning coffee!

Up there a fine Texas outfit was running horses in the open ranges. Horse-boss and waddies were a busy lot. At the crack of dawn men and mounts were up romping around, busy with this and that, waiting for the morning grub and . . . coffee.

Now, the boss of that outfit was the particularest man in Texas about his coffee. Most of the time he'd take the job off the pokey biscuit-shooter * and do it all himself.

Just remember that in the land of bow-legged men and wild steers, straight cowboy coffee in the morning, or any time, is sweeter than fiddling on Saturday night.

Would you like to know what straight cowboy coffee is? I'll tell you: Take a couple of pounds of coffee and wet it with water. Boil it for two hours, then throw in a horseshoe, boil it a little longer, and you'll get right waddy coffee.

This outfit had a three-gallon iron kettle to boil its favorite drink.

The boss man first washed the kettle to make sure it was clean. Next he filled it with clear water, set it a-boiling, and then put in plenty of fresh-ground strong coffee. Soon the pot was boiling and bubbling and the rich smell of tangy coffee floated through the air like a good spring wind.

* Cowboy cook.

All the men had sat down to biscuits and bacon, finishing with the rich steaming coffee. Every man had a good feeling of satisfaction. When breakfast was over, they got up friendly-like to get on their ponies. All but the boss, who liked to wash the coffee kettle again to make sure it was clean and ready for the next meal.

He rinsed the pot a few times and then put his hand in to make sure no grounds were left inside. When his fingers touched the bottom all around, he felt something kind o' soft and slithery. He picked it up and pulled it out. . . . Holy cows! it was a seven-inch-long *centipede!*

Ever hear of Texas centipedes? They're bugs with hundreds of legs and deadly poison in each one of those legs. A bite from one was sure death, and eating it was worse 'n drowning in a tar bucket!

That Horse-Boss was a God-fearing upright man and a good Texan. When he saw the terrible hundred-foot monster that had been cooking in the coffee, he turned whiter than a bleached sheet! That poison coffee would poison him and his whole outfit! He'd have to do what any decent Texas man would do. He let out a yowl good as a thousand coyotes for every man to come up. He was thinking hard and he was thinking fast. The men rode up.

"Men," he said, "I done somethin' awful. I cooked a poison centipede in yer coffee." He held up the limp, long bug in his hand. "Ef'n a poison bite from a centipede 'll kill a man, sure boilin' that poison critter in yer coffee made it poison coffee! It's more 'n twenty-five miles to Graham where we might git help! We'll never make it! There ain't no hope fer us. Ef we've got t' die, let's die like Texas men!"

The men got off their mounts slowly, each face set and grim. They sat down, waiting. . . . Some put their fingers down their throats to get the poison out, some used strong words that would burn holes in iron plates. One man hissed, " 'Twas the best coffee y' ever made!"

So they waited . . . waited . . . waited . . . for the centipede poison to work!

They waited and they waited. . . . An hour passed. Then slowly, slowly, the other hour crawled along and . . . nobody died! Not even a pain in the stomach.

The boss man was puzzled. "Maybe there ain't no poison in

a cooked centipede!" he grumbled. "Maybe a centipede can do no harm to a Texan pokey. I feel fine 's a ridin' son o' thunder."

"Me too," came from all around with a roaring happy relief.

"Yippee-eye-ay!" Big hats flew high up. "That coffee ain't gonna kill no waddy! . . . It was mighty fine coffee!"

There was laughing and high talk except for a few soreheads who didn't feel like joking at all.

"Boss, you bring that poison-scare willipus on us agin an' yer breakfast 'll be bears mixed with vinegar an' mange cure."

"Wal, boys, reckon it's better t' die from a cup o' the best coffee than from rheumatiz an' old age."

They all went to work full of good spirit and full . . . of good health.

The next morning the boss man said:

"I'm gonna do the coffee-making from beginning to end t' make sure no centipedes get in this time."

He cleaned that pot mighty good and put in the water and the coffee. Soon all the men were sitting around enjoying hot biscuits and bacon and—coffee.

Said Slim, the skinniest man in the outfit, "Sure this 's the finest coffee y' ever made, Boss. Betcha ye put in a good fat centipede this time again."

"Quit yer kiddin', Slim; ye'd sure lose yer bet this time. Ain't no centipedes in this coffee."

When breakfast was over, the boss dumped out the coffee grounds and . . . once again, a fine boiled centipede dropped out.

The boss man looked and looked! Some of the hands around saw it. Boss looked, then he said:

"Don't know if kind words 'll soothe a stiff Norther, but a cooked poison centipede sure makes good coffee."

Of Sam Bass

In the wide and windy state of Texas there were outlaws. Plenty of them, and there's much that's told about them in song and story.

Here's a tale of the most famous outlaw of the Lone Star State: Sam Bass. Some say he was a bad man, meaner 'n snakes. But there's many a one who says he was a man good as they come—and some say he was both. Maybe that's as near the truth as one can come.

There was prize money on Sam Bass's head brought in dead or alive. And there were many who tried to get it.

One time a bright young fellow who called himself a detective decided to earn that pile of dollars. He wanted adventure and walked with his head up, looking cocksure at the world. He was mighty sure he'd get Sam Bass dead or alive. So he traveled around Stephens County in Texas where the outlaw and his gang were leading a gay and lawless life. He traveled around the hills and woods where folks said Sam Bass, the bank robber, and his men were hiding. He carried a good six-shooter on his hip and was full of hope he would find Bass.

Walking along the road, he saw a buggy driven by a man, his hat deep over his eyes. It was Sam Bass himself, sitting there quiet as the moon on a fall night. At the bottom of the wagon a couple of good sixes were hid under some hay. The horse was going easy-like.

When the outlaw saw the young fellow he spoke up, "Stranger, goin' far?"

"Reckon I am," the young detective answered.

"Come up along in the buggy. Four-footed mule kin go faster 'n two-footed man."

The young fellow went up and sat down next to the driver.

"New in Stephens County, young feller?"

"Just came a couple o' days ago."

"In the cow or horse business?"

"Nope, I'm in man business. I'm a detective."

"Doggone, that must be a mighty interestin' business. You got to carry a good six-gun all the time to git yer man. Heard that's a detective's job."

"Ye guessed right. I got a fine six-shooter quick 'n ready, fer I'm on a tough job."

"Yowlin' painters! * Sounds as if ye're out fer big game."

"That I sure am. Folks say it's the toughest I ever tackled. Don't like to tell it loud, but I'll tell ye, I'm out fer Sam Bass."

"Wal, wal, guess ye're a reg'lar rooter dog after a hot-bitin' tarantula. Yep, ye sure got a rough cob down your throat, young feller. Don't ye think ye're huntin' big trouble?"

"I know this is a tough nut, but I've handled mighty tough cases before, an' I guess I kin handle Sam Bass."

"Think ye'll know Sam Bass when ye see 'm?"

"I'm mighty quick at knowin' outlaws when I see 'em. I sort o' smell 'em."

"Reckon ye're a mighty smart detective."

"Well, I'm young, I guess, but I've nailed every man I was after."

"What yer gonna do when ye git Sam Bass?"

"He'll come along like a lamb, or they'll carry 'm feet front."

"Wal, that's spoken like a man who's not scared of anythin'. Now, young feller, I'm gonna tell ye a thing that'll save ye lookin' for Sam Bass any further. Ye're sittin' right next to 'm."

The outlaw looked straight at the detective. With one hand he held the traces and with the other he played with his six-gun he'd pulled from under the seat.

The young fellow turned white as a burial sheet.

"I . . . I . . . Mr. . . . Mr. Bass, I really didn't mean what I said. I was just braggin' a bit. Y' know how a man'll speak . . . I got a young wife and two young children . . . I never done anythin' to ye . . . I swear. . . ."

Sam Bass looked at him, just smiled, twirling his sixer.

---

* Panthers.

The fellow's tongue stuck to the roof of his mouth. He couldn't speak. He was sure his end had come.

"Wal," Sam said slowly, "ain't gonna throw away a good lead shot on ye, an' don't want any necktie party either. Git out pronto. Am gonna let ye run along. Don't ever let me see yer face 'round these parts o' Texas again. Ef I do, sagebrush on fire ain't gonna help ye."

The young fellow jumped out and was never seen in Texas again. That's the way Sam Bass acted often—half high up and half way down.

And now I want to tell you what happened to Sam Bass at the end of his life.

The law of Texas and the Texas Rangers got him at Round Rock when he was trying to hold up a bank. One of his own gang betrayed him.

They put his body in a dray, and a black man was asked to drive the coffin to the cemetery.

Folks in Round Rock knew the body of Sam Bass was in that dray, and as it rumbled along the bumpedy road through the town, the Reverend Mr. Ledbetter, a Methodist minister, saw it.

"Ain't gonna let that misguided boy be buried without a word from the Lord. He was only an errant youth," he said to those standing near.

He followed the dray to the cemetery, and he was the only one there except the black driving man. The two took off their hats at the grave and the preacher preached good words over the body of young Sam Bass. He spoke of Sam's fine spirit when helping poor folks in need. Then he thanked the black man who had been entrusted with the body.

Those were the things that happened to Sam Bass in his wild life in Texas. And folks down there speak of him to this very day and tell these tales about him.

Horse Trading in Wichita Falls

All Texans hold that Texas is the finest state in the Union and that Texans are the smartest folks in the land. But you know there comes the day when even the smartest can be caught at the dead end of the road.

When Texans are fooled, they are so smart they can laugh at themselves. So, when Wichita Falls folks are in good humor, they tell the tale of when they were taken in like a cat in the bag. At the end there's a good-natured smile. They believe that it's only a bad *hombre* who can't laugh at himself.

That is why Eleanore Flemming of Wichita Falls told this tale. It happened in the days when the place was just a cow town, when cows and horses were its life and business. Famous buffalo hunters, cattlemen, and soldiers came there to sell, to buy, and to spend their money.

One day a British officer rode into town. He was a fine-looking man, mounted on a fine horse, and he called himself Captain Henry Navarre. Head high, he walked and spoke and acted like a gentleman. He wasn't the least scared of the good Texas sun or the devil-tearing Northers. All the people took to him in a big way.

Pretty soon he let it be known that he had come to buy riding horses for the British Army. Lots of horses. And he was ready to pay for good animals.

With a fine British accent he told the horsemen of the town that he and another officer had been sent to do the buying. But his companion had to stay in New Orleans, which at that time was suffering from smallpox and was quarantined.

"Your reputation for raising horses is famous all over," he said. "I've come to see if you can find a thousand head in good flesh. I plan to examine them first and then wait for my fellow officer to come and close the deal. He'll surely be out in the near future and he'll arrange the financial part of the transaction."

The whole town was happy and excited. Excitement among the men over the coming big sale and excitement among the women of Wichita to entertain so distinguished a British officer. He used such fine language and had such polite manners. Why, he could even speak French! Nearly every one of the two thousand citizens of the town was spellbound by him. He was invited everywhere and was dined and wined without end.

When he accidentally said that his money had given out—he spent it very freely, treating everybody—the city officers printed special coupons for him that he could use as money. A government revenue agent who happened to be in town at the time stamped the coupons with a government stamp so that Captain Navarre could use it as money.

While the distinguished British officer was spending the money generously, the men were scouting around buying horses at any price. Soon the town was full of horses. There were not enough stables to house them and they were kept wherever there was any kind of shed.

There hadn't been such excitement and doings in Wichita Falls since the day Buntin and his fearless brood of children, who, like Pecos Bill, rode wild bobcats, had settled in that territory.

On a Friday, three weeks after the British captain had come, he announced that he was ready.

"Gentlemen," he said to a group of men, "if you'll get all your animals together, I am ready to inspect them this coming Monday morning. The quarantine in New Orleans has been lifted and my fellow officer should arrive any day."

Through Saturday and Sunday hundreds of horses trotted into the town of Wichita Falls. Horses of every color, size, and stature. Cowboys led them, owners came along approvingly. They all converged in the center of the town.

Never before had there been seen a gathering of such fine animals. There was milling and stamping and pounding of earth and whinnying and shouting.

Monday morning came. Nearly all the men in town were on hand around that giant herd of horses. It was like Judgment Day. All were there waiting for Captain Navarre.

They waited and . . . they waited. The sun rose high and hot and cowboys and horses became restless. Even more restless were the owners . . . waiting. They waited longer. . . . Then one of the men was sent to the hotel where Captain Navarre had been staying and —there was no Captain Navarre!

The proprietor said the Captain had left Sunday afternoon, saying he would be back early Monday morning.

But Captain Navarre never came back. . . . The good citizens and ladies of the town were left with angry and red faces.

"Just the same, he was a fine gentleman," the ladies said after a time. And all the men could do was to smile a little wryly and say . . . nothing. They had been taken in and took it like—Texans!

Lafitte's Great Treasure

Is there a place in all the golden states of the deep South bordering the Gulf of Mexico that has not at least one tale of lurid Lafitte, the pirate? I'm going to tell you one that is told around Galveston Island, which looks with one eye at the green waters of the Gulf and with the other on the rich Texas shore.

It is a weird tale of the sea pirate in his late years, when his hair was graying and his bones were wearying.

He lived in his luxurious mansion, "Maison Rouge," enjoying life with his beautiful young wife Jeanette and permitting no man to come near her. The two lived alone among gold and jewels and the dreams of the great pirate captain. For, though his black hair was streaked with gray and some of his boisterousness was gone, he still plotted and planned attacks on ships on the high seas.

One of his eyelids was always closed and folks said he was blind in one eye. But he wasn't. He saw keenly and sharply and was ever on the lookout for adventure.

The "law" knew that well, and so a Lieutenant Kerney of the U.S. brig "Enterprise" was sent to order Lafitte to leave Galveston *forever* . . . never to return!

It was a stormy meeting between officer and pirate. Lafitte ranted and roared, but all he heard was the quiet, sharp order:

"In three days you must leave, never to return, or go to prison instead."

"My wife is ill."

"You will take your wife with you."

The officer left, and Lafitte sat for a time alone in the great, high-ceilinged room, with his head down, harassed and distressed.

Suddenly he looked up. A cold wind had "walked" into the big room like a ghost. The tall windows before his eyes seemed far away! Now a ghostly little breeze came into the silence. It ran around the heavy furniture, at the thick curtains of the high windows, as if trying to escape.

For a moment the pirate sat bewildered, vacantly staring around. He who feared no man felt a shiver go through him.

He recovered and walked quickly into the room where his wife lay in bed.

Cold! Silence! Cold! He touched her: cold! She was dead!

For a long time he stood stony-still. Then he went to the door and shouted to two men, his attendants, who were on the floor below.

"Leave and don't return until tomorrow night!"

They obeyed.

The men returned the next evening, but they did not see their master. They only heard him. Back and forth! Back and forth! Pacing back and forth! Hour after hour, muttering to himself. Always muttering and walking!

They took off their boots and went stealthily up to the door.

Back and forth! Back and forth! Heavy slow steps and muttering.

"My treasure gone! My treasure buried! . . . My greatest treasure! Under the three trees I buried my great treasure! Under the three trees."

He kept on walking and he kept on muttering. But the two had heard enough. They went downstairs.

"We must get it right now. Tomorrow we must go away with him," one said.

"Yes, he must mean the three trees standing near one another in the garden. But we must wait for the night."

Night came soon, dark and windy. They took shovels and picks and went into the garden where the three oak trees stood together. There were signs that the earth had just been dug up.

A white moon showed through the wild running clouds. The men dug fast and hard and sweat ran down their faces and bodies. Suddenly the shovels touched something hard. Carefully they moved the earth away from the box and made enough room for them to get down to open it.

The moon shone down fitfully as they raised the lid to one side.

No silver! No gold! No jewels! No doubloons! Only the waxen face of Lafitte's young wife!

Fear—cold, wet fear—seized the two. They put the lid back swiftly, jumped out, and put the earth back, shoveling wildly.

The next day Lafitte and his men left Maison Rouge never to return.

Hercules of Virginia

There's big Paul Bunyan of the woods and big Kemp Morgan of the oil fields; there's Pecos Bill of the wide plains and there is Johnny Darling of the good farms. There are other golden-rooster hero-folks of America who have done great deeds of strength and fearlessness—and Peter Francisco of Virginia is among them. Down in the Azalea State, Old Dominion, and many other states, folks talk of Peter's mighty deeds and of his bravery.

Peter of great fame came from far, far away—some even said Portugal, but that's no matter. He was found as a child on the shore, left by some fierce sailors who fled swiftly with bulging sails. That happened many, many years ago on the coast of Virginia around Hopewell, not far from Petersburg.

Luck loved the little black-eyed, black-haired boy. Kind Judge Anthony Winston who had a farm nearby took him to his fine home. There the boy grew big of body and strong of muscle and soon was known far and wide for his feats of strength. Yet he was a quiet boy, tending his own business, using his power only when there was need of it.

With every year he grew bigger and stronger. At sixteen he was near seven feet and weighed over two hundred and fifty pounds. He could hold a big man high up in each hand.

Came the days when Americans wanted their freedom from England and Peter was quick to enlist in the army.

From the very first he became famous for his power and courage. He was always in the thick of battle and no soldier distinguished himself more than Peter did. All men, all officers from generals down, knew of his bravery. George Washington had a sword made for him that was six feet long; he wielded it like a feather. General Lafayette was his good friend, and so was every man.

When the war was over, he turned to live in peace and comfort, but he continued his great deeds just the same. I'll tell you just one of them and you will see that Peter Francisco deserved every word of praise and admiration folks had for him.

One day he was sitting peacefully on the porch of his house at New Store, where he ran a tavern, thinking pleasantly of the battle he had fought with Tarleton's dragoons, when single-handed he had routed near a dozen men. Suddenly there was the sound of hoofbeats coming toward him.

"Ha! a traveler seeking food and lodging!" He looked sharply. Along came a big, blustering-looking fellow on a big horse. He rode right up to the gate.

"Good day, sir," Peter said pleasantly. "Are you seeking accommodations? We have plenty of room."

"Are you Peter Francisco?" the fellow roared out, loud enough to be heard seven miles.

"That I am. Won't you get off your horse and step in?"

"My name is Pamphlett. I come all the way from Kentucky to whip you—for nothing."

"Well, that's easy, Friend Pamphlett," said Peter, smiling. "Ho there, boy, come out." A servant came out on the porch. "Boy, go and cut some good long twigs of the willow tree and give them to the gentleman from Kentucky."

The boy hurried into the garden.

"That boy, good Master Pamphlett, will save you lots of trouble and work and you can do what you came to do."

Pamphlett looked at Peter, not able to understand why the famous giant didn't turn angry. He sat quietly for a time, then he got off his horse and led it through the gate, through the little garden that was Mrs. Francisco's pride, right up to where Peter was stand-

Peter raised the frightened animal with one mighty effort and flung it clear across the fence after its master.

ing on the porch. Pamphlett was a big, heavy man and walked clumsily. He looked for a little time at Peter there, with his head near the ceiling of the porch, then he said slowly:

"Would you permit me to feel your weight, Mr. Francisco?"

"Certainly. As you wish."

The Kentuckian dropped the rein of his horse and with all his strength lifted Peter several times off the ground.

"You're a heavy man, Mr. Francisco."

"That's what folks say, Master Pamphlett," Peter said laughingly. "And now, good Master Pamphlett, who came to whip me for nothing, I'd like to feel your weight.... Allow me to lift you to feel *your* weight."

Peter Francisco bent a little forward and quickly lifted Pamphlett off the ground. He did it twice, and the third time he raised him high up and pitched him clear over the garden fence.

Pamphlett lay for a time on the ground, then rose slowly. The fall hurt him a little, but not too much. He looked at Peter none too pleasantly.

"You've put me out of your garden," he said sarcastically. "Would you mind putting out my horse?"

"With pleasure, sir." Peter went up to the horse confidently. Hadn't he once lifted single-handed a cannon weighing eleven hundred pounds? The horse weighed less, he felt sure. And even if it didn't....

He put his left hand under the horse's belly and his right behind its tail. Then, planting his feet hard on the ground and straining every muscle in his body, Peter raised the frightened animal with one mighty effort and flung it clear across the fence after its master.

Pamphlett stood, mouth wide open. Then he said slowly and respectfully, "Master Francisco, I'm fully satisfied that the reputation you have as a strong man is fully deserved."

"Thank you, sir," said Peter, smiling pleasantly. "Thank you, sir, and call again when you come by."

Pamphlett rode off and Peter went back to his seat on the porch, smiling at the Virginia flowers and the Virginia sun.

All on a Summer's Day

I just can't tell how true this story is, but I reckon when a man goes to church regular on Sunday, he won't tell lies to strangers on Saturday. This churchgoing man told me this tale while rolling along the Mississippi on a riverboat going to New Orleans in Louisiana, and he said the tale was gospel truth.

This gospel-telling man said this happened to him when he was out fishing along the Cowpasture River in Virginia. In those days towns and folks were scarce along that river—it was just swamps and woods.

"Well," said he, "it was one of them nice warm mornin's, an' I was going down to the river for to catch some good fish.

"There was me and my eldest daughter Carol who loved fishin' same as I did. I was carryin' fishin' rods and Carol was carryin' a basket she had woven from willow twigs, that was full o' good vittles and a jug of the finest yellow dandelion wine her good mother had made last spring. She made this fine dandelion wine every spring an' I tell ye there was none better in all Virginia.

"We didn't bother takin' any bait along, figurin' I c'd easily find a couple o' worms or maybe a frog. Ye find 'em there 'bouts.

"We kept on walkin' an' I was thinkin' of politics or somethin' not worth thinkin' about, when we got to the river. We sat down in a good place and then I reminded myself 'bout the bait.

" 'Carol,' says I, 'we got to get some bait.'

"We were both sittin' comfortable as a rabbit in a burrow an' I just hated to get up. I was lookin' aroun' to see if I couldn't dig up somethin' at arm's length when I spied an elderly moccasin snake.

She was lyin' not far off, a fine frog in her mouth ready for swallowin'.

" 'A frog makes just as good bait as swallowin',' says I to myself.

"I got up, grabbed a forked stick lyin' on the ground, clamped it on the moccasin right aroun' the neck, and took the frog out of her mouth for bait.

"I took away the stick and that elderly moccasin looked at me so sadly I got a guilty feelin' in my heart. She had her mouth still wide open, lookin' with pleadin' eyes down my way.

"You know, friend, I'm a God-fearin' and creature-lovin' man an' I can't see any creature a-sufferin'. I couldn't give back that frog, for I was in need of it. Right next to me stood the jug o' dandelion wine Carol had taken out to make sure 'twouldn't spill, an' so, without thinkin', I poured a mouthful of fine dandelion juice into the open mouth of the moccasin snake.

"Well, you should ha' seen the face of that snake. If snakes kin smile with gratitude, I tell ye that snake had the happiest and kindest smile in all Virginia.

"The guilt was gone from me, for the snake looked happy, so I sat down to do my fishin'. Fish was plenty and Carol an' I soon had a mess lyin' on the grass. Carol, she was talkin' all the time, for she takes after her mother who kin talk like runnin' river.

"I was listenin' to her and sudden-like I felt a gentle tappin' on the side of my leg. I quick turned around and there was that moccasin snake a-tappin' me with his tail, head high in the air, mouth wide open with a frog in it!

"You could ha' bowled me over with a willow twig!

"That snake was a-tellin' me in snake talk: Here, mister, I brought ye another frog, just ye give me another mouthful o' that fine dandelion juice ye gave me afore.

"What could I do? I told you I'm a kindhearted man, so I took out the frog and poured some more of that dandelion sauce in the snake's mouth. But I told that moccasin clearly I had no more need o' frogs, but I had need of that dandelion juice for my vittles.

"The snake looked kind o' sad, but slithered along.

"Carol and I, we caught plenty o' fish, ate the good food she'd brought, and then went home with our mess o' fish in the basket.

"Since that time I never go out fishin' without a good jug of fine dandelion juice. It saves time diggin' for worms."

The Merry Tale of Belle Boyd

Even the sad War Between the States had at times its merry side, and there are tales of those days of horror that bring a twinkle to the eye and a smile around the mouth. Such a one is the tale about Belle Boyd.

Belle Boyd was a wisp of a girl. Not too tall, not too small, just a slip of a Southern girl, lithe and pleasing, with a mind zooming and swift as a bee full of flower-honey on the way to a hive.

From the very beginning when the "sad war" came to Front Royal in the lovely Shenandoah Valley, she was receiving and giving information to help her Southern cause.

She was friendly and flirted constantly with the Northern officers to make friends of them and so learn of their plans. She brought the "Blues" to her home, went to places where they stayed, was always in their company to learn their military moves, which she reported to the Southern officers.

No sooner did she learn of any coming actions, any new changes of attacks, than she'd carry the word to the army she believed in and loved.

Whenever she was caught—and she was caught often—she had a way of slithering out that was the marvel of her friends and even of herself. Perhaps it was her sweet youthful air and ways, perhaps her clever mind. Maybe it was a combination of all of these, but no matter what the difficulty, she always came out on top . . . to continue in her helpful spying work for her South.

The Merry Tale of Belle Boyd

There are a thousand tales told of Belle Boyd in Tennessee and every other state and I'll tell you just one that is as good as any of the others. It is a tale of courage, determination, laughter, and sadness, all rolled into one.

The Northern officers and troops had come to Front Royal and the Shenandoah Valley, planning to capture Richmond.

The headquarters were in the hotel of the town and, sure enough, Belle was around visiting relatives in a house that was near the courtyard of the hotel. But she was in the hotel proper with the officers more than she was with her relatives. She was gay, smiling, pleasant; all the young officers were enamored of that Southern belle. Often she spent her time in the upper chambers over the hotel parlor where the officers met and discussed their plans.

There was a convenient knothole in the floor through which the parlor could be seen, and through this she learned one day that a large part of the Federal army would be sent away to help capture Richmond, the capital of the South, and that only a small force would be kept ready to attack General Jackson.

Goes on the tale. Fifteen miles Belle Boyd rode through woods and scrub, through fields and furrows, to reach her own Confederates to tell them of the plan and how simple it would be to overwhelm the troops in Front Royal and capture them with little effort.

She told of her own little plan, what she would do at home to help defeat the Federals quickly and handsomely. The officer laughed, for he trusted that wisp of a girl and believed she could carry out any stratagem of war and love. They could depend on her. Home she rode, fifteen hard miles.

She put on her loveliest dress, the most winsome smile on her face, and came to General Nathaniel Banks and his officers.

"General," she said gaily, "there's a war, but there is also spring this month of May. For an evening let us forget the war and make merry. I invite you all to a ball with lovely girls, fine food, and good refreshing drink. We will prepare a fine meal and there'll be everything to bring good spring cheer."

No man could resist lovely Belle Boyd's siren smile and maidenly wiles. The Federal general accepted gladly amid the cheers of the other officers.

So in the evening there were fiddlers to play for dancing and food and drink for cheer. And there were pretty Southern girls in their best, flushed and winsome, gay and merry to charm the men in blue of the North.

The officers danced and flirted and ate and drank until mind and body were overfull. When the gaiety was at its highest, Belle Boyd excused herself for a time and rode out to tell her friends that all was going according to her plan.

Then, home again, when men and girls, tired and sleepy, were going to their beds. But not pretty Belle Boyd. She had work to do. Her mind was with the coming Confederate troops. She knew General Banks and his officers were in deep sleep, tired from feasting and dancing. Her side must be told that all was well and ready.

Again she rode her horse to signal them the news.

The first golden signs of dawn were in the east and Belle Boyd waved her white bonnet as a sign for the Grays to come on!

They came and handily captured seven hundred of the thousand men in Front Royal.

Thus Belle Boyd went through the "sad war," working fearlessly for the cause she believed was the right cause. East, West, North, South knew the girl, the heroic spy of the South. Tales and adventures of her life are told to this day, and that is why I am telling one to you here.

Two Foxes

In a dark, busy forest in Virginia, where rabbits made eggs for Easter and toads make warts for silly folk, lived two foxes. They lived near a spring from which ran a little rivulet that gave water to the animals that lived in the woods.

They were two very beautiful foxes. One was a little older than the other, and they were the best of friends. Their friendship was made of fire and water, the two great riches in the world, and so nothing could break that friendship. Other animals in those woods gossiped about it, but just as barking couldn't harm the moon, all the gossip couldn't break the friendship of these two foxes. They went their way in peace and pleasure as God wanted them to live.

Yet, though the golden sun shines warm in the day, there is the dark night with cold winds. There was no end of animals and insects in the woods and the two friends saw and heard fussing and quarreling all around them.

One day the two foxes were talking pleasantly to each other.

"It is good to be like everybody," said the taller of the two. "Maybe we should try fussing and fighting, then we too will be like everyone else."

"Maybe you are right and we should be like all other folks. I think I would like that."

"Come, let us start," said the taller.

"How do we start?"

"Let me think," said the taller. His long thick tail went down and so did his long snout. For a time he was looking down on the little running water and the glittering stones lying around.

"We could bite each other," said the taller. "I have seen many animals biting each other when they are angry."

"No, that would hurt," said the smaller.

"Yes, it would hurt. I am bigger than you and you are my friend and I don't want to hurt you. Maybe it would be better to get into an argument first and get angry at each other like everybody else."

"That would be better," said the smaller fox. "How do we do that?"

"Well, here are two nice stones lying in the water. I'll show you how we start."

He picked up the two gleaming stones with his paws. Then, raising his voice, he screamed just as he heard the others do.

"These two white stones are my stones, you can't have them, do you hear me!"

"Yes, I heard you," said the other. "If they are your stones, then they are your stones. I don't want to take anything from you. You keep them."

For a time the tall fox was quiet. "We are not getting anywhere with our quarreling," he said, a little downhearted.

"No, we are not, good friend fox."

"Well, let us try again. Let us try another way, maybe we can do better." They were quiet for a little time, then the older raised his long snout and his bushy tail and said in a loud voice, "This wood belongs to me and you had better get out of it quick."

Said the other, "I am sorry, I like you and I like you to be my friend. But if this is your wood and you want it, I will have to go out even if I don't want to. It is a nice wood and I like it. Now I will have to find another."

The tall fox looked at his friend in surprise. He liked his friend and did not want to hurt him.

"I don't want you to go. We are good friends and we like to be together and play with each other."

"I am happy to hear you say that. I didn't want to go, I want to be with you."

The two were silent for a time, then the taller said:

"Friend, we are not good at fussing and fighting and quarreling. I think it is best for us to be as we are. Let us be the way we are, not the way others are."

So these two foxes in the deep wood remained, all their lives, good friends instead of fighting enemies. And I am glad they did.

The Black Ghost Dog

This happened in the dawn days of Virginia, the Old Dominion, when the first Cavaliers came over from England.

A tale was running around Botetourt County about a giant black ghost dog. That dog was seen every night in one of the passes in the mountains near which there were many healing springs. Every night from sundown to sunrise that big black dog walked in the silent night, up and down the pass. Up and down with solemn, heavy steps. Sometimes he wailed and growled a little in low tones. But most of the time he was silent. Just doing his vigil from sunset until the sun rose in the east. Then he would disappear.

Folks often spoke about that ghost dog, but no one would go near the pass. It is not wise to disturb a ghost.

But the young are adventurous and fearless. Some young blades said the talk was just old women's gibberish, but when it continued, they decided to investigate. They would learn if it was just an old woman's tale or whether there was such a creature as a big black ghost dog.

They set out, four of them, or maybe five, and rode to the pass in the mountains. No dog! But it was still sunny afternoon and they would wait for sundown, when the dog was known to appear.

The sun dipped slowly behind the dark laurel and pine trees and the young fellows were talking gaily of this and that. The cool night air had come friendly-like, telling of animals and woods, and the moon was just coming up when one of the men shouted, "Look! Look! There!"

And there he was. Suddenly, out of nowhere! Maybe from the leaf-covered earth—or out of the rocks—there was a big, heavy, black dog! For a minute he stood silent, his big head held high in the air, then he walked slowly and heavily a ways down the pass, then came back. Up and down, up and down, along that pass as if guarding something.

"Come along," one of the watchers shouted. "Let's go through the pass and see what he'll do. Come!"

He spurred his horse and so did the others. The horses went forward and came up to the pass where the dog was walking. Then . . . the horses halted and began rearing back! All of them raised their heads, some stood up on their hind legs as if in fear. Not one would go ahead. The men shouted and dug their spurs into the horses' sides . . . but nothing could make those animals move forward.

The big black dog was marching back and forth unconcerned.

The men rode back a bit, turned around, and tried to make the pass on a run. No use! No sooner did the animals get to the pass than they became panicky and tried to back away.

The men tried again and again and finally decided to give up.

"I'll return with a musket and finish that dog," said one of them.

The whole county heard of what happened. Old men shook their heads and said, "Young fools go where old men are wise enough to stay away."

This only made the young hotheads angry, and they determined to get that dog, come what might. They decided to go to the pass again, this time with firearms.

One afternoon they set out, each one armed, determined to end that ghost dog and wipe out their disgrace.

They came to the pass just about when the cool night air came up a little shivery and the woods began to be full of night-noise life. Yes, there was that big black ghost dog solemnly walking up and down—up and down.

Firearms were raised carefully and steadily and aimed straight at the dog. The target was big enough. Bang!—shots thundered through the mountains, echoing over and over again, and when the smoke cleared away . . . there was the ghost dog unharmed, walking quietly up and down—up and down.

A little fear crept through the men, but firearms were grimly reloaded and carefully aimed. Again the thundering shots rolled back and forth in the mountains and still that ghost dog was there, calmly walking up and down—up and down.

Then ice-cold fear went sharp through the hearts of those young men and they turned their horses. They saw that it was not wise to meddle with a ghost, even in the form of a dog.

From then on, no one came near that ghost dog again; they just let him be.

So years passed and folks took that ghost dog as they took sun and wind and rain. . . .

One day a lady came into the county. She had been searching for her husband for a long time. He had left her years before to build a new home for them in Virginia. For a time she had heard from him, then . . . silence. No message, no letter. So she had set out to find him. She went everywhere in the state and finally she had come to Botetourt County where she had been told that a tall man answering her husband's description had been seen. But that was as far as it went. Then she heard the story of the big black ghost dog!

"I want to see that dog," she said. "My husband took with him a large black dog when he left. He said a big strong dog would be of help in the new land. It might be my husband's dog."

She begged to be taken to the pass and finally some men promised to take her. They went with her, and when they came near the pass, they told her she would have to go the rest of the way alone.

"I'm not afraid of ghosts. I'll go alone. If it is my husband's dog, he will recognize me. Just you wait for me here."

The men left her not far from the gap. The lady rode right to the pass and dismounted and tied her horse.

The sun was setting in seas of golden clouds, and darkness came quickly. With the darkness, there . . . suddenly, was the dog! A big black dog! A dog the lady knew well. With a cry she ran up to him and stroked him with trembling hands.

"Where is your master? Where is your master?" she said over and over again, patting his big head that rested against her. He raised his head, looked at her, seemingly wanting to say something, and walked off a few paces, looking back all the time.

She did not follow and he came back growling and began pulling her by her coat. She understood and followed.

He went to a ledge near a boulder. She was close behind. He began scratching the ground with his big black paws, looking at her, wailing and growling and then . . . he was gone!

The lady went back to where she had left the men who had brought her.

She told them what had happened.

"I would like you to dig there where the dog clawed the ground," she said.

"We have no shovels, but we'll come back tomorrow and do it."

They returned the next morning and, digging under the boulder, they found the skeleton of a man. The lady recognized it was her husband by a ring on his finger.

The skeleton was given a Christian burial and the lady left the land.

From then on the ghost dog was never seen again in Botetourt County in Virginia. He had accomplished his task—even after his master's death.

Grace Sherwood, the Woman None Could Scare

Grace Sherwood was a witch!

That is what many folks down in Princess Anne County by the sea in Virginia said. But there were just as many who said witches' talk was silly old wives' tales unfit for folk of understanding and belief. So there were battles in homes and battles in courts about this widow woman who worked hard for home and children.

Grace Sherwood was a woman of high spirit, without fear, who held her head straight and was quick with her tongue. When she was accused by Jane Ginsburn of bringing harm to crops and kine, Grace answered back that honest hard work would keep harm from crops and kine.

There were others who whispered that she had crossed the wild ocean in an eggshell to find poison plants to set before her house. One tittle-tattler, Elizabeth Barnes, said she had seen Grace change into a black cat that had jumped on her bed and had whipped her with its tail and then flown out through a crack in the door. Another said she had seen her ride on a broomstick to the witches' Sabbath. Each gossip had a different tale against that widow woman.

But the one who cried most against her was Mistress Hill, Luke Hill's wife. She believed every rumor, everything that buzzed against Grace Sherwood, and babbled it in home and church. In the end she claimed that she was bewitched by that witch woman.

Mistress Hill made her husband believe it, and so the two, husband and wife, hailed Grace Sherwood before the court.

"This time the law'll punish her properly," ran the word among the women.

There was a long-drawn trial; some said Grace was a witch, others said it was pish-posh. But there was a great shrill screaming against the widow woman who had come to the courts so many times, so that in the end the judge chose a jury of women to examine her body to see if she had any witches' signs on her.

Elizabeth Barnes was the head of that jury, which sure wasn't fair, for Elizabeth and Grace had been at odds in court before.

The women examined her and said there were the proper witch markings on her body and therefore she was a witch.

But the judge still held out against such fiddle-faddle and sent the case to the Council of State to decide.

That body didn't believe in the silly "mark findings" either. But the angry, unthinking crowd led by Luke Hill and his wife and their friends were set on getting Grace Sherwood this time. They clamored and set up a great to-do, so the judges had to promise that Grace Sherwood would be tried by ducking. If she was guilty, she would drown; but if she was not guilty she would float!

The trial by water was to take place in a pond near William Harper's plantation.

Of course it was not fair, which didn't matter to the crowd. But the judges decided to send a boat to follow Grace to save her in case she was in danger of drowning.

The sun shone bright on the dancing water. Folks from all over were sitting on the grass and on seats, waiting to see that justice was done.

Grace came between two soldiers, a Bible in her hand. Her head was high and there was no fear in her eyes.

At the pond she stepped into the boat in which four men were sitting. She sat on the wooden seat clutching the Bible in her hand.

Two men rowed the boat out to the center of the pond, and when they got there, the two other men took off much of her clothing and crossbound her. The Bible was now on the bench beside her. Then they threw her in the water.

Grace Sherwood wasn't going to drown. She was a good swimmer and no sooner did she hit the water than she began swimming.

"Ye numskull dolts," she screamed, "it's ye who should be drowning, not me!"

Then, coming to the boat, she shouted, "Tie the Bible around my neck. I want to show these blind jobbernowls that I am innocent."

One of the men held her and another did what she asked. With the Bible around her neck, she swam around singing a hymn while folks on the shore cheered and booed and screamed. Finally the men in the boat pulled her back and rowed ashore.

But the clamoring went on by those who see a witch when they see an innocent black cat, so she was taken back to jail.

She stayed for a time and was tried again, but the trial came to nought because, to the judges, Grace Sherwood was just a high-spirited woman who could be neither downed nor drowned. In the end those who were forever seeing black in the daytime grew tired and let Grace Sherwood live her own life.

. . . *Thanks to Patrick Henry*

Patrick Henry was a great patriot and a great lawyer. He was renowned not only for his famous cry that ran through all our land: "Give me Liberty or give me death," but also for his many clever deeds in life and in the courts. There is no end of tales about him running through the land in general and through Virginia in particular, and here is one I heard and like to tell. And the same can be said for many folks in Virginia, for it is a tale that brings a good laugh.

There lived in those days a young blade who fell in love with a young girl, the way it has happened since the days of Adam. But that Virginia girl was not yet of marrying age according to law. What was worse, the father of the girl didn't want his daughter to marry that young man. He had other plans. But law and father's wishes never have bothered young folks in love, not since love began.

Now, eloping, running away from town and parents and getting married, is a fine old Virginia custom. When it's all over, most of the time parents forgive and forget. But to these two, running away would bring deep double trouble. The law in Virginia said if any man ran away with a girl under the set age, he'd be put in jail for a nice long stretch. So you see there was lots of trouble ahead for these two if they ran away and got married.

The young Virginian was thinking deep about his love trouble. What to do!

Now, it so happened that he knew Patrick Henry, and his father had often said that Patrick had the smartest head in the state for law, so he went to him and told his tale of woe.

The famous man listened, and then a smile came on his face.

"Young man, you love that young lady very much?" said he.

"I do for sure and I'd pay anything if I could marry her and not have to go to jail."

"You'd pay anything, and that's a fine beginning. Would you pay one hundred guineas?"

"Gladly, sir. I can easy get the money from my father."

"We are making fine progress, young man. I believe I can arrange that marriage and keep you in your good home and not in jail."

"Oh, Mr. Henry, I will never forget you if you can do this for me."

"Very well then, come with your young lady to my office tomorrow and I'll tell you how we will accomplish our good deed."

So the two young folks went to Patrick Henry's office, the young man very eager and the young girl high-spirited, as Virginia girls are.

Patrick Henry greeted them pleasantly; then, turning to the young lady, he said:

"Young lady, one fine day when your good father who objects to this estimable young man is away, you go into the stable and pick out the finest horse you have. Then you race as fast as you can to where your chosen young man must be waiting for you.

"When she gets there, you, young man, mount the horse she has brought—behind her. Remember, behind her, so that she will guide the horse to the minister who will marry you. Remember, you, pretty young lady, must hold the reins and guide the horse while your bridegroom sits behind and holds on to you. When you are married, go to your father and tell him you are married. If the gentleman still objects and hails you to court, I'll be there to defend you. But remember, young lady, to tell exactly how you eloped, and I promise you you'll be going to your nice home instead of to jail to see your beloved. But remember to tell exactly how you two ran away to be married."

She promised. The two thanked the lawyer and went their way.

Soon as that young lady learned when her father would be away she arranged to meet the young man. The road clear, she took the finest horse in the stable and raced to where her sweetheart was waiting. He got on the horse, behind her, as the lawyer had told him to do. She rode the racing horse until they came to the minister who married them right and proper. Then they went to the bride's father and told him all about it.

The old gentleman was in a fury. He locked up his daughter and hailed the young husband to court. He wanted him jailed for life!

The day of the trial came. Since both families were among the gentry, the courtroom was mighty crowded. Besides, the word spread that Patrick Henry was the lawyer, and folks came from far and near to see and hear him.

The sun was shining and the birds were singing and the azaleas were flaming—maybe they were as much interested in the goings-on in the court as was the crowd that had come.

The lawyer for the angry father got up and had his say and it wasn't too much. Just that the young scamp had run off with a girl not of marrying age according to the law of the state of Virginia, and now the law must take its just course and send him to jail.

Then Patrick Henry got up.

"Your Honor, I have little to say in this case. I would rather have the young bride, lovely as an angel, tell the tale of the running away as my colleague claims. Then, Your Honor can judge for himself if this charming young man should go to the cold jail or to his pleasant home with his bride."

Then, turning to the young bride, he said, "Now, young lady, tell His Honor exactly what happened. Remember, tell exactly what happened and how it happened."

He had instructed the girl carefully before the trial in what she was to tell on the stand.

The blushing bride got on the stand. She was a little nervous, but she spoke clearly and without hesitation.

"Your Honor, it was this way. Last Wednesday morning I went to our stable and took out Star Prince and went to where my husband was. He got on the horse behind me. I rode the horse, he behind me, till we came to the minister who married us."

Patrick Henry rose.

"You mean to say he sat on the horse behind you and you ran away with him!"

"Yes, sir, that's what happened. I ran away with him."

There was a great laugh in the courtroom.

"Your Honor," said Patrick Henry, "that young fellow never ran away with that beautiful flower. 'Twas a clear case where the girl ran away with the man. And, for certain, you can't put that handsome young man in jail, because he did *not* run away with the girl!"

The judge laughed, the folks laughed, and even the angry father laughed, so all ended happily for everyone—thanks to Patrick Henry.

NOTES

ALABAMA

The First Tale of Alabama

This is one of the many "why" tales that are in every part of the world. When I traveled through Alabama, I heard a few explanations of the reason for the name of the state, and I have used the story I thought fitted best and that I like most.

Fearless Emma

The story of Emma Sansom's fearless deed is known and told in Alabama and all the other deep-South states as a folktale and as a historic tale. Courage and daring were the breath of life in North America and so it is only normal that the bold, brave act of a lovely young girl should be popular. I heard the tale of Emma Sansom over and over again as I traveled through the South.

Don't Drop Into My Soup

Folktales of lack of fear are common throughout the world. There is even a Chinese tale of a boy who could not learn to tremble with fear. It is a favorite theme everywhere. The story told here is unquestionably of European origin—but transformed to North American soil.

I heard it years ago at a Halloween ghost session. As far as I know, I have not seen this version in print.

Railroad Bill

Railroad Bill is as famous in the deep South as is Billy the Kid in the West. His actual name was Morris Slater, and he worked in a turpentine still. After a fatal shooting bout with his boss he fled and turned outlaw. To escape pursuers he often hid in railroad boxcars, and so he was given the name of Railroad Bill.

Stories began to be told about him, as they generally are about outlaws. He was clothed with conjuring powers; he could turn himself into any kind of animal to escape pursuers. Often he helped his friends and well-wishers in Escambia County who were in need of help. He roamed everywhere in the guise of a fox. In the end he died when he had no time to work his magic.

The legend of his deeds and wizardry has lived through the years, and stories about him are current in the state to this very day.

The Face in the Courthouse Window

Tales of faces, seen etched on glass and windows after great stress of fear or tragedy, are often found in the folk literature of the world. Here, in the North American states, they are met with quite frequently. Of course, it is easy to see how a mind incited by strong emotional suggestion and an inflamed imagination can see weird faces and fantastic animals in old windowpanes that have lines and curves running in all directions. The man who related this story swore he had seen the face with his own eyes, and I believed him. (I, too, can see weird shapes in the old windowpanes in my hundred-and-fifty-year-old farmhouse.)

This particular story of Alabama is quite well known and widely believed in Carrollton, in Pickens County, for it is based on historical facts. Skeptics call it a figment of the imagination. Believers assert that not only can the face of Henry be seen, but on stormy nights, when the winds scream in weird voices around the eaves of the Carrollton courthouse, streaks of lightning illuminate Henry's ghost as it peers out of the garret window. . . .

I heard a similar story in Maryland.

How Far Is It to Jacob Cooper's?

As I have said so often, in the early days entertainment that would bring pleasurable laughter was rare. It was therefore natural to play practical jokes or even indulge in horseplay to bring about a little merriment. Work was hard in those days and almost anything that relieved it with a laugh was welcome.

These practical jokes generally related to everyday life and were passed on by word of mouth. But many a time they found their way into diaries, biographies, and county histories. They have proven a bonanza to historians, folklorists, and novelists. "How Far Is It to Jacob's Corner?" is such a story. I heard it told as a "funny story" at a folklore meeting in Washington, and then I saw it in print. Both times it brought a pleasant smile.

The Battle of Bay Minette

Battling for county seats was a favorite pastime in the states. These struggles were numerous, and many of them are famous in lore and legend. I heard of a very unusual one in Mississippi at the time I heard the story of Minette. Men had to use brawn and brain to gain the honor for the city of their choice.

The story I have included here is based on actual facts and is still told with glee when men gather and are in the mood for swapping tales.

The Smartest One in the Woods

I heard this story years ago at a meeting of the National Story League. The main interest of the members of the League is storytelling, and so hearing tales from every corner of the land was the order of the day.

This story was told by Mrs. Adlyn Keffer, who told me she had heard it in Alabama. Mrs. Keffer was a fine storyteller and had devoted nearly all her life to gathering and telling tales.

False Alarm

The late Dr. Peter A. Brannon, who headed the Department of Archives and History of Alabama, once wrote me that Cherokee County in Alabama has hundreds of folk stories. He generously helped me with this one. He also stated that Mrs. Holmes and her children, who figure in the story, are often mentioned in early annals of the county.

This is a pure American story, often encountered at that particular period. In the *Alabama Historical Quarterly*, the Reverend Mr. J. D. Anthony wrote of Mrs. Holmes's adventure in his "Reminiscences of Early Cherokee County."

Dr. Brannon, then Director of the Archives, and Dr. M. B. Howard, Jr., the present Director, both gave me permission to use freely material from their publications. Of course I am very grateful for this.

ARKANSAS

The Arkansas Traveler

No tale of Arkansas is as famous as the tale of the Arkansas traveler. It is based on an incident that is said to have happened to Colonel Sandford C. Faulkner, and the first version, printed in 1896, was said to have been arranged and corrected by him. Many other versions followed this one, none of them quite as good as the Faulkner version which I have followed almost word for word.

Two famous paintings and many engravings were done of this scene. There is also a fiddle tune arranged for the tale, and plays, too, have been built around it.

How Red Strawberries Brought Peace in the Woods

Why and How stories are common among all peoples and the Indians have a full share of them. "How" strawberries were created by the Great Spirit is a tale that roams all over North America. There is little variation among the different versions and it must have been a common tale among many tribes. This is the Cherokee version of how the strawberries came to the earth.

The Proud Tale of David Dodd

The tale of David Dodd of Arkansas is a historical fact and a folktale as well. Rarely will you fail to hear it when tales of the Southern heroes are told.

I heard it whenever I asked anyone for Arkansas "War" tales. It surely has the ingredients of hero-folktales.

The Bull Didn't Have a Chance

Animals had a very important personal place in early American life. Many American folktales, therefore, deal with them. Some of these are tales of courage and cunning; many have a humorous turn. To this day the bull is still a subject for diverse tales.

There are many stories in New England,* in the West, as well as in the South, dealing with male bovines. Here is such a humorous tale—but not humorous for the bull.

I first heard this tale from Louis Imbert when I saw him in Florida. He told me he had heard it from a man who lived in the Ozarks, in Arkansas.

The Sad-Lovely End of Wilhelmina Inn

The charming tale of Wilhelmina Inn near Mena, Arkansas, is well known to people throughout the state, and to the endless thousands who, every year, visit Queen Wilhelmina State Park, which is on the site of the original inn. It is one of the stories that is "in the air" of the state. I am grateful to the members of the Mena Chamber of Commerce for their help with the tale.

The Judge and the Baseball-Pitching Indian Chief

Perhaps one of the most famous old-time judges in the country—certainly in Arkansas—is Judge Isaac C. Parker, the "Hanging Judge." He was a fine, just man who tried his best to bring the bad men of the day to justice. Innumerable tales are told about him and one of the best ones tells of his passion for baseball. I first heard this folktale in Bloomington, Indiana, at a folklore meeting. I don't remember who told it. I have since heard it many times.

Sam Hudson the Great

One of the great local heroes of Arkansas is Sam Hudson. It was my good fortune to find Mr. Walter Lackey, President of the Newton County Historical Society, who lives in Low Gap, Arkansas, to help me with the story. Like so many local historians, Mr. Lackey is an excellent student and collector of folklore and folktales. His parents knew Sam well, and he himself knew many of Sam's children, "down through the years," to use his own words.

The tale tells the kind of man Hudson was, the type who made the great America of today. It is still related when Southern tales are told, a true folktale built around actual facts.

* See *New England Beanpot* published by Vanguard Press, New York, N.Y.

In Arkansas Stick to Bears, Don't Mess with Swampland Skeeters

Tall tales! Whoppers! In no land do they flourish and bloom as in ours. Arkansas has as magnificent a crop of them as any state. You can hear such yarns any time you sit down with a good Arkansas man, woman, or growing boy.

"Stick to Bears" is a real nice example.

Mosquitoes have always been a favorite subject of tall tales. This is a sample of one from the Bear State. I heard it first in Florida from some men out fishing. When I came to Arkansas, the verity of the story was solemnly corroborated.

The Daring of Yellow Doc

Many history tales become folktales when they're picked up from the written books and are told by folks. I call them history-folktales. Such is the tale of Doc Rayburn. It is a good tale to hear tell.

I first heard this story many years ago in Arizona when I was on a dude ranch and the men sat around swapping stories. Then Mrs. Jerri Pirtle, Secretary-Manager of the Des Arc Chamber of Commerce, sent me the story as told by the late Mrs. Frank Norfleet, a retired schoolteacher who lived in Des Arc, and others, all of whom knew the doughty lieutenant and had a part in his daring deeds.

Mrs. Pirtle sent me a long and very beautiful artistic version of the tale which alas! I could not include completely.

The tale was also printed in the *Arkansas Historical Quarterly*.

A Tale of Steep-Stair Town

When you come to Eureka, Arkansas, for health or sightseeing, you are sure to hear the story of the woman who threw the slop down the neighbor's chimney. Somehow the particular tale has caught folks' imagination and it is often retold in the famous health resort.

Of course Eureka citizens laugh it off and say the story is not true, but then, since when was truth demanded of a folktale? It is sufficient that it has been handed down from generation to generation to this very day.

I am sure that there are innumerable clean, neat housewives in the town. But there must have been some exception to prove the rule. This was probably the exception. If it is good enough for folks in Eureka to tell, it is good enough for us to hear.

I want to express my sincere thanks to Mrs. Cora Pinkley-Call for her invaluable assistance. She has lived all her life in Eureka, as did her forbears, who helped build the city from its beginning. She is a fine historian-folklorist of that section of Arkansas.

The Colonel Teaches the Judge a Lesson in Good Manners

The story of how Colonel Walker taught Judge Rover a lesson in manners, neighborliness, and courtesy is well known and told with good humor. The Colonel's method was a little rough, but the result was perfect.

The morality theme is quite common in our land and there are parallel stories in other states. But Mr. William F. Pope in his admirable book *Early Days in Arkansas* vouches for the authenticity of the story in Arkansas, and there is no reason in the world to doubt his statement.

The Lost Treasure

The story of the Bowie knife needs no notes. The history of the knife, how it came to be made, and the man who made it, is a common tale wherever men enjoy hunting and telling tales, which includes all the United States.

A few days ago I saw in a shop window in New York City a beautiful steel knife lying in a satin-lined box with the legend "Genuine Bowie Knife."

How the formula of the steel was lost is a pathetic tale, for with the loss of it the ability to make the finest kind of steel was lost. James Black was a pioneer in metallurgy and has been known through the years as such.

FLORIDA

The Great Conjure-Alligator-Man of Florida

The great Negro cry for freedom from slavery expressed itself not only in the heart and in actions, but also in many fields of the imagination, particularly in the Negro songs and tales. Animal tales, stories of fantasy, stories of adventure, all had the same theme: freedom.

When I roamed around in Florida, I went to Maitland, where that peeress of American folklorists, Zora Neil Hurston, did a good deal of her magnificent research work. There, I, too, heard some of the stories she told. And there I heard for the tenth time stories of "Uncle Monday."

This local folk hero is sometimes called by other names and is known in different sections of Florida. The reason is easy to understand. He was a man cut out to be a hero.

As is usual with the case of the folk hero, he is gigantic in size, battling the white man for his freedom and the freedom of those near him. And he is also a great conjurer and magician. He can turn himself at will into an animal—here, into an alligator, the greatest and strongest alligator in all Florida. He is truly a magnificent character, colored by imagination and surroundings!

Possibly at some time there was a real man who performed deeds that were the foundation of the tale. I tried to trace the story to its source and then realized the absurdity of such an attempt. The origin of a folktale is in the background of the life of the people. It is in the endless hidden places of the folk-mind. This tale, like many others, found its birth in the yearning for freedom and humane treatment.

Nobody Sees a Mockingbird on Friday

The mockingbird is the state bird of Florida, so chosen by the young folks of the state. Floridians claim its song is more beautiful than the nightingale's.

The tale is well known in most parts of Florida. I heard it first in Miami, and later in other parts.

The Tale of Lura Lou

This story was told to me years ago by Professor Louis Imbert of Columbia University, who spent his last years in the Keys of Florida. He said that a fellow fisherman from a little place called Oldtown told it to him.

Pirates and phantom ships are popular themes in folk literature.

Dixie, the Knight of the Silver Spurs

This is a historical story, but it can be put into the realm of folktales because of its continuous retelling by word of mouth and in print through many years. Captain John J. Dickison is one of the beloved men in the state of Florida, and when talk and tales come around to the Civil War, the Captain's name and his daring deeds come up quickly.

I heard the story first when I was in Richmond at a meeting of the Story League of America. Subsequently I heard it in Louisiana and Florida. I cannot help but quote Mr. Roland Dean, who said of Captain Dickison: "He was an able leader of men and a dashing and spectacular character. He caused the North as much trouble in the St. Johns Valley from Jacksonville to Cedar Keys as that debble Forrest in Tennessee and Alabama."

My great thanks to Mr. Dean, of Winter Park, Florida, and to Mr. W. G. Conomos, Editor-Publisher of the *Orlando Sentinel*, for their generous help with this tale of Captain Dickison.

Way Deep Down in the Okefenokee Swamps

People the world over have ever created, through the years, in their dream life, gardens of Eden. A *Schlaraffen-land* where roasted ducks come flying straight into your mouth. Of course Negroes are no exception. To them Diddy-Wah-Diddy was the place of eternal feasts— of fried chickens and sweet potatoes that flew around begging to be eaten. There, life was perfect.

Besides all the good food one could eat, there also lived in that promised land heroes who battled for everything colored folks wanted —above all, freedom.

Naturally, this wonderful land was laid in the Okefenokee. I took the liberty of connecting three little tales that are told in the locality, Okefenokee, and which I heard when I went through that glorious swampland. They are the classic folktales of the guides who lead visitors through.

Of course, similar tales are heard in other parts of our land and throughout the world.

And now a few words about John de Conqueror, an important folk hero, a champion, a redeemer who was to free the Negroes from slavery. He is big, powerful, wise, and cunning. He wanders about like King Arthur, performing great deeds.

As usual with such heroes, there are variations of his name. He is sometimes called "Old John," echoing "Faithful John" of the European folktales. "John de Conqueror" is probably a more recent and literary transformation. Zora Neil Hurston wrote a fine, instructive article about him.

A healing root, "St.-John's-wort," is perhaps associated with him. It is a cure-all for every ailment and the morning dew off it is particularly helpful for sore eyes.

The Bridal Chamber of Silver Springs

Like many folktales, this one is part truth, part fiction. The words of Mr. Allen Skaggs, Jr., of Florida's Silver Springs, explain the "informant part" to perfection.

"The legend," says he, "is both fact and fiction. Several people in this area remember a Captain Douglas, a Bernice Mayo, and an Aunt Silla. There may have been a son Claire, but we have been unable to find concrete proof of this. Also, there may have been a love affair, because Aunt Silla is known to have told and retold the story."

I would call this a perfect example of how folktales are born and grow.

Daddy Mention and Sourdough Gus

I don't remember where I heard this tale. I first wrote the story in 1947 when I found it in my shorthand notes of tales heard many years ago when I was in "Floridy," as the farmer folk around Cooperstown, New York, pronounce the name. Since then, I have heard many more tales of Daddy Mention, one of those minor local folk heroes around whom complete cycles of stories and jests are built.

As usual with this kind of character, many stories connected with him are similar to tales attributed to other famous local folk personalities. There are quite a number of variations to this tale from the tip of Maine down to the Keys of Florida.

GEORGIA

The Song of the Cherokee Rose

There is considerable dispute about the original home of the Cherokee rose. It is the state flower of Georgia, yet other states also claim it as their own: Florida, where I first heard the story, Mississippi, and Alabama. This is so lovely a story, so sweet-scented a flower, that it deserves to be claimed by many states.

The "rose" theme recurs in many parts of the world. Stories of flowers, and roses in particular, have been favorites through the ages and it was natural for the Indians to have their own story of the rose.

Dan McGirth and His Gray Goose Mare

The story of Dan McGirth and his wonderful horse Gray Goose is known far and wide in the South. There are still arguments whether or not Dan was justified in going over to the British for the way he was treated by the Colonial officer and the Liberty Boys. Whatever the final word, the story of the fearless scout and his splendid horse is considered worthy of being told and heard. So folks say down South, and I agree with them.

Like many Southern tales, I heard this one many a time and from different folks.

I want to express my thanks to Mrs. P. W. Bryant, Deputy Surveyor General of Atlanta, Georgia, for her assistance with the story.

The Tale of the Daughters of the Sun

This Indian story is common in the Okefenokee region of the deep South. It is possible that the story was influenced by European tales.

In 1826 Chateaubriand called the Indians around Natchez "Children of the Sun." But there is no reason in the world why Indians could not create stories similar to those of the Europeans. Mirage tales are common among all peoples, and the swamps and waters of Okefenokee are certainly conducive to strange tales.

I read the story years ago when taking a course with Professor Franz Boas and making a special study of Southern Indian games. Then, while traveling through Georgia, I stopped at a wayside stand kept by Indians selling baskets, and became friendly with an Indian woman and two little girls (her daughters) who were with her. I bought a few baskets and then began talking to her about stories her girls would like. A boy came up, about fourteen, who she said was her son. It was late in the afternoon and I kept on talking about stories, telling some to her and the three youngsters. They all listened, open-mouthed. As a rule Indians are not overly friendly with white strangers, and justifiably so. But I had finally gained their confidence, and the boy repeated this story.

"Is it a true story?" I asked.

"Why not?" the woman said.

I had no answer, for I agreed with her.

Georgy Piney-Woods Peddler

Sometimes a folktale becomes a lovely folksong. Georgy Piney-Woods Peddler is such a tale. I heard it first many, many years ago—I'd say at least twenty—probably many more—and I could never forget the little singsong jingles that run through the story like a narrow silvery river through a deep-green meadow.

A story like this should really be heard only on a record with the words and rhythm and musical cadences in which is was first told to me. There is no way to reproduce in just words the rich resonant tones of the deep-South Negro. I have tried, I am sure not too successfully, to convey a little of the lovely musical quality with which it was told. The slow, rich-rolling, throaty, summery twang and intonation of words and song really made the tale. If I have succeeded in giving just the mood of the story, I'll feel well compensated.

I wrote it down for *Story Art*, the storytellers' magazine of America, and here it is with two very minor changes.

The theme of the expansion of wood due to poisoning and then its contraction due to rain is a common one in the tall tales of America.

Swapping as a business was very common in the early pioneering days. This story is also common in other lands.

The Curse of Lorenzo Dow

This tale is told all over the state. I heard it again and again when I asked for a story. It is a strange, inexplicable tale, as strange as the fascinating power this little preaching man with dark searching eyes had over the folks who listened to his words. He not only enthralled their souls but their imaginations as well.

As he wandered up and down the eastern states preaching and pleading with folks to follow the ways of the Lord, he made many converts and just as many enemies.

Many, many tales have been spun around him, as is common with a folk hero, but the one told here is based on an actual fact. There *was* a Jacksonboro in Georgia, where preacher Dow was driven out in 1830 and which he cursed. And the strange events that followed after that curse actually happened. Through the years the town suffered ordeals of fire, storms, floods, and many other tragic mishaps. Every house was destroyed, every family but one left—all that remained was the Goodall house and the Goodall family. That house is still standing, and Jacksonboro, which had been a roaring, drinking, boisterous community, is still a ghost town, cursed by Lorenzo Dow, the itinerant preacher. Sometimes fate rules over man.

I am indebted to D. Elderdice of Georgia for help with this story.

Hoozah for Fearless Ladies and Fearless Deeds

The stories of Silverheels, Captain Heard, Mammy Kate, and Agnes Hobson flourish in Georgia as do the lush flowers. They are stories that are pleasant to tell and pleasant to hear. Many people in the state told them to me as I am telling them to you.

I am greatly indebted to Mrs. Lilla M. Hawes, Director of the Georgia Historical Society, for her most helpful suggestions.

Fearless Nancy Hart

Nancy Hart is one of the heroines of Georgia. There are legions of tales told about her, and, as usual with a folk hero, the number of stories of acts she performed has grown with the years.

I heard quite a few tales imputed to her which are also attributed to other folks in different parts of the land as far as New York and Maine.

In Georgia, the Nancy Hart tales are told (as I heard them) with gusto and relish. For she lived a full life, giving aid when it was needed. Informants for the tale were numerous. I heard the story first when I was on the way to Louisiana.

Miss Carrol Hart kindly helped me with it.

And here I want to add my thanks to others, connected with the state's historical associations and universities, and other folks who helped me gather the tales: Dr. Bell I. Wiley of the Historical Department of Emory University; Mrs. Mary Warren, President of the Athens Historical Society; Mr. Stephen Mitchell of Atlanta; Mr. T. M. Cunningham of Savannah; and a host of others.

LOUISIANA

The Silver Snake of Louisiana

This is an old North American Indian "why" story. The name of the bayou is supposed to have been originally "Tenche," an Indian word meaning snake. The French changed it to "Tesh," and finally it was changed to "Teche." Some contend that the name is a corruption of the word "Deitsch," for the early settlers came from South Germany. Of course this has no bearing on the tale.

The snake had a very important place in the lore and history of the North American Indians and other peoples of the world as well. The snake holding the world; the snake the mother of man; and the snake in a thousand and one other capacities plays a very great role in the origin of folktales everywhere.

Fairy Web
for Mr. Durand's Daughters

Mr. Durand's (his name is spelled in different ways) famous feat to celebrate the double wedding of two of his daughters (it is said that he had twenty-four children) is one of the delightful tales of the Teche area of Louisiana. It is told again and again, orally and in writing, and it was vouched for to me as absolutely true. I heard it in New Orleans alone four times! And it fully deserves its popularity. Mr. Durand's feat was an accomplishment fit for an ancient Eastern satrap.

Utilization of the theme of spiders' webs is common in folk literature. There is a very beautiful South American tale, the central theme of which is the weaving of a spider's web.*

The late Mr. Herbert Asbury, the noted historian and New Orleans folklore student, also told me of Mr. Durand's accomplishments and Miss May P. Hebert of the *St. Mary Banner* and *Franklin Tribune* was also helpful. My thanks for their good assistance.

The Life of Annie Christmas

Ask any and all for a "local" story of New Orleans and next to ghost tales you'll get tales of Annie Christmas. She is as much part of the old French-Creole city by the sea as are pralines and gumbos. There is a rare magnificent grandeur around her acts and behavior. One of the interesting angles is that her stories are told by black folks and white folks. Both claim her as their own. Some say she was white and Irish, some that she was black and African.

Her exit from the world of New Orleans is one of the great American folk scenes. The late Mr. Herbert Asbury told me many tales about Annie. Later, when I was in that city, I heard many more tales about this black-white heroine.

Gray Moss on Green Trees

Thick, grayish moss hanging from green trees is seen in many states down South. It is so outstanding and popular a sight that many stories have been woven around its origin. Remember that unusual and fantastic growths of trees all over the world have ever been the incentive for folk imagination and folk creation. In the olden days, the French called the hanging moss Spanish beards and the Spanish called it French wigs.

I heard three versions of this "why" moss tale. Besides the one I used, there is the story that it grew from the hair of an Indian Princess who, with her young husband, was buried under an oak tree. According to ancient custom, her black hair was cut after her death and hung on the tree. No storm could dislodge that hair. As the years went by, the

* See *The King of the Mountains* published by Vanguard Press, New York, N. Y.

hanging hair turned gray, spinning all over its tree and other trees as well. Finally it turned into gray moss.

One amusing version I heard, in Florida, has since been turned into a modern, jingling rhyme, used on postcards. There an elderly Spanish soldier falls in love with a young Indian girl who does not favor him. One day she sees him coming toward her and, frightened, she runs from him. He pursues her. Finally, to escape, she climbs quickly up a tree, her hair hanging down loosely all around her. This then turned into moss.

I am certain there must be other explanatory tales of the lovely gray moss that hangs from the trees. Besides furnishing food for the imagination, the hanging moss has become the source of a thriving commercial industry.

The Bridal Ghost Dinner

If you come to the Mardi Gras in New Orleans, and you should, for it is one of the great social-folk events of the South, the chances are that you will hear this tale. I first heard it in the home of a lawyer, a fine bibliophile and a collector of Louisiana history and lore, and heard it later several times, slightly varied in the telling, as is natural. Sometimes one hotel or restaurant, sometimes another, was mentioned as the exact place. Mr. Herbert Asbury spoke of the story, too.

Of course the theme is a very ancient one and has been used in folktales and literary works throughout the world.

One Pair of Blue Satin Slippers and Four Clever Maids

This is one of the tales Mr. Herbert Asbury told me the evening we spent together at the Bedford Hotel. He said he had often heard it told on the Teche, and that it was based on actual happenings. There really was a Conrad family and David Weeks did play an important role in early Louisiana.

Ben Botkin, that inexhaustible source of folklore information, said that the story appeared in print, but I have never seen it. I think it is a very charming story, and the theme, the universal cleverness of young ladies when necessity arises, fully deserves print and retelling.

The Silver Bell
of Chênière Caminada

The terrible storm that almost completely destroyed Grand Isle, in Louisiana, is graphically told by the American author Lafcadio Hearn in beautiful descriptive language. Chênière Caminada, opposite Grand Isle, with which this story deals, met the same fate. If you want the full agonizing desperate feeling of those hours of natural destruction, read Lafcadio Hearn's description of the scene.

There is a great deal of lore about bells throughout the length and breadth of the world. Their music has always fascinated the folk imagination and in every land there is no end of stories in which bells are the theme. This particular tale is factually based, and, as has been said so often, fact is often far stranger than fiction.

Today the bell is in the belfry of the old Grand Isle church building, according to the Reverend Mr. Gerard Laroche, present rector of Our Lady of the Isle Church of Grand Isle. He kindly helped me with accurate information about the incidents of the story. He had heard of other details relating to the happenings but, he said, my version was pretty much as he understands it, and that "the bell may have some silver but with a mixture of other metals."

I heard the story originally in the early nineteen thirties. Visitors to Grand Isle today will still hear it told.

Three Great Men at Peace

Mr. Asbury told me this tale with a full smile on his face. He said it showed how far folktales go into flighty imagination and romantic impossibilities. I contended that however impossible and absurd a folktale sounds, there is always a germ of real widsom and wishful desire in it. And this story, in a measure, bears out my point.

Mr. Jerry Wise, also a student of Louisiana lore (and owner and editor of the Cameron *Paris Pilot* in Cameron, Louisiana), helped me considerably in pinning down this and other tales.

MISSISSIPPI

The Song in the Sea

There are numerous tales of mass suicide in many forms the world over. This particular story, sometimes ascribed to the Pascagoula or Biloxi Indians of Mississippi, sometimes to other tribes in Alabama, appears in different versions. Exhaustive studies by folklorists have been made to authenticate the tale, but unsuccessfully.

There is a version that one tribe was converted to Christianity by the priests who came down South with De Soto. But their former goddess, who was a sea goddess, lured them with her singing back into the sea. Of course the stories of the Lorelei come at once to mind.

Another version tells that the Biloxi Indians, after being defeated by the Choctaw Indians, decided it was better to drown themselves rather than to fall under their enemy's power.

In still another version it is Negroes, brought from Africa by slavers, who decide to drown themselves rather than become slaves.

The "mass suicide" tale probably has a foundation of actuality and, therefore, is justifiably fascinating for storytellers and listeners, as any story of great heroism would be.

I heard the story in many parts of Mississippi and in other states, always influenced by the particular locale.

The Living Colors of the Twenty-first

This is a true tale that is so charming and human that folks have been telling it ever since the day it happened. To wrench a beautiful tale out of the grimness and brutality of war is not a common occurrence.

The Twenty-first Regiment of Mississippi told the tale with pride, and their descendants keep on telling it to this day, and so the story has spread.

I heard it told by a man from Mississippi when we were sitting around in a fishing boat.

I am indebted to Mrs. Laura D. S. Harrell, Research Assistant, Department of Archives and History of Mississippi, for her asistance with this story.

The Ghost Wedding in Everhope

Walking, leaping, dancing lights, furniture, and dishes have always had a place in folk- and ghost tales. So have banquets of and for the dead. European and Eastern tales are filled with such incidents. In Bali, I saw the most elaborate flowers, fruit, and food arrangements for the dead carried to the temple on people's heads.

In our own land, ghost tales in which inanimate subjects become animate are quite frequent. Thus, I found that in one tale there are candlesticks walking from mantelpieces, dishes leaping off tables, chairs hopping after guests, and so on. There are many, many such folktales. The Mississippi story of the floating bottles at the ghost dinner is in the full folklore tradition.

I first heard this story in Washington, D.C., and I was told it is quite well known at Washington Lake, in Mississippi.

Again Mrs. Harrell was a guiding hand, and I am thankful to her for her help.

The Ring Around the Tree

When you go to beautiful Biloxi, as I did several times, you must visit the historical Episcopal Church of the Redeemer to see the huge live oak with the ring around its branches which brought this tale to life.

How the story began, who was the first narrator, is hard to tell. Unquestionably it is a created tale, as many folk stories are, but this does not detract in the slightest from their charm.

You'll hear this tale as soon as you get to Biloxi and ask for a tale of the city. I heard the story from the guide who took us on a tour there. Mr. Anthony Ragusin gave me most generous and invaluable help in "authenticating" the story, and I am also grateful to Mr. H. Hinman, who gave me a fine photograph of the "live oak."

Tar-Wolf Tale

There are hundreds of Tar Baby tales, and somehow other young folks and I (from eight to eighty) never seem to get tired of them. Here is a version I heard from a splendidly tale-talkative man from Mississippi, named Theopholus, whom I had the good fortune to meet. This story also appeared in the *Journal of American Folklore* many years ago.

The Tar Baby tales are as old as tale-telling man is.

This tale, though dealing with a wolf, follows the perfect Tar Baby pattern.

Mike Hooter and the Smart Bears in Mississippi

Whenever you mention bears to any man in Mississippi, the next words will be Mike Hooter. For Mike Hooter, hunter and preacher, may safely be called the folk hero of the state of Mississippi. Many stories have grown up around him and his family, and there are some delightful stories about his daughter.

He was born in Red River, Louisiana, and came to Mississippi in 1800, living in Yazoo County. As a hunter, it is said he finished as many bears as did Davy Crockett—and remember, the bears in Mississippi are very smart! The story here shows that. Mike Hooter used his head as well as his steady hand in hunting. As a preacher he was known as "The Shouter." His exhortations for folks to follow the Lord rang out like thunder in the springtime.

There are many, many stories told about him. Wherever I asked for some good Mississippi hunting tales, a story of Mike Hooter was sure to come up. Only lack of space prevents me from telling more of them.

The Sad Tale of the Half-Shaven Head

Life for Southern folks after the Civil War was far from happy. Good laughter and pleasure were as rare as hens' teeth. Many Northerners who came down South at that period tried their best to help heal the wounds of the war, but many who came put only salt on the sorrows. So when a chance came along for Southerners with a sense of humor to play a joke on one of those misguided people, they seized it with avidity. This is a tale of such an occurrence.

To this day this story is told with zest and is often repeated throughout the state, where I heard it while traveling and asking for tales. Finally I found it included in the publications of the Mississippi Historical Society. There, it is to be found in the entertaining and informative article, "Some Effects of Military Reconstruction in Monroe County, Mississippi" by R. C. Becket.

Mrs. Laura D. S. Harrell, Research Assistant, Department of Archives and History, who has been of great help to me in all my Mississippi tales, kindly gave me permission to use material that appeared in this publication.

Guess Who!

There is no question that this story is a version of the European "three" suitors, a "three"-task story integrated into Negro tales. Such stories are among the most common in European lore.

Nearly all the incidents or tasks and actions have their parallels in the European versions. The variation here is that there are four suitors and four tasks instead of the proverbial three, and that the winner is left for you to guess.

The story was in the collection of Arthur H. Fauset in the *Journal of American Folklore.* I heard the tale in Mississippi.

NORTH CAROLINA

The Savage Birds of Bald Mountain

The legend of Bald Mountain in North Carolina is a "why" story that can also be called pure fantasy. The tale shows European influence although there is no reason in the world why Indians cannot conceive tales similar to those of Caucasians.

The theme of a wild animal that devours humans (here, a bird), occurs in other tales the world over. Sometimes it is a snake, sometimes another animal. Many such tales are found in Indian myths and folktales. The Mandan Hidasta Indians who lived along the Missouri River also tell tales of children carried off by monsters. It is truly a universal theme in ancient mythology.

The White Doe

The story of Virginia Dare, the White Fawn and later the White Doe,* and the Lost Colony, has been told for hundreds of years. Many folk versions are told of the legends of her "transformation" and reappearance and I chose to tell the one found by the W.P.A. field workers. I also included some slight elements found in other versions.

* Sometimes the tales say that it is Virginia's mother who is supposed to be the White Doe.

The Tale of the Hairy Toe

The "Hairy Toe" ghost folktale is known with slight variations in many states. I heard four different versions. The main difference is generally in the type of vegetable the old man is digging for. Sometimes it is beans, sometimes potatoes, sometimes just greens.

In Nashville, Ohio, I heard a similar tale under the name of Tailipoo (I am not certain of the spelling), told by Dr. Grover Brown, the District School Superintendent. We were sitting on the "Liar's Bench" under the shady trees, and never have I heard a ghost tale more dramatically told.* I think the "classic" way of ending the tale is by pointing the finger at one particular person (it's the way I tell it) and shouting: "*You* got my hairy toe!" That was the way it was told by Jim Monahan, Tar Heel citizen, from whom I heard the tale in Phoenix, Arizona.

Dr. Ralph Boggs of Miama University has a similar version in his fine collection of North Carolina folktales.

The Revolution of the Ladies of Edenton

On the courthouse green in Edenton, there is a beautiful bronze teapot, a replica of the one the ladies of Edenton used originally to declare their independence from British tea. It was probably the first revolutionary act by ladies in the new land. Of course it is a historical fact, but it is a tale that has been told over and over again and is often related today, and so it belongs among folktales—tales told by folk.

There is a small painting, on glass, of the famous happening in the Metropolitan Museum, in New York City.

I want to express my thanks to the members of the Edenton (Cradle of the Colony) Chamber of Commerce for their helpful assistance.

Nollichucky Jack

There are some folks and happenings which are "naturals" in the realm of folklore and folktales. Such a man was John Servier of North Carolina, and his deeds have come down to us by word of mouth and in old writings.

---

* See *Sand in the Bag* published by Vanguard Press, N.Y.

North Carolina 343

The most famous of Servier's escapades, and you can call them so, was his fearless act of turning the Blue Ridge Mountain area into an independent state. It was too much of a bother to belong to North Carolina.

It took four long years for the lawmakers in Raleigh, the capital of North Carolina, to convince the Franks that Franklin, as the domain was called by Servier and his mountaineers, still belonged to the state. There was many a battle and many a tale before it was accomplished.

This particular incident is commonly known throughout the state.

Pirate Blackbeard's Deep-Sea End

Folktales about folk heroes, either local or national, grow with the beauty and abundance of wild flowers and weeds. Blackbeard, the pirate, is one of those folk idols, and the stories around him are legion. Here is one that befits that great be-bearded sea robber.

I heard the tale under amusing circumstances. A few men were sitting around after a day's fishing, well fed and well under the influence, swapping jokes and tales. Somehow I said I believed that thirteen was my lucky number. Then came a discussion about lucky and unlucky numbers and signs. Jokes and tales of these portents followed, this among them.

Let me say here that Blackbeard had thirteen wives! And thirteen was his unlucky number. That caused the strange ending of Edward Teach, better known as Blackbeard the Pirate.

The Ways of the Lord

This true tale makes the rounds all over Swanquarter. It is a most fantastic story, which by sheer repetition and popularity can be called a folktale.

This strange incident was actually witnessed by many people. Call it coincidence; call it a miracle and the will of God; or call it the harmony of land, water, and mankind; it is a fact, and was part of the life of the town. It is a mystery discussed to this very day.

The Reverend R. C. Hamilton, pastor of this Methodist Church (1964), gave me a description of the occurrence. My many thanks for his generous help.

The Man, the White Steed,
and the Wondrous Wood

Belden Crane, my neighbor, lived on a farm his family owned since about 1730. Now Belden and his forebears are in a better world than ours. Beldon loved and worshiped trees as if they were gods. He would not permit a tree to be cut on his hundred-and-sixty-acre farm. I know many stories about him and about trees struck by lightning on his place. One time when I was telling a group of men about him, the story of William R. Pool, of North Carolina, who similarly loved trees, came up.

Years later when I began my research on North Carolina, I found that J. Harden had used the story of Mr. Pool in his fine book, *Tar Heel Ghosts*. Mr. Harden graciously did not object to my retelling the tale. I don't know if Emmerson Wood, who told me the story at a cook-out at a ranch in Arizona, had read Mr. Harden's book or whether he heard the story in North Carolina, but it is a good one from the Old State and worth telling and hearing.

The Mystery of Theodosia Burr

This is a story based on conjectures and tales that have been told up and down the eastern coast from Maine to Florida for the last one hundred and fifty years: "The Mystery of Theodosia!"

I have taken the most common legend, and all the essential facts. The only additions are color, which any story needs.

The mystery has never been solved, and the tales of Theodosia's death have been speculations and conjectures mostly based on scraps of facts that have come up through the years.

SOUTH CAROLINA

Shake Hands with a Yankee

One of the great pleasures of the collector of folktales is to find a direct descendant of those with whom a story deals. In this particular tale I had such good fortune: a lady from the family of Paul Hamilton, Mrs. Margaret S. Fuller, whose husband is a direct descendant of the Hamiltons, was the good angel. Then, to make it even more perfect,

Miss Almeda Holmes, also of Beaufort and a good friend of Margaret Fuller, added her helpful words. Both gave me the full story as well as some very charming details. With two such authorities the tale is truly one-hundred percent informant-proof.

This heart-warming tale of the saving of the famous residence for the Confederate family is well known throughout the state of South Carolina and is often told.

The Tragic Tale of Fenwick Hall

The tragic tale of Fenwick Hall is known throughout the South. There are different versions of it, many of which I have heard. They vary considerably. One states that it was Mistress Fenwick who ran away with the groom, just like the old gypsy tale. Another has it that the culprit was not a groom but a pirate.

In a measure, it is a tale following the old ballad theme heard in England, Scotland, and other lands.

Emily's Famous Meal

Emily Geiger's story is one of the famous stories of the South. It has been told so often for the last two hundred years that it fits well into the framework of the folktale.

I heard the story in Richmond, Virginia, and in Florida and South Carolina.

Chickens Come Home to Roost

This is one of those pleasant frontier tales of early-American life, which I am sure is factual. Mrs. Alice J. Owen, Special Collections Librarian at Furman University, Greenville, South Carolina, who, with Southern graciousness, gave me help with the tale, thinks the same.

There is a homey ring to this story of the days when many times it was a question of beating the horned gentleman at his own game.

Ah-Dunno Ben

Two men told me this charming Southern tale in different parts of the United States: Jason Burnside in Charlestown, West Virginia, and Professor William Utter of Denison University, Ohio. Both men knew that I was ever on the lookout for folktales of any kind and they happened to know quite a few of them, particularly Professor Utter.

My thanks also to Dr. Omega G. East, Supervisory Historian of the U.S. Department of the Interior (National Park Service), for helping me with the story.

The Tale of Rebecca Motte

This is a historic-folktale. It is told down South to this day—for folks down South like to tell their olden tales more than do those up North. They are told with a cherished, personal feeling, as if they had happened to a friend or relative—and as if they had happened a week or a month ago.

Of course as these stories are repeated through the years they undergo many changes. Each teller adds or subtracts or turns a mote. But the "heart" of the story is not changed. Such romantic-historic tales become folktales by sheer constant, oral repetition.

I want to express my sincerest thanks to Mr. E. L. Inabinett, Director of the South Caroliniana Library at the University of South Carolina in Columbia, for patiently helping me with this and many other South Carolina tales.

The Perpetual Motion in the Sea

This tale is an account of something that is said to have actually taken place. I heard it down in Key West, Florida, where men had come to fish and were swapping tales.

Giant devilfish were quite common around the South Carolina waters until they were slaughtered, as so many animals and fish have been. They had fins like bats' wings that sometimes stretched twenty feet across and weighed a tremendous amount.

Tales of men seeking the secret of perpetual motion were quite common in those days.

Young Sherman and the Girl from Charleston

Many folktales grew in Oakland Mansion House and the plantation, from the Revolutionary days down to our time. Perhaps the most striking is the story focused around young General Sherman, which informs us, supposedly, of what led to his fierce behavior during the War Between the States.

Again I am indebted to Mrs. Margaret S. Fuller of Beaufort, South Carolina, for her tireless assistance in digging up facts and manuscripts; to Dr. E. L. Inabinett, Director of the South Caroliniana Library; and to Dr. Omega G. East, of the U.S. Department of Interior, National Park Service, for his informative notes.

TENNESSEE

Kate, the Bell Witch

Next to the early witch tales of New England probably the best-known witch story in our country is that of the "bell witch" of Tennessee, who not only carried on her antics in that state but in other states as well.

The story of that poltergeist is very unusual, since so many folks, often of reputable character, claimed to have "heard" her and "seen" her. She really became a "concrete" reality in earlier days for those who believe in ghosts.

The ghost's behavior was strictly according to regulations. Hounding of the wrongdoer after the death of the wronged, smashing furniture, tweaking noses, snatching away food, and showing kindness to those whom the ghost liked, etc., etc., etc.

There have been ghosts like the "Bell witch" all over the world and it is therefore perfectly normal to find such a ghost in Tennessee.

I have heard the story in nearly every city I visited in Tennessee. Quite a few books and articles have been written about Kate. Here is a small list for those who would like to learn a little more about her:

Ingram, M. V.: *The Bell Witch*. Setliff Co., Nashville, Tenn., 1894.

Miller, Harriet Parks: *The Belle Witch of Middle Tennessee*. Leaf-Chronicle Press, Clarksville, Tenn., 1930.

Bell, Charles Baily: *The Bell Witch*. Privately printed, Nashville, Tenn., 1934.

The Nashville Banner. September 21, 1930.

348 NOTES

The Best Laugh Is the Last Laugh

Playing practical jokes was one of the popular pastimes of the early North American immigrants. Anything to bring a little laughter into their lives!

The tales of Timothy Reagan are said to be true—and they probably are. This one was set down by the W.P.A. workers. Of course it falls into the class of "joke tales," which are endless in number throughout the world.

Fiddler's Rock

Fiddlers played a conspicuous role in the early days of the United States. One of the reasons was that they were *the* important source of entertainment. Hard-working settlers needed music to please their deeper feeling of folk-emotions. Let me add here that fiddlers have always played an important part in the lore of those places where stringed instruments have been known.

It is normal, then, to find many fiddler tales here. Nearly every state has a story associated with a player of this instrument.

This one was collected by the W.P.A. workers during the nineteen thirties.

Trust Not a New Friend

This very delightful tale is still told in Tennessee and in many of the other Southern states, for it is an amusing tale of war—without bloodshed.

I heard it in Memphis and I saw it in an old copy of the *Commercial Appeal*. I am sure that it is a true tale. It can be put into the category of folktales, for it is still told today when good Southerners get together and speak of old times.

Come and Laugh with Bobby Gum

Robert (Bobby) Gum was a well-known character around Memphis in the days when Clay and Polk were battling for the Presidency.

There are innumerable tales told of him to this day, and I chose this from among the many I heard.

The Ghost Who Wasn't a Ghost

This is one of the stories collected by the W.P.A. research group. I also heard it verbally in Memphis at the same time that I heard the tale of "The Ghost the Whole Town Knew." The story is said to be based on an actual happening, but this type of ghost tale is found all over the world.

I have tried hard to locate Gloucester in Tennessee, and generous and cooperative members of different historical societies worked hard to help me, but without success. Perhaps the name was recorded wrong.

Big Sixteen

This is a wandering tale. When I say wandering, I mean that it can be heard in different states and is equally true in each. Actually this story was told by Andy Johnson of Fort Cheatem.

Of course the resemblance to John Henry is obvious, and the theme of fetching the devil from hell is common all over our country and in Europe as well.

Ghostly will-o'-the-wisps or fireflies also are very common throughout the world. So, all in all, it is a tale with a universal theme fitted into the Southern scene.

The Ghost the Whole Town Knew

This ghost-treasure-mystery tale is one of the best-known stories in Memphis. Almost invariably, when I asked for a story, the tale of Clara Davidson and Lizzie Robertson and the treasure in the glass jar came up.

It is supposed to be an actual happening, if you accept the statement of the whole city, endless newspaper reports, and the word of those who heard it from eyewitnesses.

The tale, as such, runs true to the type of ghost who comes to inform one of a buried or hidden treasure. It is a tale repeated endlessly in fairy and story literature in every part of the world.

I owe particular thanks for this and other Tennessee tales to Mrs. Ralph C. Roudebush and the other librarians of the Goodwin Institute Library in Memphis. They gave generously of their time and advice. And, of course, there was always genial, gargantuan Paul Flowers, editor of the "Greenhouse" a column in the *Commercial Advertiser*

(Memphis). He knows more tales about Memphis in particular, and Tennessee in general, than anyone else I met in that state.

The Power of Woman and the Strength of Man

This is a story included by the W.P.A. workers in their monumental collection made in 1938. It is a Negro "why" tale with a good touch of modern feeling behind it. In its neatness of structure, it almost seems a literary-created tale. Keep in mind such tales are perfectly good folktales if they stand the test of time and transmission by word of mouth. Today, since the mass medium stresses the written, rather than oral, tradition, we have to accept it as our folklore expression. The folktale is a tale rich in the humor of simple folk depicting the understanding of human arguments and tribulations.

The Gladiator, the Belle, and the Good Snowstorm

This is a tale I heard in Memphis. I was told it also appeared in one of the newspapers there. It is unquestionably built on facts, though there are rarely violent snowstorms in Memphis. The story has been handed down by word of mouth for many years. Every now and then it pops up in the local newspapers.

Beale Street Folks

Beale Street is in Memphis, Tennessee, the King Cotton city. It is one of the famous streets in our land. The tales you hear of the deeds they did in that street would fill many volumes. One book has already been written about it. In these pages there are just crumbs of the doings of folks in that Tennessee city.

Cherry Malone was a real person in Memphis and became famous for her physical strength because she helped the police in many a strike. The incident told about her here, I was told in Memphis, actually happened in that city.

The catfish story comes up in many states. Stories of birds and beasts of strange appearance and personality are also well known.

There is no question but that Steamboat Bill is identical with John Henry, the most admired personality in Negro lore.

TEXAS

The Karankawa from the Great Gleaming Oyster Shells

This is another of the stories collected by the W.P.A. workers in the field of folklore. I found it in the archives of the Library of Congress. The story is also among those of the Karankawa Indian tribe.

How Joe Became Snaky Joe

This golden nugget of a tale was told by Mrs. J. C. Miller of Big Springs, Texas. There are thousands of snake tales, but I know of none with the turns and twists of this tale—all for a good laugh. Beat it if you can. It is a true American tale and, I am quite sure, has no parallel in the lore of any other land.

The White Buffalo

The northernmost part of Texas was, and still is today, a wild and unpredictable stretch of land. Once there were vast ranches there. The Indians fought there fiercely and bitterly to keep the lands that belonged to them. Now gaunt ghost towns look in angry memory at the sky. And Nature there is wild and fierce. Screaming Northers, billowing blizzards, run around in a wild race. But once it was called Buffalo Country. There were thousands of them until they were slaughtered by white men. And so it is normal that tales about buffaloes grew up in that corner of Texas, stories half-Indian and half-white. Such is the tale of the White Buffalo. It is a story befitting the place and the folks—Indian and white.

When the white men were collecting tales for the government, they heard the tale of the White Buffalo and told it, and here I am telling it to you.

The Ghosts of Stampede Mesa

This is one of the stories that was collected by the Works Progress Administration folklore workers. It is a popular tale and is still told when cattlemen gather.

The theme of ghosts haunting places—woods, people, anything—is a common and favored one in the field of folklore and folktales of every land.

Only in Texas

There are innumerable stories told about Judge Roy Bean of Texas. I think I know about thirty of them, or more. The one I am telling you here I've heard at least half a dozen times. Judge Bean is one of the comic folk heroes of that state and fully deserves the title.

Texas Centipede Coffee

This Texan-tall-tale gem was obtained by the W.P.A. during its heyday of folktale collecting. It was related by Ranger R. F. Smith, who was known as a good storyteller.

The "theme" of thinking oneself poisoned, or even dead, is quite common in folktales throughout the world. But this is truly an American tale in content, humor, and feeling.

Of Sam Bass

There is no end of tales of Sam Bass, the Robin Hood outlaw of Texas. They are still told today in camps, rodeos, homes—everywhere. With the years, they have grown bigger and better. Part of the tale told here I found in the W.P.A. archives in the Library of Congress. I also heard it at a folklore meeting when we were swapping folktales.

The theme of the outlaw who helps the poor is found in every country in the world. It is an ideal that folks have created in their tales, and which has been used over and over again. Nearly every outlaw has been a hero, a Robin Hood who robbed the rich and helped the poor, and this is also true in the folktales of the United States.

Horse Trading in Wichita Falls

This tale was told by Mrs. Eleanore Flemming, in Wichita Falls, to one of the W.P.A. workers when they were scouring the United States to collect old tales. Of course, similar incidents are found elsewhere and in other countries as well, but that does not take anything away from the validity of this story. Human beings are much alike the world over and similar incidents can happen in far-distant lands. If you want it classified, put it in the category of "trickster tales."

Lafitte's Great Treasure

I heard this tale many years ago in the Florida Keys and filed it among my notes. There is no end to Lafitte treasure stories, but I think this one is unique.

It is fascinating to see how stories "grow" around a particular individual. There must be some magic in the personality, in the name, in the knowledge we have of a person that inspires this "growth" of tales.

Such characters are called folk heroes, and Lafitte can be considered in the class of minor folk heroes of America. Enough stories of daring and fearlessness, of cleverness and strength, of cruelty and kindness, are woven around this deep-South pirate to fill a book. I know a few more Texas tales about Lafitte, but I chose this because it is so different from the usual pirate story.

I have often said that there is a germ of truth in most folktales and I believe there is in this particular one. The name of the young wife and the name of their home has been handed down in history. But that is not really of importance. A folktale can stand on its own merits.

VIRGINIA

Hercules of Virginia

Stories of Peter Francisco are legion. Many of them are tall tales based on actual happenings. I have set down here but one, though I was tempted to tell three, each just as fabulous and just as amusing. But, alas, space forbids.

That giant of Virginia accomplished great feats easily and smilingly, as if they were everyday happenings.

My thanks to all Virginians who were always eager to tell me another Peter Francisco tale, and to Dr. J. M. Jennings, Director of the Virginia Historical Society, in particular.

354   NOTES

All on a Summer's Day

This type of tall tale is very popular in our good land, the United States. It is found in nearly every state, particularly down South and out West. I have known the tale for at least twenty or more years, and heard it over again while going down the Mississippi on my way to New Orleans.

Snake tales are common among folk, and dandelion wine made in farm homes is one of the two most popular folk wines. The other is elderberry wine. This is a good tale to tell, and I've told it many times.

The Merry Tale of Belle Boyd

The story of Belle Boyd, the most famous "spy" of the Civil War, needs no comment. Stories about her and her life are too well known.

I am indebted to Mrs. Barbara J. Woodward for her helpful detailed information about the famous lady's activities.

Two Foxes

For many years I have been telling a story of how two animals refuse to fight each other for a holiday crowd. The animals of that tale speak, and their conversation centers around the question: Why do these humans want us to kill each other? One day when I told the tale at a gathering, one of the listeners came back with this charming animal story, which once again brings home the never-ceasing cry of the world, so well expressed in the Chinese saying, "The great harmony of the world is Universal Peace."

This may be a story brought from Africa or the Far East, or it may be a tale created here in our land. Whatever the origin, it is a good story, well worth telling and well worth following.

The Black Ghost Dog

This is a very old Virginia tale. Since I am fond of dogs, I am always ready to tell dog tales and listen to them whenever I have the opportunity.

On a trip to Europe, years ago, when I traveled on boats around the seas, this story came up while we were telling tales on deck. It was related by a lady named Virginia Toller, who was a Virginian, living in Washington.

Such "faithful dog" tales are quite common all over the world. This one has a somewhat European echo, but the informant said it was pure Virginian and happened in that state.

When I decided to use the story in this book, I tried to authenticate its content and location a little better. I contacted folks all over and, as usual, all tried to help me with gracious Southern courtesy. Particular thanks are due to Mr. Gay Arritt, Secretary of the *Covington Virginian*, who knew of a similar dog story that he believed was told "in Augusta County or one of the areas settled long before Alleghany County was formed."

In a measure, it attests to the fact that it was a popular tale in those parts, running around in various versions.

Grace Sherwood, the Woman None Could Scare

Somehow, I became deeply interested in Grace Sherwood when I heard her story and read accounts of her trials and tribulations set down through the years. She must have been a fearless high-spirited woman. Never did she give in to witch-baiting and maligning. She was always fighting back, and there were many persons, including judges in Virginia, who were on her side.

I owe no end of thanks to Mrs. L. Cawford Syer of Virginia Beach, who devoted a great deal of time and work to provide me with the authentic information of that dauntless Virginia woman. I also want to give my thanks to Dr. Virginius C. Hall, Jr., Assistant Director of the Virginia Historical Society, and to two Virginians to whom I am particularly indebted for their tireless work. Both gave unstintingly of their time and research to help me find the stories that are known in Virginia. One is Mrs. Paul Lowenstein of Luray and Harrisburg, Virginia, and the other is Mrs. P. C. Shiray, of Staunton, Virginia, who wrote an admirable guide book of Augusta County, Staunton, and Waynesboro, Virginia.

. . . Thanks to Patrick Henry

There is no end to the tales of Patrick Henry, admired, loved, and respected, South, North, East, and West. Get together with any group of folks who like tales—lawyers in particular—and you are sure to hear some good story in which the great orator-patriot has a leading part. I heard this story at such a gathering in Memphis, Tennessee.

1929